THE ROAD

B E T W E E N

TWO SKIES

THE ROAD

BETWEEN

TWO SKIES

LINDA FIFER

atmosphere press

To my mentor, Heidi M. Thomas, whose creativity and encouragement allowed me to take the risk.

PROLOGUE

BRENNISS' JOURNAL

I have two names: Brenniss and Maggie. Brenniss is the name I was born with, inspired by my grandmother Berniece. My mom wanted a modern variation of the Victorian name. While I was still in the womb, my dad and mom used my bump as a table to sort paper scraps with potential names while lying in bed. They moved letters in "Berniece," then wrote their favorites. Apparently, at one point, I kicked; the scrap of paper that had "Brenniss" written on it fell between them onto the covers. It was a story my mom told often, how I chose my own name before I arrived. I was the little girl with the unusual name for the first portion of my life.

Maggie is the name I got after all this happened, one of my own choosing again, I'm told. It's a down-to-earth name. It fits me like a well-worn shirt. Maggie is the love of simple, the solid earth that grounds her. Brenniss is a pretty name from a pretty time in my life and I'm grateful for her, too. Brenniss is like a favorite dress from high school. Not all of it fits, but I remember it fondly.

"After all this happened"—that's a loaded phrase. I only remember flashes. Some of the events still haunt me, like an unanswered prayer. The events crawl into my dreams, rising out of a fog; I'm not always certain of what I've seen. There are faces, still, wedges of light, cold steel pressed against my skin, ripped fabric or a sharp blade in my back. They blur and flicker like an old-fashioned film on the spindle. They taste like panic, like mud, like fire. Sometimes it's easier to think of those events in reverse order, from the most recent which are clearer and more comfortable, to the earlier moments that changed my life. Maybe that's how it should be.

Those Brenniss days were touched by something magical: my mom, my dad, coworkers, shopkeepers and baristas, gardens and picnics, fireflies and graduation. I was proud being the Lead Archivist at the New York Public Library. The memory of that work is like quickly scanning pages in a thick book, where key words pop once in a while if you concentrate on one spot long enough. Ironic, that I defined my work by things from the past. How lucky to touch an envelope with Emily Dickinson's handwriting of an incomplete poem, or an IOU written by Poe.

I was working on a famous letter at the time all this happened, one that I never saw again but imagine from time to time in my dreams. To this day, the old-world aroma of stiff paper and leather bindings, or the glint of gold along the edges of a first edition, or the sound of a book spine cracking open like a dull bullet—all that sparks something true and right in me. But like in a decade-old magazine article, some of the details are lost, despite leaving an impression on me some time ago. Walking into a library is a little like finding a lost home: the anticipation, the discovery, the reassurance of soft voices and carpeted floors, the small groups intent on words and language.

Vince was in my Brenniss life, too. We were a week away from getting married. We had just consolidated living spaces. My life, boxed and labeled, had been transported to his condo blocks from my apartment. I owned nothing at that point, if I think about it. I've not seen those boxes since. I'm not sure I would recognize anything anyway. Details lost, I guess, like a forgotten page in a book.

For months, my only recollection was a flicker of white. My mother reminded me later, the final fitting for my wedding dress was that day. She said I took her breath away, just like the first time I held you. She stood behind my reflection, and we smiled, toasted champagne while the white flowed around me like clouds. She left the reflection at some point, a tattered page I couldn't pull together for nearly a year. Just. White.

Leaving the mall that day, I know I was burdened with a briefcase, gift bags, a purse, the dress, and maybe tipsy with a little too much champagne. My head pounded as I fumbled for my phone to leave a message for someone. Hindsight tells me I could have parked closer, not tried a shortcut, refused the second champagne toast, or been a little more vigilant. To this day, I don't recall ever hearing the engine closing toward me.

The metal door rolled open like a mouth. I'm slammed by arms and bodies folding me like a dog-eared page in a phone directory. My legs buckled and my arms were emptied of the packages within a breath. I ricocheted upside down onto the scratchy floor of in the van while my white dress pooled on the ground like a waterfall. A jerk of the wheel and we screeched around the corner. I yelled for help, but my head slammed against the floor. A rough hand slapped across my mouth. Three faces swam in front of me, but I didn't remember much beyond that for a year. Brenniss became lost in a random moment, a fragile fluff of dandelion scattered only to disappear.

But I discovered, what I lived that next year, was how I created the survivor in me.

CHAPTER
ONE

Brenniss Tripham stared at her collected life in the messy condo living room and craved coffee in the worst way. The parade of her boxes and belongings to Vince's condo was a weary memory, dying a slow death sometime after 10:30 last night. Vince had collapsed on the floor but not after removing his smudged white tee shirt and waved a sign of surrender. They somehow sank between the covers an inch before midnight.

After they dressed for work the next morning, she stared at the unforgiving living room again. Stacked boxes were like tanks readying a maneuver for an upcoming attack. Her boxes demanded attention a week before the wedding, along with everything else she had to do last minute. But instead, she wove her way through the barriers toward the kitchen to set up the coffee maker, the one that put the fear of God into Vince. All one needed was the water and the coffee pod, then press the button. If Vince only would—

"Bren, where's my blue tie?" Vince called from the bedroom. "I put it with my shirt last night."

Living on her own, she heard only muffled conversations. Maybe the toaster popping a quick breakfast, traffic outside her window, the neighbor's baby wailing at 4:00 a.m. She never had an actual voice so close to her in her living space. Just now, Vince's voice interrupted her thoughts more loudly than the subway. That difference, of hearing that familiar voice within the walls instead of on the phone or in a restaurant, surprised her. Clarity had opened the door for her again. This new life.

"Check the floor. It may have fallen from the chair." She chuckled. "I'm making coffee. We don't have time to go to Merry Beans on the way to work today."

"Maybe tomorrow," Vince added as he approached the kitchen. "I like this, better anyway. Having breakfast our first morning together."

She sighed. "I can't believe this mess."

Embracing her shoulders from behind, Vince's head slid next to hers. "Look, it's not forever. If we don't get this done before we leave for the honeymoon, we'll have plenty of time after we return. You've got to admit, Maui sounds much better than unpacking boxes."

This she loved, the proximity, the sound of his breathing in the room, the warmth of his arms. How he put things into perspective. She felt him lean back to finish his Windsor knot.

"How about a bagel and some eggs?" He reached for the pan as she made Vince's coffee.

⌒

Brenniss' confidence rose with each step toward the New York Public Library, the grand, historical lady that housed her work. Heading the Archival Department buoyed her, as she anticipated the discovery of the recent acquisition: a previously unknown letter from the Revolutionary War attributed to Alexander Hamilton. He had not only Washington's ear but also his back, with recommendations regarding support for the voluntary army. Brenniss had the rare opportunity to authenticate that particular letter she held last week.

The mystery surrounding the letter's long absence in historical circles would not be something she could detect in the text. But she could reach into the past and find clues from the brittle paper, the faded ink, to the artful cursive requests for funds from Congress to support General Washington. Knowing he could have held the page, could have dipped the quill into the ink, could have formed the sentences, dotted and crossed and punctuated, was like shaking hands with the man himself.

On the other side of the Archival Office door, the lab report on the letter's paper and ink samples sat squarely on her desk, the only thing worth noticing in the room. Her staff members, Grayson and Jennifer, crowded into her office doorway as she picked it up. Her hands felt as paper-thin as she released it from the envelope and read the first two lines.

"Bingo! Take a look, you guys! The lab says the paper contains linen authentic to sometime after the 1760s and, according to the graph—see? See that spike?" They crowded closer, holding breaths, looking at the spidery lines. "The ink contained iron gall. That means the ink is authentic from that period as well!"

"Holy buckets!" whispered Grayson. "It's the real thing!"

"Well, all we *can* say is the paper and ink are from that period. Now, it's time to look at the script itself. So, get the samples of Hamilton's signature from the Smithsonian! We've got work to do!"

She knew well the elaborate, almost lyrical curve in Hamilton's pen, unlike Madison's squatty signature. Hamilton's was known for tall slants and flowing beauty: the open loop on the capital *R*, the connection of his *A* in his first name to the curve of the *H* in his last, followed by the downturn of the *n* at the end of "Hamilton," as if waving goodbye. She smiled. *And some are convinced that cursive is dead.*

Checking her calendar, she was distracted by two appointments. Lunch with Vince was purely to keep her sanity. The other was her final dress fitting. *Wait...today? Already?* Thankfully, that was at the end of the day, an appropriate comma to catch her breath before the hectic week that followed. If she could make it to the mall within an hour after work, she'd still have time to focus fully on Alexander Hamilton, the other man in her life right now.

———

Had Vince Caldwell not lost his parents in that drug store shooting while he was in college, he might not have been as focused on order in his life: his socks folded just so, his shirts almost compulsively organized by color and season. If he lived by order, kept focus instead of dreams, then organization, not memory, could be his guide. It all stemmed from his parent's dream vacation to the Caribbean and that simple stop at the drug store to get last minute essentials. Little did he expect two officers meeting him in the dorm office telling him his parents had been killed in one of those nonsensical mass shootings. His face remained stoic, his focus on classes remarkably sharp, and his unwavering graduation plans allowed his emotions to skim the surface while his grief dug a hole. Having no siblings, he gratefully managed with the tidy cushion from his parents' estate.

Backup plans made more sense than dreams anyway. No surprises or upsets. Do the preparation, don't get distracted, stack the emotions in the loss column and stay with the logic, inning after inning, month after month.

He joined the financial planning branch of the firm of

Whitten and Mast after college, which planted his feet where he needed to be. Clients appreciated his focus, his drive, and that desire to have things fit perfectly. In turn, they talked to their bosses about the serious young man who was working hard toward securing their money, as fluid as mercury. That "dedicated Caldwell fellow" rose quickly at Whitten and Mast, all the while, pushing away sentimentality toward holidays, recalled birthdays, and the anniversary of that freakish shooting that suffocated his parents' lives. Such a focus added talent and skill to Whitten and Mast's income. No one saw the flat face of denial, the anguish of a broken life that connected to no one.

He hadn't wanted the disorder of doing research at the New York Public Library. His desire to "zip in and zip out" probably contributed to the speed when he turned a corner beside the stacks to ask for assistance. He met a young woman carrying leather-bound books up to her neck.

"Can you tell me where I can find this reference?" He showed her a hand-scribbled note. She craned her neck over a volume labeled "Hawthorne." No luck. The handwriting was atrocious.

"I'm sure you could ask the librarian at the desk or check the card catalogue." She nodded in both directions. "I don't work in the library directly. But Mariette is very helpful. Tell her Brenniss sent you." She smiled and wished him good luck. Turning, she tipped the books slightly, and all fell to the floor. He helped her pick them up, thinking about the weight of the books, a good five pounds each, and that his stupid question caused such chaos.

"Are you all right?" she asked, looking directly into his face. She checked the leather bindings for damage, her gloved hands rubbing the books as if they were suffering. At that moment, chaos dissolved, maybe for the first time in many years, into a desire to be one of those volumes.

"Oh, gosh, I didn't—I'm so sorry, uh, Brenniss, is it?" He leaned back, feeling the surprise of the connection. "I'll just..." he motioned toward the librarian's desk. "I'll just...thanks again."

She smiled, then continued around the corner and disappeared behind the door marked "ARCHIVES." His written apology on personalized stationery arrived days later, an invitation for coffee at Merry Beans. Then followed dinner not long after. For good reason, Vince usually didn't like surprises, but this unplanned introduction to kindness at the library couldn't be ignored. Then came other dinners, other conversations, and another surprise: how awesome it was to be five minutes late for an office meeting because the coffee and companionship were delightful.

His heart took the risk, the new perspective, never seeing fails, flaws or red flags. Brenniss and Vince both realized how isolated they had been. Much like a tango between Vince's Orioles and Brenniss' opera, they created order for the next week and the next. Then plans into the summer and fall, then past the holidays.

Meeting Brenniss' parents, Milt and Betty at Thanksgiving dinner, Vince discovered two things: the onset of an untimely fever left him with no appetite that night, and more importantly, he didn't remember how to interact with parents, not having parents in his life for nearly ten years. As an adult, his only conversations were about fiduciary funds, prime rates, and retirement plans, not the new city council or the price of Betty's remodeled kitchen. A sense of foreboding swarmed over him. Additionally, he failed to see was how pleased Milt and Betty were that Vince would go to any length to please their daughter. They welcomed him back, the young man with such focus.

By next spring, during a weekend at the beach, Vince had decided to propose. Perhaps Bren already had an inkling he might ask her, but her surprised face when he knelt in the sand was as if she were doused with a bucket of stars. The sun was setting. "I can't let another day pass without asking you to marry me. You're the woman I love; I want to combine my life with yours. Before the sun sets, please say 'yes'."

How could she say "no"?

———

The magnifying glass emphasized the coil at the beginning of the "A" in the signature. Brenniss held her breath, superimposing it over the Smithsonian sample.

The phone rang.

"Brenniss, we've got a staff meeting in five minutes," her supervisor Henry Lloyd droned. "You definitely need to be here. Head of the library wants to know if we should be calling a news conference about the Hamilton letter. Oh, and the New York Times editions from 1901—are they ready yet? We need—"

"Oh, crap! I forgot to pull them from the archive this morning. Grayson can and I'm on my way," in one breath. She pressed her fingers along the bridge of her nose, the announcement of one of her migraines. She was so close to matching those *As* of Hamilton's... "Grayson? I need you to drop everything! The New York Times 1901 editions? I guess I needed them about ten minutes ago."

"Holy buckets! I'm on it!"

Lunch with Vince was to be the quick serving of tranquility she needed today, but...she used her speed dial.

"Hey, Vince."

"Okay, what's up? You wouldn't be calling this close to lunch if you weren't cancelling."

"Sorry, but Lloyd sprang a staff meeting on me in...three minutes. I'm not organized, and I've got a killer headache coming on, too. But that's not new."

"Well, how about I make your day a little more challenging? I just got wind that the gang here at Whitten and Mast is throwing us a wedding shower tonight at Trendz. It's a surprise, so meet me there after work as soon as you can."

"No way! I can't! I have my dress fitting after work!"

"Tonight? Well, how long does a dress fitting take? Everything should fit, right? You try it on. Everything looks super. You change clothes, pay the rest of the payment, and come back to Trendz, right?"

"It's a drive to the mall and back. It's a little longer than that, but..." she took a breath, "I'll get there as soon as I can."

"Maybe we should have eloped all along." He chuckled.

"I gotta go, Vince. The meeting, I'm sorry."

"I'm sorry, too, sweetie. I'll see you later."

CHAPTER
TWO

If Trendz could talk, the bar would tell stories of a gentleman's club with cigars and brandy, bankrupted by the onslaught of gin and flappers and, later, Prohibition. But Trendz was a survivor in its own right, cementing the essence of each decade to survive: confrontations, celebrations, and conversations from Gehrig to DiMaggio and Mantle, to Berlin and Bataan, to James Dean and Brando, to sit-ins, men on the moon, disco and 9-11. Now, the gentrified bar with its microbrews and original punched tin ceiling, the exposed and seasoned brick walls and pub-like friendliness was the most comfortable friend for the Whitten and Mast crew even for a wedding shower.

At least, that's how Tess had convinced him. Sometimes Vince's assistant seemed clairvoyant, or maybe she was organized to a fault. That fit Vince like a glove, made her a valuable part of his team especially when she didn't ask for a spotlight or credit. Tess had secretly organized the wedding shower until Vince discovered Tess' wayward memo in the copying machine. For once, she couldn't explain it away and begged him to pretend to be surprised. He chuckled while she shrugged.

Without Brenniss, he felt more awkward walking into Trendz' meeting room brightened with balloons and fluffy paper flowers and a vinyl banner wishing the "Best for Vince and Brenniss." He feigned shock, even felt a little overwhelmed by the thirty-odd staff members yelling "Surprise!" Tess loyally stood close to Vince until Brenniss would arrive to take her place.

"Did Brenniss leave you already?" someone called out. "Smart woman!" another teased. The laughter disrupted the quiet of the moment, until Vince spoke.

"No, no, really, she'll be here. Of all nights, this was her final dress fitting. She'll be here once she can get back from the mall. So, on behalf of Brenniss, I will say thank you once again for celebrating with us."

"To Vince and Brenniss!" a voice rang out. "A long, happy life together!" Glasses raised above the voices and cheers.

Vince absorbed himself among friends and well-wishers, avoiding the empty embarrassment. Another hole in his life worming at his confidence.

"So, where is she, Vince? We want to talk some sense into her!" a new arrival called out.

"Honest, Brenniss is coming. I bet she's held up in traffic." He kept the smile, the charm, the ease.

More arrivals entered. Tess warmly welcomed new arrivals, always returning to Vince a whisper's width away.

"You enjoying the surprise?" She winked at him. "Thanks for going along with this. You looked pretty convinced when you walked in here. How about I buy my boss another drink?"

"Sure! Another beer? Why not?"

As others arrived, Vince juggled the laughter, goodwill, and his concern for Brenniss artfully, accepting this disruption as an expectation. Tess set the beer next to him on the counter, but he already had moved toward coworkers Kent and Dave.

He covered his concern with a smile, although wondered if her migraine had overwhelmed her. Maybe she was lying on a couch somewhere in the women's lounge at the mall or maybe her headache had advanced enough she was seeing double and unable to drive.

"Tell you what, I'll call her cell." *Maybe she had just driven home.* He steadily watched the doorway as he used his cell. The celebration had gone on for nearly an hour with no Brenniss. He got her voice mail, instead.

"Hey, Bren! Lots of folks here at Trendz asking about you. Just give a call to let me know how much longer you need."

"Standing you up?" Tess teased.

"Oh, no, no. It's just a busy time, you know. She'll be here soon enough."

But after another hour, some were drifting toward the door. Brenniss' absence was more than uncomfortable. Vince felt stiff smiles and spitwad glances in his direction. He didn't need more beer or crab puffs or to open any gifts. He needed Bren to walk through the doorway, profusely apologizing. Conversations lost their focus, topics repeated. Still no answer when Vince called the condo. Even Mr. Witten seemed a little nervous about the situation with his awkward "thanks for a nice evening, Vince" as his goodbye.

A few gathered trash, empty beer bottles like bells, a sure sign that the night was over. He tried Brenniss' phone: mailbox full. Tess sat down next to him a little too closely, sipping a new drink.

"Hey, what are you drinking, anyway?" He grabbed her glass and sipped. "Rum and Coke? Are you old enough to drink that?" He pushed the drink back toward her.

"Hey, how old do you think I am? Of course, I'm old enough. I couldn't have come in here to decorate if I were underage!"

"Sorry, sorry. This was supposed to be a special night. You

planned things perfectly. Too bad we didn't have anything planned when the guest of honor didn't show."

She giggled, running her finger against the moisture of the glass. "You know, Vince. I always had hoped that someday—"

His cell shattered the remaining conversations in the room. A little too loudly, he said, "Finally!" and brought the phone to his ear.

"Hello, babe. I've been waiting to hear—What? Hello?"

His voice caught. For once, Trendz held its breath.

"Excuse me? Oh, hello, sir." Another deep pause that painted a silence across the other tables. "Yes, Yes, I am. Is there—is there some kind of—What?"

His face blanched. The last friends stopped their thoughts and focused, as he felt the collective kick in the gut.

"Are you sure? Of course! Of course! I'll be right there. Thank you, officer!"

Vince pocketed his phone in slow motion. Then, he ran towards the door, around tables and the remaining couples staring at him.

"Something's happened to Bren! I gotta..." But by then, he was out of Trendz while a single balloon broke free against the high tin ceiling. Trendz really couldn't offer anything at that moment, not a gasp or sputter. Nothing.

Jumping into his car, he barely noticed those staring from the sidewalk or his friends squeezing into the window wells, shaking their heads, shrugging their shoulders, and casually looking at their watches. His hands absently flicked the steering wheel, waiting for an opening in traffic. Yet another red light. Didn't they know he was in a hurry?

He replayed it. "Are you the fiancé of Brenniss Tripham? Were you expecting her this afternoon? I'm sorry to tell you we believe she's been abducted late this afternoon from the mall..." Abducted? *Abducted?* Who gets abducted these days? Maybe in Iraq, but at the mall? Certainly that wasn't anywhere in their minds when they were having breakfast. I'll go to the mall for my dress fitting and then I'll get abducted. Have a nice day. No, she probably took a wrong turn, put down the briefcase momentarily then left it behind. Her headaches did that sometimes, played with her memory. Or maybe she was stuck in the restroom at the mall, right under everyone's noses. Sure, it's a mistake. She'll be there by the time he gets to the mall. The honking behind him intensified, and he realized the light had turned green.

Agony. As traffic ticked from one block to the next, he imagined Brenniss being in the next car, because *her* car broke down. Good God, he didn't even remember what she was wearing today. He pounded his fist against the steering wheel. Please, Brenniss, let this be a horrible mistake, something they could laugh at later. "Remember a week before the wedding when we lost you?"

His blinker ticked his intent to inch onto the ramp, finally picking up speed along the curve. Instinctively, he turned on the radio to alleviate the uncomfortable edge of silence in the passenger seat.

"...Once again, police report a missing woman possibly abducted this afternoon from the Whisper Tree Mall. The woman, Brenniss Tripham, is 5'7" tall, in her mid-thirties, brown hair, brown eyes, last seen in the vicinity of the northwest corner of the mall. She was abducted in a dark blue or black van. If you see an older model dark colored van..." He flicked the radio off. Damn, it's on the radio. What the hell?

The stone in his stomach rode with him until he reached the mall. Police were diverting cars at the front entrance, and he was told to drive toward the back where he parked in the far lot. He was aware of how bizarre it was to run across the grassy, manicured, curved drive of Whisper Tree. Joke's on them, he thought. I've had four beers and the whole police force could arrest me right now for DUI. Yellow police tape, like CSI cornering around a nearly empty parking lot; the police cars parked outside the lines as if they never learned to color in grade school, yet some police are talking without panic.

A voice called out. "Hold it, son! You can't go past this tape. It's a crime scene."

Crime scene! His brain screamed. "No, wait. I'm Vince Caldwell. I was told to come here—"

"You the fiancé?"

"Yes, yes! Officer Michaels told me to meet him." His voice sounded far away, something he couldn't claim.

"You mean Detective Michaels? You got any ID?"

"You've got to be kidding!" His thick fingers fidgeted with his wallet, then finally threw the wallet toward the police officer. His eyes were drawn sideways toward red and blue strobe pulses. In the midst, a tow truck raised a white car onto a trailer.

"Wait! That's Brenniss' car! What the hell are you doing—?" He felt a sturdy hand push his wallet against his chest.

"It's still a crime scene. Watch your step." He was waved inside the tape.

One foot led the other across the asphalt lined with impossibly perfect trees in grassy plots. There on the ground, an unexpected still life: shopping bags, a collapsed wedding dress, a briefcase, a purse scattered, her cell phone blinking alive with voice mail messages—likely his from Trendz—her wallet oddly distant in the trail left behind. No wonder some thought she'd been kidnapped. This didn't look much like a mistake at all. Her "perfect" dress lay against the black asphalt drive but turned at an uncomfortable angle away from the waist, as if having second thoughts or catching someone's attention, the chiffon flaking up and down against any breeze, conjured by the officer taking pictures. It took his breath away.

"Vince! Vince!"

"Brenniss?" He looked around, hopeful. It was her voice, wasn't it?

"Vince! There he is, Detective, see? Vince!"

He turned toward the voice. Her mother, Betty, frantically waved as if erasing the stunning display. Her tiny figure was bolstered by Milt's lanky arm. His empty expression told Vince that they had heard the worst already. Vince's wooden legs turned, forcing heavy footsteps until he reached the couple with Detective Michaels.

"Thanks for getting here as soon as you could." The detective spoke solemnly. "I'm very sorry for this. What we believe has happened is that your fiancé was kidnapped, but we don't know who or why. We're hoping for a ransom call soon. But we do have some security video we think captured the incident. We need you to take a look, if you don't mind. Maybe you'll recognize a face, a mannerism...something that the abductors did. Come with me."

The detective led Vince into one of those invisible service hallways toward a makeshift office to view the video. He realized only then, as he sat down in front of the monitor, that the last time he talked to Brenniss was during the rushed conversation before lunch. And he'd never told her he loved her.

The grainy video jumped a frame or two, then revealed a young woman. His hand cupped the screen. *Brenniss, my Brenniss.* She had too much to carry, that's what happened: briefcase, purse, some small shopping bags, the dress draped across both arms. He drew a sharp breath. *Stop, now. Go back and ask for help.* The next frame showed Brenniss awkwardly attempting to use the keypad on her phone. She stopped only for a second, but just as a dark van turned the curve behind her in the upper left portion of the screen. She had tried to place the phone near her ear, but the bags shifted against the dress. She stopped to adjust it all.

The van approached closer. She briefly stepped sideways. The van slowed; the side door slid backward. Two men jumped out. One grasped her head and bent her forward, off-balance. The dress was strewn one direction, her belongings scattered. The other man grabbed her waist and shifted her in one smooth motion, folding her like a leather billfold or an origami crane into the van. The door closed as the van disappeared off the lower left screen.

No! Vince swallowed hard. He didn't recognize the men whose faces were shielded by hooded sweatshirts. He viewed it again. And another time. Again and again. Each time, Brenniss slowed at exactly the wrong time. She didn't turn back, she didn't jump, or arrive one second later. Each time, it wasn't the hooded sweatshirts he studied, it was Brenniss. That surprise of being pushed off-balance, losing her footing, her mouth open in a scream. Until the screen went blank and Vince's heart went numb.

CHAPTER
THREE

"How you can get that line tangled after four casts is beyond me! I swear that fish was winking at you!" Griff Hensley's chuckle could make a friend out of an enemy, could relax the most anxious. Riley Bedarte smiled. The worst fish story ever. His gray stubble from an afternoon's relaxing on the river caught white in the setting sun. They loaded their gear haphazardly after chasing that one last catch. Which he lost. Griff's beater truck with the worn finish, the rebuilt engine, and a bumper sticker that said "Duct Tape don't fix Stupid" was used for gathering wood, hunting, and fishing trips such as this. However, the truck reserved judgment on their talent for fishing.

"I'm out of practice. I got no excuses." His eyes lifted to the late sunset and the river snaking below the road. "Damn, it's pretty out here. I'd forgotten."

"Sure glad to see you back on the river again."

"Don't start, Griff."

"No, I'm just saying the river was happy to see you. Gave you two fish!"

Riley raised his catch for a better view. "Yeah, they're beauts. Here—why don't you take these fish with you? You and Hannah can have dinner."

Griff reluctantly took the fish, then smiled. "Okay, on one condition. You come by for a fish fry tomorrow dinner. Come join us. Like old times."

Riley removed the fishing vest and laid it on his other gear, then eased into the truck. Griff placed the key in the ignition.

"It's been over two years, Riley. Grace wouldn't want—"

"You got me out on the river. I enjoyed myself. I gave you two fish. Let's leave it at that." Riley's words snapped like a twenty-pound test line. His eyes closed for a moment. He still saw Grace's face—the beauty of her—not the battle-torn, weak woman after the chemo. "Sorry, it just isn't in me yet, I guess."

"So, come to dinner, tomorrow—no big commitment."

Griff started the throaty engine of the truck. He backed away from the river's edge, now enclosed in pale gray dusk and headed onto the dark washboard road that paralleled the river.

"Come by about 6:30 tomorrow. That'll give you time to feed the horses, right?"

Silence.

Griff tried another tact. "Speaking of horses, how about training more for search and rescue? The town council thinks you're stalling. There's going to come a time we'll need three or four sure-footed horses for rescue. We can't get them trained anywhere except this area because of our terrain. Hell, *I* can help you train them!"

"Griff, you know it's a twenty-hour a day job. You can't devote that kind of time. I just don't have the support, the way that Grace—"

Riley had lived on the ranch more than fifteen years, most of that time considering Griff his best friend. In fact, Grace had been the one who saw the property first, who dreamed of training quality stock, who named all the horses, who rode early and stayed late in the barn. He began to love the animals, too, and now every nicker, every gallop made him think Grace was right beside him, stepping off the porch to the barn.

"Search and Rescue training worked because of Grace. She was the glue that held the program together. You know that. I need someone just as reliable as she was. You know someone?"

"Hell no, but I thought I'd give it another try."

Riley peered ahead into the darkness, the remains of the sunset in his rearview. "Okay, 6:30 tomorrow." He tipped his hat back and reached for the thermos of Hannah's coffee when he called out, "Hey! What's that ahead?"

The movement along the shoulder came from a dark van, maybe black, no license plate, with three men carrying what looked like a log, then tossing it down the embankment.

"Damn kids throw their trash along the road," Griff muttered. They wore hoodies that covered their faces, but their movements were quick, much like a surprised deer. The threesome jumped back into the van and peeled away, just as Griff's headlights fixed solidly on the vehicle.

"I'll call it in; let's take a look."

"I can't quite make it out in the dark. Hand me that flashlight!" Riley said, balanced sideways on the shoulder. He lowered himself step-by-step down the incline away from the road, into the dark. "Looks like it caught on some saplings," he yelled to the road. Riley's gaze sank into the shadows while Griff shone another flashlight. Balancing, he bent forward, pulling back thick braids of carpet. He smelled dirt, beer, cigarettes.

The carpet disintegrated between his fingers as he pulled fabric layers, some so full of dust, his hands slipped. There certainly was something solid wrapped inside. Pieces pulled away from the rug like bits of old insulation. First, carpet, then a thin blanket was pulled back, slowly, until he encountered hair—a bear, maybe, not a deer. Then, to Riley's surprise, something more human. A nose, a chin, an arm...

"Good God!" Riley recoiled and nearly lost his balance. "We've got a body, Griff. Or the remnants of one. A woman!" Something swift and sure in him knew he could help. He couldn't help his wife Grace, but now, his purpose was focused. He pulled more fabric away to check her pulse, the way he'd check Grace's pulse in those last few weeks, to radar her life more closely. He pulled that from deep inside for this stranger.

Griff careened down the incline, sliding just short of Riley, the inertia and adrenaline driving his body. "Is she alive?"

Like Grace, the stranger was dependent on him for the next few minutes. He willed a heartbeat, however faint. "She has a pulse." He breathed. "Barely, but I can feel it." He leaned toward her face. "Shallow breath."

"County emergency: this is Sheriff Griff Hensley. We'll need an ambulance and investigative team on Stryker Road at..." He glanced down the road, "mile marker seventeen. Unknown female in extreme distress, weak pulse, unconscious, appears to have been assaulted. County emergency, I repeat: immediate call, mile marker seventeen on Stryker Road..." Griff's training kicked in, by the book, following procedures to keep this woman alive. The two men levered the soiled rug past the snag of saplings, while Griff checked off in his brain the protocols. Emergency services, crime scene protocols, keep the victim breathing, warm and as alert as possible. Emergency services was only half a mile away. Clearly, this unconscious woman's right eye appeared permanently shut, her face the color of ripe plums. Blood and fluids stuck ooze along her lips. Her dark tee shirt and slacks had been ripped and blood was caked around her upper thigh. Her right wrist bent sideways. Every inch of exposed skin was blemished with cuts and bruises. He hardly recognized her as human. "How could anyone...?" His breath slid out unfinished. He didn't dare feel anything more, just get communication to the right people to do their jobs....and he did his.

The sirens pierced the darkness, a banshee wailing a sadness that pulsed fear. The ambulance screeched to a stop and spilled humans like a clown car. EMTs prepared for transport to the hospital. Griff saw how difficult it was to start an IV, yet oxygen slowly increased, improving her chances toward the hospital. As the ambulance swallowed the gurney with the motionless woman, Griff pulled Riley toward the truck. "We'll follow behind."

The silence hung between them while outside the siren led to town. A large curve brought them to Copper Station's small community hospital. Doc Mattheson met the ambulance, his white bristle hair standing in surprise, his clean profile barked questions.

"What have we got here?"

In one clean movement, the gurney extended onto the drive, while EMTs bulleted the scant information. Racing through the ER doorway, they were swallowed into the brash light of the hospital.

Griff and Riley followed the group, but when stopped by the closing ER door, the exclamation point to their efforts felt sudden and useless. Powering down their adrenaline, they stood like aliens in the florescent lights as the door glided shut, a vacuum of silence. No sirens, no shouts, no monitors beeping, no racing over dark roads, no panic to hold onto that thread of life in a still body, just a hospital hum. They sighed in the stuttering silence, heartbeats racing.

Griff turned to the receptionist. "Do you have some paper and pens for us? Might as well write our statements while we're waiting."

While driving west on Stryker Road at approximately 8:00 p.m., three males dressed in hoodies were witnessed alongside the road... Griff's hands were stained with mud, dust, and whatever-the-hell might have been in that rug. He had cast that last line into the river with the same two hands that now stalled over the white paper. He remembered the burn of the bright truck headlights against the moonless night, the shock of seeing a barely alive body in the folds of the blanket and rug. Then, making mental notes to catalogue evidence with a small village of volunteers to measure tire marks, snap pictures of the rug, and write down the brand name on the blanket.

...the rolled rug was observed being pushed over the shoulder along Stryker Road, falling north down the embankment approximately twelve feet from the road, when it stopped...

He looked at Riley as they wrote in tandem. This must be tough for him, he realized. Maybe the first time back at the hospital since Grace's last admission.

...unrolled the blanket to reveal a white female, approximately mid-thirties, with severe contusions about the face and body, broken wrist, collarbone and ribs, unconscious, with a thready pulse measured at 40 bpm...

Her wounds were purposeful and defensive. There was more to the story than finding her along the roadside. His mind clicked scenarios that tap danced across his report.

...dispatched to the scene were EMTs who provided emergency care to stabilize her for transport to hospital...

And, slim to none, even if she survived, how could he put the pieces together?

Riley leaned forward, elbows on his knees, paper extended toward Griff. "Not sure I can remember any more." He slid his statement toward the sheriff. "Now, why don't you go home to Hannah. I can stay here. Pick me up in the morning or bring my truck."

"Oh, God! Hannah! I never called her! She has no idea where we are!" He clicked his cell phone open.

"Go on home." Riley waved. "I can stay."

———

*Strange being back here. After Grace's battle, and it was **that**, being inside these antiseptic floors and walls again. Even that same urgent look in Doc's eyes tonight; yes, the same when Doc met Grace at the emergency room that last time. Yet here he was. Waiting.*

Two years ago seemed like yesterday, watching the last of Grace, a film of her former self, sleeping away. At one time, she angrily vowed that, when she died, she was taking the damn cancer with her, her own angel of death. He was proud of her battle but terrified that she was right.

He and Grace had moved from Chicago, what?—seventeen years ago?—ready for their second career in their late thirties then. Their lives had brought them enough prosperity that they wanted a second career. Grace had always hoped for a ranch. On a trip to Arizona, they wandered the blue highways and happened by Old Man Fletcher's place. The "For Sale" sign waving them in. He saw it immediately in Grace's eyes—the barn had good bones, the pasture could be teased back to life in a couple years, the 1900s farmhouse, with that huge wrap-around porch—it all could be done. She was optimistic that way.

That first day he and Grace drove to the place, high summer toasted the road. Grace opened the doors and windows because the house had held its breath long enough. She wiped down those pitiful dusty oak floors. They hadn't seen a broom or mop since Old Man Fletcher had died on his front porch, loading his rifle for fall hunting, the locals told it. Keeled right over—heart attack—dead before he hit the porch floor. But, by dang! Didn't that rifle discharge when he fell and shot an un-suspecting turkey ambling down the driveway? Always was a good shot, they said.

Griff got around to introducing the idea of search and res-cue horses soon after. Those first horses, Sage and Buck, held an officer proud in the saddle and helped locate runaways and lost tourists. The training often dissolved into dinner with Hannah, Griff, Riley, and Grace when the sun was never warmer, never seemed to set at all. Search and rescue expanded their friendships and their mark in the Copper Station commu-nity.

Grace found the lump under her left breast when Riley was overnight at a Tucson horse auction, late spring about three years ago. She attributed it to hard work, a pulled muscle, maybe nothing at all really, until the mammograms showed she had trouble brewing in her chest. Riley knew the size of that lump and the pain were devilish. Then the call came back a few weeks later. But by then, Grace already knew.

Just like her to go full-bore into surgery, chemo, and radi-ation so she could be better by the fall. The surgery went well, Doc said, we got as much as we found. Before long, when Grace's eyes grew larger against her sunken cheeks, she knew the guarantees were lost.

The damn stuff had spread, a mind of its own. Riley aged while Grace withered, for nearly two years, cell-by-cell. She still had many good days, the horses always refreshing her strength. But gradually, she was making more plans for Riley and the place than for herself.

That last race to the emergency room, after Grace col-lapsed, was much like tonight, an eerie comparison. Riley picked up the scarecrow his wife had become from the front seat of the truck. She was so lightweight; Riley thought death might not notice and pass her unnoticed. He handed her over like a broken doll to Doc, as if she could be put back together *one more time. Doc's face had that look of "Oh, no, not yet," no matter how many times he'd warned Riley that she only had weeks. The end came in a room that smelled like bleach, the white sheets framing Grace's form. She just forgot to breathe, a quiet, soft nothing in her lungs, her heart making no effort.*

Remember with Bliss? he seemed to hear her ask. I had a feeling about that horse, didn't I? And I was right. Proved to be a strong runner. So, how could you treat this young woman any differently? I have a feeling about this one...

"Riley? Riley?" He felt someone at his shoulder, pressing again. His eyes snapped open, the progressively bad coffee still stuck to the roof of his mouth. Grace was nowhere to be seen. *No, wait...Grace...*dawn inched through the window shades. Next to him sat Doc, intent, but weary.

"Didn't think I'd see you here." Doc smiled. "She's out of surgery, Riley. She's made it through, somehow. She had broken bones and horrible damage done to her vaginal cavity. I doubt that she'll ever have children, the damage was so severe. But she's a survivor."

Who was he talking about? Grace? She was just—

"Let's see...broken ribs, broken clavicle, broken cheekbone, broken wrist, dehydration, contusions, bite marks, scratches, and," he swallowed, "if that weren't enough, signs of multiple rape and vaginal tears. She likely would have bled to death in a matter of hours if you hadn't come along." He wiped the fatigue along his face. "I'd never seen anyone so battered. We've got a rape kit for the sheriff when he returns."

Riley, even in the fog of waking up, felt a rise in anger that pounded his head. Doc reached for his shoulder. "She's still critical, but she's alive. She's stable enough on IVs, antibiotics, and supplemental feedings. When she wakes up, she may not remember much, you know."

"No, Doc, I'll stay. Seems it's not right to leave someone like that after all she's lived through. You'd want that for your kin, wouldn't you? If she woke up...well, don't ask me why. Just point me to her room."

"Honest, Riley, she's resting now. You don't need to—"

"Where's her room? Just give me a chair and a few pints of that awful stuff you call coffee and I'll be fine." Riley's face was more stone than fatigue and he meant every word.

CHAPTER
FOUR

Riley watched the woman sleep, looking for the sparrow of a pulse in her neck. He did that with Grace those last weeks, watching her heart defy death with each beat. The woman's hair had been washed, the matted hair combed out, now drifting past her face and onto her shoulders. Her face was cleaner, too, although the purple and blue along her cheek and throat were more noticeable against white sheets. He settled again into the chair.

A nurse entered into the room and checked the IV, the wounds, the surgical sites, the tube feeding routed through the woman's nose, the oxygen hissing into her lungs. "Anything I can get you, Mr. Bedarte?" she whispered.

He shook his head.

"She's holding her own. Blood pressures stable, the bleeding has stopped, she's breathing well with good oxygen levels. You a friend?"

"No, we just found her along the roadside, abandoned. It just didn't seem right to abandon her here again."

The nurse smiled. "She's lucky. She has a friend and

doesn't know it, yet." She looked back at the woman. "We're doing checks every fifteen minutes, so I'll be back soon. Let me know if she—or you—need something."

He sighed and closed his eyes. Why was he sitting in a hospital room, beside a woman he didn't know, hoping she survived whatever happened to her? She was as lost as he'd been these last two years. With Grace, he watched pieces of her die. With this woman, he watched for any signs of recovery. Funny how both took the energy from him like the slow leak of a tire. Maybe this time, his efforts would bring a different ending. The woman needed to heal. So did he, come to think of it. So did he.

He was pulling a log tangled in fishing line from the river, then scratching at the bark to find bare wood. He peered past the marks on the wood. He found a face, inside.

"Riley, Riley," he heard against the shadow of that dream. "Riley, wake up."

He opened his eyes to see Griff and Hannah between the bed and his chair. A deep sigh brought him to a wakeful place, away from that cold river and rough wood, a place with words instead of confusing images telling a nonsensical story.

"We brought your truck so you could get home. Poke and the horses are probably wondering about you." Their voices were hushed, lullaby low.

Hannah let her eyes slip toward the bed, tried to find the words, but stayed silent.

"Nurse says she's hanging on. She's a survivor, Doc said."

"Yeah, I saw the doctor's report and got the rape kit," Griff whispered.

"I can stay awhile so she won't be alone. You go on home," Hannah offered. "We won't leave her."

Riley pressed his fingers to his eyes, trying to erase that initial shock of pieces of a human being, swaddled and hidden in a dirty rug. "I do need to check on the animals. I can be back later—"

"Take your time Riley."

As he turned into his drive, Poke pushed his head around the corner of the porch, then lay back down. His tepid welcome let Riley know it wasn't Poke who was in the doghouse.

"Sorry, fella. If you'd seen what I did last night, you wouldn't have come home, either. Somebody needed my help." The familiar antiseptic smell drew Poke closer. Riley rubbed the dog's forehead. He could smell it, too.

"Naw, Poke, it's not Grace you smell. Sorry, boy. She won't be back. No, this was someone else who needed a friend." He thought of the woman's whisper breath, each cycle building cells and bone. You'd think he'd be used to those monitors and respirators by now.

"Let's get you and the horses taken care of."

The two-story home retained the cinnamon fragrance Grace loved, a bit of her just a breath away when he walked through the kitchen door. The morning light invited a second cup of coffee or conversations about the price of feed or how high the river would crest this spring. Poke took his favorite spot on the floor that gathered sun most of the morning, while Riley poured kibble into a bowl. This was the familiar. Last night's nightmare was far enough away, now. He could breathe into his own pace. He was home.

"Hey, Bliss, how's the day? Morning, Cartwheel." The roan and the dun were the last two horses Grace had named. Restless in their stalls, they showed him they were ready to stretch, run, and breathe deep the morning air. Both nickered at his presence, although Cartwheel, the younger, kicked her head back in mild reproach. Each day, they'd learned to accept him without Grace's presence, but even after all this time, certainly they missed her touch. Given an open barn door, they ran into the pasture with no cue, preferring the open to any one person. He didn't take it personally.

Bliss flowed like unraveling yarn toward the open, never hinting at the rough start in her life. The days Grace and he spent with her, after her life in the shelter, now seemed like a few ticks of the clock. She'd been collected from a farm further east, one that neglected twenty horses including Bliss. She arrived with weak legs and a muted appetite, having learned to make do with little food. Her mama had to be put down at the shelter, having given all of her energy and nutrition for her foal. But Bliss had the will. Grace saw it in her eyes, and instantly named her. "She has a serenity, a bliss about her." They brought her home, so she'd know love, too.

Bliss' coat was a dull chestnut when she first arrived, and she spent her energy like a miser. They rubbed her flanks, brushed her coat, and massaged her neck and legs for hours. She eased into their friendship. They never forced a path to win her trust.

She took food at first only if hand fed to her. A handful here and there, or an occasional gentle touch while these new people brushed her neck or chest, to open her heart to tenderness and trust, until her fear evaporated. Now Bliss looked forward to time with Cartwheel, the companionship she craved. Grace put her soul into Bliss, something left behind for Riley to touch every day.

Cleaning the barn had been his and Grace's time. They had talked about the daily things like bills and their plans while Grace could still manage. So fresh, still, what she might say, expecting to hear her take a breath in to start a sentence or to cock her head as if to question. Each day, he'd start first with a whisper about their life together, but today, that whisper was about that broken woman.

"I know your heart would go out to her, Grace. You were

always drawn to someone torn apart. She's just lying there, less than recognizable. A dog or a horse that beaten? You'd put it down. But a person? Different set of rules, trying to keep her going. Doc says she's holding her own. She's got a long way to go, though."

Now he was pulling the straw farther out the door in great sweeps, his voice above the soft gathering. *"Okay, so I don't know her, but nobody knows her story! Maybe she won't want to tell it, but there's a story there. You'd want to know it, too, once she got on her feet."*

He looked up. Poke was wagging his tail as if in agreement.

He heard a car horn by the house. It was Lester with the mail. He waved a small box and clipboard into the air. Riley left his mental soapbox to walk toward the mail truck.

"Les, how you doin'?"

"Got a package you need to sign for." Lester nodded and shoved the clipboard enthusiastically in Riley's direction. "Medicine for the horses?"

"Looks like."

Les wasn't the most socially adept postal worker, took his job rather seriously, in part, Riley believed, because he favored his uniform and the major responsibility of everyone's mail. He was approaching forty, never been married, despite being on speaking terms with nearly everyone on his route.

"There's a church social next Sunday, Riley. You ought to go. There're some fine fillies you could have your choice of." Les' smile broadened as if a wink were on its way.

"They've got horses at the church social, do they, Les?"

"Well, no, I mean the ladies!"

Riley flipped the clipboard back to Les. "No self-respecting lady I'd want to know would want to be referred to as a 'filly', Les. Have a good time, cowboy."

He pushed his postal cap further up on his forehead. "Cowboy, huh? Just trying to help you out, Riley." He shook his head while Riley returned toward the barn to put the medicine in the barn fridge. Poke cocked his head. "Filly, my ass," Riley grumbled.

But riding the horses diffused his disgust toward Les. "Come on, Cartwheel." He encouraged the horse to cut back and to the side. He brought her to a halt, backed her with gentle knee pressure to align with the corral fence. He moved the horse gently forward, then into a canter and repeated the process again. Cartwheel was methodical with Riley's guidance, a solid horse for turns and for endurance.

He whistled for Bliss who bolted enthusiastically from the pasture toward the corral. "Your turn, girl." He swung the saddle onto her back. Grace had planned to train Bliss for obstacle courses. She loved to run and trained to the details, except for one thing...

"That horse can't jump!" she'd called out, picking herself up from the Arizona dust. Her hat had rolled toward the creek she'd planned to use as a water hazard. "She out and out refuses," but she said it with a crinkled smile on her face.

"But where would Bliss need to jump?" Riley remembered asking.

"Just wanted to challenge her." She swiped her hat against her thigh. Damned if she didn't give that horse a carrot, anyway.

Riley, you need a challenge, too, he heard her voice in the back of his brain. You're getting set in your ways. Said you never wanted to do that. Grace's voice—well, it certainly wasn't *his* voice—showed up at the strangest times, he had to admit. She was rarely wrong in these discussions they weren't having.

"Poke, I'll finish up with Bliss, then get the horses settled. You want to stay in the house or the barn tonight?"

Poke looked toward the barn.

"The barn it is."

In another hour, he'd be on the road back to the hospital with Grace's voice in his thoughts.

Her face was the color of blueberries and plums, with a sickening green tinge in some of the margins. The white sheets, white curtains, white walls brought that out easily. White wasn't Grace's color, either.

He advanced slowly into her room, hearing pumps and the vitals monitor beep. She was six ways to broken, lying still to let her bones settle, with no evidence of that battle going on inside her body. He automatically looked at the screen, heart rate a little high at eighty beats per minute, but blood pressure and respirations were good.

"Um, hi there, young lady," he whispered. "Sorry I don't know your name. I'm Riley. I met you yesterday." The words didn't matter so much as his tone of voice, letting her know kindness was near. Grace had taught him that. "You know, I'm really sorry you were treated like this. You didn't deserve this, no one does. I stayed with you through the night and you're doing well, considering..." He looked at the screen again. Her heart rate had slowed to sixty-five.

Later that evening, he was near asleep when he heard a rustling. He looked toward her in the green light of the monitors and saw her hand, the unbroken one, flick up and down. Her toes nodded against the blanket, as if running an imaginary race. Then a soft whimper channeled unnaturally between the tubes in her mouth. Her eyes remained shut, as if the nightmare had just started.

"Hey there, hey there, young lady. What's wrong? Easy, easy..." He touched her arm, and it flailed weakly toward him, random, like a piece of straw caught in the wind and with as much strength.

"Easy...I won't hurt you. I'm here to help. Here, let me take your hand." He lay his hand flat against hers. She slowly inched her fingers into his.

"There, that wasn't so bad, now, was it?" He let his hand rest a full ten seconds before he touched her fingers. She flinched.

"Easy, now," he soothed. "Honest, I won't hurt you. I don't know what others did, but I'm not like them. I want you to know you're not alone." *Damn! If it weren't like Grace and Bliss. Waiting for that horse to approach her took every bit of patience Grace had.*

The young woman's face softened.

"Now, you've had a lot of surgeries, and I bet you're mighty sore." He leaned over toward the night table. "Here, how about I put some lotion on your arms? Hannah brought this for you today. Grace used to love lotion massages. Grace, she was my wife."

He opened the bottle as he spoke. "Just a little lotion, you'll see."

The mild lavender fragrance enveloped the room as Riley applied lotion on her papery hands in slow small circles, then small drops around her fingers and swollen knuckles. He tried lotion on her lower arms, achingly slow around the tender IV sites and the casted wrist, pushing the lotion carefully and gently up her arm. She pulled at times, still letting Riley ease the sore bruises, softening the scars with the relaxing lavender.

"There, Sunshine. See? I'm not hurting you. I want you to feel safe and comfortable. Easy now. Gentle...gentle... Sometimes I massage my horses after a long day. You can tell when their muscles are tight. You'd like them, Bliss and Cartwheel." His voice reassured like an evening rain, like a summer's breath. He placed his hand on the fist she'd made, and she relaxed her hand flat. It took a good thirty seconds, like a mainspring of a watch as it let go its minutes.

He slowly retreated to the chair, clicked on the news flickering across the screen, with no sound. Grace rested in his thoughts again, tucked into white sheets, willing survival in the battle of T-cells, white counts, and red blood cells.

He saw her face briefly, her healthy face. She led Bliss through the pasture, not by the reins, but merely by the strength of her walk. Bliss, so close, watched Grace's next steps, stopped when Grace did, walked when Grace resumed. "See? See, Riley? She knows what I'm thinking," *he heard her say.* "Such a pretty girl," *she cooed as she rubbed Bliss' forelock.*

Then they rode along the river. An eagle dipped into the far shore, pulled out a silver fish that slapped against the talons. The sun warmed his skin. Cartwheel stopped to sip cool water. Grace turned back to Riley. "You know, I'll need to go on ahead sometime...without you for a while..."

"Maybe not yet," *he thought.*

"Sometime, though, when it's the right time."

He drifted a little, watching the river wash by, sounding like a soft hissing, cycling in and out with the breeze.

He awoke a few hours later, initially looking for Poke, then rubbing his own neck where the stiffness crept in. He recognized the windows, then looked at the bed. A comma of a figure still as a whisper under the sheets. No, not Grace. The nurse smiled, indicating the woman was doing well. *Sometime, he thought, I'll tell you about Grace. I think you would have liked her. I have a feeling she would have liked you.*

CHAPTER
FIVE

"My name is Vince Caldwell." He white-knuckled the edge of the podium for support. Bright lights, digital recorders, and microphones intruded into any level of sanity he was trying to hold on to. "Two days ago, my fiancé Brenniss Tripham was kidnapped by a group of men in a black van. She was leaving the Whisper Tree Mall, just having completed her final wedding dress fitting. We are to be married in a few—" His voice broke, like a stick bent too tightly. He bowed his head, hacking two sobs past his voice.

In response, cameras click-clicked for a close-up of his emotion. He looked briefly to see Betty pull her head against the crease in Milt's shoulder. They both had the same sobs, unable to speak, mouths frozen by grief. Cameras continued to flash incessantly, lightning quick and nearly as bright.

"Brenniss and I are to be married this weekend," he continued. "The police are looking for you, Brenniss. If you hear me, please know we will find you. If anyone saw her, we need you to step forward to contact the police department. Please, please do the right thing and help bring Brenniss home."

Vince's breath was not really his own, more a ghost's than a voice needing to be heard. A nightmare even saying these words. He felt Detective Michaels grip his shoulder as his voice exhausted. He had peeled away layers for Brenniss just now, something he'd never done for his parents. Later that week, he would be haunted by newspaper photos showing his eyes, news anchors hinging his life to another unexplained loss in his life.

The TV screen showed Brenniss' young face, with a frame noting "Kidnapped Bride." One of Betty and Milt's favorites from the hundreds they had. Maybe it would make Brenniss look twice at the screen, make her pick up the phone or get someone's attention.

"Thanks for coming today." Detective Michaels' clipped speech was officer material, more logical than Vince's raw heart. A speech pattern someone might expect to calm when the emotions spilled over. "Our investigation has few leads just now and we need people to tell us if they have seen Brenniss Tripham. She is 5'7," in her mid-thirties, about 130 pounds, shoulder-length brown hair and brown eyes. When last seen at the Whisper Tree Mall, she wore beige slacks and a black tee shirt. She has a degree in library science and has a wide knowledge of archival books and collections. She most recently was involved in verification of a rare letter purported to have origins with Alexander Hamilton. That may have some bearing in her case. She may be wearing an engagement ring."

News clips later showed Detective Michaels reading his statement while Vince stared at the ground, his jaw clenched. His recall of the days' events was now scraping through his bones. *Was Brenniss watching now? Could she just walk out the door, find a reasonable citizen to get her home?* Had he only found a seam in that day where they had an extra minute on the phone that, like falling dominoes would have delayed her walk out of the bridal shop at that particular moment. Maybe she could have dropped her keys, and someone would have stopped her. He certainly would have.

Detective Michaels accompanied Brenniss' parents and Vince through a narrow hallway toward a parking garage at the police station. "I think that went very well. You were convincing, Vince, sincere. That strikes a chord with viewers. Someone has to remember something. You got them thinking—that's good! It's still early."

"Early?" Vince's voice turned sour. "It's been two days!"

"I know it's two days too many, but a criminal might wait longer to set up a ransom, for instance, to increase your anxiety and force your hand. Plus...we think we found a black van abandoned in the rail yards..."

"Oh, God!" Betty cried out.

"But certainly, you realize that because this is a kidnapping, the FBI is involved, already checking out the van and some other leads."

Betty shuddered. "Do you really think she's been kidnapped?"

There it was: that denial that helps some cope. In every crime Michaels dealt with, someone had a cloudy denial, not ready for the reality of the world he dealt with each day. It was kidnapping all right, for whatever reason. It usually came down to money. The sooner he used the word "kidnapped," the sooner families could face the other choices.

"Yes, ma'am. All the evidence at this time supports kidnapping. The FBI's resources will help us greatly."

"Betty, sweetheart, they must do this to get Brenniss back. It's the only way." Milt's voice was as thin as a paper window shade fighting off a thunderstorm.

"Do me a favor—all of you. Go home, now. Screen your

calls. Your lines are tapped by the FBI, so if any calls come in, there are agents listening in and can trace the source. Give yourself a break from this media circus. I'll call you when I know more."

Their fragile moth wing arms supported each other toward a car that would soon be trailed by the press.

Vince's heavy footsteps led him toward the modern condo door, and he grasped the slick metal pear-shaped handle that he swore he needed. Now it mocked him with his blank reflection. Hope flicked on his heart like a light switch. Brenniss certainly was on the other side of the door. She had heard his plea, escaped, waited here. He turned the key, a sound similar to a bullet slipping into the chamber.

Sure, she's there in bed, exhausted from those men, resting from that migraine that didn't let go, or maybe freshly showered after her ordeal, ready to tell him about it. "Oh, gosh, Vince, you won't believe..." The door sucked open to reveal the gray moonscape of the living room, still stacked with Brenniss' boxes.

"Brenniss? Brenniss?"

Go home, Michaels said. Go home and rest, he said. Really, is that what I do next? Vince's breath caught somewhere in the back of his throat, a painful choke. *What can I possibly do next to make one foot move ahead of the other?* His brain played the grainy video from the mall security camera. She juggles the dress, the phone, the briefcase, the packages...*who in the world was she calling just then? Why would she make the effort to call someone right at that critical—?*

Vince sucked in a sharp breath as he sank onto the couch. *The reason she'd slowed down, to use the phone...was to call him. Of course, she was letting him know she was on her way* to Trendz. *She'd been thinking of him up to the last moment, distracted by him. If she hadn't paused...*

"Please, come home, Brenniss, please!" he wailed, a siren against his loneliness, burying his head against pillows. *What he needed right now...her breath on his shoulders...that little hum she made when she drifted to sleep.* Those little things gave him comfort in the past. Those were Brenniss, more than the wedding, more than her boxes of belongings or the wedding gifts that remained unopened, or the cancellation of the flowers.

His eyes fluttered. He'd slept, somehow, all of forty minutes, with his phone in his hands, waiting for the improbable call from Brenniss. *"Vince, call me. I'm stranded, so come pick me up..."* but the screen showed 10:30 p.m., the battery cautioning orange.

He shuffled down the hallway toward the bedroom, then the bathroom. Splashing cold water along his eyes increased the tears. Then, his lungs jolted and convulsed. He slowly slid to the floor, curling onto the cool rigid tiles, the only thing just then to prevent him from slipping away.

———

Vince napped on the couch, hand clutching his cell phone. He awakened slowly in the foggy sadness that had overtaken him, watching the moon's pale angles along the gray walls. She walked by the couch and leaned on the back.

"Do you want coffee at Merry Beans today?"

"Brenniss?" He sat upright.

The dream ghosted through the closed window to catch up to the moon. It was the air conditioner's breath he heard.

His heartache bled into early morning. But, as in college, his heart determined work heals. *If he left right now, crosstown traffic would be minimum. Walk into the office, untouched, not needing to say anything to anyone except maybe the cleaning crew. Busy himself with files and proposals. Put order into others' lives, as he always did, at the familiar desk with the glassed view of the city. Client folders stiff in his hands were easier to manage than this pain, and no one would know.*

He let the shower flow over him, a gentle reorientation. He distracted his mind by listing his clients in alphabetical order: Amberly, Anderson, Cotton, DelFrisco, Immel...then their birthdays in chronological order as he dressed. He opened the closet for a fresh shirt and there she was...not Brenniss, but her essence, her fragrance lingering as if she'd walked through the room to pick up a magazine. His heart could have easily been stabbed and pulled through his chest just then and still register less pain.

He entered the office at 4:00 a.m., the cavernous conference room down the hall, the break room ready for that first pot of coffee. His eyes slid through puffy eyelids toward dawn's shadows, hoping to erase the agony. Another day. His computer hummed to life. So, that's what the first week will be like, he thought.

When coworkers gradually arrived, he tolerated the gasps, the whispers, the unsure greetings, mostly by pulling the shades that separated his glass office wall from the others. His emotions had no compass point—anger, betrayal, boredom— all the same, no true north.

He attended the 8:00 a.m. conference amid furtive glances. They waited for his juggling act to drop the dishes, to make a mess that everyone understood and would help clean up. Yet later, among themselves, they admitted that the Immel presentation was "remarkable, comprehensive...considering...How did he do it?" And yet, the conversation jammed when he entered the break room for his fifth? cup of coffee. He was cool, strong, dedicated, wasn't he?

Tess saw through all the bull, a little angry with the whispers and gossip. She brought him spreadsheets for Anderson and DelFrisco, making feeble attempts to break his gaze from the computer screen, to let him share how broken he'd become.

"Hey, boss, how about the Orioles?"

"They didn't play last night."

"Oh...well, is the team worth their uniforms this year?"

"Hardly."

"More coffee?"

"No...uh, yes."

God knows, she tried. She sifted through his day, unnoticed, but as determined.

Vince forced his absorption onto the spreadsheets, as the others left for the day. A pencil rose to between his teeth, focused his concentration while his fingers tapped computer keys and completed two more intake interviews. By 8:00 p.m., the window stared at the darkening canyons below. He knew another agonizing night waited by the elevator, then riding home, opening the condo door, the hollow moon cursing into the living room. Maybe he'd catch a burrito from the vending machine and review another file. At some point, he'd push the chair away, turn off the light, nap on the break room couch. That's what he'd do next.

CHAPTER
SIX

My arms and legs are alive. I feel clean and swollen and raw and sore and stiff. My heart threads into my ears. My mouth is dry. I'm breathing. In, out, in, out, hiss, hiss.

It's the nothing I notice. No sound, no engine, no tugging or pulling, no knives or cramped muscles. No movement because I don't need to. No screams. No sleeping on the floor. No stale beer smell.... I smell...what's the name? Lavender. When was the last time I smelled that? Someone used to love lavender. Did I?

I swim toward murky waters. I stop for air. I feel a light touch, a swift breeze, an adjustment to the left, to the right. Voices flit in, voices, quiet ones, not forced, not demanding, not assaulting. The voices, like a warm shower, like someone brushing my hair.

There is one voice I notice more than the others, a gentle, soft voice. A safe voice. Easy...easy, it says. A voice like opening a door, like grass under my toes, like a warm thaw after winter when it's okay to go coatless.

My brain doesn't know me. I'm a stranger waking up in a

padded world. I won't fall, I won't spill, I won't bleed. I'll open my eyes soon, coming up for air, tasting the sky again, floating away from the tangled web, like breaking free of reeds in a thick pond. I don't know how, but I know I can.

There is something I know. It's something I'll awaken with, floating around me like a life preserver. It's solid knowledge that was given to me some way since the time I've been floating in the dark.

This is what I know about someone named Grace:

She was someone who found good in everyone and every-thing. She never used revenge. She loved animals, thought they communicated with us and had souls purer than we ever thought possible. She was comfortable in herself, strong in every sense, but still would weep for an injured barn cat. She cared more about what a person believed than what flag he waved. She was quiet with sunsets but whooped it up when her horses ran. She didn't have a favorite color; she liked them all. She loved to cook and found friendship in the smallest of smiles. She had fire in her soul, an ache on a moonless night when she stared at the sky, paused when an eagle slipped across the water and caught a thermal, gave her horses a drink first and loved waking to a soft breeze tickling across her skin. She hated balancing her checkbook because money was never perfect. She like fresh-squeezed orange juice, her favorite boots, barley soup, and Duesenbergs. She danced with a smile on her face. She liked potluck suppers under the stars, fiddle music and Benny Goodman.

She hated dying because she had too many things unfin-ished. She let go because her heart said it was enough.

Don't ask me how I know these things. But because I know these things, I'll wake up soon and these things will be in my blood. Maybe an angel told me. Maybe, it was someone telling me that it was finally safe to open my eyes.

CHAPTER
SEVEN

Griff Hensley hated domestic violence as much as he hated seeing a fish gasping in a polluted river or a dog chained to a garage. It was all waste. He hated the neglect, the misfire toward a human being. But his judgment always remained cool when required of him. He never laid a mean hand on his prisoners, as much as he entertained the thought, sometimes. He respected those arrested as someone with a story he hadn't heard yet.

He approached Doc in the hospital corridor near the woman's room, expecting a single sentence and a period at the end.

"Actually, she's got a day and a half under her belt," Doc said. "Some of those wounds had been established for a while...days, at least. Oh, and the toxicology report? No drugs in her system. No alcohol. Now the labs from the rapes *did* show evidence of multiple partners."

Griff winced. "No clear DNA, yet. Counting on the state crime lab." Doc shrugged. "But I'll tell you, this kind of trauma may result in loss of memory. She may not be able to give any clues."

A crime. Stacked on another crime, and maybe another, and increasingly, it appeared the woman provoked none of them.

"Is she awake yet?"

Doc shook his head. "No, but blood pressures and vitals are stable. You can go in if you want." He nodded Griff toward the door.

Griff walked in, pulled back a white curtain, much in the same way he had pulled back the carpet and blanket that night. She lay motionless. Tubes for breathing, her nutrition, her antibiotics, and medications, and tubes drew her urine from her. The harsh florescent light didn't belong on her face, the color of ripe purple plums, the quiet survival trickled into one breath, in, out, in, out. And he thought she was already dead that night. She was a fighter, a survivor that much he knew about her.

Thank God Hannah could read him quickly after that night at the hospital. She calmed him, just by listening. He'd jump up from the couch, stamp his fist into his hand, run his hand through his hair, shake his head, shrug his shoulders; she nodded and listened. She willingly put up with his anger and frustration so he could relax enough and extend his strength for another day.

Griff couldn't help but be grateful for his life in Copper Station, for the woman that became his wife and the trust the town had given an outsider. He knew their frank looks, not wanting big city ways to interfere with their town when he first arrived. Many were cautious. But he was dedicated, straight-forward, with no agendas other than what the law required. And win them over, he did. His hands-on approach was welcome. Fewer bullets, more negotiation, because after all, a person deserved respect from the law, just as much as the reverse.

Fitting in was like a first pair of cowboy boots. Nothing gave, all stiff and awkward. Sometimes the baseball cap that said "Sheriff" was enough, especially with the teens and a few kids from the reservation who found their way into town. A cowboy hat seemed to add so much distinction to his office, because people were more likely to talk to him when he wore it. Copper Station took in his fairness, his honesty, and his integrity. Griff felt a coin or two of accomplishment deposited into his pocket, slowly each day.

He was one of many who got an invitation to the new art gallery in town, almost threw it out, then realized it was yet another opportunity to be visible. A graceful woman approached to shake his hand when he walked through the gallery entrance. She had black hair falling like a shiny ribbon past her waist. Her turquoise necklace was a bit of sky against her skin.

"Hi, I'm Hannah. I sure appreciate law enforcement making a presence tonight. Well, face it." She chuckled and looked around at the empty gallery space. "I'm glad *anyone* is making a presence tonight! I apologize for the mess; in fact, I'm hanging a few pictures that just arrived. Feel free to look around."

"You need help?" Griff offered.

"You got to admit, that's pretty tacky to ask a guest to help, but I'm not proud." A turquoise bangle slipped forward on her wrist, and she cupped his hand. "Over here."

He'd never seen a more beautiful woman.

Hanging pictures was the best way for him to start an awkward conversation and not be blamed for it. He held them in place while she eyed the positions, nails in her mouth, hammer at her side. He stared at her because his eyes couldn't move. She nodded, approached him and hammered two or three times, then hung the picture. He smelled sage, a little paint thinner and oil paint when she brushed against him.

"There! Now that looks better!" She made a quick nod.

"Ever see anything so striking?" She looked at the photographs she'd placed on the wall. He looked at her. "Billy Eagle Wing in this one: the hoop dance. Look at the position of his arms."

"That's...that's some detail."

"Well, at least I owe you some cider and refreshments. Normally, I have to pay someone when they help me like that." She smiled, showing white teeth that reminded him of seashells in the summer. "Glad you could make it, Sheriff!"

Her smile continued to brighten the room as three more people entered the gallery. He looked around, noting the variety in the artwork, drawn to a sturdy pottery mug, a spotted brown glaze with a flash of copper toward the lip, like a bolt of lightning. It would hold a second cup of coffee along with the first. But beyond that, the fine woman Hannah shaking hands enthusiastically as others entered the gallery.

Before leaving, he downed three more cups of cider. The gentle wave of conversation moved from shelf to wall, not the loud punctuated laughs you'd find in a bowling alley or a bar or even at the home football games. These were easy conversations and an occasional tip of the hat to the sheriff who cared about such businesses. He carried the mug long enough to commit to it, having a more difficult time of bumping into Hannah as the crowd grew. His tongue failed him when he was close to say something meaningful. He took his purchase, was swallowed by the crowd that had gathered by that time, feeling rather anonymous as he drove home.

"Is this Griff Hensley?" The alto in the voice on the other end of the receiver a few days later was as smooth as a late summer river.

"Yes, ma'am. Sheriff Hensley here."

"Sorry to bother you, Sheriff. This is Hannah...from Ten Winds Gallery?"

"Oh, oh sure! Hello, Hannah. What can I do for you?"

"Gosh! You caught me off guard! I thought I'd get an

answering machine."

"No, there's always someone here alive and kicking. Do you have something to report?"

"Report?"

"A crime? Somebody break in? Steal something?"

"Ohhh! No, no!" He could hear a chuckle pass through her breath. "Oh, no, I wanted to talk with you."

His heart effervesced into his brain. "About?"

"The other night? At the opening? You left your pen behind when you wrote your check. It's a nice one. I'm sure you didn't want to lose it."

Griff immediately patted his shirt pocket. *THAT's where it disappeared!*

"Well, I'll be. I just couldn't figure out where I left the darn thing. I can just walk over to get it." He blushed. "You'll be around the next hour?"

"Sure. The coffee's brewing, although I can't compete with Marta's coffee next door."

As he walked toward Ten Winds Gallery, he slipped into Marta's to ask what the gallery owner Hannah always ordered. He ordered two, as thanks for finding his pen. His legs felt loose and floppy, not quite fitting into his hip sockets while his heart danced a jitterbug that didn't keep time with his feet. And somehow, his face had taken the color of too much sun. All for a pen?

No, it was more. Griff resolved before he opened the gallery door, he would ask this woman to join him for dinner.

Now in a hospital room, while watching this unknown woman, he couldn't help but suck in a deep breath as to his luck, maybe serendipity, when connecting with someone as powerful as Hannah. All of this came to mind as he stood by the woman's bed, watching her breathe in and out, pumps of mocha-colored fluid entering the tube through her nose that dripped into her stomach, the monitors pulsing numbers and lines every few seconds. Hannah was the sweet in his life, especially when the day was too long. From day one, she seemed to know him better than he did.

"Griff?" Hannah walked up behind him, wrapping her arms around his shoulders, the very ease he needed just then. Her hair gathered down her shoulder and arm. "Thought you'd be here," she whispered.

"Thank God, she's a fighter." He pulled her arms closer like a shawl around his shoulders. "See those marks on her hands and arms? Defensive wounds. Probably broke her wrist trying to get away." He shook his head. "If she survives this, she's going to need a lot of help."

Hannah leaned further over Griff's shoulder. "Where do I start?"

CHAPTER
EIGHT

Hannah's next steps took her to two thrift stores for clothing for the young woman. What a journey. A small platoon of folks counted on her waking up, getting on with breathing, eating, and walking. It's the kind of thing Grace would have done, come to think of it.

A bit quirky, Grace. And the same could be said for Hannah's journey to Copper Station. Disillusioned with the success of her art gallery in Phoenix, she had no clue that a toad and a flat tire would change her life. Quirky. That's what she named the toad, too.

She didn't recognize her Phoenix self, focused on art as business rather than the artists. She was more the abstract painting with lines and dots and circles that didn't articulate and didn't make sense. She had set her favorite camera aside, lost the trail of creativity for sales slips and contracts. One day, she locked the gallery door for an adventure, armed with her camera bag and a dozen or so rolls of black-and-white film for a day trip along the blue highways.

Caught up in safe landscapes and weeds, she recognized

how she'd lost the edginess she craved in photography, the clarity that pulled her eye past the need for color. During one of her roadside stops, she encountered a toad near the driver's wheel. Clarity...he was large, stubborn, certainly not handsome. *A craggy mesa or an eagle? That was easy to capture.* She spent maybe forty minutes with that lazy toad, working on close-ups of his eyes, his profile, his shadow made long and thin by the morning sun. Nearly thirty pictures later, he hopped off into the spare grasses, ready to tell his family what happened to HIM before lunch.

Driving farther from Phoenix, the rediscovery of photography opened like a blossom, the merit from a toad, no less. Fascinated by the bumps and warts of it all, she missed a turn, which led her toward Copper Station. No sooner did she turn toward the town, she heard a pop! on the driver's side and limped her car carefully to the gas station at the town's edge. For the first time in her life, an unscripted mistake was about to open a door.

She ran her hand along the deflated tire that had frop-fropped her to the station. *A woman traveling solo? An unfamiliar town?* She smelled a major expense that could freeze her credit card.

The service station owner took one look. "Barbed wire. Happens a lot on that road. No worries. I can fix it in an hour." He wiped his mercilessly gray hands on a towel. "Nice coffee shop a block down and Rosa's is open for lunch." He nodded toward a marked car. "Got the sheriff's car to finish up," he reassured her. "But your tire is an easy fix."

*Well, if the sheriff's car was here...*she took her camera and purse and wandered the few blocks toward what looked like the main street—covered by the most intense of turquoise skies, framed by earth the color of tanned leather, and a breeze that carried the fragrances of sage and espresso into the wind chimes.

Pictures were easy to take. A Navajo rug, the solidly square brick buildings, the weather-worn faces of residents, a horse glad for her attention as its owner bartered for a new saddle. Her feet were slow to return to the gas station, dreading the cost as inflated as her tire. An hour passed quickly and she returned to the gas station, pulling out her wallet.

"Oh, no charge, ma'am. Barbed wire takes out two, maybe three tires a week. I just do better not charging for it."

"At least let me buy you a cup of coffee or lunch."

"Oh, no, ma'am. You just come back, sometime."

By the time she started up her car, she knew she would do just that.

Within seven weeks, she sold her Phoenix gallery, returned to Copper Station, and purchased the empty storefront next to Marta's Grind—the earthy coffee aroma an inspiration. Her vision was to bring attention to people's art, while gaining confidence to avoid the neglected f-stops in her life. She sought artists tucked on the reservation, hosted art classes for seniors and high school students after hours and included a few retirees who had found the high desert the heart of their creativity. In all, ten artists met with her to establish an artists' cooperative. Ten Winds Gallery was born.

That first open house showcased pottery, paintings, photos, and papier-mâché animals, with more than half of Copper Station showing up, including the sheriff.

By the time Hannah and Griff were married, she ran the gallery full time and continued to inspire artists from grade school through retirement. Tourists had made connections and found their way from Phoenix past the barbed wire to seek out the variety she featured at Ten Winds. Enchanting day trip, worth the drive, she was told.

Once again, her camera sat farther back in a drawer as the gallery became her life. But in her office, an eight-by-ten black-and-white toad face she named "Quirky" stared back at her every day on the wall to remind her of the risk she took, the chance wrong turn that mangled her tire and brought her to Copper Station. Those round toad eyes, if she looked closely enough, reflected back a tiny portrait of Hannah squeezing a shot at the toad's defiant and distorted wisdom.

When she returned to the hospital room, she folded the clothing into the closet then sat silently on the edge of the bed, watching this woman beat the odds with each breath.

"Hey, Hannah." Riley's soft voice eased past the creaking door.

"Riley." She nodded toward the woman. "She's breathing pretty steadily, no sudden changes. You eat anything yet?"

"No, I'm kind of addicted to the hospital's excuse for meat-loaf. I'll get something later. I'm planning to stay again, to-night. You know, just in case she wakes up."

"How about I swing by later and bring you dinner? Hey, I could even feed your horses tomorrow morning, if 6:30 isn't too late."

"Now, that I would appreciate, too, Hannah. Dinner would be nice. I admit, I don't taste much of what I eat here."

Riley moved closer to the woman's bed while Hannah stood. Stunned. Riley hadn't accepted help or even acknowl-edged that burdens could be shared since Grace had died.

CHAPTER
NINE

By the fifth night of watching the woman's spirit running from the demons in her fractured dreams, Riley brought some of Hannah's leftovers to the woman's room for dinner. He opened the woman's door, set down his dinner, then looked up.

The woman was standing. Two feet from her bed, back to the door, her eyes open, staring out the window. Her head was slightly bent as if mid-prayer. She was taller than he figured. The hospital gown hung shapeless and tent-like over her shoulders, tied loosely at the back.

"Um, oh, um, hi...uh, ma'am. Excuse me for walking in like I did. I'm Riley. I've been visiting you...uh..ma'am?"

He expected her to startle, wouldn't have blamed her if she'd screamed or turned wildly to defend herself. Instead, he slowly eased toward the recliner that had been his territory the last few days. Once there, he saw her eyes dart toward the chair, then the wall, toward her feet, and back to the window. Her hair hid most of her battered face.

"Hi, Riley. You see our Jane Doe woke up this afternoon.

Pulled out the feeding tube herself, so we'll try dinner to-night." The nurse placed the dinner tray on the table. She smiled toward the woman's back. "Hasn't said a word...maybe she'll talk to you." She closed the door quietly behind her.

Riley waited a lifetime of seconds before taking a breath.

"Well, let's see what you have for dinner." As he approached the tray table, the woman cowered. "Easy, easy...just taking off the lid, here...well, look. It's chicken, see? Mashed potatoes, green beans. I love green beans myself. Got a garden full of green beans. Now, I'd say that's a pretty nice dinner. And it's all for you." He purposely kept his eyes on the tray, talking a soft easy pace to let her know where he was. "Here's your milk. You know, you've got a few broken bones—your collar bone, some ribs, your wrist—you'll need the calcium."

Easy talk filled the spaces between them, voice low and effortless, just as he'd done with Bliss. The tone of his voice, not so much the words he chose, was more important. He didn't wait for a reaction while he placed butter on the potatoes. "Now, me? I like coffee—a little bit of cream to take the edge off. But I'll warn you now, the hospital coffee needs more than milk to rehabilitate it."

"I bet you didn't know you're in a hospital. Bet you didn't know you were in Arizona. But you're safe now. We've all been taking really good care of you. Doc, the sheriff and Hannah, his wife. We've all been here..." *Easy...easy.*

The woman backed slowly toward the bed, then slid onto one corner as if wary of offending the sheets. She glanced sideways at the food tray.

"Yeah, that's your dinner. I brought mine—right there in the bag. I'll eat later. That chicken looks worthy of a try..."

He reached slowly toward her knife to cut it. She slapped her hand on the Jell-O container, and said, "I want that. It's pretty."

He stopped a split second. Her voice wasn't exceptionally

strong, but it startled Riley all the same.

"Now, see, that's Jell-O. Looks like it might be cherry." He nodded, not missing a beat.

"Jell-O...Jell-O..." She tried the word, her mouth playing the sounds. "Do I like Jell-O?" She didn't look at him.

"Everybody likes Jell-O. Try it."

She held it like a jewel to the light, slit open the lid, then smelled it. "It doesn't spill." She shook the container. "What did you call it?"

"Jell-O."

"Jell-O...Jell-O..." she whispered again, as if gently mashing the word against her tongue. She scooped a bit with her spoon, her face splitting from the dark into instant pleasure.

"Ohhh! This is good! This is my favorite! This is so good! Jell-O? Oh, I like Jell-O. I know this—I know Jell-O. It's like...nervous pudding."

Just as she took her third bite, Griff knocked softly on the door and peeked in. His eyes splashed wide with surprise at the scene. The woman immediately stopped eating and slipped the Jell-O cup under her covers.

"Riley. Ma'am." Griff tipped his sheriff's cap.

"Ma'am, this is my friend Griff, the sheriff I mentioned. He and I found you the other night. He's kept you safe here. He won't hurt you."

She slowly withdrew another bite of Jell-O from the hidden container.

"How's it going?" Griff's question was directed toward no one.

"She woke up. Still a little confused and cautious. But she likes Jell-O." Riley smiled.

"Ma'am, I hate—"

"Why do you call me that?"

"Ma'am?"

"Yes. 'Ma'am.' Why do you call me that?"

"Well, honestly, we don't know your name." Griff nodded. "Can you tell us?"

She stopped her Jell-O intake, let her eyes scan left and right in search of..."Well, it isn't ma'am!"

Griff swallowed his smile. "I hate to interrupt your dinner here, but for nearly a week, you've been the greatest mystery to us. I'm afraid we don't know you and we want to help you. You from around here?"

He wasn't certain if her hesitancy were fear, or just allowing the Jell-O slide down her throat, a cool, slick, sweet river.

"We just want to help, you know, get you back home or wherever you were headed," Riley added. "Griff, here, wants to help, and he's my best friend, so I know he won't hurt you."

The fearful silence in her turned over empty. "Have I done anything wrong?" she whispered.

Riley leaned forward a quarter of an inch. "No, nothing as far as we know. But you've been through a lot, and we don't know anything about you."

"So, what happened to me?"

"We're not certain, other than finding you near the side of the road a few nights ago."

"A road?"

Griff offered more. "We think someone was...trying to...get rid of you. You were wrapped in blankets and a rug."

"I think I know that." Her eyes closed. When she took a big sigh, she winced from the rib pain. "Could I have more of this?" She pulled out the empty Jell-O cup from her covers. "More red?"

"Of course," said Riley calmly. "I'll find you some."

Griff walked away from the bed toward the window as they waited for Riley. "You've been beaten pretty badly, young lady. Seems someone didn't want you around for some reason, and that someone may still be in the area. You're safe, for now, here at the hospital. I don't like seeing anyone hurt the way you are. It's my job to protect you. And if I can find out who you are, that may lead me to who did this and why, so I can arrest them."

"Am I arrested?"

"No, ma'am, you are not."

She heard a snippet of a voice. *Hey, girlie girl. Don't fight so much. You'll like it.*

"I...I really don't know... blankets?"

"Yes, ma'am."

She squinted at the floor. "I think I remember blankets. But, I don't remember being called 'ma'am'."

Griff nodded. It would come with time, he hoped.

Riley returned with more Jell-O. "Here you go, Sunshine."

She smiled at him. "Jell-O. Thanks." Another bite slipped into her mouth. "Why do you call me 'Sunshine' and not 'ma'am'?"

"Because you're awake now and that's sunshine to me."

It was something, to catch that flick of her smile. After all, she was talking.

CHAPTER
TEN

Hannah's waist-length black hair shifted along her back as she met Riley in the hospital corridor, his hands warming against the first cup of coffee of the morning.

"What's up? I heard a rumor." She smiled.

"She's awake, talking some, remembering little. She's alert. Little eye contact yet. She's not sure she can trust us, a little hedge high." He leaned toward the door. "Come on, let's see how she's doing," Riley urged.

The young woman sat up in her bed, jaw swollen blue, eye socket enlarged and asymmetric, a heavy tape across her clavicle and a cast on her right arm.

"Hey, Sunshine, this is my friend Hannah."

"Hey, look at you," Hannah whispered. As she leaned forward at the foot of the bed, a skein of her black hair dangled forward over her shoulder.

The woman's left hand slowly rose, nearly touching the edge of Hannah's hair as it moved. She tried to form a word, a predictable word like "pretty" or "soft," but she only stared. Her eyes switched to the wrinkles in Riley's shirt, placed there from another night in the recliner. Her eyes reached a little closer to his face today. Progress.

~

Hannah was right. When he walked toward the corral, he saw Bliss and Cartwheel running circles through the pasture. Poke's eyes were trained on them both. Riley let out a whistle that brought the horses toward him as if that whistle were a rope tied to their halters.

"I haven't treated you very well." He opened his hand with an apple for both horses. "I need to apologize. My routine turned upside down because of a young woman in the hospital. Maybe we should do some riding today, all of you. You too, Poke." The dog sniffed the familiar sterile clean on Riley's shoes. He pulled blankets and saddles from the barn and prepared both horses. His touch settled them, like a four-year old tucked against a pillow. Situating Poke on Cartwheel's saddle, he sat astride Bliss and took the horses across the road along the river.

Grace and he had ridden this same area, letting the water sing nearby. Nice ride, she would say...or this is my favorite spot. They'd stop and trace clouds or check the breeze right then and there.

I told you I had a feeling about this one. Grace's voice interrupted his reverie.

"She's waking up," he said aloud. "But she's so afraid."

You need to do something, she pestered.

"What the hell? I'm there every night. What else can I do?"

You'll know when the time is right.

Damn, thought Riley. Is she always right?

~

Doc stood near the woman's bed, shared by Hannah.

"Ma'am, it's nice to see you up and awake," he reviewed the chart, "and eating and drinking fairly well. I'm Doc Mattheson. I met you when you came to the emergency room last week."

The woman drew the pillow instinctively closer to her neck. She looked at the foot of the bed. In the leaden silence, she heard the voice again. *Do what we say, Princess. Don't fight so much. Keep your damn mouth shut.*

"Doc probably saved your life," Hannah said softly. "He's been taking very good care of you."

"From the road." The woman recognized part of the story, now. "Did I do something wrong?"

"No, not that I know of. In fact, you've been doing everything right this past week. You've been hurt pretty badly. You probably hurt all over."

"But you're getting stronger each day." Hannah cautiously stroked the woman's hair.

"So, would you let me examine you? See how much you've healed?"

"Can I have some Jell-O later?"

"Absolutely. How about your wrist?"

"Which one?"

"The one with the cast. It was broken."

Her brow creased. *Look at that fancy, pretty little ring. Bet we could buy a new car with that.*

As Doc leaned toward her, she mildly drew away, while watching his hands. They were clean and didn't smell of gun metal or beer. He didn't move suddenly but moved her fingers in slow motion against the rim of the cast. Doc draped the gown sleeve back toward her shoulder. She withdrew slowly, and he continued his caution by not getting so close. He extended his hand again and rotated her arm slowly as if winding yarn.

"Does that hurt?"

"Not bad."

"Does something hurt more?"

She didn't want to tell, not to give it away. That's where he would go first, to the painful spot. And she wasn't sure if Hannah would intervene if things went wrong. She slowly pointed toward her gut.

He sighed. "I suspect you do have a great deal of pain. You've had quite a bit of trauma inside your body. Would you let me check there?"

She remembered a fist bulleting toward her eye. Her head snapping back. "No! No more!" She looked toward Hannah. "Tell them to stop," she pleaded, squeezing Hannah's hand. Her voice punched the walls with panic.

Hannah rubbed between the woman's shoulders. "We know there were some bad men that did bad things. Doc wasn't one of them, though. Did they ever let you say 'no'?"

The woman groaned a sob. "It was loud...their hands kept...at me...all over..."

"But you told them 'no'—"

"It didn't matter!" she screamed. The silence fell into defeat immediately. "It didn't matter."

The woman, sucking sobs until she was breathing evenly, leaned against Hannah's shoulder. "But you know what *we* do?" Hannah whispered against the woman's cheek. "Doc and Griff and Riley and me? We support each other, we hold each other up, we try to take the pain away, we hold tight and don't let go. We do that with strong hearts for the circle to heal." She let a slow breath out. "Of course. I'll stay and make sure Doc stops if you say so."

The woman nodded "yes."

When Riley arrived that evening, the woman was standing again, looking out her window. Something was different, though, as if an explosion had detonated just moments before, as if gunpowder were still fresh in the air. He approached her slowly then produced a cup of Jell-O and a spoon from his pocket.

She reached for it, eyes tacked to the window. She breathed sadness, a heavy flag resigning to the wind.

"I like this stuff. It's so good." Her voice was tired, flat, and dry as the desert floor.

"Are you okay?"

"I don't know. I don't know what 'okay' is." As she swallowed the Jell-O, Riley imagined the sweet liquid baptizing her pain. "Where are we again?"

"Arizona."

"Ar-i-zo-na. Do I live here?"

"No, this is a hospital. We brought you here—"

"—because the men wouldn't listen to me when I said 'no'."

Riley sighed. "You were pretty bad off, that's true. We don't know where you live."

She licked the spoon. "Pretty bad off. I was hurt. Inside. The doctor called it 'trauma.' I told him 'no' today, so he stopped his examination and Hannah helped me heal in the circle."

The puzzle pieces didn't quite slide into place, but Riley formed a picture.

She finished her Jell-O and held up the empty cup. "I like this. I like Jell-O."

She slept free that night, tube free, curled like a comma, her hands coiled like fists at the ready near her chin. The devil had passed by.

"Riley, I was hoping I could catch you," Doc whispered from the doorway. He tip-toed toward Riley's chair while glancing at her chart. "Been a long day."

"Hannah told me, but she seemed to be okay when I showed up this evening."

Doc tapped his pen on the chart. "I'm not going to lie to you. This woman is challenging. Broken everything, it seems, scratches, bruises, swelling, contusions over eighty percent of her body, multiple vaginal wounds from those rapes. Physically, she is healing. The bad news is she sustained all these wounds around circumstances we don't know and who knows what emotional scars will reveal themselves? Her memory can be a problem, those bits and pieces right now."

"All good, right?"

"You tell me: where can she go? She likely will become a ward of the state and move to a state hospital, but she needs care that could help her recover. And who knows what kind of support she might have there."

Riley glanced toward the window, rubbing his chin, a second and third time. He sensed the next few questions. *Grace said I'd need to do something, when the time is right.*

CHAPTER
ELEVEN

The woman opened a stiff book with blank pages and poised a pen over the first lines. She frowned and then scratched the words.

"Doc gave me this journal and it is for my re-memories. For when I write things down. I might remember more. When I remember, I write more things down.

"So, I'm in a hospital in a town in Arizona. People are nice here. The doctor scares me a little because he touches me where it still hurts. He scares me sometimes into dark places, but he's always nice and quiet and stops when I say "no." He checks stitches and teeth and x-rays and blood. He says I'll be better.

"And Hannah has beautiful hair and brings me clothes so I don't have to wear those thin gowns anymore. Her hair is black silk. She has a bright smile. Someday, maybe I can smile like her.

"Griff and Hannah are together. Griff is the sheriff who helped me. I was living on a roadside and he found me. He has questions I can't answer. He wants me to think about the dark place I'm from. The faces that I don't know because I can't remember. I can't tell him, yet, how the gun felt against my skin or inside me. I told him they had teeth, they yelled, they had hot breath, they were heavy. That I remember. But it's like a veil drawn over my face. It brushes up against a memory and the pictures change.

"And then, Riley. He's a nice man. He smiles. He knows I'm scared, so he reminds me I'm safe. I don't tell him that is important to me. He doesn't pull, tug, or jab. He doesn't come toward me too fast, and he lets me think slow. He doesn't get angry or slap me or call me "bitch." He's the kindest of all, so I won't break. He believes in me more than I can myself right now. He calls me "Sunshine" because I can talk. And he brings me Jell-O. Which I love. I think I remember Jell-O from sometime.

"I remember white. I'll write that here, too. There's something about a white space around, spilling softly downward, a fluffy fall, soft and pretty. Someone is smiling. Maybe it's me. The white is perfect. Maybe I'll find it again sometime. The white, I mean.

"I want a name like Griff, Hannah, Riley, and Doc. I'm tired of being called "ma'am." I want a name that's comfortable and safe, that belongs here. A name that fits with Arizona turquoise, with suede jackets and jeans and boots. People wear those here. I'm not ma'am, not Jane Doe and not young lady. Sometimes Riley calls me "Sunshine" and I think I like that, but I'm pretty sure it's not my name. I don't know my name. I try to think of a name, but I get a hollow tunnel with no clues.

"I know this, though. I hurt inside from the stitches and healing, where I should have a soul. I have a broken wrist and bruises and an eye socket as big as my fist. I'm sore when I stand too long, or if I laugh at Riley's jokes. I like Jell-O more than pancakes. But I like chocolate cake and oatmeal and pickles and milkshakes and chicken, too. I don't know yet about fish or pizza. Maybe tacos. I don't remember much about my life or who I am. Someday, Doc says, a light bulb will go on and I'll start remembering. I tried it with the light switch in the closet in my hospital room. All I remembered were my feet."

CHAPTER
TWELVE

"Hey, girlfriend." Hannah peeked around the white curtain. "How about trying on those tee shirts I brought you?" The woman held up a hot-pink tee shirt with a drawing of an artist using paintbrushes. It said, "Doodle till you drop!"

"It's my favorite. I'll try this one. But don't come here," the woman said. She pulled the curtain. "Don't."

"I won't. And I'll make sure no one else does. I'll give you privacy. Just tell me when you're ready."

"Privacy. That's good. Okay, I'm ready."

Hannah pulled back the curtain to see the gown gathered like a tossed rosebud around the woman's waist. But the shirt fit great.

"Okay, I've got some jeans, too."

"Can I have some privacy again?"

"Here you go." Hannah smiled and drew the curtain. "You know, just about everyone around here wears jeans. You'll fit right in. If you need help with the zipper, let me know."

Zip it, princess. Zip it. Or I'll close your yap for you. She remembered a haze of pain when she took clothes off or put them back on. Days and nights blended together, a gas station looking out over flat prairies and seeing her face in a scratched mirror for the first time.

"Riley wears jeans. You wear jeans. Doc doesn't wear jeans. Okay, I'm ready."

Hannah peered past the curtain. "Hey, they fit! I just guessed at your size." She pulled a jeans jacket in view of the woman. "Now, this is cute. See? That flower on the pocket?"

The tee shirts and jacket told stories to her enough to smile past the swelling and bruises.

"Kind of like Christmas, huh?"

The woman looked at her. "Say that again."

"Like Christmas?"

The woman's brow furrowed. "Christmas. I know something about Christmas...Christmas...it's cold like Jell-O, Christmas. It sounds familiar. Is it Christmas now?"

"No, not until December. Summer just started."

"Christmas is December," she repeated. "But this is like Christmas, because—?"

"It's like Christmas because you're getting presents."

"Ohhh! These!" She scooped up the tee shirts like ice cream. Her mind clicked into a place and for a second she saw a platform, then remembered stepping up to a mirror. There was white everywhere. Then she looked up: the same bed, the tee shirts spilling from her arms.

"I remembered doing something like this before."

Hannah sat alongside her cautiously. "What, like trying on tee shirts?"

"It's white, something white."

"Snow?"

"Like December...white...like..." She shook her head. "I don't know. It just slid out of my head."

Griff and Riley knocked softly and entered the room, Griff mid-sentence. "...so I'll go to Eddie Hamilton's on Tuesday.

You're welcome to come along—" He glanced at the woman. "Well, lookie here!"

Lookie, lookie, princess. But more loudly, she heard, "Hamilton." *Who was Hamilton?*

"She just remembered something, Griff."

"Is that so? What did you remember?"

Lookie here, she wanted to say, but instead, she looked at him and said, "White."

"White, like this room? Like snow?"

"White. I'm standing up and it's white."

The silence begged for more. White opened a door with no further definition.

"So, is it cold?"

"You did remember that Christmas was cold. Was that the 'white?'" Hannah suggested.

"It's...white...but you said 'Hamilton' too."

"Eddie Hamilton? You know him?"

"No, no, something else."

"A town? Your name?"

"No, just Hamilton."

Griff tried on a smile. "Well, good, good. You're starting to pull some memories up. Doc did say bits and pieces. We can't expect it all to come back in one day."

"I have my memory journal Doc gave me."

"What's with the fashion show?" Riley asked.

"Oh, Hannah gave me this tee shirt and these tee shirts and these jeans and a jacket and some privacy like Christmas in December." She smiled.

"Pretty darn nice. I bet that feels good." He leaned against the wall. "Doc's thinking about letting you leave here, soon."

"I can't stay here?"

"Naw, you're getting healthy and strong. You don't need a hospital."

"Do I go somewhere else?"

"Actually..." Griff drew a breath. "There are some nice places in Phoenix or Tucson you could—"

"Sunshine, do you like horses?" Riley interrupted.

"I don't know."

"Do you like dogs?"

"I...I'm not sure. I think so."

Riley shifted his weight and leaned slightly forward. "What do you think about coming to the ranch with me?"

"With you?"

Griff and Hannah stared in surprise. "Are you out of your mind?" exploded Griff.

Riley waved Griff off. "It's a nice-sized ranch, plenty of room and you'd have your own room."

"And privacy?"

"Yes, ma'am."

"In Arizona?"

"Riley, there's a place in Tucson for young woman—"

"Hush, Griff," Hannah spoke up. "Let Riley finish."

"It's just a few miles out of town here. I've got a dog named Poke, some barn cats that don't have names—"

"—like me."

"Well, yes, I guess so. And I have two horses named Bliss and Cartwheel. You can stay there as long as you need until you can figure out your future."

"Friend, is this wise?" Griff broke the silence before the woman could answer.

"I don't think I've been on a ranch before," she said under her breath.

"Maybe we should discuss this," Griff whispered.

Riley's face beaded onto Griff's. "Way I look at it, the ranch is safe, she'd be protected, she'll be near her new friends, she'll make a few more friends, and, frankly, there isn't much more therapeutic than caring for the horses."

"He's got a point, Griff. She goes to Tucson or beyond,

she's right back where she was two weeks ago. No telling who might see her or recognize her. Who knows if the wrong people are looking for her?" Hannah added.

"But I mean settling into a home that isn't hers? Isn't that the same thing as taking away her identity again?"

Just then, Doc peered around the open door.

"Good morning! Good morning, young lady. I'm glad you're all here, actually. Looks like we need to talk discharge plans."

Riley nodded. "She had a good doctor."

"And great friends who kept her going, too. So, I'm open for options."

"Just talking about it," Riley spoke up before Griff could mention Tucson or Phoenix or any other *wherever* up his sleeve. "My place is clean, has lots of space, it's safe until she can make better plans. I can take her home with me, if she'd like. I've thought about it, and it seems the right thing to do."

"The ranch?" Doc asked, his eyebrows raising with interest.

"Any problem with that? Way I see it, she can have her own space, it's a good place to heal, even though Gracie—" He stopped abruptly, swallowed. Took a breath. "Okay, I don't have much but the ranch, but I'm rattlin' around there. I can look after her. It's a sure sight better than some anonymous state group home or shelter, don't you think?"

"There's rehab in a few of those places, Doc," Griff interjected. "And she could make new friends."

Doc countered. "But she's starting to remember things, Griff. She's more likely to remember things if she has less stress in her life. And won't that help your investigation? You know you won't rest until you know who she is."

Hannah, Doc, and Riley all looked at Griff shaking his head. Once in a great while, Riley showed his stubborn streak and usually had logic on his side. Hannah wanted to be a comfort to the woman as she recovered more. And Doc, well, Doc's vote seemed to count twice.

"I'm glad you're remembering things, young lady. That's a great start. What do you think about all this? After all, it is your choice." Doc caught her gaze.

"Well...I don't know what a Tucson or a Phoenix is. I don't always remember Copper Station, unless it's written out where I can see it. But...I had like-Christmas today and privacy. I think these are my best friends. Why would I leave that?"

Doc chuckled and nodded enthusiastically. *Indeed.*

"My concern is we don't know who she is or where she's from. We may be creating false roots here. It may interfere with her remembering, complicate the decision to leave when the time comes. There, I've said it." Griff's flat and professional voice weighted the room.

"Good point," Doc continued. "But research shows that memory is more likely to return in a situation where trust can be built. She's starting that already. Moving on to somewhere, you have to have some form of identity first, sheriff. Let's not fool ourselves. There are few perfect solutions. And we don't know if we're making a good decision until after we've made it and seen it run its course. It really is up to you, young lady."

"I'll go with him. He has horses."

"Pretty fine ones, too, but be careful, he'll make you work for him." Griff added under his breath.

"Well, she'll need to take it easy for a while," Doc added. "But once the interior stitches heal, once the cast is off, no telling what she'll want to try." He wrote a scratchy note across the paper, amplified by the metal chart.

"How does the end of the week sound?"

"Great." Riley slapped his hand on his thigh.

"Now, there's one more thing," Doc added. "Since you've been here, we've been calling you Jane Doe. Do you remember anything about your name?"

"I know I'm not Jane Doe. I'm not Ma'am and I'm not Young Lady. Say some names, maybe I'll know."

"Well, there's Amy, Angela, Abby, Alexandra, Aubrey, Adelaide, Alice—" Hannah chuckled.

"—or Barbara, Bitsy, Belle—" Riley exaggerated each name.

She giggled. "Stop!" She grabbed her gut, her laughter hissing through her teeth. It was the first laughter any of them had heard in her room for over a week. They all absorbed the wonder of her. Alive.

She opened her eyes, caught by the piles of clothes on her bed. The jeans jacket lay with sleeves apart as if awaiting a hug. Inside, the label read "Maggie's Threads."

"How about 'Maggie?' Maggie's a good name. I like Maggie."

"Maggie, it is." Riley's eyes lit from inside, something she'd never seen before. "I agree. Maggie's a good name."

"Okay, then, Maggie. Home with Riley on Thursday. How's that?" Doc wrote a quick note in the chart, then closed the metal cover.

As Doc approached the door, Griff leaned to Riley. "Good thing that label didn't say 'Liz Claiborne'," he whispered.

Riley's first night sleeping back in his own bed felt like an island compared to the hospital recliner. He almost felt an apology on his lips to the empty house, a guest in his own bedroom. The horses settled in the barn, knowing he was home. Poke found his spot in the bedroom, his familiar worn cushion that showed his particular curve before he rotated one, two, three, and lay down.

What am I thinking, Riley asked himself. *What kind of person opens up his home to a complete stranger? Who knows? Maybe she's a Bonnie Parker or harbored a drug problem or kills people for a hobby, or—*

We always seem to take in strays, you know that. Hasn't

backfired yet, he heard Grace say.

A stray? Is that what she is? Come on, now, her memories are those demons that haunt her face and darken her voice. Just today, she gave herself permission to laugh and damn! It sounded great! Doc says she may have more dark days before the good ones, but it will come back. She can find that purpose and that laughter here. She can be happy here. Why send her—?

But she'll be safe. Griff said so.

"She won't be happy!" he called out against the dark. He snapped the light on to see Poke's head abruptly pull toward Riley's direction. "Sorry I woke you, fella."

Then you answered your own question.

He walked across the hall to the guest bedroom, the room that tomorrow would capture the morning light in the curved corner window. He and Grace loved this room because the breeze sifted across the window seat, the room they painted a soft green, where Grace sometimes read when she couldn't sleep. Where, on hands and knees, they cleaned the years from the surface and found honey-colored oak floors. Memories from the move to start a new life, a welcome room...for any-one...for any guest.

Off in the distance, he heard a thick screech, echoing through Mitchell Canyon. It came two, three times more. His spine shivered ice water. Many Devils was active again. Sounded closer than ever. He hadn't heard Many Devils since before Grace passed. Walter McKay had complained of a mountain lion threatening his cattle, then. But when Walt showed Griff the paw print, the one with the slice through the pad, the one the size of a dinner plate, along with two calves destroyed, people drew the legend of Many Devils back into life again. Despite Walt's electric fence, the cat now had a taste for a beef. Many Devils on the prowl was always a bad sign.

He looked through the curved windows, reassured the

horses were locked inside the barn. Truly, a closed barn door likely wouldn't deter the cat either, but a human being could. Maybe tomorrow he'd build another scarecrow made of metal cans. Many Devils was skittish that way. By then, the cat seemed to be sulking back into the canyon; that God-awful screech faded against the night breeze.

He looked around the room in the moonlight. He saw himself dusting, maybe changing out the sheets on the bed, sweeping the floor. It wouldn't take much for the room to welcome this woman named Maggie...

I told you; you'd know what to do when the time came. He heard a soft chuckle in Grace's voice.

CHAPTER
THIRTEEN

Poke watched Riley pull the quilt from the mattress on the guest bed then fold it like a flag. Riley had stripped the bed a few months after Grace had died and left it bare, with naked pillows and the quilt draped across the top until now. He flipped the mattress, somewhat preserving the last of Grace. He chose fresh sheets, lowering them like a snowfall against the mattress top. His hospital corners were never as sharp as Grace's. Pulling the linens up along the chin of the pillows he finished with the quilt folded along the foot of the bed.

The dog sneezed, shook his head, then rubbed his face.

"So, what do you think, boy? About having a guest in the house for a while? She'll recover here until she gets her strength back, maybe even help out a little if she liked."

Poke leaned forward, head resting on his paws.

"She's got a lot of healing to do, don't get me wrong. And by then, maybe she'll have her memory back and she can move on. Maybe even find some happiness. Face it, you, Bliss, and Cartwheel have all missed a woman's touch."

He glanced around, adjusted the throw rug by the bedside.

"Okay, maybe a couple months at the most, but she'll like it here, right?"

The dog looked up.

"No more nights away from home."

Poke stood tall, tail wagging, ears attentive. Riley wasn't sure who was more nervous.

He watered and exercised the horses under Poke's watchful eye, then looked around. The place looked welcome enough to him. A new adventure, kind of like a new horse or a new client. He just didn't know what to expect. *Maggie gave herself a new identity, but in a way, she gave me a new one, too.* This risk they both were taking had no past to shuffle through or blame things on.

He drove the large curve of the river, Poke in the truck bed, looking through the back window at Riley. The dog waited there until Riley returned from whatever errand, but certainly was curious regarding all the fuss.

When Riley entered Maggie's room, Griff was in serious sheriff mode, with Hannah casually packing Maggie's clothes.

"Anything else you can remember?"

Maggie bit her lip, eyes darting, eyebrows pulled into a net to hold something...anything. "There were three men, I think." She couldn't catch the flickers and shadows that skittered across her brain: a face, perhaps, a birthmark, a gold tooth, or a body piercing maybe. Then, she shook her head free.

Griff glanced at Riley with enough question in his eyes, then shook his head slightly. "Three men. Any names?"

"No, no more."

"Hey there, Sunshine," Riley spoke cautiously. "Looks like a party." Her smile was lopsided, jawline still purple, eye socket allowing her eye to be more visible, despite how wickedly bloodshot the eye appeared. Her cast boasted Hannah's signature and a sunshine doodle.

"Come help me, Maggie, with the tee shirts and jeans," Hannah offered.

As if on cue, Griff stood and pulled Riley toward the window.

"You sure you want to do this? You still can change your mind."

"I sure didn't hear any better ideas."

"Okay, what if this young woman—"

"Maggie—"

"Okay, 'Maggie'. What if she doesn't want to leave once she figures out who she is?" Griff's whisper was more urgent.

"Isn't that up to her?"

"Look, I get the benefit of her being here so I can work on this crime—"

"So let her recover at the ranch while she clears. But right now, she's not ready to be shipped, sorted, flagged, identified, fingerprinted, transferred, or reestablished. She'll know when she is ready, and we'll make arrangements then."

Griff shook his head. "I've got a feeling about this."

"Yeah, I've been hearing that a lot lately."

Hannah opened the bottom drawer of Maggie's nightstand. "What's this?" She outright laughed.

"Jell-O. I saved some."

"You certainly did! This drawer is lined with unopened Jell-O cups!"

"Go ahead, pack it up." Riley smiled. It wasn't like she didn't have room in her suitcase.

A quiet knock announced Doc, clipboard in hand.

"Okay, it's official. This room can hold more than five! Maggie? You ready to get out of Dodge?"

Her eyes narrowed. "I thought I was in Arizona."

"Yes, yes, you are. I'm sorry—figure of speech. I'm asking if you're ready to leave the hospital."

"I'm going to the ranch with Riley in Arizona. He has Jell-O and so do I."

"Okay, then. Maggie, promise me you'll write in your

memory book, every time you remember something, good or bad. These bits and pieces add up, may help us track something from your past, something important. Bring it with you when I see you again. Show it to Riley, Hannah, or Griff when you add something. Promise?"

"Okay."

"Now, Riley, here're the final instructions." He gave Riley a checklist which were more DON'Ts than what he wanted to hear. He zoned out briefly as he watched Maggie try to brush her brown hair. No longer tangled, it was getting its soft shine back.

"...and, thanks, Riley, for doing this. I know she's in the best of hands. But I'm only a phone call away." They shook hands, like at a football game after the coin toss.

"Now, your signature here...and here...and initials here...and you are good to go." Riley's signature in less than four seconds turned Maggie's life over into his hands. Griff had warned him, and for a second, he thought maybe Griff was this side of right. But then he looked at Maggie and saw a bit of sunshine in her smile that reminded him this was the only and right thing to do.

Maggie felt the magic of being wheeled away from the white room, down the wide corridor, past pictures on the wall of large open landscapes that invited her outside. Shafts of light filtered through the window and beyond, an atrium as wide as the blue-water sky. Her eyes looked up, something she'd not done in a while, and she wanted to taste the outdoors. She looked up because no one told her she couldn't.

Trees danced a breeze just outside the door. The automatic door slid rhythmically open, letting the breeze spill past her neck and hair. Her hair rose away from her shoulders momentarily, a sensation of flying. She heard Hannah's light footsteps, Riley's boots, and Griff's steady shoes behind her, not running, but clicking steadily through a wide plaza. Birds, breeze, sunshine, shadows all teased her memory just then, as the group approached Riley's truck.

The outside was so...big...so full of other.

Maggie looked up again. This time she saw a furry face staring down from the truck bed.

"Maggie, this is Poke." The dog pawed against the truck bed for a better view.

"Hey, Poke. He's cute."

Warily, with Riley's support, she stood near the passenger door, then slowly stepped to enter the truck. But then she heard a pounding, felt hands tugging on her, yelling over who should go first...

"No. No." She backed away.

"Go on, Maggie, just take it easy. Let me know if it hurts."

She placed her hand inside, put her hand on the doorframe of the truck. She saw a face in her brain. A gun. *Don't you scream again, bitch.* She stepped back.

"No, not again," she whimpered. "No, I can't." She looked toward Riley, a dark fear solidly between her eyes.

"Maggie?"

"They want me in the truck. I hear them." She choked.

"But you're with me, remember? My voice is the one that counts. I'll help you into the truck and then we'll go home to the ranch."

"Okay, okay," she whispered. Her left hand grabbed the doorframe and steadied her cast against the truck door. She licked the dry fear from her lips. "Okay."

Again, she leaned forward, foot slightly raised toward the truck. *I said stay on the floor, you're mine now, Girlie girl ...*

"No! No! Leave me alone! Don't touch me! Stop!" Her arms flew up against her face, hiding panic and fear. "I can't. I can't!"

Riley looked at Doc, stunned.

"It *is* the first time she's been back into a vehicle since her ambulance ride..." Doc paused. "But I think I have an idea that might work. Maggie? Could you ride in the back of the truck, if we lifted you in there?"

She tilted her head toward the truck bed. "With Poke?"

"You bet; he won't mind." Riley clasped his hands together, holding the solution tight so it wouldn't blow into the wind.

"Give me a few minutes." When Doc returned with two orderlies, they carried a mattress and linens. "We're getting rid of these anyway."

The mattress was lifted into the truck bed, sheets tucked and secured so the mattresses wouldn't pin Poke or place torque on Maggie's fragile healing.

"Now listen, Maggie. I'll help you up into the truck bed. Will you let me lift you there? I need to touch you under your back and your legs. You trust me?" Riley searched her eyes for any panic.

"Okay."

She was like a newborn colt, all legs and fear. Up onto the tailgate, she sat, then once Riley joined her there, he lifted her again onto the mattress. Her head propped up against the pillows under the cab window.

"How's that? Any soreness?"

"No."

Poke slowly moved into a pocket by her legs while Riley settled into the cab.

"You ready, Sunshine?"

"Yup, Poke is, too."

He waved at Doc, Hannah, and Griff as he pulled the truck slowly onto the street.

"I'll go slow. You just stay on that mattress, and I'll get you home in one piece."

Maggie thought about what "home" might be. A ranch, a house, Ar-i-zo-na, a privacy, a person, a dog, some horses, a bed, warm blankets, clean sheets, a jeans jacket reaching toward her, a name, and certainly Jell-O. That was what she knew so far. A home was *not* loud music, not things pulled away from you, not bruises, guns, and worse. She had come from dark and nothing before that. Whatever home was, she was willing to try Riley's brand.

The sheet covered a bubble of air by her arm. Briefly, she remembered a white flake of fabric against a black backdrop. Then, something about miles, people talking about miles and routes and how to save time and when to get gasoline.

She felt the truck shift, and for a second, she was waiting for a face to appear, for a sudden push. But it was only a small easy curve. Poke raised his head. A fist of wind punched over the cab, past Maggie's shoulder, then skidded onto the road.

Riley looked in the rearview mirror. Her hair whipped like soft, thin flames rising to investigate uncertain air. Then he saw her left hand rise up and cup the air in her palm and let it go—again and again, like a bobbing sail on an invisible sea. Maggie's arm tattooed with bruises, darker than any sky, was weaving effortlessly against a pocket of wind, then relaxed to let the air fly free. That arm, feeling the sky and back again, letting it go; a small victory in a fingerful of wind.

CHAPTER
FOURTEEN

Riley cornered the truck slowly into the driveway, a small cloud of dust kicking up from the tires, briefly shadowing the blue sky. He watched Maggie's mirrored reflection in the truck bed behind him, but Poke's face bobbed into view. They were home. The engine cut clean.

"Okay, Sunshine, wait right there." As Riley dropped the tailgate, Poke jumped to the ground, a tiny pirate claiming the land. Riley met Maggie's eyes, waited for permission with her slight nod, then lifted her carefully again onto the tailgate, legs dangling like she liked to do from her bed. She met the ranch.

"Here's home, Maggie. We have a real nice porch for sitting in the evening. That's the kitchen by the door there, and the other end is the living room and study. That, straight ahead? That barn? That's where the horses sleep. They've been cooped up this past week, just like you. You'll meet them later. They'll like you." He smiled.

She raised her casted arm against the wash of the noon sun, squinted against its light.

"Your house. In Arizona."

"And that," he pointed to the turreted corner, "is your room."

"My privacy."

"Yes, ma'am. See? It looks out over the river we followed from town. You can see the barn when you sit in the window seat. My room is over here."

"Your privacy."

"Yes. Yes, I suppose so. I own all this." He spread his arms up. "Up past that mountain, the pastureland, all the way over there." He pointed behind her.

"Arizona."

He sat near her on the tailgate, not too close.

"Maggie, you've been through a world of hurt and it may not be entirely done. I don't know all the demons chasing you or why. But while you're here, I hope you can feel safe. Understand?"

"It's black."

"What?"

"Your truck is black."

"Sure, under that layer of Arizona dust."

"Like the other one was too."

The color sank into him like an ink spill. Of course, she wouldn't get into another black vehicle. Of course.

"See? That's one of those fears still haunting you. That's something we'll tell Griff too. We may not have all the answers, but we'll do our best to get your feet under you."

She wiped the dust from the edge of the truck. Black.

"Okay, so do you think you want to ride inside the truck someday?"

"With you? I...I don't know how."

"Maybe I can help. Are you willing to let me help you?"

"And Hannah and Griff and Poke?"

"Yes, and Poke, too." He started to reach toward her back, in a natural way to reassure, but then checked his hand.

Gentle. No surprises.

She looked at Riley but did not flinch. She took a deep breath, stretched her arms wide like a funnel pouring the sun into her.

"I like this Arizona better than the hospital Arizona, so far."

"Okay, let's go inside. So that means I'll lift you from the truck. I'll set you on the ground, right here by Poke. Ready?"

That nearly invisible nod brought him closer, slowly, no sudden moves. He lifted this small broken stranger who had interrupted his life onto the ground. He looked at her feet.

"Those sneakers comfortable?"

"They're part of my memory. Doc said so."

"Well, that may be, but if you're going to be around the horses, they won't be enough. Hannah's bringing you boots tomorrow."

"Like cowboy boots?"

"Gotta have 'em, Sunshine, if you're in Arizona." He lifted her suitcase.

She smiled. "Arizona even has boots."

Maggie stared out the door while Riley made sandwiches. She sat at the dining table as Riley had asked, wary of going anywhere her skin wouldn't allow her. He set the plate before her then added a cup of her hospital Jell-O.

"So the truck was scary, huh? Were you in a black truck or car or van?"

"I think it was bigger than the truck. What is that?"

"Might be a van. I'll let Griff know. But you remember 'white' too. Was that in the van?"

"I don't think so. The white was something happy, I think. The van was dark and loud." *Hold your pee 'til I say you can go.*

"You like red Jell-O, don't you?"

"It's my favorite." Like that, the demon dissolved, and the dark patterns lifted the shadows.

"Think you can walk out to the barn after lunch? We'll visit the horses in the pasture."

"Do I like horses?"

"Don't know, but I don't know too many people who don't like horses. If you lived in the country, you might have had horses."

"I lived in a house. Until I lived on the side of the road when you found me."

Pretty simple, he thought. Her life in two sentences. His life with Grace could fill a book.

She looked at her plate. "I remember celery and salsa. It danced hot on my tongue. People were laughing."

"In the van?"

"No, when I was happy."

After lunch, the two walked slowly toward the barn. Maggie still felt tender while walking, choosing steps as if her legs were glass. They turned toward the corral.

"Wait here." Riley blew a piercing whistle that brought the horses running toward him. One by one, the nickers and heavy-footed steps turned into shiny coats, manes, and deep brown eyes.

"Here." He handed her a few carrots. "Open your hand flat, like this." He held an apple half in the flat dinner plate of his hand. "They'll take it from your hand. Don't curl your fingers, keep your hand flat. Like that...right."

He smiled. "This is Bliss. She's a gentle girl, a little bit of a diva. Bliss, this is Maggie."

Maggie extended her flat hand but squinted her eyes away from Bliss as the horse drew closer. Like that, the carrot piece was gone.

"It tickled! Where did it go?" Bliss' crunching was the only answer.

"They won't hurt you as long as you're gentle with them. Now, this over here is Cartwheel. She's pretty spirited. Try another carrot with her."

This time, Maggie watched the brown head sweep toward her flat hand. The horse parted its lips to show giant teeth then delicately plucked the carrot.

He chuckled. "See? They like you, now. You're their friend for life."

"Horses and cowboy boots and carrots and apples and Jell-O," she whispered. She looked at Riley. "It's like magic here."

"Yes, yes, it is."

Bliss leaned forward toward Maggie, searching for another treat. Maggie backed away, her hand pushing back.

"She's being a little greedy, don't you think?" Riley said. "Here. Bring your hand up here between her eyes and her nose. We call that the 'forelock'. She likes to be petted there. That's it. Easy, easy."

Maggie extended her arm, for a second catching a flicker of a man's head leaning toward her, then lost it as quickly, when Bliss nudged her hand. She let her fingers spread a circle across the spot.

"She's soft and warm. She likes this."

"She likes you, Maggie. One of the best ways to communicate with Bliss or Cartwheel is to use a gentle touch like that."

The horse leaned closer, and this time, Maggie felt her brush her face. The vote was in. Maggie's touch, a forgotten woman's touch, was familiar to the horses. Maggie passed inspection.

He saw Maggie's body bend a little, giving in to a cramp as they returned to the house. He led her to the soft couch and placed covers and a pillow for her rest, while he curried the horses.

When he returned, Maggie was asleep. Her easy breath rose up and down in a rhythm of cowboy boots and carrots and Jell-O, secondhand clothing and an empty suitcase. Those small pieces of her story, next to nothing really, made pictures for her, something she could remember when she awoke. *What would he have done if he'd ever forgotten his life with Grace? It was bad enough remembering Grace and not having her with him. But it was even worse now, needing a photograph sometimes to remember Grace's eyes or mouth.* He took Maggie's suitcase to the guest room, put her spare, secondhand clothing with a lost history into the dresser drawers.

At dinner, Maggie's fatigue hit her like a dropped theatre curtain. She stared at her plate, face blank. Riley sensed she wanted the comfort of welcome company and a dog at her feet, but she gave in quickly. He guided her wobbly legs up the steps toward her room. He stood near her in the bathroom when she brushed her teeth and washed her face, oriented her to her room: the bed, the lamp, her clothing in the drawers. She settled, her door slightly ajar, and Poke nearby. Riley turned away.

He sat on the porch, long enough for the moon to scrape past the canyon on the outside curve of the river. Long enough for a hoot owl to inquire about his new resident. Long enough for Riley to count the stars, listen to the cricket and frog choruses. Long enough to visit doubt about what he was doing with a stranger upstairs who needed to set days between the devil and any happiness she might someday own.

He stretched, locked the door behind him. For the first time in more than two years, he turned on a night light in the kitchen in case Maggie tried to wander downstairs, as he did for Grace when she couldn't sleep. He climbed the stairs. A sliver of light from Maggie's door reached nearly as far across the hall to his door. Poke guarded the door.

He tapped on the open door and saw the sweetness meant for this room. Maggie was asleep, but not in the bed. She had pulled the blanket and quilt and lay cocooned in them on the floor. Her hair, coiled slightly around her bruised face, her face tucked against the pillow. Poke walked into her room softly, nudged near her feet, determined to protect her, as she fought the dark places in her dreams.

CHAPTER
FIFTEEN

Riley overslept by thirty minutes because Poke wasn't there to wake him up. He showered and walked past Maggie's door. The dog looked up as Riley peeked in, then tucked his head back down, nose to toes. Riley had walked this same limbo before, while Grace slept, almost second nature to him how he could slip back into stealth. Riley motioned Poke to join him in the kitchen. The dog hesitated.

What was up with Poke?

The aromas of fried eggs and toast rumbled hunger in his own stomach as he prepared Grace's favorite. Certainly the aromas would pull the most stubborn of sleepers from their dreams. Certainly Maggie would be walking down the stairs any minute now. But not even Poke made an effort to tiptoe toward the kitchen. Instead, Riley buttered toast, put a small pocket of Hannah's apple jelly, and a container of Jell-O on a covered plate then carried a breakfast tray up the steps, reminding him of Grace's last months. He placed the tray by her door and turned for the stairs.

Poke emerged from the room and sniffed the tray.

"I don't think so, Mister. Your food is downstairs. You comin'?"

Poke looked up, stretched and dog-moseyed his way toward the landing.

"What am I suddenly—chopped liver?" he whispered as they entered the kitchen.

To say that working with horses was therapeutic came from Riley's personal knowledge. Grace's loss was more bearable due to Bliss and Cartwheel. The horses needed attention, gave him reason to leave the house, to focus on someone other than himself and Grace's absence. When he had a hole in his life, he needed the routine of feeding Poke and caring for the horses each day. But the routine of caring for Maggie was tangled.

He opened the stalls with new energy, as if Grace urged him on, feeding the horses, giving them baths, and spoiling them with apples. Bliss leaned toward him, Cartwheel focused on the pasture as they walked outside. The sun spotted the sky overhead. Poke, ever the guardian, switched devotion from Maggie to the horses and disappeared into the pasture's tall grasses.

But Riley's curiosity got the better of him. He returned to the house, his gloved hand carefully brought the screen door closed, listening for movement in the guest room overhead, in the adjacent living room, in the bathroom. Nothing. He carefully walked up the stairs, quiet boot falls, not to disturb.

Tray, still there. Eggs, toast, jelly, and Jell-O, gone.

He knocked on the door.

"Yeah?"

"Maggie, it's Riley. Can I check to see if you're okay?"

"Uh, yeah, sure."

He opened the door to find the bed made again, Maggie looking outside, knees to chin, sitting on the window seat.

"I saw you with the horses, not cooped up."

"Yeah, we had a good morning. Did...do you want to go outside?"

"Am I allowed?"

Riley's insides crushed. There, Maggie sat, afraid of leaving the room, no, not even afraid. Just not even aware she had any rights yet, because it wasn't too long ago that she didn't. She'd earned every bit of freedom with broken bones, scars, and bruises.

"My God, Maggie, you're welcome to join me for breakfast, lunch, and dinner, help me with the horses, use the bathroom, take a shower, eat a snack, pet Poke—who incidentally has fallen head over heels for you—honest, you can leave the room any time, you don't need to ask."

"The door was kind of closed."

He squeezed his eyes, his fingers tight along the bridge of his nose. "For your privacy. I want you to feel safe, but this room is not a prison cell."

"Not like the hospital."

"Right. Now, I want to be close by when you take the stairs, and if you need help with your cast, but all you need to do is call out. Then, you can have your privacy, again. Is that—? Does that work for you?"

She nodded.

"Sleep okay? Any pain today? You probably should take your medicine."

"Okay."

He turned to leave then leaned back. "I'll walk you down the stairs. Feel like visiting my garden? I've got some weeds to pull, and I bet there are some tomatoes ready, too."

She looked out the window again. "There's Poke, head over heels," she said. "Does that hurt him?"

Riley smiled. "No more than Bliss taking an apple from the palm of your hand."

For the first time since yesterday, Riley saw her smile.

He pointed her toward the porch and around the back of the house.

She brought her hand across her forehead then nodded. "Nice size garden. And it's green here. There's so much brown up there." She pointed toward the mountain.

"Well, some of that is weeds. The garden looks much better when those are cleared out. Ever do any gardening?"

"I don't know."

The plants whispered soft against her skin, the garden breathing. She looked up because she could, and no one would hit her. Riley attacked the tall green stalks like an enemy.

"Weeds," he said. "Makes you wonder what God was thinking of when he created weeds."

"Is this a weed?"

"No, that's a tomato plant."

As he crossed from his line of dirt to Maggie's, she stepped back quickly. *Back in the van, bitch, on the floor, now.*

"Okay, here's a tomato...right...under here." He wove the leaves back, and she forgot about the van or the voice she just heard. There, by his thumb, was a red, baseball-sized thing he called a tomato. And then, it was something she remembered. Just like that.

"This plant is loaded with them. It will be tomato city in another week or so. We can make salsa, if you want."

"I thought we were in Copper Station, Arizona. When did it become tomato city?"

Riley's smile pulled her back to the plant. "What I meant was that the tomatoes will be so plentiful, it will be like a whole city of tomatoes settled in here. Lots, and I mean lots, of tomatoes."

Tomato City sounded important, but she hadn't figured it out, yet.

"So, don't pull up the tomato plants. We want to get rid of the weeds. Like these..." He held up some that he'd uprooted.

"We've got lots of these."

"Weed city," she said.

Riley laughed, a big laugh that flew up into the sky like a bird. Riley's laugh could make all the voices and dark places disappear for darn near forever, it seemed to Maggie.

"Good one, Sunshine. Good one."

Once back in the kitchen with a basket of tomatoes, her cheeks remained warm, a souvenir from the midday sun. She'd forgotten her skin could do that, a little warm and prickly against the bruises.

"How about some lunch? You can help. Ever do any cooking?"

She looked at him, taking a bite at his question.

"I think so. Kitchen feels familiar, but I don't know why."

"We'll just make some sandwiches. I have some ham in the fridge. Sandwich and soup?"

Sandwich and Soup sounded like horses' names to her, but she nodded yes, anyway. Maybe Sandwich and Soup were friends of Bliss and Cartwheel. Sandwich and Soup. It was like saying Ar-i-zo-na. Sandwich and Soup, with a pop at the end of it.

He reached for a can opener and a pan and in one movement, then opened a drawer. He pulled out a knife.

There you go, pretty, pretty. We can cut your hair short, so everyone will think you're one of us. She flinched at the voice and walked backward to the chair.

"Uh, Maggie, no, no, it's okay," Riley said softly. "I need to slice the ham with this. See? I'll use it on the ham." He shielded the ham from her eyes as he sawed thin slices like pink paper onto the plate.

"Okay, Maggie. I'll put the knife in the sink and wash it later. See?"

Her eyes followed his hand as he released it into the sink. *Okay, okay, easy,* she thought.

"Why don't you reach into the fridge and get some sandwich makings? I'll heat up the soup."

She opened the fridge, as he had said, but "sandwich makings" didn't ring a bell. The door fanned cool air across her warm face that surprised her body into a shiver.

"Sandwich makings, sandwich makings," she whispered, searching the fridge, the door, the cold space for something labeled "sandwich makings." She used to play "I spy" with someone older than she was. *I spy something blue,* she suddenly remembered. *I spy sandwich makings.* She was pretty sure Riley wouldn't hit her just because she couldn't decide what it was she was looking for. *Hurry up, pretty, pretty. We don't have time for your skinny little ass to find yogurt. Get a damn donut and get outa here.*

She reached for Jell-O. She knew that.

"Here it is, Sunshine." He had quietly approached behind her while she was hearing that voice. He reached past her shoulder to the second shelf of the fridge. Maybe the hand looked like a fist. Maybe it was a little too close to her shoulder, her neck, her face. Maybe she heard a different voice, *pretty, pretty, bitch, get out of the way.*

Fast as lightning, she screamed. A wail, a stab of a voice as she jammed her body back against a wall. Terror escaped red, raw, jagged, her eyes seeing nothing but that hand, nothing of sandwich makings at all, but rather hands reaching across her throat and shoulder ready to punch her down again. Her legs gave. She slid down the wall until she solidly met the floor, knees peaked like mountains to protect her.

Then silence.

"Easy, Easy, Maggie. I just wanted the mayonnaise and mustard. See?"

Her tears burned shame and terror against her prickly

skin, afraid to look toward the nice man Riley.

"Here, in the door. Sandwich makings." He wiggled them in his hands then set them on the floor between them.

"Maggie?" He used the same soft voice he used with Bliss. "Maggie, you with me?"

She couldn't catch her breath, sobs bouncing against her heart.

"Breathe for me, Sunshine. You're all right. I moved too fast. That was my fault.

"Okay, I'm going to close the fridge door. We'll just sit here a while." He moved in slow motion. The door closed slowly, the latch a period at the end of a paragraph. Her breath split into gasps, then staccato whimpers that slowly let air escape in little puffs.

"I was too close, Maggie. I wasn't thinking. Somebody back there hit you hard enough to believe it every time. But it wasn't me. In your heart of hearts know I will never. Hit. You." Each word was a bullet, solid with meaning, dropping on the floor.

In the flickers of fist and flesh, she held the terror like a fresh slice of bread. But the silence told her it was all over, whatever just happened, it was over. She finally remembered words that made things better.

"I'm sorry, I'm so sorry, Riley," she whispered, looking at her feet. She looked up because she was sad, but then because she was brave. She saw Riley's head dip sideways, but there wasn't hate, there wasn't rejection, just the sadness they both held. The soft-voiced man just made a promise stronger than paper, one that he would never tear to pieces or toss in the trash when it was convenient. She looked at him again, maybe for the first time. She remembered another word: apology. And another word: forgive. And another: grateful. Then: healing.

"Am I all right?" she whispered.

He smiled. "You bet." His voice was solid as rocks in his mountains.

Poke padded to Riley's foot and sniffed the Jell-O cup that had fallen from her hand. She felt a brief softness, something that once belonged in her life. Somewhere, a soft thing she liked. Then, it slipped like a drop from a faucet before she could name it. Poke lay his head on her knee.

She got it, just that perfect quiet moment after the thunder.

"Oh, I'm safe, right?" she whispered.

If he hadn't smiled, she would have missed the tears in the corner of his eyes. All she could think was, he's a nice man; he doesn't hurt me after I made a mistake.

The sun set with a tangerine glow in the wide blue sky. The softening gray fell around them like a comfortable sweater. They sat on the porch after such a long day.

"You're nice to me and I don't know why."

"Not sure there is a 'why', Maggie. It's just something a person chooses to do. A person has choices. I'm one of the people who found you. You needed help, and I knew I could do that. It fits together."

"What was my choice in the van?"

"You chose to survive."

"Did I do something bad today?"

"No, no, I don't think so. You reacted. You still have reactions in your brain that helped you survive. I moved too fast and too close. I reminded you of some other situation and you reacted. Doc said I need to expect that, still."

She shook her head, going through the motions. New rules, now. Even though it wasn't home.

"So, tomorrow will be better. You'll remember more.

There might be something to remember or something you'll choose to forget. But each day gets better."

"I believe you, Riley."

The words wrapped around him like a ribbon.

CHAPTER
SIXTEEN

Riley finished readying for bed while Poke padded softly to Maggie's room. He had just pulled the covers near his chin when he heard a night-splitting screech echoing from Mitchell Canyon.

Many Devils. Again.

Blood prickled his skin, then ran cold along every bone. The screech razored through the canyon again, ripping the very sky apart. The slash of the prowling cry sounded as though the cat had been injured but was still standing his ground.

Many Devils was such a legend, some said for upward of thirty years. Likely, several descendants claimed the name, but everyone agreed to his size and threat. However true, legend said Many Devils could take down a sixteen-hand horse in one flash of a leap, teeth dug deep into the jugular.

The barn door was locked, he remembered, before he and Maggie sat on the porch. He scanned for Cassiopeia, the constellation that Grace loved. With each step back to the house, he looked at that lazy double *U*; that queen reclining back catching a peek at herself in the mirror. Maybe she was catching a reflection of Many Devils, instead.

He pulled the covers up further, eventually dozing in and out of Many Devils' imagined trip across the sky to land on the house roof. A growl, a wail here and there in his dream convinced Riley that Many Devils still was doing something sinister under Cassiopeia's eye.

But that sound persisted, as if Many Devils weren't ready to leave his dreams. It was the sound of pure hell. Riley sat up in bed, the sound now closer...closer...it wasn't outside. It was across the hall. Many Devils? *No, Maggie.*

He opened her door and heard her in the darkest of nightmares, screaming, sobbing.

"No, no, no!" She kneeled on the floor, tugging the blankets and imaginary attackers.

Riley took careful steps between the shadows into her room.

"Maggie? Maggie?" His voice eased toward Maggie's crouched form. "Maggie? Can you wake up for me? It's Riley." He squatted near her.

He was fully aware the last time he was this close, she screamed, believing he was ready to hit her. Sure enough, her hand and casted arm were waving, pushing away her demons. He saw her hair damp with sweat. It had been a fight, already.

"Maggie? It's Riley."

"No, no, go away!"

"Maggie, wake up now. Maggie—"

Her casted arm swung from the shadows toward the side of his face. He caught her arm in time. But she started backing away on her knees, now trapped against the side of the bed.

"I'll turn on the light, Maggie, so you can see where you are." He reached toward the bedside lamp, but she hit his leg with the other arm.

He held both arms, not tightly, but securely as she

dissolved her strength into a whimper. He realized only then that they likely held her down, all of them, to get what they wanted. He hated doing the same thing, watching her resist up until that moment. Riley's stomach turned toward his throat.

"No, not the gun, no…" her face slick with a perfect storm of tears and panic.

Held her down at gunpoint? Good God. "No, Maggie. No guns, listen, listen. It's Riley. You're safe, remember?"

She went slightly limp, her breath still pounding from her lungs. But there in her eyes, a wild fear slid slowly back inside. She blinked once. Twice.

"Maggie, you awake?" He let go of her arms.

"What? What? Where am—?"

"You're here with me. Remember? Riley? Poke? At the ranch? Where you're safe? You had a nightmare, Sunshine." She slumped against the bed, gasping for breath. She blinked in the shadows, taking in the sudden quiet against her pounding heart. *You can cry all you want, princess. We still deliver you at the right time. So get on your knees.*

"Sunshine, I held your arms so you wouldn't hurt yourself. But you are still safe, here with me. You know I wouldn't—"

"They came back," she sobbed. "They came back and hit me and—" She gasped again.

"But, they're gone now, see? Look around the room. Just you, Poke, and me."

Those long dark moments let her settle into stable breaths. She wiped her cast along her face, then pulled back the wet strings of her hair. Riley shifted to sit in the light.

"I don't like them," she whispered.

"I don't either." He slowly raised his hand toward her shoulder. Then, as slowly, he rubbed her arm, something she allowed from not so long ago. Lavender.

"I don't know them." Her voice strained. A pulse of breath

released. "I don't want them to come back."

Riley blew out a slow breath. "I'll do everything I can to prevent them from coming back, but I can't keep them away from your dreams. I'll be here when you start a new day tomorrow, take a new step, breathe in the Arizona morning, and look beyond the dark places."

"Can I do that every day?" She looked at him.

"You and me and Poke? We're pretty strong, aren't we? We took out the weeds."

"Tomato City." She nodded in the shadows, more a hiccup than a sob.

"How about I help you back to bed? You deserve to sleep on the mattress, not on the floor. How about that?"

She nodded.

"Come here, we'll go slow." He leaned toward her then scooped her up in the secure bowl of his arms to place her on the covers.

She held on, leaning back and forth while Riley rocked her back to sleep.

CHAPTER
SEVENTEEN

MAGGIE'S JOURNAL

What I know

    The days here are quiet and strong.

    I have a name—Maggie.

    Poke is head over heels my friend.

    The nice man named Riley makes sure I'm safe.

    I'm allowed outside anytime.

    I can look at the sky.

    Riley has a nice smile.

    He has nice eyes.

    His hands are gentle along the horses' necks.

    I like the horse, Bliss.

    I'm in Arizona.

    Doc took care of me and told me what I needed to do in the hospital.

    I'm afraid of the voices I hear, jabbing at me, tearing me into pieces.

I have a purple face with green stains, but I don't know how they got there.

I can't get my cast wet, so my arm wears a plastic bag when I'm showering.

Hannah gave me privacy for like-Christmas and Riley gives me privacy every day.

I wear cowboy boots.

I'm sore inside and I can't lift much to help Riley.

I like the tomatoes from tomato city.

I like my hands on the horses' necks, too.

I like the smell of straw.

The river is silver outside my window, but I have to look across the road to see it.

I feel trust in my hand when I give Bliss a snack.

I'm happy when I remember something from the day before, like Riley's name or the feel of Poke's fur against my arm or the sound of the horses in the barn.

I'm happy when my face can smile because the bruises squeeze my face tight.

I'm happy I can live another day in the sunshine with the nice man Riley who keeps me safe.

Sometimes I forget there's tomorrow, but Riley reminds me, and I am not afraid.

CHAPTER
EIGHTEEN

Maggie

When I wake up, the windows let the easy breeze tease the curtains like a strand of hair against a wide face. I feel something like a gear turning a circle to get me started. I see the ceiling, the closet door, back to the windows. I hear the horses whinny. It must be morning.

The gears slip forward. I remember now. I came here with bruises, but now there are just shades of green near my jaw, the swelling by my eye is gone. I see better. I remember this is a place I like. I feel safe. It doesn't hurt here, and I can move around without someone hitting me, pushing me, licking me—

The gear slips forward again when I hear a car on the road or the kitchen door open. I sit up to be part of this life. Poke leads me to the bathroom. I wash up, including the unfamiliar face as it stares back from the mirror. I feel clean as the rivulets follow the crease along my nose, around the corner of my mouth. I want that sure fit when I pull on my boots, that solid wall of leather kicking up the dust or dancing high steps into the pasture.

Another slip forward and I dress, the tee shirt leaving the cast on my right wrist untouched. Riley says my farmer's tan will need some fixing once that cast is off. I remember that comment every day as I feel that sure fit when I pull on my boots, that solid wall of leather dancing high steps into the pasture or walking down the steps to the kitchen. I know the morning sun bathes my face when I walk to the barn, but what is a farmer's tan?

"Morning, Sunshine," is another part of the gear, one of the pieces I like. I remember I'm something good like the sun, how there's a smile on his face when he calls me that and how, somehow, he manages to flip a pancake or a waffle or a fried egg and still pour a cup of coffee with a little bit of cream—just the way I like it—and set it at my place setting. He knows not to approach me too quickly at first, or the gear will fall off-center from the cog and everything will stop.

Another click into place, and he'll ask me if I remember.

"Where's Poke's food?"

"In the pantry."

"And the scoop?"

"In the dog food bin."

"How many?"

"One, two scoops into Poke's bowl."

"And what else?"

"Fresh water."

"Atta girl."

He says I'm helping him. He somehow does this all while he's toasting whole wheat bread from Marta's Grind and Bakery, or finishing up the biscuits, keeping all the gears into place, moving breakfast and the morning like a purring machine. No glitches, no surprises, nothing sudden or threatening or hurtful or something that erases me.

"Shall we take care of the horses, Sunshine? You ready?"

Why wouldn't I be?

—

The faces...or actually parts of them, I see in a flash. Doc tells me to write it down. How do you write a shadow that lightens into part of a mouth or fingers or thumb, or elbow or lips? Lots of times, the voices are disconnected from the movement, a bug against a window that didn't see it coming. The voice...behind me or on the floor, or splat against the window. There's black and shadow and lights. Voices pick up like a lost radio station as the waves fade at 1:30 in the morning, then I feel the suffocation of breath and bodies and another slice of pain.

Doc says if I write it down, it will help my memory. Why would I want to remember anything like that? All I feel is being smothered and the fear of losing myself during the interruption.

I don't expect him to understand, but Riley does, somehow. Even without talking about the shadows, just sitting, and rocking against his heartbeat until the voices fade, until some point I can put those voices aside like a used tissue and lose myself to sleep.

I sleep in the bed now because Riley reminded me I could. Forget the scratchy floor, the tightly shut windows, the closed-in rhythm of the music and the bodies. That's not worth remembering now. Riley reminds me that I had a normal life once, with doorways and windows and sunshine and fresh air, just like when I wake up in the morning. That is something worth remembering.

CHAPTER
NINETEEN

Riley nursed his coffee while Maggie opened the Jell-O package. Breakfast Jell-O. He grinned. Go figure. He watched the first bite slide down her throat, then her smile.

"Have I eaten this flavor before?"

"It's raspberry."

"I like it. It's my favorite."

"You like Jell-O, period."

"It's good. It doesn't hurt to eat."

These last few weeks had given her a makeover. Her jaw and eye socket were nearly normal color, now, her eye wasn't bloodshot, and she didn't squint as much when she looked around.

"I want to try the truck again today," he said.

"But we did that yesterday."

"Why don't you practice sitting inside the truck, too. I need to take you to Doc next week for a follow-up appointment. I'd love it if you rode inside."

She stared as if he'd just pronounced a death sentence. Inside the truck. It sounded hollow like a cave, a hard scratchy floor, and windows that didn't open. Inside. *Get back in the truck. Don't even think you can fool us. Get in now.*

"If we do just a little more every day, you might be able to get to town with no worries."

Inside the truck. No worries. *What did that mean?*

"I don't want you to be afraid, Maggie. Sometime, in the future, I might need your help with the truck, with the horses, maybe, or with Poke. But you need to trust me."

"I trust you. I don't trust the truck."

"You and me, we'll go easy. We'll try a little today, a little tomorrow." He drained his coffee. "Just a titch."

Her head snapped up. "Say that again."

"Just a titch?"

As brief as a whisper, she heard a shadow voice slip through her brain. Just a titch. Not the mean men, but some-one measuring—coffee? Sugar? Flour? Just a titch—she closed her eyes to bring the word closer to her memory, a voice from somewhere safe before Arizona. A titch of this, a titch of that...how much is a titch? Enough to land on your eyelashes and blink it away—

"Maggie?"

"I can't bring it to my heart," she whispered. "I know that word, though...titch...it belongs in the kitchen."

"This is one of those memories I bet is a good one."

"But why do the good ones take so long to come back?"

Every day when she walked to the barn with Riley, she looked away from the black truck parked near the kitchen door. She walked on the opposite side of the drive, she closed her eyes, she counted to ten, she said Poke's name over and over, anything to distract her from the black. She helped Riley feed the horses, with her back to the truck. She lifted the toe pick or the shovel so her hand covered the position of the truck in the distance. She wiped down the saddles, never looking out the barn door so her eyes wouldn't land on the black surface.

Maggie watched Riley work the horses in the corral, knowing the truck was behind her, waiting for her. He sat high on Cartwheel, the gypsy horse who teased and liked challenges: left, right, left again. Cartwheel responded quickly, a game of short and long steps, a lurch, a balance, a slow pause. Cartwheel anticipated Riley's commands with quick, sharp turns, keeping focus on Riley and nothing else. Maggie needed to do that, too.

Bliss' turn. Her footing was careful but sure footed. Riley had her circle the corral, first to the left, then the right. She stopped to his command, then held her head high. Look at me, this is how it's done. Maggie looked up to the sky again because Bliss showed her how.

He let them gallop out to the pasture, school children breaking for recess.

"They work hard for you. They're so focused."

Riley gathered the rope and leather. "That's how they trust me. So, let's try the truck."

"I was hoping you'd forgotten."

"This is what we'll do. Open the door like we practiced. You'll put your foot inside. Then, you'll lean partially inside. Like this—" He opened the passenger door, stepped his foot inside on the floor. He pretended it was a bug that you squished with your foot. He leaned forward, not really sitting, but getting ready to. So easy, when Riley did it.

"It might be a little tricky, might throw your balance a little because of your cast. So, focus on me."

It was already in the eighties outside, but Maggie's stomach turned to ice anyway.

"Let's try together." His hand carefully cupped hers on the silver handle. She pressed the latch to release the door. She opened the passenger door and felt the stifling heat rush from the interior.

"That's it, that's it. Now, your left foot. Bring your cast

above the door like this."

She leaned forward to place her foot, searching for that imaginary bug that perpetually needed squishing somewhere on the floor. But instead, she felt a pounding deep in her brain. Her leg was shaking. She was holding her breath. She jerked outside.

Riley closed the door. "Nice, Maggie. Very nice try. Okay. Again."

Her distorted face swam in the silver handle against the dark current that pulled her away. The first part was easy, opening the door; that part she'd learned the other day. She brought her breath back more quickly. She pulled the door open, he guided her placement of her foot, then she briefly sat on the seat and stood again.

"Wow! Look at you! Again. Both feet now, inside."

She searched an invisible list right behind her eyes as to why that wouldn't work, her eyes darting like flies.

Her balance suffered without flexibility in her right arm. He guided her again...door handle, pause, pause again, foot inside, breath, lean back, sit, the other foot... But at the same time, those invisible voices that drummed to only her brain were stronger still. *It's my turn now. Get on the floor.*

"Maggie, focus. You are doing great—"

She spilled out of the passenger side, coated in sweat and screams. She ran past Riley, trying to catch her breath, bending over, gasping.

"Holy horseshoes, Riley! Everything all right?" A voice floated from behind him. He turned. Lester, delivering the mail. He walked tentatively toward the couple, a box in his hand, all 5'7" of him in postal blue. Lester had a perplexed twist to his face.

"Gosh, Les! Didn't see you drive in!" Riley's brain switched into high gear. "Hornet's nest! There's one around here, somewhere!" He waved his arms convincingly scaring whatever hornets away.

"Those hornets sure scared the little lady." Les moved closer to Maggie. "I'm Lester. I bring the mail and I never fail." His smile broadened as if that had been the first time he'd ever used that line.

Of all times for Lester to show up...

"Brought the equine meds you ordered. Need to sign right here." He pointed his finger absently to his clipboard, but his eyes were on Maggie.

Ignoring everything except her hair clinging to her scalp, she lifted the tresses to let the dry breeze wash across her neck.

Lester stepped annoyingly close to her. *Was he someone she knew? Was he being friendly?* "Ma'am." Lester nodded, his voice dry as the air. His smile had not quit, as if it were stuck on his face.

"Now, where are my manners?" Riley exaggerated his voice. "Maggie, this is Lester Manning, our postal carrier. Comes by just about the same time every day." Riley's face twitched slightly, wishing Les could be, just this one time, one of those imaginary bugs that Maggie's foot squished on the truck floor.

Lester reached out his weathered hand. "Maggie. Uh, I didn't catch your last name."

"Maggie." She pulled from his hand, staring at her shadow stuck to the soles of her boots.

Of all times to come face-to-face with a last name for Maggie. Of all times to make up a past...with Lester...

"Well, this is Maggie..uh..Fletcher. You remember Old Man Fletcher. You remember, he had a niece back east..."

"Well, now, I don't recall, no, I can't say."

"Oh, sure. Rhode Island. She wanted to visit the old place—"

"Oh, sure!" Les nodded an unexpected recognition. "Sure, I remember now. I met you when you were this high." Les extended his arm straight out past his waist. "Yep, I can see the resemblance now that you mention it."

Maggie's bewildered glance toward Riley met with a slight headshake.

"Now, don't tell me you fell off one of Riley's horses and broke your arm!" Les chuckled.

"I won't," Maggie said, staring at the cast.

"Well, by gum. She's even got Old Man Fletcher's sense of humor. That's a good one!" Les' chuckle sounded a bit like a chicken clucking.

"You bring the mail every day?" Maggie asked.

"Not on Sundays, no ma'am. Now if you order something, like this medicine here? I'll deliver right to the door."

Maggie tightened her lips in discomfort, looking toward the mail truck door with no one inside.

"So, how long you here for?" Les moved a step closer, twisting his way into Riley's stomach. He saw her flinch slightly with Les' movement toward her.

"I guess I'd better get these meds into the fridge. Maggie, why don't you help?"

She stared at Riley in pure confusion.

"Maggie?" He nodded toward the kitchen.

"Sure, sure."

"See you, Les." Riley waved the box in the air. "Thanks!"

Les' blank face indicated he had forgotten he was delivering the mail.

"Oh, and watch out for those hornets, Les! Hope one didn't settle into the mail truck. They sure can be a nuisance."

Les tapped the bill of his cap and looked quickly into the corners of the truck before getting in.

Maggie stared at Riley in the kitchen. "Wait a minute! You know who I am?"

"No, no, wait, Sunshine..." He rubbed his eyes.

"You know my last name? I've been here before?"

"No, Maggie, I lied to him. Les is a busy body, a gossip. The last thing I want him to do is try to hang around here to get to know you better, let alone tell everyone about you."

"So, Fletcher—?"

"I couldn't very well say 'this is Maggie, but we don't have a last name for her' because we don't know who you are."

"So I don't know the mailman?"

"No, and if I have my way, you never will."

"But he said—"

"He pretends he knows more than he does to look important. I'm pretty darn sure he's never met you."

"I'm not from Rhode Island?"

"No, not that I know of..." He sighed. "I'm sorry, Maggie. I think I just created a huge mess from a lie I used to cover up your past, whatever it is. Maybe it wasn't such a great idea."

"So, there's no Maggie Fletcher?"

"No, I suppose not, but a representative of the US Postal Service believes there is."

"Then, who am I?"

Riley's body sank against the counter.

"Good question. When we found you, you didn't have any identification. You couldn't talk to us for nearly a week. Doc tried to match your dental records, but that's been a dead end. We just don't—"

Her brain took her back to the hospital room, the clothing on her bed, the Jell-O cups, something about lavender...she remembered that.

"Okay, here's what I do know: you're quiet, curious, you're observant, you love the horses and Poke. Your favorite food is Jell-O, especially cherry, although it appears the raspberry you had today at breakfast came in a close second. Whatever happened in that van is buried so deep and painful that it erased who you were. But as far as we know, from the day we first met you a few weeks ago, you didn't do anything wrong. You may or may not have family. You may or may not have someone still wanting to harm you. You work hard when I ask you to do something, you make coffee better than I ever imagined and we don't know why. You don't always remember, and when you do, it's a horrible nightmare that I can't always pull you out of. But, right now, you're safe here."

For the second time in an hour, Maggie had been holding her breath. She let it out slowly, like a string pulling itself free from a skirt hem.

"I want to be somebody, a name that makes sense, the holes filled, glued together, tied into a package that I can hold it and live with it. Maggie Fletcher sounded like a good name... Soooo, I guess you don't like Lester that much."

"He's a necessary part of my daily routine, to get my bills, the horses' medicine. But I try to keep my interaction with him to a minimum."

...enough to land on an eyelash and blink it away...

"Oh," She smiled. "Just a titch."

Riley showed Maggie the storage shelf in the barn refrigerator for of the medicine. She matched the expiration dates and inventory numbers on the labels to the customer receipt. The older vials that had expired were pulled from the fridge.

"I know this." She paused. "The process, I mean, checking back and forth..." her eyes stared at the numbers waiting for them to tell a secret about her. A slice of recognition cut across her face.

"Inventory? Maybe you've done inventory?"

She slowly shook her head. "No, no, not so much the numbers, but this...checking back and forth...I remember something about it...checking...checking for..." She lost the connection.

Riley closed the refrigerator door. "Maybe you did research. A college? A pharmaceutical company?"

She squinted again at the inventory sheet. Paper and pens, lines, figures and words, in Arizona, but somewhere else, kind of like this. Paper, maybe pages and pages of paper, but not always blank, maybe with letters and paragraphs, too. "There *is* something familiar about it, but it's so far away, and not big enough of a memory I can sink my teeth into." She sighed. "Maybe it's better to be Maggie Fletcher, even though it is a lie."

"Tell you what: you can help me with inventory each month—" He looked up at another car pulling into the driveway.

"Hey, Griff!" Riley called. "You've been a stranger!"

They sat in the cool kitchen, a welcome oasis from the late-morning heat.

"I practiced with the truck. I got both feet inside," Maggie announced.

"That's good, isn't it?"

"We're working on getting Maggie used to riding in the truck. Tomorrow, we may try having her sit inside for a few seconds. A little at a time."

"I must say," Griff smiled, "you are looking healthier than last I saw you. Hannah would be surprised."

"Yeah, maybe we can all get together," Riley added, "sometime next week. Dinner maybe?"

"Actually, I'm here on unofficial business from Hannah. We were thinking maybe more like tomorrow night. I've got an errand to run, and Hannah will bring the food here. Which, of course, means her cheesecake—"

"Ohhh, Sunshine, you are in for a treat. Hannah makes cheesecake that tastes like clouds in heaven. So what should we make?"

"We have tomatoes from tomato city," Maggie said. "Can we use those?"

"You bet. Riley's tomatoes are the best. A salad will be just fine."

"She's remembering more, Griff. Like today, she

remembered doing something like inventory."

"And 'titch'." Maggie's face squinted into a smile. "I remembered the word 'titch', from sometime before." She smiled proudly, although Riley recognized them as just pinpoints of fact that didn't connect.

"Well, good." Griff stood. "Oh, and Hannah might have a few more clothes for you—"

"Like-Christmas."

"Yes, and I'm probably going to discuss search and rescue again, Riley. Look friend, we'll need to retire another horse next year. Sure would be nice to train a couple to take its place."

Riley reluctantly walked to Griff's car. "Look, you know as well as I do, Grace was the trainer around here. I assisted."

"But you know more than anyone else."

"I'm not ready."

"I've got three city council members who are. They'll approve money to purchase new horses, pay for the training, their food, their care—"

"I've got enough with Maggie, right now—"

"Maggie can assist!"

"I don't know if she can even ride a horse, and she certainly doesn't have the all clear from Doc, yet. Let's be realistic, Griff."

"Okay, we'll table it for a month. But once Maggie's cast comes off, once she's healthy enough, we'll talk again."

You need to listen to him, a voice filtered into their conversation. *You can do this, Riley,* Grace's voice said. He sighed again. She was a little like Les, showing up when he didn't expect.

Griff's smile faded as he prepared himself to tell Riley the rest. They walked outside, away from the porch. "I needed you to be out of earshot from Maggie. Got a call today."

"Someone who knows her?"

"No, nothing that easy. Some back country horsemen came across the remains of an accident at the bottom of Mitchell Canyon. A van. A black van. No license plates visible from the road. Human remains, although we haven't gotten to the bottom of the ravine just yet. I didn't want to say anything in front of Maggie. We're taking a helicopter out early tomorrow to check it out. Dollars to donuts, it's the van we saw that night. I may know more tomorrow night when I meet you here for dinner."

CHAPTER
TWENTY

If the river were a dragon's silvery spine through Copper Station's valley, Mitchell Canyon was its teeth. Deep granite jaws rose from where the ancient river carved. Rock hounds looked for agates or rumored gold, historians sought Indian caves and painting, climbers provoked the sides of cliffs and rough verticals with chalk-white hands, hikers and campers found pockets and cavities in unforgiving extremes. The heat spewed dry flames in summer, the hot breath from the dragon head, and canyon bones slept, dusted with snow in winter.

Griff's department included search and rescue, which is why he preferred the horses to any air-conditioned, leather-upholstered SUV. Vehicle accidents were rare in the canyon because tourists stayed away from the narrow, convoluted service roads. Traffic didn't disturb the dragon. Maybe an errant rock was tired of hanging around and took a walk across the road, but Griff could count on one hand the number of vehicle crashes he'd encountered, let alone with human remains. But something like this needed a helicopter.

Charlie, Griff's pilot, eased the helicopter along Redtail

Creek into Mitchell Canyon. The rocky front edged its teeth toward the helicopter. Charlie predicted where the updraft patterns were, flew close enough for a view, but not so close to be sucked into the hot dragon's breath of the canyon winds. Griff trusted no one else with the helicopter.

"What on earth was a van, of all things, doing way out here? All the vortices are in Sedona," Charlie joked.

"It may match the description of one I saw a few weeks ago. Not campers, but I suspect some illegal activity," Griff called into the headset. He looked down to see a pack of coyotes along a ridge. "That's not good," although he was thinking of Many Devils.

"Looks like it's up ahead." Charlie pointed. He saw telltale buzzards circling above a ravine, just off Service Road 21, one that followed the canyon all the way to the other side.

"How close can you get?"

"This is a tricky spot. That ravine picks up a wind gust that can turn this bird sideways. I'll try to get a little closer."

The metallic flash below caught Griff's eye. He pulled out binoculars, then his camera to take overhead pictures of the crash, then spoke into the radio receiver.

"Nine-five-zero, this is Graybird; can you go south on Service Road 21? I think about five miles in. We'll stay in the area to mark the location. Copy?"

Within ten minutes, two state and FWP vehicles arrived and waved Charlie off. They readied their equipment to rappel down to the site like ants on a string. While Charlie located a spot—a nearby mesa above the service road looked likely—the team planned to take pictures, samples, locate remains, if any, and inventory the collection of evidence. Routine for Griff's staff.

Charlie was the best, a former Vietnam helicopter pilot who knew how to set that baby on a dime. Nowadays, he ran the local airport—more Piper Cubs and Cessnas than anything else. He volunteered for the sheriff's office in cases like these, just to jump at the chance to fly this copter through the arid landscape. Cutting the motor, he let the Arizona wilderness seep into the cab.

The canyon and its mysteries fascinated Griff, never totally certain a ghost might wander from an undiscovered mesa. Trees were rare at this elevation. The service road was no more than a line of dust, curving like a rattlesnake throughout the rocks.

Once at the service road, Griff looked for tire tracks. *Must have gone around the corner too fast, misjudged the curve,* his first thought. The desert and this canyon had no LEDs overhead, so you relied on your headlights at night and a feel for the road during the day. The crew lowered themselves over the edge, a measured freefall along a web of sturdy rope. Griff was grateful someone else loved to do that.

His eyes picked up a curious detail. The tire tracks were there, but the configuration was all wrong. The tracks appeared to have stopped, with deeper indentations in the roadbed, then an awkward sharp right turn as the van had moved forward, then over the edge. Why would a driver stop, then drive over the edge? *It must have been night. The driver stopped, maybe, thought he figured out the road but found the cliff edge rather than the road.*

Griff peered over the seventy-five yards to the bottom. Still, no other tire marks and no skid marks. More and more, it was obvious the van was purposely driven over the edge once it had stopped. *No one could have survived that.*

"Chief! Check this out!" a voice squawked over the walkie talkie. "No license plates and we can detect at least three bullet holes in the side of the car."

"Show me!" He peered over the edge while one crew member pantomimed the direction and location of the bullet holes. It was the side of the van that would have faced the road, if the van were heading out of the canyon, facing east.

"And we've got remains," the voice continued. "But they're pretty compromised. This van is flat as a pancake...Wait a minute..."

He saw a crew member put on protective gloves, then lean closer. "Looks like Many Devils has been through before the coyotes and buzzards. We've got body parts missing."

Griff calculated this "accident" could have happened over a week ago.

"Something else, Chief. We've got one...two...three remains, I believe and you're not going to believe this...at least one of the bodies has a gunshot wound to the head. Can't tell about the others."

"Wanna take a guess at the caliber?"

"It's the same as what hit the van. Most of the skull was blown away. The whole van needs to be lifted out of here, with the bodies inside. The boys in Phoenix are going to love us."

"So, they were dead..."

"...before the van went over the side."

"Well, I'll be..." Griff whispered, rubbing his chin. "Okay, listen up!" He looked around at the scant crew near him. "We've got a crime scene! I want you to bag anything—hair samples, buttons, fingerprints, clothing, bullet casings—anything that doesn't belong in a canyon. Get pictures and measurements of these tire tracks here..."

All the while, Griff felt that ghost riding through the wind, perched on a rock somewhere laughing at him. Or maybe it was Many Devils.

Two more vehicles arrived to assist while Griff stepped back. He looked behind along the edge of the road. No other tire tracks, no other footprints. In fact, too clean. The wind Charlie spoke of came up from the ravine and dust pushed away from the road. Farther away, a good ten feet, exposed rock lined the ravine edge. But where the van had been, sand filled in between the edges. A sandy footprint would have held a shape with the wind blowing from the ravine over to the inside curve. He spied wisps of tumble weed and picked them up. They had been recently cut, sliced clean with a knife, not torn or broken stems from the wind. Small bits of sand stuck between the tinier branches.

"Bag this." Griff pointed. "I bet somebody swept the road. Let's get a picture of this, and up this road, too."

He saw it more clearly, under a new layer of sand: the side-to-side sweep from the road, then up the steep path to the plateau where Charlie had landed. He gazed up at the plateau. Funny, he couldn't see the 'copter from where he stood. The angle was too sharp.

"Wait a minute."

He walked across the service road to the edge of the ravine. Still no 'copter. He carefully retraced his steps back up the sandy path of the mesa, then turned and looked down. He imagined the van's position. He aimed an imaginary gun. Hell, somebody could have picked off the victims from here. If the shooter were low enough, if the sun were just right... He crouched.

"Channel 3, channel 3, do you read me?"

"Yes, chief."

"I'm waving at you near the edge of the mesa...above you. Can you see me?"

"No, sir. Negative."

"Well, I'll be."

Griff scanned the mesa trail, left and right, for a toothpick that could provide DNA, a rivet from a pair of jeans, a lost button, leather glove, a pattern of crushed weeds toward the road. He pulled a flashlight to wash away the shadows from the rocks. People came to these places, sometimes for target practice, so it wouldn't be unusual...

"Well, I'll be," he muttered again. There, in a natural *V*

between two boulders, Griff pictured the perfect support for a high-powered rifle barrel without being seen from the road. He bent down, squinted his eye through the *V*, as if lining up a scope toward the road. It was a clear shot to the van from his exact position.

Further sweeping his gaze along the plateau, he focused on dry grass blowing sideways. He leaned back and caught something. His flashlight beam spotlighted beige-on-beige sand, but wedged below...not a bottle cap between the grasses, not a pull tab, but something more shiny, sitting upright so only a rim could be detected...a shell casing, fifty-caliber. Certainly not for target practice. It was bright enough, not weathered. The casing was recent. Someone got sloppy. *Maybe with luck, he could pull a partial print.*

Good spot to target someone on the road below. No weeds were broken, but they definitely had been pushed by solid weight, right up against the rock, and against the wind that scooped up from the ravine and service road. But either the shooter was three-feet tall, or he'd been lying against the boulders. He stepped carefully back, placing his flashlight parallel to the floor of the plateau, looking for a scant shadow, an uneven surface...

"Bingo," he whispered.

Extended six feet or so from the *V* formation were two small indentations, about eight, maybe ten inches apart. Perfect match for the toes of two pointed boots, the kind that cowboys prefer, to kick at the rocks, to nudge the ribs of a horse. *If someone were lying on his belly, leaning against those rocks, extending his legs out, those indentations would fit a tall man.* The shooter had just thrown him some clues, including the greater oval on the right-hand portion of the sand where someone might lean. *He was tall, he wore cowboy boots, and was likely left-handed. Three shots, at least. Maybe shot within an angle of no more than ten degrees, to kill three victims. This* guy was trained, maybe a sniper at one time, someone who wouldn't flinch at firing three fifty-caliber shots in rapid succession. *So, this was planned.*

"Hey, Griff—what do you think?" Charlie pointed near their helicopter. "I count two."

Griff had forgotten Charlie had been left alone on the mesa's plateau. His eyes, blinded by the glare of the midday sun, followed Charlie's finger toward the impressions in the sand.

First one, then two parallel depressions about eight feet apart and fifteen feet long.

"Looks like we weren't the only helicopter to land here." Griff grunted under his breath. He held up the fifty-caliber casing in a baggie.

Charlie whistled. "I can't tell you the last time I saw one of those."

Griff, hands on hips, mentally listed the required logistics. *He'd need to close off the service road, tons of evidence bags, rappelling officers, evidence from three different sites...all because someone with a fifty-caliber rifle fired undetected from that V formation, took out three unsuspecting guys and forced the van over the road into the ravine. And what for? A payoff? A meeting that went wrong? A negotiation? A drug buy? Somebody with money was tied into helicopters, snipers, and perfect timing. A sudden move, an argument, a sniper's whim shoots the passengers, he loads the bodies into the van, pushes the van over the edge, sweeps the road clean and takes off from a helicopter to God knows where. A hell of a lot of money.*

Griff knew they had six, maybe seven hours of light left to get the evidence and pull the logistics off to helicopter a pancake-looking black van onto the road and truck it to the state lab in Phoenix. He had to get as much as possible out of here by nightfall. Many Devils was counting the hours, too.

"What do you need here, Sheriff?" Two crew members

approached him up the mesa trail.

He smiled wearily. This was going to lead into a long night. That ghost out there must be enjoying this. Maybe Many Devils. Maybe they were one and the same.

CHAPTER
TWENTY-ONE

"Again."

Riley closed the passenger side of the truck, watching Maggie turn away from him, not in anger, but with shoulders sagging, that overwhelming, unsaid "I can't" on her breath.

"Maggie, you're getting the hang of it. You can get one foot in, and now you're sitting down on the seat. All you have to do is swing the other foot up. I'll leave the door open. I'll be right here."

"You make it sound easy."

A person gets into a car or truck every day. Sure, it's easy, he thought. A person who has been raped multiple times in a black vehicle getting into another black vehicle? How can that be anything good?

"So, what can I do to make it easy?"

He willed her to try again. She must have been manhandled multiple times, slammed around in the van. With practice, he might push aside the dismal shadows that always seemed to bump right up against her. His strength seemed to link into her once more. One more time might be all she'd need.

"Again." She sighed.

Open the door, breathe, rest her casted hand on the door, hold the door jamb with her left hand, bring her foot onto the floor. Squish that bug. Breathe. Exhale and sit down. One foot in, one foot out. That part she had, now, but the voices taunted her. *They don't got salads here. Eat the damn donut or I'll jam it down your throat.*

"Talk to me, Riley. Tell me what to do, tell me louder than the voices." Her voice shook.

"Okay, Maggie, you've got this, just swing your foot up and back. Into the car, then back outside. You can do that." He stood by the door, squatting to her level, speaking in his calm voice. Focus. Breathe.

Hey, girlie girl.

"Your foot, Maggie. Move your right foot in, then bring it right back out."

She shut her eyes, held her breath and did just as he suggested. In and out.

"Terrific! Look what you just did!"

As soon as her right foot slid next to the left, the voices backed away. She had done something new and right and perfect.

"Again?"

"You bet." Riley smiled. "Just do what you did. Foot in, then out."

She stayed with one foot on the floor, seated on the comfortable truck cushion, the cab window open behind her. Then the right foot slid inside, next to the left. Just the way feet are supposed to be.

"Now, let go of the door, so you can sit back," Riley whispered. "You've almost got it."

Her casted arm was heavy, hadn't budged but was aching to move inside. Just for a second.

"My hand is stuck." It wasn't really. But she knew what was next: the door would close, which she wouldn't like at all.

Riley cradled her cast like a baby and brought it downward, slowly, an elevator pace, until it rested against her.

"Look at you," he whispered again. "You're sitting in the truck."

Her eyes closed, and for a second, she heard the soft breeze through the Emory's oak, a few birds chirping against the coming heat. When her ears sorted the sounds, she heard the river swishing by the house on the other side of the road. She heard Cartwheel whinny.

Hey, girlie girl.

She shot up again, out of the truck and bent over, gasping for breath.

"You stayed in there for five seconds!" Riley's voice flashed victory over such a little thing. "That's a good place to stop before Hannah arrives. Why don't we call it a day?"

Maggie slowly stood upright. *If this was success, why was she shaking her head?*

Riley had seen that face before. Grace shook her head when she knew she was defeated by the cancer. She shook her head, not quickly, but slowly, letting the defeat bleed into her a little more deeply, knowing she was licked. Maggie's face raised toward the sky, leaning her head backward, breathing in the day. Then she looked directly at Riley.

"Again," she said.

———

"Hey, you, two!" Hannah called toward the corral from her yellow car. She sliced her wave through the air, as if they hadn't seen her. Even the horses perked up their ears. "I've got dinner!" She pulled a large stockpot from the trunk and went into the kitchen by the time Maggie and Riley joined her.

"Here, take this, girlfriend." Hannah smiled. It was a bag of clothing just for Maggie, like-Christmas again. "And you can take this."

Riley took a large round metal pan and held it up. "Ohhh, Sunshine! Killer cheesecake! You are in for a treat." He chuckled all the way into the kitchen.

"What's a killer cheesecake?" she asked, washing her hands.

"Hannah is famous for her cheesecake, all different flavors—Oreo cookie, caramel fudge, vanilla raspberry—whoever heard of lemon basil cheesecake? But she had me hooked at the first bite."

"So, what is it tonight?"

"Now, that, young lady," he tapped her nose, "we'll find out when we get to dinner." His smile warmed her like Bliss' coat after a day in the pasture. He hadn't let go of that smile since earlier when she sat in the truck.

He turned his head. "Do I smell chili?"

"I figured that's something we could keep warm, no matter how late Griff is tonight. He'll be awhile....Hey, let me look at my girlfriend!" Hannah opened her arms, taking in Maggie, standing on the other side of the table.

"Oh, my gosh, you are looking great! Ranch life agrees with you. Don't you think she's looking good, Riley?"

"Bruises are almost gone; cast is mostly a nuisance. Doesn't need a refill on her pain meds, either. Going to go see Doc next week, likely."

"Great! Make sure you have Riley bring you by the gallery, then. I'd love for you to see it." She pulled tee shirts and a sweater from the bag to show Maggie. "Thought you could use a few more."

Maggie balanced herself up the stairs steadily as she took them to her room.

"So, how is it going?" Hannah turned her steely gaze on

him. "The truth."

He tucked his head once. "I really didn't know what to expect. First few days, she hid in her room, but once she realized she wasn't a prisoner, once she found Bliss and Cartwheel wouldn't run her over, she seemed to settle in fairly well. Not so much at night. She still has lots of nightmares. You know, when Grace fell asleep, my fear was she'd never wake up. With Maggie, I wonder if she'll have a full night's sleep."

Ready to offer something, Hannah's hand reached for his arm.

"But it's good she trusts me. That's what's been injured more than any broken bone or bruise. She had her trust destroyed."

"Not like Grace, huh?"

He retreated into a memory of watching Grace lying in bed, her bones more visible than her skin, her breathing shallow, then slowly blinking her eyes open and looking toward Riley. Looks like you've got another day with me, cowboy, she'd whispered.

He shook his head so slightly, not wanting Grace to leave his memory. "Let me...uh...let me get some greens and tomatoes for a salad. Chili and salad..."

"And I have cornbread, too. We'll have a feast!"

Riley tilted his hat back and walked around to the back of the house, just as Maggie came down the stairs.

"Those tee shirts fit fine, Hannah. Thanks so much. Riley didn't look too happy just now. Is he mad?"

"Oh, no, no. Just a little memory popped into his head. Come over here and try the chili. I want to catch up with you. Haven't seen you for a few weeks!"

"Is Riley sad?"

"What makes you think that?"

"Grace still makes him sad. He talks about her. He wants her back here."

"Well, he misses her. We all do. She was my best friend. She gave and gave till she gave out. She gave her attention, so you felt as if you were the only one she was talking to. She gave her time, even when she didn't have it to spare...said, 'Life is too short not to spend it with your friends.' And everyone was her friend. She gave knowledge, skill, she was tireless. She had a reserve to keep us all going, sometimes into those late nights with the horses, after the coffee had given out. She gave her love to Riley, to Griff, to me, never thinking about getting something in return."

Maggie sniffed the cornbread. "No wonder he misses her."

"But let me ask you something, Maggie. Since you've been here, how many times have you seen Riley smile?"

"He smiles with the horses, when we walk to the barn, when I practiced today, sitting in the truck, when he feeds Poke—"

"Exactly!" Hannah slapped her thigh. "You've brought his smile back, even in the little things."

Maggie lifted the lid on the stockpot and raised a teaspoon.

"You know, this chili recipe is Grace's. Riley gave it to me after she'd passed. Thought it would be nice to bring a little of her here, tonight. But..." Hannah stirred the tomatoes, beans, and meat slowly. "There's something missing. Try it."

As soon as the thick liquid hit her tongue, Maggie heard car horns blast in a corner of her brain, people talking and laughing, then gone like a flash of lightning. "Chili! I know chili! This is something I've had before." She drew back. "With lots of people...outside...I just saw it for a second. I know this!" Maggie's face splashed a big smile. "This is great!"

Hannah took a taste. "It's good, but there's something missing. I don't know what."

Maggie tilted her head. "That's funny. When you taste the chili, you taste something that's not there. When I taste the chili, it brings me a memory, something more than I had before." She giggled. "Does it taste like Grace? I mean, do you hear her laugh or see lights or pictures or people when you taste it?"

"Mmmm, sort of, I guess. It's like she's close by."

"So, if she's close by, Riley wouldn't miss her as much. Why don't we have more meals, then?"

"I don't follow."

"Grace made other food, right? So, why not have a dinner sometime with favorite dishes that Grace made? Then Riley and you and Griff wouldn't be so sad."

Hannah's eyes popped with delight, dark brown saucers big enough to catch the sun and the moon in one blink. "Oh, Maggie, what a perfect idea! What a sweet, generous, perfect idea!"

It was the darker side of 7:00 p.m. when Griff finally drove into Riley's driveway, the others waving from the porch. Long day. If he unburdened the day, Maggie would know things he wasn't ready to share. At least until he figured out how it all fit.

"You sure are lucky we didn't eat yet!" Hannah called out. Griff's face had wrinkles ironed into place from the day's sun and dust. Pieces of his soul returned drop by drop as he walked slowly toward the porch, uncertain where reality was in the evening sky.

"I'm looking forward to a big bowl of that chili, woman." His voice pushed toward happy, but there was a leak, a little like a three-day-old balloon.

"Come on in," Riley said. "We had just about given you up."

"Bad accident," Griff said almost under his breath. "Crew is working most of the night on it. Told them to call me if they needed something."

"Then, let's eat," Hannah said. "Take a look at Maggie's new shirt, Griff. Doesn't she look great?"

"How's things going?"

"I have a new name—"

""Uh, Maggie—" Riley wheeled around from the sink.

"I'm Maggie Fletcher!" She beamed.

"Is that so?" Griff turned to Riley who, he swore, was wincing.

"Well, I for one, like it." Hannah ladled chili into pottery bowls.

"You gave her Old Man Fletcher's name? What on earth...?"

"It was Lester's fault," Maggie continued. "He kept asking questions."

"You know how Les is." The hand towel dangled like a limp excuse from Riley's hands. "All gossip. You can imagine if I couldn't give her a name..."

"But he's going to tell everyone!"

"Did I say something wrong?" Maggie's eyes darted to Riley.

"No, no, Sunshine. It's a good thing, honest."

Griff pulled Riley outside. "What's this Maggie Fletcher business about? A last name? Come on, Riley, her life gets more entrenched here every day! Why is she here—for her safety or for your happiness?" His voice hissed against the evening sunset.

Riley seethed a stare. "If you weren't my friend, you would have been decked on the ground by now. I don't know what you—"

Griff's hands flew up. "I apologize. It came out wrong. I didn't mean how it sounded."

"So let me ask you this—if not Lester, then what? Doesn't it look more suspicious to be just 'Maggie'? She knows I lied to cover her memory. For God's sake, she can't really say 'I don't know my last name'."

"I was out of line, Riley. I'm tired, my brain's muddy. But this accident..." The two inched toward the truck, their voices lowered into husky drafts.

"So, there was the van, mashed like a sardine can, bullet holes along the side, bodies inside carrying bullet holes, too. There was a direct line of fire to those bullet holes from some rocks on the mesa above." Griff scratched his hand through his hair, as if it were part of the memory. "I can't imagine there are that many black vans around this area right now. With partial remains inside the van, we might get DNA."

"You think these might be the guys that we saw getting rid of Maggie?"

"There were three in the van, as best we can tell. But the connection to Maggie? I don't know yet. But what were they doing in Mitchell Canyon? It wasn't a leisurely van drive through there. The van was facing east, coming OUT of the canyon. The tire tracks show the van had stopped, turned, then moved over the edge."

"Somebody wanted them dead."

"And if that person knew Maggie was still alive, would he want her dead, too? There's only one reason to show up in Mitchell Canyon on a service road in a van in the middle of the day—"

They both said it at the same time. "Money."

"Hey, gentlemen! Thought you were hungry!" Hannah called from the kitchen door. "You gonna talk all evening or you coming inside?"

"Keep this under your hat, Riley. Maggie doesn't need to know."

If the chili were indeed Grace, then the three friends cherished that Maggie enjoyed each bite. Salad from Riley's garden, cornbread, butter...all were connections to Grace, but also to each other, bite by bite.

"I remember chili," Maggie said. "I had a memory, but I can't bring it back."

Hannah shook her head. "But there's something missing, I keep telling her." As soon as Hannah said that, her breath held, hoping no one would say the obvious.

Riley took another bite. Grace had taken three tries to get this recipe right. The first batch nearly burned when she checked on Bliss in the pasture. The second try, she added her homemade salsa for more spice, an improvement, she thought. The third time, she accidentally splashed her coffee into the chili when she'd poured a second cup...a fluke, a spill, an accident...

"Coffee," he said absently.

"You want some coffee? I've got some made—"

"No, it's coffee. That's the secret ingredient. The recipe I gave you didn't have the ingredient because I promised Grace I'd never tell. Seemed important at the time. Always used Marta's Double Blend because she thought it was bold enough." He looked at Hannah, half-lowering his eyelids, in embarrassed apology for the deception that somehow kept Grace close to him. "Just doesn't taste quite right without it, though."

There was an empty hole where Grace could have spoken up.

Riley leaned toward Maggie. "We used to have meals here, sometimes a couple times a month. She cooked like a mad scientist, all burners going at once, her hair flying..."

"So, why don't you do that again? I bet Hannah's hair could fly, too."

Hannah laughed outright. "Riley, Griff, listen to this, Maggie has a great idea! Grace meals. Your favorite meals that Grace made."

Riley was about to speak up to say "no."

"It's a wonderful idea, Riley. You liked that sweet potato casserole, Griff, remember? You still have that recipe, don't you, Riley?"

Riley stared at the table, a little too raw at this point in the meal, maybe. His voice was an empty pocket that couldn't be filled. "Why?"

"Because it's good food and we like her food," Maggie offered simply. "And she needs to bring your smile back. Because you love her." Her voice was casual, as if listing groceries or ordering fabric for a new dress, as if she'd turned a page in a book to finish the sentence.

"Sunshine..." but before he could say the next word, his mind went blank. He couldn't think of a single reason to force that grief back to the table. He stared at Maggie, at Hannah, at Griff, maybe looking for that one way to give permission. But, he realized, they already did.

"Grace meals, huh?" He watched Griff nod slightly as he downed another bite. "Okay, so promise me one thing. I'm not cooking. You'll have to do that."

If Hannah had her camera, she would have secured that priceless moment. Riley's soft surprise in his face at how easy it was to agree. Griff shaking his head. The fresh breeze whispering up from the river, past the Emory's oak and in through the kitchen door let them breathe easy, look a few days ahead, toss out all those eggs they'd been walking on the past two years.

"Well, I'll be," Griff shook his head again, a smile creasing his face. "Careful, Maggie Fletcher, he may reconsider training search and rescue horses again."

Somewhere between the bites and easy conversation that followed, Riley couldn't help but hear Grace's chuckle. It's about time, she was saying.

CHAPTER
TWENTY-TWO

Vince heard a noise, a shuffle, a door closing, barely looking up when Tess closed her cubicle for the night. He detected a slight nod from her as she turned. His eyes slid to the photo adjacent to his computer, a selfie of Brenniss with him from their engagement, the sand and ocean drifting away behind them to an indistinct horizon. Her hair was loose and tangled from the beach wind, her smile full.

New York City was immediately outside his window, a place many aspired to be. Every time he left work, he was reminded of their last morning together, how Brenniss walked out the door so casually. They both expected that she would return in eight hours or so.

Briefcase and jacket in hand, he locked the doors, rode the elevator, mercifully alone so he wouldn't have to tell someone how he was doing, then turned into the parking garage. He let grief seep back into his gut, missing the woman he loved and their perfection. Yet, he wanted to feel the pain, having hidden it all day long. The pain was the only thing that connected to Brenniss, right now.

This late, he tagged at the end of rush hour, a pleasant negative in his life. There were others, too. A life in limbo, until he heard a song on the radio, or see a sweater of hers in the closet. Or her boxes stacked in the living room because he hadn't the nerve to open them, yet.

He opened the condo door, knowing there was no way he could throw them out. She could just as easily be back tomorrow. Collapsing into his Eames chair, he realized he'd put his watch on upside down this morning. All day, upside down time. Like his life. His body shifted, sinking into the chair. He'd forgotten his body could do this. It had been nearly six weeks since he hadn't felt just two breaths away from exhaustion. But his cell phone startled a heartbeat in his shirt pocket. "Hello?"

"Hello, Vince. It's Milt. Just checking in on you to see how you are doing. We've been thinking about you. We left a message on your machine, but when you didn't answer, we thought we'd try your cell. Sorry for a call at 7:00 p.m."

"Brenniss?"

"And, well, um, we got a call." Milt paused, a deathly pause, the worst sound possible, that dead air. Just plain paused. "From the FBI. They want to meet with us. Can I bother you to drive from the city to our home as soon as possible?"

"I'm leaving now."

Vince recognized the car in the driveway of the Tripham home only as an official vehicle. He felt odd ringing the doorbell, when usually Brenniss and he walked into the front foyer together.

"Good to see you, Vince. Glad you could come so quickly." Milt's hand guided Vince toward Betty into the den, where two somber-suited gentlemen sat on the couch.

Milt remained the unflappable, a calm, stoic host. "Vince, I'd like you to meet Special Agents Walter Reynolds and Carl

Stanley, from the FBI."

A sinking fear speared into his stomach, the reality of two FBI agents before him. Always two. Like the pair of agents who met him in his dorm lobby, solemn faces telling him, regretfully, that his parents did not survive the drug store shooting. Such news hung low inside bisque-colored walls and correct manners.

"They think they have a lead." Milt thinly cleared his throat.

Vince heard a gasp. His own. Then he saw the sorrow in Milt's and Betty's eyes.

"First of all," Reynolds began, "we wish to extend our sincere sympathy for these last six weeks and how trying it has been. We also want to thank you for helping with the investigation so far. You've been cooperative with the most sensitive of issues."

Stanley opened a map on the coffee table. "Until now, we've concentrated our resources in this area." He tapped a triangulated web of the city but spoke as casually as looking at a menu.

"This area includes your condo, Vince, the library, and your office. But we didn't check *here* until our lead."

They all peered at the same time to the point where Stanley's thick finger pointed.

"Railroad tracks? Whatever for?" Milt asked.

"One of our informants recently sighted several young women being moved to railroad boxcars—and our investigation found human remains, sir. We're completing our analysis on those remains now."

"Oh, Milt!" Betty grabbed her husband's arm.

"We found clothing, but none that fit the description of Brenniss that day. We *did* find something, though, that we need Vince to verify. This engagement ring." Stanley pulled a baggie from his pocket. "Maybe you could tell me if it's Brenniss'."

Vince backed away two steps. That small voice inside shook denial. What he determined could be so final, the period after a long joyous sentence. He looked at Milt and Betty instead, then back at both agents.

"I'm sorry, son, I need you to look at it." Agent Stanley folded the bag calmly into Vince's hand.

Grief crawled up his throat until he brought the bag closer to stare at the ring.

White gold, single teardrop diamond, less than a quarter carat, small enough to be fairy dust. It was dainty, a simple ring. But it *wasn't* the full one-carat diamond with the baguettes on either side that he gave to her. His relief was certain. "This is *not* her ring, Agent Stanley."

The agent cocked his head.

"I still have the receipt," Vince said defiantly. "Hers was an oval diamond, and larger than this one. It's not Brenniss', honest." His smile broke past his tears.

"Thank God!" Milt called out. "That means she's still alive, doesn't it?"

Agent Stanley nodded coolly, as he placed the ring back into his pocket. "All we know is this is not her ring. The investigation is ongoing, sir."

"What are you thinking, then?" Milt persisted. "What can we help with?"

"Well, frankly, when we've seen this kind of pattern of women grouped together, it usually revolves around prostitution or sex trafficking, unfortunately..."

Vince stopped listening at that point, his pulse picking up altitude.

"...could be in another state or even in another country."

"No!" Vince said a little too sharply. "No, Brenniss would not be involved in anything like that."

"Sorry, Mr. Caldwell, but this is the ugly part of the job—"

"Betty and Milt have experienced enough for one day,

don't you think? I think we're done, here. You need to leave right now." He tugged on Stanley's suit sleeve.

Reynolds looked sideways at Stanley and folded up the map. "Well, then, Mr. and Mrs. Tripham, Vince, we thank you for your time. The good news is that she's still out there some-where. We'll be in touch."

Yeah. Vince blew out a breath that had built in his lungs. *And the bad news is...she's still out there somewhere.*

CHAPTER
TWENTY-THREE

Vince's office chair fit like a favorite baseball glove, even at 7:30 at night. Hunched over his computer screen, he was as intent as a pitcher in the ninth, full count. The chair was the only comfortable thing in his life right now, twelve hours into the day. Maybe he'd stay until 11:00 tonight, get the quarterly done.

He stood, his eyes drifted toward the office window, losing focus on the computer screen's green glow. His arm braced against the glass. He missed their life, the one they didn't get to have yet. Picking out the condo together—that was *their* condo, the one he's a stranger in now. Unfinished business in pieces at his feet.

He was doing it again, staring out the window, watching for a jacket, a scarf, a familiar pattern of walking on the sidewalk below, one that would tell him Brenniss was back. *Concentrate, Caldwell,* he told himself as he returned to the keyboard....*let's see...quarterly numbers...*the screen before him blinked a silent metronome. He typed in $1705 on one line, entered it, then checked the copy.

"Damn!" He'd transposed the numbers.

He erased $1750, added $1705, but hit the key twice: $17055.

"Damn it!

He erased it again, typed in $1705, and then ENTER. The page erased.

"What? Don't erase! Don't do that!" he yelled at the screen, as if waiting for an apology and self-correction. As if the Hindenburg had just exploded into nothing. But in the next breath, he realized this would keep him from going home as quickly. *I've got all night to correct this...*

"Wait! Don't touch the keyboard!" Tess' voice emerged from her cubicle. She came running in from the darkened office, her stocking feet noiseless on the carpet. "You can UNDO the mistake."

Where had she come from?

"You didn't touch anything, right? After it erased? You just yelled at the computer?"

"Uh...no, yeah..."

"Okay, watch." She pressed two computer keys in succession, the screen blinked and returned to the original financial schedule, now with the corrected $1705.

"Oh, my God, Tess. You just saved my life!"

"I know, it's magic," she teased. "UNDO."

"What the hell are you doing here?" he demanded.

"Oh, I had to update the conference room schedules, and I figured I could start on your narrative on the Oertner account. You're not the only one who works late, sometimes."

"Scared the hell out of me! Why didn't you say something?"

Uninvited, Tess sat in the chair opposite his desk.

"Look, Vince. We all miss her, too. We miss *you*."

"Go home, Tess. I'm not in the mood for lectures on how I should feel. I'll be a little late here. No need to stay."

"No later than other nights, right? You've been coming in way too early and staying way too late. We've all noticed." She leaned forward. "In case you think I'm meddling, I'm actually trying to help. You don't have to isolate yourself. We're your family here."

"Tess, enough. I just want to get this—" He looked at her with dog-tired eyes, suddenly craving sleep.

"Just let us help. We may not know what to say—"

"You think *I* know what to say?" he exploded. "Every day, I want to say the perfect phrase to make this nightmare... UNDO." He choked. "How can I expect you to deal with this if I can't?" He caught his breath momentarily. "I can only manage one minute to the next. Believe me, work is the only distraction I have." The corners of his eyes stung with fatigue.

She shrugged her shoulders. "Okay, so we both have more work to do," Tess continued brightly. "How about I go to Moose's down the block for takeout?"

He stared at the screen. "Not tonight." But just then, his stomach betrayed him with a short growl.

"Moose's it is. Think of it this way: do one thing this week, just one little thing that you did before all this landed on your shoulders. You like takeout from Moose's, right? And I'm pretty sure you've eaten one too many bean burritos from the vending machine. So...that's one roast beef on rye with mayo, mustard, extra tomato, pickle, and a bowl of minestrone, right?"

"I hate their pickles."

"I know, it's for me. And how about an iced tea instead of root beer?" She smiled, but he stared at the screen. "Tea or root beer?"

He sighed. "Iced tea...with lemon."

CHAPTER
TWENTY-FOUR

TESS

As Tess gathered herself in front of the mirror, brushing her teeth, she felt the bold strokes defining her. She was sure more than ever that she could land right where Vince would need her again this morning. Her thoughts pinged energetically.

When I wake up, I think how I can be helpful, no, indispensable today. Like getting to work early, getting a head start on one of the proposals. I shower, fix hair and makeup in under seventeen minutes, so I can look over my own agenda while I make breakfast.

Oh, yeah. I'm organized and efficient, and he's starting to notice how I save his bacon. Need the car washed? Let me get that. Spot on your shirt? I'll order another one from Bailey Brothers because I know they'll deliver. Bring your coffee before you know you need it, get you a refill for your pen so your client won't hesitate when signing a big deal, know when to offer a bottled water or a soda, remember your clients' names and their wives' and eventually which son likes baseball, which son scored the winning touchdown or who had the hat trick at the Rangers game last night. Oh, yeah, I can do that and more.

Watch me.

I'll be so damned important, he won't imagine a life or success without me. We're a team.

I can make appointments, rearrange schedules so he'll have an extra fifteen minutes at lunch for a breath or two of Brenniss memories. He still needs that for now. But, he won't much longer. Unlike him, I know when to give, even though it hurts and rips me raw. And I can make his life easier right now. I really do know what I want.

Watch me.

CHAPTER
TWENTY-FIVE

Tess arrived at her work cubicle at 8:00 a.m. sharp and was astounded to see Vince with files edging up four inches on the corner of his desk.

"Hey, boss, anything you need? I wrote the Foraker summary for you."

"You did it again, thanks." His smile was a quick flash.

"That's what I'm here for."

He artfully hid his struggle from workplace rumors. He now allowed himself an occasional break on the balcony patio to savor the sun and traffic and the pungent aroma of food carts on the corner.

By late July, it was a habit, safe and comfortable, to come to work at 4:00 a.m. and leave at 11:00 p.m. And to take his breaks outside on that high-rise patio to insulate himself from the gossip he fully knew was part of others' habits. Or maybe it was to feel the sun touch his skin without asking anything in return. Tess joined him sometimes, not every time. Was that a habit, too?

He liked how she never talked about Brenniss, only

listened and nodded. Then, back to her book or filing her nails or drinking her coffee. She didn't interfere, didn't preach. She might say something like, "Orioles coming to town. You going?"

"Naw."

She got it. Takeout lunches served no words, just munching or sipping, crumpling wrappers and turning pages, the traffic below, an off-beat jazz session of horns and thunder.

Habits don't guarantee happiness, just the illusion of order. They can corner you, inflate your hopes, dash you to pieces. Sure, he once owned that, but it wasn't the same without Brenniss. But with Tess, *that* habit of relying on her, well, that was something that opened a sliver of light to him.

Tess got that he couldn't laugh and the devastation of why. The only things she asked were to check the reports, check the appointments, and if he could take line two for a call. For that alone, even if their communication was comfortably minimal, he looked forward to those few safe minutes with Tess each day.

A habit.

CHAPTER
TWENTY-SIX

Vince curled his body into an uncertain question on his sofa while the night deepened. The cell phone rested on his chest, a habit that defined his restlessness these days. Brenniss ghosted his dreams at times when he bought sleep with his fatigue: a clip of her laughter, a flash of her hair, her slow-motion entry into Casey's to approach their table. He always seemed to awaken before she sat down. His air conditioner sighed into life, gauzy curtains barely acknowledging the breath. To this sedate moment, the vibration of his phone danced across his chest. Vince's eyes startled open as he swiped the screen.

"Hello?"

He heard nothing at first, as the sleep evaporated from between his ears.

"Hello, Brenniss?" Nothing again. He automatically looked at the screen for a clue about Brenniss. The number on the screen registered as familiar, but with only ten seconds removed from a deep sleep, he couldn't place it.

"Hello?"

A sniff.

"Hello?"

"Vince? I'm sorry for calling you so early. I didn't know what else—"

"Brenniss?"

"Oh, dear, I'm so sorry. No, Vince, this is Betty."

He sat upright on the couch, tie askew, shirtsleeves exposing goosebumps on his arms. *What was it? 4:00 a.m.?* He was late for work.

"Is it Brenniss? Have you heard something?"

"Vince..." He heard a dreadful sob. His feet turned to cement.

"No, no, it's not about Brenniss. It's Milt." Betty's thin voice filtered through his confusion.

"Milt?"

"Yes, he got up early to visit the bathroom and...he...well... he had a heart attack."

"Are you at the hospital?"

She paused again while her soft sobs pulsed into the receiver.

"No, Vince, he's dead. He died."

"What? He was just—" Vince choked a breath. What else could he say to Betty she didn't already know: he just talked to me last week, we drank coffee at dinner. Disbelief steps in before you get body-slammed by reality. He was in the same place again: his parents, Brenniss, now Milt.

"You're at home, Betty? I'm on my way." Saying something personal and direct like that, meant he understood, when really, he didn't, he didn't at all.

All too familiar now, the dark, blank corridor he moved through. The car slipped through lanes with little traffic while he thought what he could possibly say. Reassurance, like a ribbon, tied things together for a while, a little like a prayer to buy time until the feelings settle in. He dialed Tess to say an emergency had come up. She reassured *him* that she'd get the copies to everyone at the meeting. No worries.

He approached the familiar Georgian home as he felt his shoulders take on Betty's grief, while he put his for Brenniss on hold. After all, she was the closest to family he had. Such a sorry connection, but the best he had.

He waited for Betty to answer the door, enough time to imagine Milt on a gurney, a passive ragdoll jolted toward the ambulance, oxygen mask covering his face, furious chest compressions pounding at his heart. Betty opened the door and never looked so fragile.

He pulled her close, found his voice to guide her into the den. Just a few days before, the room had been cramped by Agents Stanley and Reynolds, their maps, theories, and facts. Milt could have easily been in another room just now. *We all do it, try to reverse time to remove grief as a full-time job.*

"The stress," she began, then shook her head. "When those hoodlums kidnapped Brenniss, they good as killed Milt. He held me together. What will I do now?"

Vince felt a coil of purpose rise in him. A poor substitute for Milt, he might get the chaos under control, be the force of comfort and decision. Betty relaxed against his shoulder.

Betty's dear friends stepped forward to honor Milt: bridge club, garden club, the neighborhood association, the country club. They gave her rides, held her hand, phoned the minister, brought casseroles and salads and baked hams as if one tiny person could eat it all. They smiled and supported Betty while Vince stood sentinel next to her. But, once the casserole dishes were cleaned and returned, the visits and phone calls slowed, people got busy, forgot to call. Sadness can't be invited in too often.

Vince remained.

He had dinner with Betty a few times a week now, purposing her to find a recipe or a dessert that would fill her time. He sat across from Brenniss' chair in the formal walnut-paneled dining room, drinking iced tea from a glass that surely Brenniss had held sometime. He walked with Betty in the garden, tightened a screw on a towel bar, or put away the stockpot in the uppermost shelf, a reminder that Milt's tall frame would be missed for such jobs.

He sorted Betty's bills until she made sense of them. Milt had developed monthly computer spreadsheets for their budget, thankfully Vince's language for such matters, but a language Betty didn't use. Vince introduced Betty to the computer.

"Oh, Vince, I'll never get this." She shook her head. "I mean, all the keys? What's DEL again? And FN?" Her eyebrows framed her eyes, extending her head slightly so that she could see more clearly through her bifocals. *There, there it was again, that same face Brenniss wore when information overwhelmed her. It was almost worth Betty's confusion to see that face again.*

"Here, this one." Betty pointed to the HOME key. "If I hit this key and type in Milt's name, will it bring him home?" She leaned on her fist and stared at the screen.

CHAPTER
TWENTY-SEVEN

Vince looked at his reflection, the final reluctant touches with his tie. His smile was forced. *How did it happen again? Joining Tess for dinner? What the hell was he doing?*

It started when Tess had walked into the office with the finished proposal for Gilfadden. The perfect simulated leather cover with gold-stamped lettering enhanced the ordered numbers, charts, the late nights, the pages with columns and lines. They had sandwiched hours between funerals and meetings to correct, delete, omit, addend, print, collate, all while Vince provided some sanity in Betty's life.

"Here. I wanted you to check this before you left tonight. Oh, and page six?" She leafed through the virgin pages. "I added the paragraph you wanted."

He skimmed through the page, although truthfully, he looked at her narrow fingers, instead, and the dynamic blood-red enamel on her nails.

"Mmm-hmm, yes, yes, that fits in nicely. Thank, Tess. You've been an angel through these last weeks."

She shuffled the pages again. "One more question: page

twenty-four? You wanted that chart here?"

He looked again at the chart. Magic numbers. Talk about shock and awe. Gilfadden will be bowled over. Where *did* she find that impossibly perfect color of red? That glossy, attractive, almost as smooth as a BMW-hood-at-a-stoplight finish. That red required a second look just to make sure there was no other red like that in the world.

He was staring.

"The chart? Vince? Is that what you wanted?"

"Yes, yes...yes, sure...uh, looks great!" He nodded. "Great!" He blew out a breath as he lifted his gaze out the window. He looked for that exact color of red somewhere outside, just to distract himself. He wanted to see it again, but he didn't dare stare.

"Well, good." She closed her fingers along the dark brown cover, the red more pronounced, like blood leaking from the leatherette. "It's done, then. Anything else for tonight?"

"Hmm..." His eyes slid away from the window, back to the color and the red exclamation points of her nails. "Well...I...uh..."

"Yes?" She smiled at him, a shrug, not yet completed at her shoulders.

He took two breaths. How could such a red, the purest of artery-reds, shudder him to a halt?

She sucked in her lips in anticipation, then blew a quick breath. "Well, I can think of something. You've been putting in months of blind devotion to your work and to Brenniss' mom. How about no midnight typing or speed reading unfinished reports? How about we take a break? Aren't you ready for a change, Vince?"

She crossed her arms, but her right hand splayed upward along her upper arm, those red fingernails impossible to ignore, poking between strands of her hair. Her hair...not golden, not a deep brown, after all, but more of a warm honey, something that just occurred to Vince.

"So what do you say, Vince? Let's celebrate Gilfadden's proposal and have dinner. That one thing, remember?"

"You mean...like...a...date?"

"Oh, gosh, no. Like what we've been doing for weeks now, only we called it takeout and stayed in the office." She pulled her bangs back with those red nails, playing hide-and-seek between the strands. "No, just a friendly dinner, like you've done before and will do again whenever you finish a big proposal. I'm saying, let's get OUTSIDE the building for a change." She cocked her head, as if that were a simple option to consider.

He sat, leaning back in the chair, admitting to himself he hadn't seen this coming. It's just...Those red nails were patient. He tipped his favorite pen onto the desk.

"Okay." Just like that.

Okay? Okay? Really? He stood before the bathroom mirror, a cheesy smile fading, now fully aware there were no 'loose ends' to tie up at dinner, nothing really to celebrate.

But then he'd reserved a spot at Casey's of all places, only because it was on speed dial on his phone. *What was he thinking? All because of that incredible, desirable red on her nails?* He loosened his tie. It was all wrong. Sure, it was just a meal. He heard Tess' voice again: *We sit, we order drinks, we order an appetizer, our meals are served, and we talk about work. We're just talking about work but with forks in our hands.*

He continued having regrets, reinforced by the waiter, familiar with Vince's patronage, with someone other than Brenniss at his table. And feeling betrayed by Tess: the sophisticated red had been replaced on her fingernails with a delicate shell pink. How she spoke mindlessly of nights out with the girls. That she initiated the toast to Gilfadden. Clearly, he was not prepared for tonight.

"Your appetizers." The waiter interrupted his thoughts. "For the lady." He presented a plate of wafer-thin vegetables, cheeses, and crackers for Tess, and a display of shrimp for Vince.

She opened her hands much like holding back applause. "I honestly don't know how I should eat this—it's so pretty!"

Vince pulled a shrimp from his bamboo skewer and let the savory sauce float across the small curve of flesh. "You ought to try this, Tess. The shrimp is so tender."

"No, thanks. I'm good with this. Really."

"The sauce is out of this world."

"This is quite tasty, too."

"I know you've never had this combination before, sweet and spicy." He reached a shrimp across the table. "Just one nibble. Just one."

"No, no thanks, Vince."

The coil inside him turned tighter, ready to spring for some reason, the fuse about ready to spark.

"Here, smell it. Now taste..." He reached the shrimp to the corner of her lips. That perky little corner that revealed a white set of teeth, a corner that he just discovered when she sipped her wine. If only she would part her teeth, take the most petite of bites—

"I said NO, Vince!" Her hand pushed the shrimp in such a swift motion that his wrist nearly toppled the water goblet. "No, I can't! I'm allergic to shellfish!" Her lowered whisper was still a hiss, a puncture in the flow of the evening.

His hand hung midair, suddenly connected to the back of his arm and his body, the useless shrimp dangling from his fork. His biggest regret of the evening amplified more with other patrons staring.

"Sorry, sorry." He sampled the shrimp, although the texture felt like cardboard, stiff in his mouth and difficult to swallow. "Sorry to create a scene. I didn't know."

"No, you wouldn't. I've never needed to tell you about my allergies, right? And imagine, I grew up in a fishing town in Maine!" She shrugged the embarrassment away.

"Maine? Really? But you don't have one of those quaint accents."

"Been in the Big Apple for a while, you know. I mean, who wants to spend the rest of her life in New Harbor, Maine? The biggest restaurant is 'Chick's Pizza'. Not like *this*." She waved a cheese slice in the air.

The waiter returned. "How are the appetizers?"

"This is fantastic, and Vince has been raving about the shrimp," she said matter-of-factly.

"Excellent, excellent. Please enjoy."

Vince took a short breath. "Look, Tess, I'm sorry about—"

Her flat hand raised toward his face. "No more, Vince. So, let's talk about you."

Months, it seemed. Months since he'd talked about himself, he almost forgot who he was. Yet, he slid easily into a conversation about himself. A few times, she laughed, a genuine laugh. He'd forgotten that sound.

"So, in five years, where will you be, Vince?"

Not fair. He was in the small talk groove, where it didn't hurt to touch on things with little meaning, actually smiling again. But the question hit him like a bullet.

"I guess, well, in five years, I'd hope that Brenniss and I would have been reunited, gotten married, and maybe even had started a family."

She nodded, tapped her fingers on her cheek, then sipped her wine.

"Not planning to be a partner? Surely, you've thought about moving up in the firm. You could do it, Vince. You've got the clients, the motivation, the connections. You haven't thought of it?"

"Well, sure. Being invited in as a partner would be ideal. Of course, sure." His voice faded. He'd thought of it early in his career, then switched gears when Brenniss became his focus. Somehow, Tess made it sound desirable again. His eyes flicked again toward the entrance, as if Brenniss could be found easily, maybe seated at another table, waving him over.

"I get it, Vince."

"What's that?"

"I get that Brenniss is still 'number one' in your life. You live for that phone call or a postcard in her handwriting that says, 'Here I am!' All your hopes were put on hold those umpteen weeks ago. Your heart is broken and no one, and I mean no one, can take her place. Dreams die agonizing deaths for the very reason they are dreams, that one speck of hope can fill your whole day."

"Okay..."

"So, I understand that you still wait for Brenniss to walk through any place that has a door. But don't let those dreams get in the way of what you can do, whether Brenniss is there or not—"

He sucked in his breath. *How dare she say that?* His brain reverted to that reflection in his mirror earlier, the unsure smile and blank face.

"—because I'm your friend and I can talk to you like this and you'll know I'll be there tomorrow to keep the pencils sharpened and have your coffee and newspaper and schedule ready, and even a clean shirt if you need it...and to pick up the pieces if I need to."

She exhaled slowly, then downed the last of her wine.

"Have I been that much of a jerk?"

"No, you're that much of a dreamer. And that's something, God help me, that's what I like about you. You could be a partner, or you could piss it all away by putting your life on hold while the rest of the world keeps turning."

He let the air leak from his lungs, while that fizzled fuse dropped onto his plate next to his unfinished breadstick.

"You don't know what kind of a friend I can be, either." She twisted her wrist so carefully that, somehow, he was cupping her hands now, the pink-tipped fingernails and all. He had forgotten the touch of a hand within his. "I can encourage you, talk to you honestly, the way you need for there to be a tomorrow for yourself."

She was right. He'd been littering his life with regret and blame. Tess recognized that he still could look ahead. He was poised in the middle of his grief, deciding which road to take. By the time he dropped Tess at her apartment, *he* was laughing, a feeling he'd been craving for months now. As he drove home, a tiny fuse sparked a connection to a portion of his old self. He might like going back to that.

CHAPTER
TWENTY-EIGHT

RILEY'S CONVERSATION WITH GRACE

Riley stood in front of the mirror while shaving that morning, knowing a connection with Grace could eat away the empty. She'd be proud of Maggie's strength, knowing when to guide her. He sledded the razor through the foam on his face as he tried to bring Grace back into focus.

When I wake up, these bones of mine forget the soreness for a few minutes. I wash up, looking forward to breakfast. I used to make a simple breakfast and then graze through the day. Even Cartwheel would have been jealous. But having Maggie here, I must admit, there's a little more meaning to pouring some orange juice or cracking a couple eggs into the frying pan.

I know not to rush her. And, by damn, she is gentle. She shows respect for the animals, absolutely loves Poke. Well, it's mutual. That dog knows to protect her, a constant by her side.

It's better not to ask Maggie those details—she's been

through hell. They bubble up, enough, after a nightmare, or some association I didn't see coming. She remembers a tax-stamp worth of something, and it's usually a slice of something horrific. The elephant in the room just stands there, lumbering around the perimeter. But I know better to let it investigate the corners. I've been there when she's broken into pieces, held her when she trembles like a young colt. I've seen the fear pierce her eyes. But truthfully, I'd rather see that—a turn of recall, as painful as it is—than the dead look she had when we first met her, six ways to broken.

I learned a degree of patience from you. I just don't mind taking the time when Maggie needs it because I believe her needing help won't be forever. Sometimes, she'll remember enough and know where she's going and what she needs to do; I think that's a given. She's not a project, she's a human being, a survivor, and amazingly strong woman who needs the best opportunity...

Well, yeah, all that sounds noble. You'd say so, too...

What Griff asked me: is Maggie here for safety or for my satisfaction? Oh, we're all fond of her. So there's no difference, right? But it's my problem if I care too much. So what if she has two names now? It's easier to call her Maggie Fletcher, than just Maggie, if someone asks. She gets better because we give her a gentle re-introduction to kindness. I look forward to drawing those bones out of bed in the morning because they don't seem to ache as much anymore. The day holds more for us: a cup of sunlight and green for tomatoes and rust-colored skin of the best horses ever. And I sure as hell don't mind serving Jell-O for breakfast. Smiling comes a little easier these days.

Is that so bad?

So, the other day, we're walking to the barn and the horses are whinnying their excitement, stomping a dance of who goes first? from the stalls. It's pretty much all we hear. And she stops like the idea forming in her head is suddenly as clear as her last breath.

"They like me, don't they? The horses, I mean. They like me and know me, right?"

Thought she'd never ask.

CHAPTER
TWENTY-NINE

Overhead, the eagle flew past the Emory's oak, away from the river. Riley recognized it circling, perhaps trying to make sense of the game they were playing. Open the doors, both sit in the truck at the same time. Maggie jumps out like a trout taking a hatch. The eagle circled again, maybe taking a closer look as he and Maggie approached the truck at the same time. Her uncertainty made her fear of the truck tangible. She sat for one heartbeat, two heartbeats, three heartbeats, maybe another before her feet caught under her. Riley saw the terror repeat itself in her breath, in her eyes. An eagle knows when to nudge the fledglings toward the edge of the nest. Humans hang on.

"That's enough for today." Riley closed the truck doors. "You're sitting longer, Sunshine. You're able to sit and talk through the voices. You'll be able to close the door soon, and then we can go see Doc."

She raised her casted arm. "This gets in my way."

"I'm sure it does. But you're getting better at feeling safe, too. Now, how about we make some Jell-O for the fish barbecue tonight?" Her sunshine smile broke through the clouds and echoes faster than a tick on a dog.

The crease tucked along her eyebrow, her concentration focused on reading the package while the water boiled. She remembered the hot water, this time, unlike a few weeks ago.

Riley pulled a stoneware casserole dish from the cabinet. "Want to put the Jell-O in this? Grace bought this at Ten Winds Gallery a few years ago. I bet Hannah will get a kick seeing it put to use. You ready to pour?"

She eyeballed the measuring cup, checking it once, then again as Riley suggested, to be accurate. Then, slowly, the hot water streamed into the bowl, coloring the bowl with the Jell-O powder.

"What's next?"

"The cold water?"

"Check again."

She read earnestly, mentally checking off the steps she'd completed.

"Mix it! Of course! That's the magic!" She carefully dipped a fork into the bowl. "And you stir for—?"

"Two minutes." She set the timer and the crease in her forehead relaxed. The water transformed into a liquid ruby, red clouds swirling into jewel. She felt the sugar grit melt, passing the fork gently into the corners of the dish where the sugar migrated.

"Almost done?"

"I've got to add the cold water," she said confidently. "And then, refrigerate it."

"Atta girl. I'll clear a space in the fridge."

"They'll love this, I know they will."

Look at her smile. She *made* Jell-O.

He handed her a basket as they entered the garden, where Maggie seemed to enjoy the surprise of fresh vegetables just for the taking.

"So, we've got fish, from the night we found—" Riley interrupted himself. "Griff will bring fish and we have Jell-O and now we'll pick veggies for the salad. Of course, there's cheesecake."

Maggie's eyes grew wide. "I remember. Killer cheesecake."

"Well, this time, it's cherry cheesecake. Hannah already told me."

"I like cherry Jell-O, so I know I'll like cherry cheesecake."

He chose cucumbers, lettuce, while Maggie found tomatoes, remembering the tangy flavor.

"So, why don't we visit them sometime?"

"We will, once you feel safe riding in the truck. When you're ready, we can go to town, visit Hannah's gallery, get some fancy coffee, get that cast off—"

"Oh." Her childlike voice, so fragile while the dark fear rode her. Being in the truck seemed like forever away. Once she could sit, then sit a while in the seat, once she could ignore the voices...She looked at the tomato she'd just placed in the basket, the most perfect tomato ever, the perfect and uniform red, round and plump in the right places. It was a shame to pluck it, to take it away from the sunshine, but Riley knew it was ready.

"Do you think I'm ready?"

"Almost. You've come a long way. You can sit in the truck and almost close the door. Once you do that, we can start short rides, like riding to the barn or around the pasture. But you'll know when you're ready. You'll tell me."

While Riley rinsed the vegetable at the outside spigot by the garden, Maggie let her eyes slide toward the black truck. Maybe...maybe she was ready...She looked at the tomato. How does a tomato know it's ready? It falls from the vine.

Riley rarely used Grace's recipe box that he now lifted from the shelf. He remembered her applying three roosters on the lid, as if placing wallpaper, with intent concentration. For the life of him, he couldn't recall the significance of those roosters. He stared at them, as if they would cue him. He was forgetting part of her. A shadow paused behind his eyes, then moved away.

"Pimentos are funny animals," he heard Maggie say. She pointed to the jar sitting next to the coffee pot. "Who knew something soft like that is more for color than for flavor? You can't put pimentos in Jell-O."

Riley chuckled. "Maggie, you go on and get ready. I'll get ready later. Wear something nice."

He'd automatically said that to Grace, maybe just as absently: put on something nice. He could easily have said "take your time to look special—I've got this" or just plain "Griff and Hannah will be here soon, you run along."

Maggie took a deep breath as she no longer needed Riley while walking up the stairs. She felt better than the fuzzy white days in the hospital. Still, she stared at her face as she washed: face, neck, left arm, right hand around the cast. The cast frayed at the edges, a smudge here and there, Hannah's heart and good wishes faded from weeks with the horses, and often, right by the thumb usually, a few strands of Poke's fur clinging like feathers. She looked in the mirror, not sure how to put on something nice. Sure, tonight was special, maybe her face could be framed with something other than a tee shirt. She smiled for a second. The smile reflected back. It took her by surprise. She didn't know her face could do that. Then, a brief flash of looking at her face in the mirror, a time when she was happy or showed it with such a smile—then gone. Her face darkened. She saw that in the mirror too. She liked the smile better. Just as quickly, she had a flash of white around her face. Then her reflection smiled again. "Who are you?" she whispered. "Where are you from?"

Wear something nice.

She padded into her bedroom. Quiet, white. Something

about stepping up and into something white. Something nice. That brief flake of color was no more than a pinpoint of her life before.

She opened the drawers of her bureau. Tee shirts, tee shirts, the perfect thing to work with the horses or to make Jell-O or to feed Poke. They were nice, but they were tee shirts, all the same. Her eyes followed to the sliding closet doors, a place full of somethings nice, she supposed. She'd never looked there, but just then, heard Griff and Hannah pull into the driveway below, their laughter not far from something nice as well.

She pushed through the hangers with nice, colorful, and lovely choices. One top had short, ruffled sleeves, inviting a barbecue on a warm summer afternoon. The Emory oak caught a breeze and sent it through her window while the curtains slid like leaves against the wall. The top she saw drew blues and greens together, just like the sound of the cool breeze. She slipped it from the hanger, held it up, and it certainly looked nice, but she couldn't remember if this were her blouse or not. Something nice. She could see herself talking with Hannah wearing this blouse, laughing with Riley and Griff and drinking iced tea while wearing this. Being someone with two names in something nice.

She lifted the fabric over her head, dressed her casted arm first, sleeves playing a pattern against her arms, hem falling loosely at her hips. She felt not just useful. She looked again in the mirror. Despite the scars healing along her arms and collarbone, the bulge lessening near her eye, despite the emptiness of who this image was, Maggie realized she felt pretty.

"Hey, where's my gal pal?" she heard Hannah say.

"She'll be down soon."

Gal pal, that's what she was. Hannah, the woman with a silk river of hair down her back, the woman who brought her clothes, who smiled, who talked about summer and Grace.

Hannah was her gal pal, too. Maybe tonight, with her something nice on, while they ate fish and killer cheesecake, Maggie would say something in conversation that was important, valued, memorable. She put on her boots with her jeans and something-nice top, hoping no one would notice her boots were creased with Ar-i-zo-na dust.

"I swear—isn't that the same damned hat you wear fishing? Is that the only one you have?" Griff teased.

They laughed about simple things. Their laughter floated up to Maggie's room, all the way from their memories. She hadn't heard that much laughter in some time, bubbles of it, popping quick from the group just below her.

She looked in the mirror again, trying on a smile. Her face felt odd, free of wrinkles and darkness, safe, magical, and effortless. She could laugh too, just give her a chance. She wanted to remember happy and maybe she could tonight.

"There she is!" Hannah called to the stairwell as Maggie emerged. A magic for Maggie happened right away, a smile, removing the clouds from over her head. She hugged Hannah.

"I heard you had cheesecake," Maggie giggled.

"Griff, look! Her bruises are all gone!"

Riley had washed the vegetables and didn't see Maggie's arrival, but while drying his hands, his smile was cut, a raven wing of anger storming a shadow across his eyes, carving away his joy. He stared a dead wall, stone and rock forming toward Maggie.

"Riley, she looks better every time I see her," Hannah gushed.

"Take it off!" his voice rasped through his throat. "Take it off, NOW!"

"Riley!" The silence was rock solid.

"Go upstairs and take it off!" he hissed. "Right now!"

"Riley, what's up?" Griff reached for his friend's shoulder.

"Where did you get that? Did I say you could wear that?"

Riley's eyes pushed right through Maggie as if no one else were there.

"What? It...in my room. In the closet." Maggie recalled a snippet in a convenience store, maybe grabbing the wrong do-nut or soft drink that would cost her later. It swam to the sur-face and evaporated.

"You mean, in Grace's closet?"

"Oh, no," Hannah groaned. She remembered now, a night much like this, with Grace starting to waste away, with Grace cold by the end of the evening because the blouse wasn't warm enough. "Wait a minute, Riley. You mean you haven't gotten rid—"

"Go upstairs and put it back," Riley's hoarse whisper was ragged and cold, giving no clue to the heat outside beyond the porch.

"It's something nice..." Maggie spoke through her confu-sion, like saying it's something healthy, or it's something re-freshing to those men cornering her by the beer. Tears seeped from her eyelids. She turned and ran upstairs.

Riley blinked suddenly, bringing him back. Griff and Han-nah were stunned into stillness in the room. Hannah pulled slowly away from Griff, then bounded up the steps.

"Hey, friend, she didn't know, did she?" Griff offered. "Let's take this outside."

"I can't let her wear that!" Riley's fist balanced on the porch baluster.

"Hey, calm down, cowboy."

They heard Hannah's voice above them in Maggie's room, a hum of quiet and comfort, then Maggie's voice rising in rhythm to her sobs. "Don't make them come after me. Keep them away, keep them away..." All those weeks of improve-ment dissolved like sugar.

Hannah's soothing voice spoke again. "Maggie, come back. Come back to me."

Riley rubbed his face trying to erase the ghost he just saw. How dare she? How dare *he*.

"Talk to me. Talk to me about what's going on. So what if Maggie wore one of Grace's—"

"She didn't have the right."

"Listen to yourself. All of the clothes she has a right to these days are second hand. You bring Maggie home, give her a place to stay, but she can't go near the closet in her room? Did you even tell her not to touch them?"

Riley's reddened eyes blinked tightly. "I didn't think she'd look...Oh, my God, What did I just do?"

"This is more than Maggie wearing a blouse, friend. You still love Grace, we know that. That blouse wasn't so much about Maggie as it was about Grace. You know that, too."

"I told her...I told her to do it. I told her what I always told Grace. 'Wear something nice.' It never occurred to me she'd look in the closet."

"What's really going on?"

Riley felt a piece turn around in his heart, feeling a drop or two of rain moistening that stone wall he'd just built. "Oh, my God, Griff. I said the same thing that those hoodlums did. Oh, God, she'll never trust me again, after all I tried to do to build that up. I was...I was surprised to look up and see Grace, I mean, Maggie standing in the kitchen again. I'm...I'm starting to forget her." Riley shook his head. "I could find Grace in a crowd, now I can't remember how tall she was. I can't remember if she parted her hair on the left or the right. I can't remember why he had roosters on her recipe box. I don't always remember her the first thing in the morning or tell her I love her at the end of the day." He wiped his eyes. "I'm losing her. And seeing Maggie just then, was just like a flag of defiance. I know she didn't mean it. I just went off half-cocked." He wiped his eyes.

Griff sighed deeply. "Let me ask you this—be honest,

friend. Does Maggie's being here create a problem? You know what I've been advocating all along, but now, she's a little more aware. You know, someplace where she's safe, protected—"

Riley raised his hand. "No, no, I won't punish her. It was my mistake, not hers and I over-reacted. I expected to hear Grace's voice, but it was Maggie's instead." He suddenly looked at Griff. "What do you mean, 'safe and protected'? I won't harm her, if that's what you mean."

"No, it's the Mitchell Canyon business. I'm waiting for ID on the deceased males. I don't know what may be out there, still. There may be others watching her...or you. I'm saying it's not too late for her to live elsewhere."

"She doesn't need somewhere else. I see her getting stronger every day, she loves the horses. They're good therapy for her. And Poke? Talk about protection! And did you see how she hugged Hannah? That wouldn't have happened a month ago. No, no, she stays here, but she needs to feel safe...and I need to make things right, again." He squinted toward Maggie's room.

"Do you want Hannah and me to leave?"

"No, certainly not. I'll get the barbecue started. Maybe I can salvage this yet."

"What did I do? What did I do?" Maggie wailed.

Hannah's hair slid forward as she leaned toward Maggie. "Nothing. You did nothing wrong. It's Riley. He was surprised by the blouse you chose. It was one of Grace's. He was mixed up when he saw you wear it."

"I couldn't remember...if it was mine. I couldn't remember. Now he hates me, hates me. He'll come after me, it'll be bad." She sobbed tightly.

"Oh, no, no, Riley doesn't hate you. It was a mistake.... okay, remember last week when Lester showed up? Remember how Riley tried to protect you from Lester? Remember how he kept you safe these last few months? Maggie, don't throw out the good he's done just because he made a mistake. Listen. He just read the situation wrong, like Lester did, thinking he remembered meeting you when you were younger. Griff is talking to him now, and we'll still have the barbecue and things will get straightened out. You'll see. Just give Riley a chance to explain."

Maggie's eyes stared down the closet door.

Within a half-hour, Hannah came around the back of the house the platter of fish in her hands. "She was pretty bad, at first. She had some flashbacks—"

Riley shook his head, the regret knotting his stomach. "I knew it—"

"But I spent some time calming her, reminding her that you were one of the good guys." She hugged Riley. "Look, I know it was a reaction to seeing the blouse, but she can't sort all that out. She didn't remember if it was her blouse or not. All she saw was anger, thought she was being threatened. But you know, Riley, you're just the one to put her at ease. She needs to hear your voice."

"You think she'll listen?"

"Go try."

His footsteps, heavy and slow, advanced up toward Maggie's room. He wouldn't blame her if she never spoke to him again. Poke, ever the sentry, wouldn't even look at him. He knocked softly on her closed door.

"Maggie? I need to talk to you. It's Riley." No answer.

"I need to apologize. I won't come in unless you invite me. I want to explain, although I'm not sure I can...Sunshine, I'm sorry I got mad at you. It's just...well...that was one of Grace's favorite blouses. I saw it and for a second, I thought Grace had just walked down the steps. I know that doesn't make sense, but I reacted, and you didn't deserve it. You're so strong these days, I forget that you can still be fragile; I have no right to take that safe feeling away. I'm sorry I scared you. Nothing you did was wrong, honest. Sunshine?"

No answer.

"I didn't do a very good job, did I?" He tried again. The other side of the door was dead still, his voice bouncing off the door, into the hallway. He rested his hand flat on the door, as if trying to reach through it.

"We...we are still having that barbecue. You're welcome to join us. We want you to have dinner. Griff's looking forward to your Jell-O, the salad with the tomatoes you picked—" His eyes filled with tears, his voice choked. His hand lingered on the door, flat, like a starved blessing against the wood.

"I can't say it enough, Maggie. I'm sorry I acted like an ass. You join us when you want. You can leave that blouse on for tonight, hell, any night. You look nice in it. You can...well...it's up to you."

Maggie heard his sad slow steps fade down the stairs, then out to the back. Low voices rose as the three talked together. He didn't sound angry anymore. Hannah said he was just confused. *She'd been just confused a lot, so why couldn't Riley be confused, too? He meant it, really, when he apologized. Those voices never apologized. But Riley did. Riley wanted to give her a chance.*

She remembered the tomato, dressing the salad in blood-red triangles, the juicy irresistible cuts that gave a sharp sweet flavor. The tomato in her hand was warm at the vine then she cut it later while she laughed with Riley. She had placed the tomato chunks into the lush lettuce, next to the translucent coins of cucumber. They belonged together, the flavors. That tomato knew it was ready.

It was up to her, Riley said so.

Nothing had been up to her in a long time. She didn't have a choice about being called bitch or the music that drove like motorcycles from the radio, or the junk food she forced down on the dark scratchy floor or how they owned her. She wasn't asked if she wanted to be found, the hospital or the color of the cast, or later about which apples to feed Bliss, or what room she moved into, or even what to eat for breakfast.

It was up to her to move with the horses and dog and Riley. It was up to her to walk down the stairs at some point. It was up to her to look toward the sky because she could. It was up to her to go to town with Riley. Inside the truck.

It was up to her to walk through that doorway of sadness. No fear. She could do this.

CHAPTER
THIRTY

She wiped her eyes once more, then stood and looked past the still curtains, staring at the truck. She knew she was ready, too, right at that very moment, never surer. As sure as a man who apologized for words he'd said, for a misunderstanding. Right at that moment, it was up to her. Riley had said it.

She opened the door softly, intent now on showing her face, giving herself the chance, fighting brave. Each soft step forward and down the steps, then forward onto the landing, gradually lowering herself each sure step, the next and the next until each step placed her onto the kitchen porch.

Step one, two, three, onto the driveway. Slowly, she walked toward the truck. Her left hand touched the shiny black finish as she saw her reflection approach the passenger door.

It's up to me, she thought. *Whoever "me" is.*

Her left hand folded under the handle and released the door open. The interior was shadowy and hot. The truck console held receipts neatly. There were no cigarettes or joints or beer cans. The floor was clean, no wads of used napkins or

Styrofoam containers from truck stop lunches. There was no smell of smoke or urine or semen or her vomit. Clean. Inside the truck.

Her casted hand rested on the open door. and she placed her left foot onto the floor. *Pretend you're squishing a bug.* She planted sure, to take away any spiders or bugs or cigarettes or faces, so they wouldn't move beyond where that foot remained. She shifted slightly and lowered herself slowly onto the seat.

Still quiet. Inside the truck. No pounding music, no voices telling her to sit, to lie down, to spread her legs, to open her mouth, to thrust, to squat...no none of that. Quiet. *It was still up to her.*

She shifted again, pulled the other foot inside, where it belonged. She reached out against the sunset and pulled the door shut. Her brain counted *one, two, three, four, five...*

Riley heard a noise toward the front of the house as the fish sizzled. He paused from the barbecue to peer around the corner to see...Oh, my God. Maggie. All on her own.

Her brain kept going...*twelve, thirteen, fourteen, fifteen, sixteen...*

He tentatively moved closer, past the porch. Surely she'll slam open the door, she'll jam short steps into the dirt as she runs away, she'll bullet out of the vehicle like she'd done hundreds of times before. Surely, any time, now.

...*twenty-nine, thirty, thirty-one, thirty-two, thirty-three...*

She felt the sweat forming on her neck, a sure sign. She focused outside the window, swinging her eyes upward, because she could. An eagle rushed the sky in play overhead, while the clouds forgot to move. She tapped her foot as she counted each number.

...*forty-two, forty-three, forty-four, forty-five...*

Riley swallowed the dry claw in his throat. *Was she okay? Was she going to hurt herself?*

...fifty-eight, fifty-nine, sixty.

She opened the truck door and felt a breeze dive past her neck toward the receipts in the cup holder. She swung her legs in unison sideways, awkwardly outside the car, because the cast threw off her balance. She looked up again. The eagle had circled and now dove towards the river. She realized she paused, not rushing out as she'd always done, never paying attention to how a real person gets out of a car. She had been breathing all along, no pressure to release a build-up from her lungs. Her legs stabilized. No one poking or yanking or tossing her out. *Hurry up, bitch, and use the toilet.* No, none of that, just a distant splash of the eagle winning a fish from the river. Her ears were clean with the silence that followed. No voices, no taunting, no ringing, no foggy haze. She looked up and caught the evening sun. A deep breath. Standing. No panic. Standing, by herself. It was all up to her. She could probably do that again.

She turned toward the house, when she saw Riley facing her, the proudest grin swiping his face. Within two steps, he was next to her. He put his arms around her in a hug, not tight, not to break her or to force her into silence or to lift her to the back of the van or to grind her onto the floor. Riley wasn't like that. No, it was a hug that covered her like a comforter. Telling her she recovered something she used to be.

She felt the breeze blow across the top of her head as she tilted her forehead to his chest. No, it wasn't a breeze, it was his breath, he was that close. No, not his breath, it was moist, a teardrop. No, wait again. It was the gentle touch of Riley's lips on her hair.

CHAPTER
THIRTY-ONE

Vince flashed that charming smile when Tess handed him reports for the morning meeting. Her eyebrow curled up as he pulled out her handwritten note. *Dinner tonight?*

"Sorry, Tess. Wednesday? Dinner with Brenniss' mom Betty? You know, since Milt died."

"Oh, yeah."

"I don't know when I'll get away. Sometimes it's a long evening." His eyes switched to those preparing for the meeting. As if trying not to look too obvious, he took Tess' note and nodded as if reading a phone message.

"Sure, sure, I understand." Her smile didn't miss a beat.

He looked through the stack of files as if reading the details, while stuffing the note into his shirt pocket. "How about Friday, instead? Or Saturday?" His murmur didn't sound any different than as if asking about a client phone number or a correction in the file.

"Oh, like—a date?" she whispered, opening one of the files and pointing.

The charm worked through his smile. "Chinese in—and a

DVD?" He looked up and saw Kent point to the conference room. "Be right there!"

Tess grabbed the top file as if studying a correction. "Pick something I would like for a change. I'm ready for a comedy." She nodded as if finalizing instructions.

She watched him walk down the hallway, then close the conference door behind him. She'd been to a few baseball games herself. She never forgot that chemistry, the way your arteries stung when the glove sucks in that perfect catch.

As if Brenniss were in the passenger seat on his way to Betty's, he talked about work or another vacation together. He scanned radio stations for Brenniss' favorite jazz station, definitely not country or hip-hop.... He didn't dare say out loud that Brenniss wasn't even here. It would have sounded like getting twenty-to-life, that final slap of the gavel.

Miles Davis. It was a blue drift of smoke up through the evening. He thought about sitting on the balcony at work, with Miles drifting notes from the thin nasal trumpet. He saw himself sitting with a cigarette in his right hand. Even though he didn't smoke, Miles made him believe he did.

What would Tess say, watching that smoke?

He nearly slammed on the brakes. Wait a minute! How did Tess show up in his thoughts?

He pulled out his favorite Eagles CD and finished the drive with Fry and Henley.

"Vince, this is so nice that you drive here each week. I really look forward to it."

"I wouldn't miss it, Betty, you know that." Their meals focused on a large serving of Brenniss, keeping her alive in the topics they chose. Betty and he walked by the formal dining room with a table that sat eight, but dwarfed two, and onto the patio where the glass-topped table reflected blooms from Betty's garden. This time, it showed two place settings, not three or four. That one detail made all the difference. "I talked with Agent Stanley last week." Betty served a favorite salmon salad of Brenniss'. "He still seems to think Brenniss is still in the country."

"How does he know?"

"I guess the FBI looked at tapes from security cameras at airports, bus stations, train stations...honestly! I can't imagine sitting in front of a screen trying to concentrate on an image on all those miles of videos. A face might turn away, a shuffle, a coat, a profile—it's all important. If someone blinks or yawns, he could be identified as a terrorist, for heaven's sake!"

"So, he thinks Brenniss might be in another part of the state?"

"Or part of the country."

"Did they ever locate the van? Seems like that would be a clue."

"That van seems to have disappeared. Off the radar. Isn't that what the kids say now?"

He shook his head. "I'm glad he keeps *you* informed."

She lowered her fork to her plate, like an elevator. "Oh dear, Vince. Here, all along, I thought you were getting updates, too."

"No, it's what you share with me." His jaw jutted forward, that he sometimes wore when he dared someone to do better.

"Well, then, I'll make him tell you everything I know. You have such a good heart." She tapped his shirt pocket, where they both heard the crinkle of paper from the pressure of Betty's hand. Tess' note. *Dinner tonight?* He'd not remembered to throw it out.

Betty's smile faded. "You were so close to being a son-in-law." She tapped his pocket again. "I can't think of you any other way."

Each tap, each crinkle brought Betty close to Tess, alarmingly so. Betty sat back and took another bite of salmon.

The sunlight emptied during their meal, amplifying those

summer sounds of motorcycles buzzing streets, school-less children yelling down the block, a jogger's tap-tap footsteps as the run was completed, the crickets sawing a one-note symphony in the grass.

As she poured coffee in the den, Betty asked, "Do you think of the future, Vince? I mean, when Brenniss comes back."

"Not much else. We'll still marry, if she returns—"

"*When* she returns—"

"Yes, when she returns, I'll hope she'll be as happy as she once was."

"But, well, what if she isn't, though? Happy to some degree, I suppose. But the same person?"

"I don't follow. Of course, she'll be happy she's home."

"Perhaps you're right." She took a slow sip. "People can change, you know, in situations they never thought they'd be in. Milt changed from who he was before the war. I still loved him. There was never a question that I would rethink marrying him. No not at all. Still, he was...hmmm, a little more closed off."

Vince's brow furrowed. His discomfort with the topic recoiled 'happy' in him.

"Betty, she's out there, I know she is. And she's the same wonderful, sensitive, and sweet Brenniss we've always known," he said half to himself. "Brenniss hasn't changed."

Her patrician stoicism dissolved like ashes before his eyes. Her shoulders shuddered with short percussive sobs. At the same time, he felt clumsy with the coffee cup, set it down on the table, and brushed his own grief somewhere to the basement of his reserve, just to pull Betty close.

We hold each other, he thought, holding on for dear life, trying to feel for solid ground when the ground offers nothing but movement. Holding on, holding out, holding up—they all meant the same thing, didn't they? Waiting...waiting for a reason for one more day. Betty's breath controlled the sobs that overtook her from time to time, then she shifted her head upward for a deep breath and rested against Vince's shirt pocket.

Crinkle.

CHAPTER
THIRTY-TWO

Puzzles are usually fun. I've built my career on figuring out puzzles. Griff waited to be connected to the state forensic lab. *Puzzles work best if all the pieces are there, but if no one is aware a piece is missing, a body grows blinders. He only sees what he wants to. Forensics must be a messy business to get all the pieces and then need to locate the one that was missed all along.*

"Hello, Sheriff? Sheriff Hensley?" The young voice in his ear started him back to the phone. "Yes, this is Griff Hensley, Copper Station, Arizona. I got a message to call you."

"Sheriff, I'm Dan Washesky from the Arizona State Forensics Lab in Phoenix. We've found a few things for you regarding the van you discovered in the canyon. I wanted to give you what we found so far. Now, your report describes a late model van found at about seventeen miles from Copper Station, in Mitchell Canyon, right?"

"Correct, at the bottom of a ravine."

"And an elevated mesa nearby, where you found landing marks from what you thought might be a helicopter. You think the two are related."

"Correct, because the bullet casing found near the helicopter evidence also matched the bullet holes discovered in the van."

"You really did some thorough combing of the area, Sheriff. You made our job a great deal easier. Now, we're far from finished, but I've got a few answers for you."

"Talk to me."

"Okay, the helicopter. Based on your pictures and measurements, we determined the skids of the helicopter matched those of smaller, privately owned ones. Although, I have to say some state agencies have smaller ones like this one, too."

"Do you have a make or model?"

"Not specifically, but we can narrow it to two or three. We'll be faxing a report to detail those. The spray of sand from the rotors wasn't a wide diameter, which also means the pilot had pretty good control when setting down and taking off."

"A professional pilot?"

"I'd say a seasoned pilot. He'd have to have control enough to fly into canyon terrain, let alone land on top of a mesa with all the wind currents."

"So, how many people in the helicopter?"

"The private ones hold two. Three if you hold your breath and you carry no supplies."

"So, one of the passengers had to be the shooter."

"The pilot wore a size eleven boot. You found a partial print by the skids. His cowboy boots matched the other depressions you found near the rock outcropping."

"The pilot was the shooter?"

"And he was left-handed. The pictures and measurements you sent showed depressions a little deeper on the right. So he leaned on his right to fire his rifle. When the shell ejected, it was to the right of his body position."

"Well, I'll be." Griff drew a quick diagram on his paper.

"Anything else about the shooter?"

"Likely he was trained as a marksman or a sniper, say in the military. Only one elbow and two toe indentations; that's a trained balance maneuver. Based on your pictures and measurements, we can estimate he's about 6'5" and around 240 pounds."

Griff wrote quickly. "Big dude."

"Now for the van. You noticed the VIN number had been filed down—"

"We couldn't see well because the dashboard had caved in when the van impacted the canyon floor."

"I'll be honest," Dan continued. "We haven't gotten very far into the van at all. Still taking it apart. But what we see is no identification, whatsoever, no VIN, no plates, no prints—"

"You're kidding; no prints whatsoever?"

"So far, the surfaces we have investigated show no fingerprints. It's been wiped clean. Someone didn't want this thing to be found or pursued. Now, we've got hair, and we can reconstruct the bodies, once we have freed them from the wreckage, despite the decay. But the bodies were dead before the van hit the bottom of the canyon."

"Let me guess." Griff looked at the picture of the single spent cartridge. "Fifty-caliber."

"That's right. Three males, between twenty and thirty years of age. One shot in the back, entered the heart and severed the aorta. The other two were shot in the head, one frontally, one posteriorly. Their faces and dental work were pretty much obliterated."

"No question, this wasn't an accident."

"Our report will likely conclude they were shot from a source approximately thirty to forty yards away. Preliminary exploration of the wounds show a downward angle—"

"From the mesa—" Griff had already calculated a direct line from the van's roadway position to the mesa. "How does

38.5 yards sound?"

Dan chuckled. "Close enough."

"So, who *are* these guys? Anything distinguishable?"

"As you know there wasn't much left of the exposed parts of the bodies. We found two bodies in the front, and one prone in the back of the van. When the van went over the side of the road, the bodies were somewhat airborne, jostled inside the space. The van collapsed inward onto them at impact and pushed the bodies toward or through broken windows, then kind of, if you will, stapled them into place. The exposed body parts were pretty much licked clean from scavengers. One hand was completely severed—"

"From scavengers? Or was it the shooter trying to remove identity?"

"No, we found teeth marks, large ones, not a clean cut you would expect from a saw or cleaver. You got any large animals in the area?"

"Oh, a few." Griff chuckled. "So, no identification on the van, parts of bodies are missing, no reliable dental records, the van is wiped clean, at least so far, and you may have to destroy evidence to tear apart the rest of the van." Griff ran his hand over the top of his head.

"Now, we still may find something. Just two days ago, we were able to lift the van roof and remove the remains. You never know—a window frame, something on the floor, the undercarriage—and we have body parts."

"Which means?"

"Maggots."

"Did you say what I thought you said?"

"Maggots, Sheriff. Those tiny little active buggers are a wealth of information—and admissible in court, by the way."

"Maggots."

"These maggots, and believe me, we have a great collection of them, have been very busy taking care of the flesh they've been eating."

"What? Destroying the evidence?"

"The maggots seal the evidence inside their bodies. We can dissect the stomachs of our maggot population, remove the contents, and test the DNA."

"The DNA of the maggots?"

"No, Sheriff, the DNA from the stomach contents. What the maggots chewed on...our victims."

Griff let a maggot-sized sense of hope wander into his thoughts. "So, by running the DNA of the stomach contents from the maggots, we'll be able to determine the DNA of these three guys?"

"Very possible. Then, we'll run comparisons against any DNA matches on file."

"You can't do that with bone fragments?"

"Believe it or not, maggot stomachs have a higher degree of reliability."

"Well, I'll be." Griff shook his head.

"As for dental matches, for the female you mentioned, so far, no luck. We still need to check the Indian Reservations, too. Some DNA may show up with her, too, for all we know, once we can get to the van floor...a single hair, an eyelash, maybe we'll find a weapon that was held against her...if we're lucky, a blood sample."

"Dan, you've really made my day. How soon can I get this report?"

"Hate to say. We may need a few more weeks for completion."

"I'll be looking forward to it. I have to confess, I don't envy your having to look at maggot stomachs."

"Takes all kinds, doesn't it, Sheriff?"

Maggot stomachs. Go figure.

Griff walked toward Ten Winds Gallery, sun to his back, avoiding thoughts of maggots, especially if he were buying Hannah lunch.

"Hey, there, my love," he said opening the gallery door. "You were hoping to have lunch, right?" He kissed her softly.

"I'd rather have lunch with you than anyone else," she whispered back.

"So, I'm buying—"

"But I can't leave the gallery. You'll never guess! This is the best news!" Her smile slid open. "Get this! I just got off the phone with the governor's office!"

"I told you to file your taxes," he joked.

"No, silly—listen! Seems that Ten Winds Gallery has been awarded the state's Entrepreneurship Award!"

"What?"

"Yeah, and the governor himself will be here to present the award! I've got to set up an open house, get things really spruced up—"

"Whoa! First, congratulations. I'm so proud of you." His broad smile erased the last of the maggots. "But when did you apply for it?"

"Well, that's the curious thing, I didn't. You're *nominated* for it. Remember the open house in March? Remember meeting Molly Swanson from the state arts board?"

"Vaguely. Didn't she buy a wall hanging of yours and—"

"That painting of Ronnie Philpot's, the one of a spot in Mitchell Canyon. That was her. Seems she took those pieces back to Phoenix, talked us up and then submitted a nomination for Ten Winds! I had no idea!"

"So, you can celebrate by having lunch with me."

"Well, here's the deal. I guess some of the governor's advance people will be here next week to help plan—you know, measure space, make enough room for cameras—Cameras! Like TV cameras! All the logistics."

"So?"

"I have to plan! Call in all the members, have a meeting, choose a theme, pick a date, arrange inventory, choose pieces—"

"So, you still need some nourishment. I'll run over to Rosa's and bring us something to eat here. You can do all that and still hop around here like a grasshopper on a frying pan."

She let out a breath. "Oh, you're right. I'm hyped. It's such a surprise! You bring lunch and celebrate before I get into uber-planning mode."

"Before?" He put his arm around her. "You know? That's the best news I've had all day."

CHAPTER
THIRTY-THREE

A lazy distant fog lifted beyond the river as Riley and Maggie stepped onto the porch. She clutched her memory journal like a talisman as they walked toward the truck.

"So, I thought after seeing Doc, we could visit Hannah's gallery. Maybe even lunch with Hannah and Griff. What do you think?"

"Will I have Jell-O?"

"If you want, Sunshine, if you want."

He talked of the future as if it were an easy thing to tick off on a list. All she was aware of was riding in the truck. For maybe twenty minutes. All she saw was something she had only accomplished for three minutes, with the windows open and with plenty of stops to catch her breath.

"You ready?" He smiled.

"Am I Maggie Fletcher today?"

He paused. "We'll talk to Doc about that one. At the clinic, they may call you Maggie Fletcher. You need a name, Maggie, but I just don't know..."

She opened the truck door because it was easy, because

she had done it before a thousand-million times, but mostly, because it was up to her. She let herself slide onto the seat. She waited until Riley started up the truck, closing her door only then.

"Ready." She nodded, but her voice sounded wafer thin, less than her intended bold affirmation. Her eyes darted, then she opened the window.

She knew by now, she counted to nearly two hundred fifty before they reached the curve by the neighbor's orchard and another three hundred before following the curve along the river. She felt the air suck her hair like a thin balloon, bouncing against the glass. She felt a little like flying, the dark ghosts unable to catch her.

"...seven, eight, nine, ten, eleven..."

"I bet Doc will be pleased with your improvements. It's been over a month since I brought you home. Can you believe that?"

"...thirty-six, thirty-seven, thirty-eight, thirty-nine..."

"Copper Station's a nice little town. The clinic, the hospital, a few churches, a hardware store, a tack shop, library, Marta's—the bakery I told you about with the fancy coffee—of course, Hannah's Ten Winds Gallery..."

"...one twenty-two, one twenty-three, one twenty-four, one twenty-five..."

Her hand tapped her knee with each count, more prayer than numbers. Her eyes had fallen to some middle place just below the window, near the fresh air vent. Hidden way deep in the sound of the wind falling through her window she heard it. *Hey, bitch, lie down, I said it's my turn.*

"Sunshine? You're here with me, remember?"

Her eyes snapped back up to the river. "Hey look!" Her heart skipped upward. As the river curved parallel to the road, an eagle appeared, carefully turning as if drawing circles in the pale fog.

"That may be that eagle family that comes in every year from the canyon. Fog might have pulled him in too. He's looking for fish."

"Like when you and Griff go fishing."

"Well, yes, but that eagle is far better at catching them than I am."

They strained to follow the circular gliding, the swoops, the powerful wings pulling him back up.

"How you doing, Maggie? Want some music? I'll turn the radio on really low."

"...sixteen, seventeen, eighteen, nineteen, twenty..."

Instead of the loud percussive anthem she'd expected, the music was guitar with a soft teardrop wrapped inside a female voice.

"At night you hear it rising and chasing through the trees:

The great windhorse riding and galloping free.

You hear its hoof-beats rolling

Slowly coming for you at night.

Then just as easily, riding on, galloping into the sky.

Sometimes you swear your compass by the wandering stars:

But, an ocean of dreams can't find where you are.

So, listen, very carefully:

That windhorse breathes a sigh,

Then turns again to climb the moon, galloping into the sky..."

"...One eighty, one eighty-one, one eighty-two, one eighty-three, one eighty-four...I like this song. She's sad, but you can hear her heart...One eighty-five, one eighty-six..."

"That's Bonnie Meacham, she's one of *my* favorites. You know she started out as a concert pianist? Played in bars for college money, then ended up in country music."

"...two oh six, two oh seven...Do you know her?"

"No, but if I had a chance to see her in concert, we'd drive all the way to Phoenix to do it."

"...The windhorse is a legend that no one ever sees.

It plays along the road, past your window, through the trees.

When you least expect it,

That horse will catch your eye.

You'll ride it past the mountains, galloping into the sky..."

"...two eighty-four, two eighty-five...It's sad, but it doesn't pound. It doesn't yell or growl. It just sings. I like that."

"I do believe, Maggie Fletcher, you are a fan of country music." His chuckle was replaced by the wind. "Not long now, Maggie. You need to stop?" She was rocking slightly in her seat, kneading the shoulder harness with her casted hand. Her foot taps rode all the way up to her knee.

"See? There's Griff's office, there's Marta's, there's Ten Winds Gallery, the grocery store...up ahead, does that look familiar?"

"...four sixty-one, four sixty-two, four sixty-three...It's a big building. Is that a school?"

"That's the hospital where we brought you the night we found you. The clinic is the flat part next to it. That's where Doc is today."

"I had a room there. The sheets were clean. Everyone was nice...four ninety-nine, five hundred, five oh one, five oh two..." Her fingers gripped the door handle, an airborne soldier ready to jump. Her foot ached, her palms sweat like someone condemned. She'd counted, listened to country music, looked for that eagle, even counted red cars as distractions that worked for seconds. But the fear flooded her heart.

"You're almost there. The clinic's after this stop sign."

She felt the breath collect in her lungs because she forgot to breathe. Breathe, forget the numbers, breathe. Riley pulled into a parking space and stopped the engine.

"There you are, Sunshine! You made—"

But she'd already opened the truck door and bansheed twenty feet into the lot before exhaling. She looked worn, but not defeated as her breath ran in short pulses. *Not bad for a first try,* he thought. She looked up to see his clear eyes.

"Jell-O's inside, I promise." He smiled.

The hushed comfort of the clinic waiting room whispered small dramas. Sitting in sentinel-like chairs, a mom and two children chose bright colors for the houses they drew. Another man, awkwardly stabilized on his crutches, reviewed his precautions with a nurse. An elderly couple sat holding hands, staring out a large window, a pamphlet about cancer treatment protruding from the woman's purse.

"Hi, Twila," Riley said to the receptionist. "Got an appointment with Doc at ten. We're a little early."

"Is this Maggie? Oh, my! You look great! How are you doing?"

Maggie nodded but stepped back to be invisible. "Do I know you?"

"Oh, a little. You're famous around here. We all were pulling for you when you were here at the hospital. Do you remember that?"

"The sheets were clean," she offered, then looked at Riley.

"That's okay, she's being friendly. It's okay to talk with her, Sunshine." They sat in a pair of chairs opposite a television, while Riley picked up the newspaper.

Alexander Hamilton Letter Authenticated

New York City—The letters are broad cursive swirls in iron-gault ink on a small piece of parchment, barely eight- by eight-inches. But the letter's content and its author made history today...

Maggie thumbed through a pretty gardening magazine, while Riley reassuringly rustled the newspaper. Now those are tomatoes, she thought, looking at the article "A Better Tomato—in YOUR Garden!" *Who names tomatoes? Well, maybe tomatoes needed names as much as she did. Once they leave the vine, they still need to know who they are.*

She folded the magazine under her journal, then opened the pages of her first days. Her writing remembered a flash of white, the heavy rhythm that turned her stomach into knots, nightmares, and more recently, learning to sit in the truck.

Ahead of her, a wall-mounted television silently flashed commercials and news, a correct waiting room courtesy. She realized a television was familiar, but from somewhere else. Riley never watched TV. They never had time.

"The Archival Department of the New York Public Library has authenticated a previously unknown letter written by Captain Alexander Hamilton, dated May, 1776 to Washington, where he detailed need for increased resources to support the Revolutionary War, as the English approached the fort in his command..." Riley read silently.

White words in a blue caption line ran at the bottom of the TV screen: "Governor announces reelection bid." *It must be a hot day*, she thought. People in tank tops, shorts, enthusiastically carried banners, sometimes applauded the speaker.

"He was an advocate for Washington's effort and recognized the need for continued American support to unite against the British troops," stated Greyson Nicholas, assistant in the

archives department. "We were given this letter anonymously by an interested citizen who claimed it had been in the family for generations. We wanted to authenticate it, starting with the ink and the parchment, which we found authentic to that period of history," he continued... Amazing, thought Riley. *If they could just trace Maggie with iron-gault ink...*

The TV screen filled with the man's earnest face. His white smile flashed as he spoke. A rally, she thought, suddenly knowing the word, although hadn't thought of in...forever. A man with white teeth and black hair got all this coverage, and she remembered that, at one time, she may have carried a sign or supported a candidate like that.

"...Not until the actual signature could be matched and once Captain Hamilton's presence was verified in the New York area in 1776, could the archival team determine the letter as authentic..."

She looked back at the television. There was something...the man speaking looked sincere, but that wasn't what drew her eyes back to the screen. His hair, black and slicked, was familiar, too, but there was something further...an eerie feeling curled through her blood. She felt her wrist snap again, the pain shooting as she stood up, walked across a driveway. The man's face turned to one side, his left profile intent on a promise. She didn't notice at first, too busy reading the caption: *Governor leads opponents.* But there it was. Again. The something familiar. *His voice, something that scraped against her soul.*

A mole on his left cheek. It reminded her of a fly landing amid his five o'clock shadow. That mole...she'd seen in before...on a hot day. He wasn't happy, he was angry, mean, judgmental, and cruel. *What did you do to the merchandise? I can't have damaged goods.* She blinked, turning her head slightly as if that single movement could lock in memory. *Damaged goods. She wasn't what he wanted.* The long gravel driveway, a big door opening slowly, the cool temperature indoors denied to her, not even a drink, those sharp words...she was part of a deal, something she hadn't agreed to...a pain inside that kept her sharp even though she was used up...

The talking man stabbed fear all the way through her spine until her bones ached. She turned to Riley, his face hidden by the newspaper. Her mouth, stunned open, tried a breath, but she couldn't form any words.

"...*Authentication of the historic letter was delayed, in part due to the abduction—*"

"Riley? Maggie? Doc is ready for you. Come on back."

"But..." was all Maggie could form. She stood, she looked back just as the crowd swallowed the talking man, the speaker. She was frozen. He was the boss of all her hurt.

"Nothing to be afraid of, Sunshine. It's Doc," Riley urged.

She looked from Riley back to the TV screen, her mouth open, her forehead furrowed. The voices had held her so long, and now this face was the one who told the others to throw her away. The one who made decisions, put the others in their places. Walking down the softly lit corridor two steps behind Riley, she looked backward at the screen which now a laundry advertisement. No talking man was there, but he followed her all the same.

Maggie sat across from Riley in the exam room, not aware that Grace and he sat in this very room a few years ago, awaiting new tests, only to find out in a matter of minutes, that nothing more could be done.

"Riley?"

"What, Sunshine? Now, don't worry. Doc wants to see how you're doing. We'll go to the gallery afterwards."

"But I just saw—"

"Hey, you two!" Doc Mattheson emerged from a hallway, an enthusiastic handshake for Riley and a hand grazing Maggie's shoulder. He sat next to her, the rolling stool his best toy in the room, as far as she was concerned. Just as quickly, she saw herself on a scooter, braids snapping behind.

"Remarkable recovery, it truly is, Maggie! Let me have a look at your face. I'll bring my hand up to your eye. Ready?" He felt her eye socket—a little tender when he pressed—felt along her clavicle, then ran his fingers along her jawline. "That night you came to us, Maggie, you were barely breathing. I didn't think you'd survive the night. Ranch life sure was a good choice for your recovery, wasn't it?"

"She's been helping a little, too, Doc, but no heavy lifting."

"Any pain in your face? Any headaches?"

"No, sir."

"Now, let me look at your wrist. Do this for me..." He bent his hand forward and back, then side to side like a windshield wiper. She had more movement, now, she was sure. "I brush Bliss every day like this," she showed brushing motions between herself and Doc.

"And any pain?"

"No, not really."

"This is good, Maggie, really good. We're going to take some x-rays of your clavicle and your wrist. Then, I want to check your inside stitches."

She thought about the talking man, turning his head to his right, the mole on his left cheek. He never checked her stitches, he never did anything. She looked for Riley's reassurance.

When Doc met them back in the exam room, he lifted the gray films against a screen. "Here's your collarbone, Maggie. See any breaks?"

"No."

"See that jagged line? That squiggle line *was* your break. It's healing nicely. Now, this picture is of your wrist."

"Is that the break?"

"*Was* your break. Looks like your healing is fairly complete now. You know what that means?"

"Can I ride horses with my cast tomorrow?"

"No, not with your cast."

Her face fell.

"*Without* the cast. It's coming off today."

Her smile spilled past her teeth, up into her face and jumped into the corners of the room. Riley had the same smile, one she hadn't seen too many times.

"Okay, let's do one more thing. I'll have Riley step out—"

"No!" Her face went dark, the fear rising a cold flood through her body. The talking man stepped into her head, his stern dissatisfied face, while her happiness slithered away through the doorjamb.

"Maggie, this is one time, while Doc does his exam that I can't be here. I'll be right outside the door. I'll be that close. Remember, Doc will explain everything. I won't let him hurt you."

Maggie's toe tapped the floor, like a steady drip from a broken water faucet. She heard her heart saying *"Don't-don't, Don't-don't"* in her ears.

"You trust Doc, right? He helped you survive." Riley's voice led her to a smaller place. She looked at his sad eyes.

"I trust them, but not the talking man."

"Who's that?"

"On TV, the talking man with the mole on his cheek."

"You saw someone on TV today? In the waiting room? But he isn't here, now, right?"

She looked at Riley, at Doc just to be sure. "Right."

"Okay, so I'll stand right outside the door and make sure he doesn't show up. Then you can get ready. How's that?"

"How's this? I'll take my time and tell you everything I'm going to do. If you tell me stop, I will do that," Doc added. "You'll let me know when you're ready. It's all up to you."

A smile tickled recognition across her face. That's what Riley had said.

207

Outside the door, Riley heard the comforting voice at first, the kind words, the swish of paper along the exam table. Grace's voice complaining, *"those damn paper gowns, you're cold enough as it is..."* But as soon as Doc explained lying down, what else would Maggie think? Her panicked "no, no" became more a wail, coyote lonely. Her voice thinned with fear. But she didn't struggle or fight back. No, she probably had learned a broken spirit has no fight. Every instinct in his heart told him to open the door and take away the shadows.

Maggie whimpered softly, agreeing with Doc. Riley took slow breaths and stepped back a few minutes to "the talking man" with a mole. *What the hell? Why would she freeze about someone on TV? Was she having a flashback from a commercial? An actual person interviewed on a talk show? A celebrity? Something had spooked her enough to rocket her anxiety.*

"Good job, Maggie," he heard Doc say. "Those stitches are hardly visible, now. Let's get that cast off now." By the time the exam door opened, Maggie stood, staring at her arm, rubbing the skin as if it were new. Her smile was tepid, but a smile all the same. She had just faced down a memory and came back strong. She was the bravest person he knew.

"Look, I have my arm back!" Maggie waved at Riley. "Now we can do search and rescue."

"Hold on! Who gave you that idea?"

"Griff...and you! Talking about when I healed; when I got better. When I got my cast off."

Riley smiled as he walked with Maggie toward the truck. "Damn, I can't hide anything from you, can I?"

He started up the truck and pulled slowly onto the street. "Tell me again, Maggie, about this 'talking man'. You recognized him?"

They drove slowly with Maggie tracking the sky toward Marta's. Her arm buzzed alive with the breeze on her arm, the sun warming her right side directly, the clean Arizona late morning welcoming her arm into movement again.

"He was on TV while we were in the waiting room. He was talking. He had black hair, really shiny black hair, and white teeth that made you stare. And he had a mole...right here." She pointed to her left cheek, then rubbed her arm again. Her hand was tan, but her arm was pale. A farmer's tan, she remembered.

"Was he on a TV show? Or a commercial?"

"He was on TV talking to people. They were cheering."

Riley's brow pulled a quick squeeze together.

"They liked him. They clapped. But I knew I wouldn't. I didn't like him at all..."

"Was he someone you recognized from before you came here?"

Her memory didn't work that way, making connections like that, from before-to-now. Pieces slid and shifted through her head, like a thin curtain folding onto itself, blocking the view, distorting what she thought she saw. She'd try to recall it, but the curtain folded differently and much too soon. The image faded with the lost light.

"All I remember is standing in a driveway. It was hot. He was mad at the others because the deal was bad. He smiled today, a lot. But I don't remember his smiling before. There was a big door, but I couldn't go in."

"Anything else?"

"I was afraid of him."

Riley nodded. "We'll tell Griff about this, okay? This sounds pretty important that can help him. But in the meantime, why don't we celebrate that cast disappearing? A mocha and a raspberry scone at Marta's?"

"Say that again."

"A mocha and a raspberry scone?"

"Mocha sounds like something I would visit."

They parked by Marta's. She opened the truck door,

evenly, no panic darting through her. Maybe she left it back with the cast. Her heart curved a happiness around the order of fancy coffee, something she may have tried before. Once inside Marta's, she heard voices calling out impossible combination like vanilla frappe or Americano grande, two shots. The musky aroma of coffee roasting smelled like the earth itself. The scrape of chairs, the music in the background, the tables along the wall snapped her eyes from one group to the next, as if looking for someone familiar.

"It's like merry...merry..."

"No, it's Marta's, not Mary."

She had done this fancy coffee thing before, not here, but somewhere before with tall windows and people in leggings or suits or jackets, with tiny billfolds, headbands, and credit cards. Sixteen-ounce cups with sleeves, the thump-thump behind the machine, a young woman swooshing something frothy...merry, merry something. And when she took a sip of her mocha, the insistent and perfect chocolate and coffee mixture slid along her palate, a warm sweetness, a titch of bitter to get the day started.

"It's not Jell-O!" she called out against the thumps in the background. "This is from before. I know it, Riley. I know this coffee from before." Her excitement pushed her outside, then a dead stop on the sidewalk. Riley grabbed the pastries and ducked past customers to find her next to the truck. First one foot, then the other back and forth holding her balance, holding the coffee cup with both hands.

"I know this, I know this! I'm not sure where or how, but everything, everything was familiar. This?" She raised her coffee cup. "This is heaven. It's my favorite, coffee and chocolate. This is the best, the best."

"I'll order mochas from Marta's more often!"

"It's one of my good memories, Riley. And I don't remember it all, but I remembered it just like that as soon as I took a sip. Oh, this is so good!" She took another sip, then savored it before swallowing. "I haven't been here before, have I?"

"No, but I bet you've had mochas before, by your reaction. So, let's go find Hannah and tell her the good news."

She held on tightly to the cup, feeling her right arm as a partner to the left, her right arm working as it should to hold that cup. But even more, she wanted to keep that connection, the complete circle that ran through her arms and into her heart, the connection that she existed before Arizona, the connection she just discovered.

CHAPTER
THIRTY-FOUR

MAGGIE'S JOURNAL

I had lots of surprises today. Going to Copper Station in the truck with Riley, with no breaks to catch my breath. Seeing the eagle. Seeing Doc and getting my cast off. Seeing the talking man scared me—my heart ran over mountains, into the canyon, going fast and far away. I didn't like how I felt, looking at him, and yet, I wanted to look at him until I figured out who he was to me. I can't connect him yet; he made me think of knives and flat, calculating voices. Gave me chills. Still does. Yet I need to know.

Oh! And mocha! That was the best. I know it by a different name, I think. Merry something, but for now, I'll go with mocha. Talk about a connection. For once, I knew something from before Arizona and don't ask me how. I felt that I belonged somewhere, that I had others in my life.

Ten Winds Gallery. Well, Hannah is never sad especially at the gallery. She sweeps her happiness toward anyone in the room. *Look at you, kiddo, where's your cast?* She asks right away. I say it loud, "I got my arm back today." I smile, waving my arm at her; my arm feels fifty pounds lighter, and I know that's an exaggeration, but that's what it feels like, anyway. Anyone would be happy at Ten Winds. I see weavings and paintings and cups with a black matte finish, cups with freckles in the glaze. The glass mobile in the window lets me watch the light dance through it, like frozen bubbles rotating in slow motion on the walls. I would go again, sweating the ride, just to see the beautiful things.

There are sad pictures, too. One ran cold chills through me—a black-and-white photo of an abandoned gas station, the shadows cleanly angled through the gas pumps. In the background, rough walls of rocks and stones nearly filled the sky. The road was there, but it was tiny, smaller and smaller so I knew I couldn't fit on that road if I tried. But it was no place anyone should go. I know because I was there, once. I don't know when, but I felt old panic as soon as I saw that photo of a gas station that really should be torn down for all the horrible things that happened there.

But Hannah hugs me, wants to know what I like about the gallery. I tell her about the sad picture, that I'd never want to be there again. Riley almost says something. If the van were parked just right, no one could see it, I think, but I don't say this, because, with no sky in the gallery, I don't know if I can look up. *Lookie, Lookie,* a voice says, reaching for his belt buckle.

The pictures are part of a new show, featuring Michael No Trees, Hannah says. *You remember him, don't you, Riley? He was a teenager when he came out to help after*—and she doesn't finish because Riley knows what she means and she's embarrassed. It has to be about Grace. That's what always happens; they always say something but don't say her name. She pulls another one from the floor. But look at this one, a black-and-white picture of horses. Recognize anyone? She hints. I look at the white and gray forms in the photograph. Bliss heading toward the pasture, but had turned partially back, tail mid-swish from flies. Cartwheel peers over Bliss' back near the barn door. Michael No Trees calls it "My Friends," and I like that picture because they are my friends, too.

Griff is bringing something from Rosa's for lunch, that's another surprise, too. I haven't been out to eat forever, it seems. And I get mocha and Rosa's all in one day. Hannah, Riley, and I walk to the back of the gallery, through a secret back door and onto an outside patio, another surprise. A courtyard of sunshine and vines and a picnic table with a brightly colored runner on top. Lattice makes a lacy roof, and tiny white lights weave through the holes. The sun makes thin line shadows along the tabletop from those overhead slats. I want to adjust our paper plates to sit on the shadows, but the shadows move almost like ghosts. How silly to hold a shadow.

"You should try this," Hannah says, "I made it myself." It's not killer cheesecake. She hands me lemonade. I remember someone handing me lemonade, too, near a white table, roses nearby. A kiss of summer like watermelon and strawberry shortcake, too. But I taste it and for a second, that sharp citrus fills my mouth and my lip buckles. Then an instant surprise.

"That's the cinnamon I add. Like it?" she says.

"It's the best lemonade ever; it's my favorite." Now, I want more summer in my mouth.

"I think she likes it," Hannah says, looking at me but talking as if I'm not there. And maybe I'm not really. But I forgive her, because a tail of her long black hair travels past her shoulder and slips straight like the truth down past her collarbone. She pours again, her arms sparkling with tiny sliver bangles that catch the sun like stars, tracing the sun in thin arcs across the table. She pretends to squeeze lemons when describing her *lemonade, and her hands are strong.*

*She looks up past my shoulder and says, "There he is."
Griff carries large bags with foil-covered pans past my ear to
place them on the table. He moves by me quickly, but I don't
jump, because Hannah warned me with "there he is." That's
how I knew. They lift lids: rice, beans, chicken, tortillas, cheese,
corn, and salsa mix their aromas right up to my nose. "You've
never had this before," Griff assures me. And, it's true; I'd not
eaten since breakfast.*

*Riley sits next to me and tells me his favorite is enchiladas.
"No," Hannah says, "the soft tacos." They discuss pinto beans
or black beans, and why do they call them "turtle beans" anyway? Griff laughs. I watch as if my life depends on these details.*

*"Here, Sunshine, try this." Riley places an enchilada on my
plate.*

*"How about Rosa's tortilla soup?" Hannah asks, her spoon
suspended. "Isn't that the best?"*

*"I don't know," says Riley. "It needs more tomatoes, I
think."*

I giggle. Leave it to Riley to think of tomatoes.

*"Taco Canyon's soup is spicier," says Griff. "But this will
do."*

*How do they remember so much? He adds more sauce and
already his forehead has formed a small army of sweat to fight
back the sauce.*

*I look up from my enchilada to see Riley's strong eyes turn
into crinkly blue smiles. He tips his hat back. They laugh, the
musical lift of an ordinary giggle climbs past the walls and
vines. I want to laugh like that, too. It's been too long. I'd forgotten how the rush of air pushes from the lungs in pulses, not
like when I cry. It's bigger when I laugh, that giddy slip of escaped air. Their laughter is stronger than the black-and-white
photos, the talking man with black hair and white teeth. Their*

laughter snakes orange, green, and aqua through me to help me remember this time again and again. Turquoise sky, the solid wooden table, the warmth of the sun on my new right arm, and the laughter coloring the corner I've just turned, walking away the sad.

Griff, too, heartily laughs. He makes a joke. They're turtle beans because you eat them slowly. His head tilts back, his mouth wide open, eyes slit shut, that rush of air full of happiness reaching toward the sky, giving God a breath.

CHAPTER
THIRTY-FIVE

Griff's laughter calmed his early frustration. He needed a normal meal with his friends to pluck him out of the weight of evidence in Mitchell Canyon. His rancher friend, a testament to friendship, and Maggie, now with both functioning arms, sat dissecting enchiladas. Maggie was still clumsy and weak with her right hand, but took it in stride, while Riley's patience was a condiment he shared more frequently now. Griff found his way back to sanity and the ease of a smile relax his face.

Yet, he couldn't shut off his memory, a slide show of evidence he was juggling: bullet casings, a bullet-ridden van, mystery helicopters, Many Devils photo-bombing the evidence of the bodies, mix-and-match DNA. Then, the maggot stomachs. He needed another laugh or the headache slowly forming at the back of his neck was going to take up permanent residence.

All because this young lady sitting across from him, who some may think is dead, is at this very moment contemplating whether to add salsa to her enchilada. Normally, he liked puzzles.

Instead, he laughed. He kicked back that tight neck to sift the headache out of his body.

"Riley tells me you're remembering a little more." The salsa triggering a mild sweat that Griff felt across his forehead.

"Like the talking man?"

"Who's that?"

"Someone she recognized on TV today when we were waiting at the clinic. I didn't see him, but Maggie said he was familiar. Remembered details about others with her and a long driveway. The man had black hair, white teeth, and a mole on his cheek."

Griff's eyebrows shrugged. "Maybe now's a good a time as any to browse through the mug shots. Maybe that face is there. That's a lot to remember all of a sudden."

She seemed so small, later, sitting across from Griff's desk, the mug shot books closed to keep her attention.

"These notebooks have pictures, portraits of men when they've entered jail or prison here in Arizona. If you look through them, maybe a face will stand out, help you remember." Griff pushed the first notebook toward Maggie.

"You ready, Maggie?" Riley stood behind her, so proud of her accomplishments this long day. Now, he was asking her again, not so much to get permission or to give reassurance, but more of a reminder that, in looking at these pictures, ghosts might jump from the pages and beat her home.

She looked at Riley as he leaned against Griff's open door. "Okay."

The book creaked open to a set of somber faces staring at her. Most were sad, but some angrily focused their eyes, accusing those who look their way. No one smiled, though, to show white teeth. No suit jackets or ties or banners waving. Her happiness from the lemonade and enchilada slowly drained with each gray page. Each picture had a story, as unknown as her own life. She wasn't casual, either, studying each picture, running a finger along a jawbone or hairline, staring into paper eyes that always stared back. She looked at the eyes first, then the whole face. But she found no connection, certainly no reaction like today with the talking man on TV at the clinic. With one final deep breath, she closed the books.

"Nobody," she said. It was kind of like a sad joke because she was a nobody too. And every one of the pictures were nobodies if you thought about it. "I don't see anything here." Her deep exhale was neither disappointment nor relief.

"Okay, okay." Griff nodded. "Well, believe it or not, that's something. Truth is, I think the men that held you in the van were working for someone else, and came from someplace else, too. But they won't bother you anymore."

"You know that?"

"They were killed a few weeks ago. They're gone."

"Oh."

"But, they held the secret to who you are. Maybe the talking man, does too," Riley added.

"See, the van was in a crash and pretty banged up. What I could do is show you pictures of the van, as we found it. Do you think you might recognize it?" He pulled a brown envelope from his desk. "I gotta ask you, Maggie, these pictures— look familiar?"

He spread the van pictures across his desk, trying not to guide her toward confirming anything. They were gruesome, not your everyday crime pictures. But he carefully selected ones that didn't reveal body parts.

She tilted her head as if it were falling sideways. Her furrowed brow hid her eyes as she scanned the pictures of distorted, crumpled metal, the door in an accordion squeeze slammed against the side, the bullet holes, the shattered glass mixed with shards of mirror, scattered against the floor of the ravine.

"What *is* this?" she whispered.

"We think, Maggie, you were in this van."

She gasped, eyes widened, pushing the pictures away, then gradually pulling them closer, one by one, as if to fall into the photo herself. She inched through each section of the photos: a crushed frame that once held a windshield; the roof peeled back like the top of a sardine can; the flattened driver's seat, the door gaping open like a grave, the remaining portion twisted like a version of car yoga. She stared at the back seat, again, then again. She noticed a seat belt tied like a knot. Her eyes slammed, stunned by that fabric.

She heard her screams again, felt the struggle. *Stay here, little princess, don't fight.*

"Here," she whispered. Riley leaned forward stroking the nape of her neck briefly. Her breath quickened. The images were coming at her too quickly, much too dark at first. Then, she sucked in a deep breath. She would identify this, if only once.

"Here, this seatbelt. This...this knot...They used it to tie my hands, so I couldn't fight. That's how I broke—" She raised her right arm, her arm able to speak because her throat wouldn't let her. At the same time, she reached up near her neck, finding Riley's hand. The warmth of his fingers, just then, clipped her heart open, feeling vulnerability like a torn quilt.

"You could swear to that in court?" Griff's urgent voice continued. "You sure?"

She nodded heavily. "I remember that."

The speed at which Griff grabbed the telephone and dialed the state lab's number by heart told her she just said something important. Everything else for her was a slow-motion movie.

"Dan? Hey, it's Griff. I want DNA from that back seat belt on the driver's side. The one with the knot? I want it today."

Dan replied in a squiggly voice, just as Maggie suddenly

put her hands to her face. Riley's hands rested lightly on her shoulders.

"You've been very helpful, today, Maggie. I know that wasn't easy. I'm sure we'll get a break here, soon, and catch the guys that set this whole thing up. Maybe what you remembered today will be the connection to your past."

Memories don't work that way, she wanted to say. *You can remember that you like one kind of bean or a certain kind of chili, or that your favorite lemonade has cinnamon in it. I don't always remember what cinnamon is, let alone if I had breakfast. Other than Jell-O. I seem to remember Jell-O really well. But that's not like remembering a seat belt and these men raping me over and over again. Connecting to my past may be one of the most gruesome things I ever do, like seeing that sad photo at the gallery today. I knew I'd been there. My memory and connections are tricksters, sometimes.*

"I'll get the DNA report and see if there is anything new on the dental records."

Maggie felt beaten for the second time today.

"Let's head home, Sunshine. I bet we've got some horses that want a little attention." Riley tried to sound happy, but Maggie read what his face told.

Griff grabbed his hat from the coat rack. "Sounds like we're done here, then. I'll let you know as soon as I hear something." He pulled the door closed behind him as the others exited.

In the silence that followed, a car's windshield reflected the afternoon sun onto Griff's wall where the door had been opened, onto something that had been hidden. Like a spotlight highlighting a soliloquy in a play, the reflection highlighted a picture of a man in his forties, black hair pulled away from his face, a solid winning smile showing white teeth, just a hint of a mark on his left cheek. The picture could be found on all state offices, placed prominently on the walls near the state seal of Arizona. The portrait of Governor Boyd Mullengrath.

CHAPTER
THIRTY-SIX

"Your turn to feed Poke," Riley said, finishing up breakfast at the stove. Maggie had learned the routine: open the pantry, open the food bin, one-two scoops of food into Poke's dish, then let the dog snowplow toward the food dish to gobble up his breakfast.

"I forgot something." She paused.

"Poke's water." Riley nodded, pouring the juice and coffee. "He'll need water outside, too. Don't forget his water bowl in the barn." He looked up, her hands working together with ease, it seemed. The bruises were a memory, much the same as her cast, yet her memories were still spare when she reined in her past. She was energetic and devoted when it came to Bliss and Cartwheel.

She sat at the table, eating with her right hand more consistently now, less awkwardly. She had ridden Bliss a few times already, only when Riley led the horse around the barn and into the pasture. She sat as tall on her chair right now, looking out the window, the way she often did, in anticipation of the day.

"Are we riding again today?"

"Maybe later on. We'll feed the horses and clean the barn first."

Her head dropped a floor or two.

"But a late-afternoon ride is a treat, don't you think?"

She smiled. "Dibs on Bliss."

"So, Maggie, I gotta ask you. You mentioned it the other day. And Griff's been dogging me about it. Search and rescue. Do you understand what that entails?"

"Horses." She chewed her toast.

"Well, yes, but other horses, not just Bliss and Cartwheel."

"That's good, right?"

"It's more work and special work. We have to train younger horses, ones with a little more spirit and spunk, to get comfortable with walking through lots of terrain, in water, using their instincts to help track people who are lost or hurt."

"Like you and Griff when you found me."

"Yeah, just like that. But now, it's a horse AND a person working together. It's a lot of training. Do you think you could help me?"

"I don't have a cast anymore. And I'm stronger, you said so yourself." She swallowed juice.

"It takes more than strength and you'll have to do what I say. It won't be easy, but it's very rewarding work."

"You're teaching the horses to find people that need help. That's a good thing. So, why don't you want to do it?"

Riley's face twisted slightly. "Who said I didn't want to do it?"

"Because you've never said 'yes' when Griff asked you." She stopped and stared at Riley.

The coffee swallow wouldn't push past his throat. He had confidence that Maggie could do anything he asked of her. No, it wasn't Maggie, it was who was missing. Grace wasn't here to guide them both. His tongue pumped tiny swallows until his throat opened up. Funny how Maggie was the only one who was allowed to talk about Grace so freely. And while he was caught off guard when Maggie approached Grace in some way, he still was relieved that someone else gave him permission to talk about her and to keep Grace in the room.

"You know, Grace did most of the training before. I just helped."

"So now it's up to you," Maggie nodded. "That makes sense, right?"

"Yes, Sunshine, it does. But can *you* help *me*, is the question. Can you be available to help with the training, the feeding, the cleaning, the shots—?"

"We do that now, don't we?"

For the life of him, Riley was not able to talk Maggie or himself out of this anymore. Search and rescue needed to be continued. And, by some freaky coincidence, Maggie was here at the ranch to help him do it.

Gloves. That second skin that picked up wood, dug soil, lifted fence poles, and adjusted the bit against the soft corners of a horse's mouth. When he needed to, Riley bit a fingertip and pulled his glove off in one movement, often to have a better feel for rubbing a forelock or applying a shot. He'd tuck the gloves in his back pocket or throw them on a hay bale, then damn! Like an errant sock that walks from the laundry, a glove came up missing. What did it do—handstands up the road? Dog paddle across the river? Hitch a ride into town?

Grace would laugh. *You're as bad as me*, she'd chuckle. We probably go through a pair of gloves every other month. Between us, we'd have a pair of gloves a blind man would use.

He watched Maggie pour water for Poke, then scoop the food for Bliss, suddenly realizing she had no gloves. Not the good kind, but the leather ones that grow to fit like a good personality.

"You know, Sunshine. We're gonna have to go to town today."

"What for?"

"I need some groceries, and I need to meet up with Griff...and... look at your hands!"

She put down the feed bucket, her face pursed over her flat palms. "What?"

He walked toward her extending his hand, slowly. "Here, see that? That's a callous."

"So?"

"You need some decent gloves. What do you say?" He smiled. For a second, a thought passed through his head. He still had Grace's gloves. *What if Maggie's gloves outlive her stay? What was he asking her about leaving or staying or just going to town?*

"Are you getting new gloves too?"

"I guess I'm gonna have to, if we get search and rescue training started again. That's what we'll talk to Griff about. I'll need new gloves, too; new chapter, huh?"

"For real? We're training Griff's horses?"

"I can't deny, Maggie, you've got a real connection with the horses. You're capable and devoted in lots of ways. Two more horses wouldn't be that much more with you working with me."

He put his mind into checklist mode as he drove: meet with Griff, clean the barn, straighten the empty stalls for new residents, order hay and feed, find a good horse auction...Insurance, he'd forgotten that. Oh, and the medicine. He might have to order more.

Grace's voice whispered through Riley's thoughts. Didn't I tell you things would work out? You're getting back into life.

"Okay, okay," he muttered.

"What's okay?" Maggie asked.

"Uh, well, getting back into search and rescue, of course."

Of course, Grace chuckled.

As they curved around the river's bend, he noticed Maggie wasn't holding her breath, wasn't counting, she relaxed, her arms not spring-loaded to jump from the car when they slowed. The passenger window open so she could look up at the sky, drink the wind because she could. She leaned into the curve around the river, not stiff like a two-by-four. Other than her active tap in her foot, she seemed to be enjoying the ride.

You buy gloves because they'll tell stories. They darken with use, mold to hand fit. It doesn't take much to trace fingertips and bite marks and scratches and the sweat of a hard day's work or the rain of a thunder wash on a pair of gloves. So, here's someone barely a story, getting her first gloves. What will those gloves tell about her? Will Maggie see the story in her hands before she finds it on her face?

It's just a pair of gloves, Riley.

That's true, he thought. But what if those gloves are more to me than to her? What if those gloves stay behind?

They're gloves, Riley, Grace insisted between his ears, not a wedding ring!

"Jesus!" He hit the steering wheel.

Maggie flinched. "No, don't!"

"Sorry, Maggie, sorry. I've got an argument going in my head. Ever have one of those?"

"Maybe...is it like the voices?"

"No, not at all like that...but I'm not winning." He chuckled.

"Maybe you need to listen again." Maggie relaxed into a smile.

Good girl. I like her, Riley, Grace added.

He pulled into the parking space in front of Copper Western Store. "Ready to be a ranch hand? Let's get some gloves, some that fit really well."

They entered the air-conditioned store, wood floors creaking with their weight toward the counter. "Let's have Hank measure your hand. You might be a medium, I'd guess."

She pulled her hand immediately away from Hank's enthusiasm, not because he might hurt her, she could tell that better now, but because he moved with too quick a smile.

"Let me," Riley said softly. She placed her hand toward Riley, a small but trusting gesture. He took two quick measures, then, for a second, her small trust rushed into his throat and choked him. She'd come so far from fighting those lavender massages.

Hank nodded, brought a pair of fresh leather work gloves. "Helping Riley with the horses?" He smiled.

She tugged on the gloves, something she'd seen Riley do before and now understood why. Gloves had a little fight in them. "Yeah, the horses. Everything." She snugged the corners between her fingers, then made a fist, like Riley's.

"Is that good?" Her face lifted, eyes squinted against the seams, her hands extended. "What do you think?"

"Looks like you're officially a ranch hand." Riley smiled.

She still tugged the gloves, tucking the spaces between the spaces when they left the store, walking toward the sheriff's office.

"Those are mighty fine gloves," Griff said from across the street.

"Hey, Griff. We were just coming to see you."

"What's up?"

Riley shuffled his toe, as if his foot were ready to apologize for such a delay in what he was about to say. "I...I mean, we...Maggie and I were talking...we, well, we are ready for some horses...for search and rescue. You've been after me for a year to start up training, and you need new ones, you said yourself. Since I've got someone to help me, well..."

"Well, I'll be. That's great news, Riley!"

"I've kind of been out of touch with things, so I'm not sure when the next auction is, but I would like you to come along."

"So, what did you have to do, Maggie, to convince Riley?"

"I got my cast off. And I have gloves."

"She's getting pretty good at riding, too, Griff. I can clean out the empty stalls probably within the week—"

"All right! All right!" Griff's hands flew up. "I'll talk to the council members, see when the next auction is, and we'll go from there."

The two men shook gloved hands. Then Griff offered his hand to Maggie. Her gloves met his, a firm powerful shake of hands with that stronger right arm. A connection through the leather: to shake a hand in agreement, a willingness to partner in a new adventure. Her adventure. A new chapter, Riley called it. She was officially a ranch hand.

CHAPTER
THIRTY-SEVEN

Hannah's written grocery list for the upcoming Grace meal held Grace memories, not just tomatoes or mushrooms or buttermilk or enchiladas. Her handwriting on the recipes, the splatters from previous meals across the cards, the additional notes in the margin in her hand ("Hot sauce packs a wallop!"). Grace was right back in the middle of the room. Maggie thumbed through her recipe box with Hannah one more time before the trip to town.

"This recipe box is jammed full and you know? I can't help but think I've done something like this before," Maggie said softly.

"You mean cook? Plan a dinner?"

"No, something else." Maggie flipped open and shut the lid of the recipe box, the roosters on its lid disappearing then reappearing in the exact position each time. "No, it's the recipe box."

Hannah shook her head, the list temporarily pushed aside.

"My life. Before...had something to do with boxes like this." Maggie held the box above her head, twisted it from side to side as if she were looking for a Rubik's solution.

"She loved cooking, trying new ones, saving recipes...they were like little journeys for her. Maybe *you* were a chef."

"But, you notice, she didn't organize them. Look—here. What's the first recipe under chicken?"

Hannah tugged a card from the section. "Lamb stew?" She giggled. "Maybe she made a chicken stew with some of these ingredients."

"So, why not rewrite it? Makes no sense."

"Oh, that one I know. It took too much time." The kitchen always seemed to be a flurry of activity when Grace was there and not just cooking. She could feed Poke, call the vet about Bliss' meds, and check on Riley's clothes in the laundry, all while she was making chicken—or lamb—stew. "She was amazing," Hannah summarized. "But I'll save that confusion for another day. We've got to hit the road, so we can get back for all the prep. You sure you'll be fine going to town with me?"

Hitting the road sounded like a difficult thing to do. *Had she hit the road before? Did Hannah use a hammer or a tree branch or a steel rod or a rope? If they were in a hurry, wouldn't it take extra time to stop and hit the road instead of drive on it?* So, while Hannah pulled the baseball cap low over her eyes, squished the car keys and grocery list in her hand, she pushed open Riley's kitchen door. Maggie followed to hit the road. Hannah's yellow car with "Ten Winds Gallery" printed on the side doors wasn't a black threat. Not like Riley's truck. Riding to town, despite hitting the road, would not be a problem.

If Grace had a journey cooking recipes, Maggie was having an adventure going to the grocery store. The automatic door rumbled open when someone walked by or into the store, knowing how long to pause, then closed with a cough. Maggie remembered grocery stores by the time she entered the produce aisle. *Wouldn't Riley's garden be jealous!* All these fresh foods for the taking, already picked, in unison, letting Maggie know they were ready. She remembered sitting in the upper seat of the cart and reaching for pretty cans. But it never made sense to sit backwards; you only saw where you've been.

"Maggie, you all right?"

"Mm-hmm. Been a while since I've seen a grocery store. I remember grocery carts and the sound they make. You always find one with a lazy wheel that's stuck to the floor a half beat longer that the other wheels."

"Kiddo, I bet ours will be darn near filled to the top by the time we leave."

"Attention, shoppers! Today at Kerr's Food Mart, look for deli turkey on special for just $1.49 a pound. Your sandwiches will be a hit during the summer days with our great-tasting deli turkey! And thanks for shopping Kerr's Food Mart!"

"Do we need deli turkey? That voice made it sound important."

"No," Hannah's voice faded around the next aisle. "No, we'll get chicken."

Deli turkey, deli turkey, Maggie thought. She must have had deli turkey at one time.

In her thoughts and distractions, Maggie fell behind, looking at the cans, remembering peas, Hamburger Helper, apricots. She knew she once likely bought those things. Something about reaching across a high counter for something delicious and inviting, wrapped in thin paper, too. She looked at yellow packages, red cans, blue wrappers, at cookies or canned milk or beans, stunned by the pure volume of items on the shelf; items she felt had to be in the cart, at least one of each of them to be sure she remembered them all.

"Good morning from Kerr's Food Mart. How about a special touch for your meal tonight? Garlic bread in our bakery is featured at $1.89 for a two pack! Stop by the bakery for a

sample. *And thanks for shopping Kerr's Food Mart.*"

Garlic bread. Surely she'd had that before.

She wandered toward the back of the store, where Hannah was scouring the dairy case for sour cream. "You get lost?" Hannah chuckled.

"It's all...so...new and big," said Maggie in a soft voice. "It's amazing; people eat all this food." She had a flash of a convenience store where cookies, snacks, and chips were the main staple. That and beer. You didn't have a garden of produce before you, let alone five kinds of lettuce or berries. She remembered craving something green. *Look, bitch, get the damn donuts so we can hit the road.* Ohhh, that's right. *She's hit the road before, and she didn't like it.*

But with Hannah, she didn't hit anything. "Let's head to the meat department. You know what we'll find there?"

"Deli turkey?"

"Naw. Chicken! For the enchiladas!"

"Can we buy Jell-O?"

Maggie liked how Hannah cruised up and down the aisles, carefully eyeing the shelves, while the cart's belly filled with more items. Near the beer cooler, Hannah slowed for microbrew choices. That's when Maggie heard—not the invisible voice overhead—but a pulsing, a pounding, a strained voice pushing out syllables like tiny explosions. It was the sound she despised, the rhythmic alternative to music she'd heard when she hit the road, an excuse to beat her, slap her, rape her.

Two young teens walked by, one with this rhythm calling out from a sleeve on his arm. Maggie's feet peeled from the floor, her arms trying to fly as she ran up one aisle, then across the next. A door, a door, some place where she could get away this time, they couldn't follow her in this big space. Her feet pounded against dense linoleum-covered floors, a slap-slap that burned through her feet and let them fly farther from that excuse for music. The van felt right up against her skin as she ran, the scratchy floor, the piss and alcohol smell. She swore she heard the invisible voice overhead.

"Attention shoppers! Thanks for running in Kerr's Food Mart. We want this woman to get away before the door closes. Attention, don't let her get caught. She'll lose herself all over again and you won't even know she's missing. And thanks for running in Kerr's Food Mart."

"Maggie!" Hannah's panic swiveled her head up the aisle watching Maggie flee from whatever it was that strung her into running away. "Maggie!" she screamed and chased her up the aisle pushing the cumbersome cart, now resistive to quick movement.

Clearing the entrance at the front, now crowded with shoppers and full carts and traffic entering the store, Maggie was oblivious to the stares and approaching cars. Horns blared and angry faces stared at her when she stopped and started unpredictable directions, running, running, her breath seizing her lungs.

"Maggie! Stop! Maggie!" Hannah shoved the cart to one side, food juggling for position. She snaked through the pedestrians staring at the wild woman in the lot, the chaos none of them understood. Her hair swooped from her head like a dark angel wing cutting the corner toward her friend.

"Maggie, slow down!"

Another car with windows open, spilling out that same pulsing beat, shook Maggie's heart. The car's youthful inhabitants wanted the prime parking space where Maggie was standing. "Hey, move it! Get out of the way!" ...*'bitch, you're going the wrong way. Get your ass over here.* The pounding and yelling wouldn't quit now. She ran behind the car, gasping so deeply, her lungs were catching fire.

That was enough of a pause for Hannah to close in near a fence of cars at the back of the parking lot. Maggie was doubled over, her legs throbbing from the speed of her heart rate, her lungs piercing with sharp breaths.

"Maggie!" Hannah ran up behind, quick steps that Maggie's brain heard as chasing. She turned quickly, her left arm instinctively pushing Hannah away with a scream. Her hand rose toward Hannah's throat.

"No! Stop, Maggie!"

Hannah's voice etched something, a scratchy needle playing a familiar record in an attic. The voices and pounding faded, Hannah standing before her just as out of breath as she was but holding Maggie's hand in midair.

Hannah had learned early in her art classes with the high school and rez kids that sometimes the images didn't agree, the paint or clay was misunderstood, and tempers ignited. Griff taught her some nonviolent de-escalation techniques that helped restore the class, while still fostering independent thinking and creativity. The de-escalation for Maggie needed to be immediate to notch things down.

"Maggie, it's me, Hannah. You're with me, remember? I'm going to let go of your hand, slowly. That's it, that's it."

Maggie's heartbeat slowed with each word, with each familiar line of Hannah's face coming back into focus, the black hair scooped back catching a breeze here and there.

"Oh, Hannah," she whispered. "What did I just do?"

Hannah slowly inched closer toward Maggie's shoulders then carefully hugged her. "You panicked, kiddo. I don't know what it was that set you into panic mode, but you were out of that store before I could turn the cart around. But you're back, right? You're with me, right?"

Maggie nodded, her face flushed with tears.

"You still able to shop with me? It's busy today. You probably went into overload."

"There's no van, right?"

"No, kiddo, no van. But we still have to pay for our food and take it home. Can you focus on that?"

Maggie nodded, but she wasn't sure she would ever hit the road again.

MAGGIE'S JOURNAL

It's called rap.

I hate it. I hear the pounding and I feel their bodies pressed against me, pushing toward me, in me, out of me. Again. Again. I hear screams and wailing. It's me, pleading, no, please, no. They won't stop, the music, if you call it that, won't stop. I can't hear the words. Why would music sound so angry and mean?

I hate it.

It turns me into a liquid panic, where running isn't fast enough to get away. I know I embarrassed Hannah today, and I embarrassed myself, and I probably embarrassed Riley when Hannah told him what happened. I don't remember much, other than running like hell. Panic shot through me like rocket fuel, and before I figured out what was going on, I nearly hit Hannah when I landed. If felt like I was running through a never-ending street with nothing but regret in my exhaust.

Poke wouldn't like rap, I know. Riley doesn't, he told me. He likes the sad country songs where tears wash midnight and feel the long-forgotten touch. The words are true in those songs, and you can understand the heartbreak in each one.

Hannah likes Native flute music. She played it for me on her CD player on the way home. It sounds like canyon echoes and feels like smoke from a lazy campfire. Griff loves rock and roll, she said, and once in a while, I hear a song on the radio that reminds me I used to like it too. He smiles and nods his head in time to the radio, she said. Before you know it, you forget he's a sheriff, more like the guy you'd be sitting next to at a concert.

You know what Riley said? He said I had every right to run away, because my heart still wants to run from the guys who did this to me. He said it's too bad that it scared Hannah so much. It's too bad Copper Station didn't understand at the grocery store.

I told him about hitting the road, and he chuckled. Know what he said? He would never hit the road again. Sounds good to me.

CHAPTER
THIRTY-EIGHT

Riley squinted against the cobweb shadows as they whispered beneath the planks and the sawhorses. He had purposely stored them in an empty corner of the barn to avoid them, in the same way Grace had been tucked into his memory. Those planks seemed a little like a monument to late summer with Grace and friends. And now Maggie wanted to exhume her memory with a Grace meal. Well, come to think of it, maybe he did too.

The planks, the foundation of their outdoor dining table, were personally chosen by Grace for their rustic sturdiness, not because they could be neglected and still have function. He rubbed away the dust, as if erasing those years were that easy, the treasure of Grace, still there.

Grace had been reading *Sense and Sensibility* those last months when she still could follow the plot. Entertaining, she'd say, a way to escape cancer's own story, a way to keep busy when she lost the energy to walk to the barn. At some point, she put the book down, a ribbon as a bookmark, a third of the way through the eighth chapter, a reminder to pick up and continue. But she never did. After her death, it became too much of a heartbreak to see that book unfinished, much like her life. When getting Maggie's room ready, Riley finally wiped the leather cover of dust, then stored it with her leather work gloves in his third drawer, ribbon untouched.

And now, because of Maggie again, he brushed the planks, pulled them into the sun, hosed them down and did the same to the sawhorses. The wood had grayed. It was no surprise they needed attention, but still willing to be Grace's table again. A deep sigh. A page had turned, and Riley held the book.

"How's that arm, Maggie? Think you can help me rub oil into these planks?" He showed her how to oil the surface, then swipe with the rag in the grain's direction. Maggie watched the dull gray transform into a warmer brown.

"I smell Christmas." Her eyes widened. "Why would I do that? Why would I smell orange oil and think Christmas?"

"Sometimes people bake at Christmas or cut up oranges for Christmas breakfast," Riley offered. "Some people think oranges smell something like a fresh-cut Christmas tree—"

"Christmas trees! That's it! I totally forgot Christmas trees!" She stood, upright in the pure gold of the sun, thinking about ornaments and lights. "I had a Mickey and Minnie Mouse ornament, when I was little. And a silver bell, too. I loved Minnie's polka dot dress." Her voice filtered into a breath. Maybe she was lost somewhere in a snow drift or amid boxes with ribbons, but like all the other memories, faded quickly. "Wow, all that from orange oil."

Riley brought Bliss from the barn. "See, Sunshine? All those aren't bad memories. Christmas trees, Minnie Mouse, fancy coffee—" Maybe they don't connect yet with bigger memories that people with two names have. Our memories move in the same room as we do, Riley thought, but for Maggie, it's something like watching a screen.

Just then, they heard an eerie half-cry, half-scream, like a giant comb scraped across the mountain. The echo chilled her spine, again and again.

Riley squinted under the shadow of his hat, looking north into the outcroppings above his pasture. "It came from up there," he whispered. "Sounded like Many Devils. I've never known him to come this far east out of the canyon. It's a little peculiar."

"Many Devils?"

"I've mentioned him before. A mountain lion almost as big as the truck. He's quick, he's clever, part trickster, part athlete, part mystery. Don't think he'll come down this far in daylight, but we'll keep our eyes open as the sun goes down. We'll watch the horses...and Poke."

The sound came again, muted and faded like a nightmare evaporating. Many Devils was canyon-bound again, likely, but it wouldn't be the first time a person was tricked by the cat.

"See Bliss' ears? Tipped forward like that? She's alert. She doesn't like Many Devils, either. Know what? I'll get the horses into the barn and give them water in those buckets for now. We'll just keep listening. If it gets quiet, we'll let them out a little later. I'll get my gun. For now, keep on oiling those planks."

She wanted to say, *we don't need the gun. In the shadows, there was a gun.* She felt the cold metal along her face, then under her chin, along her leg, then... Her heart raced tears to her eyes as she rubbed the oil along a second plank. She still heard the bullet click into the chamber, like a lock in place, the metal pressing against her ear, then hands pushing and yanking her onto her stomach. She didn't want to see a gun, not even be near one. She would fight off Many Devils herself if it meant no gun. She hurried too quickly with oil, got a splinter, but couldn't see it to pull it out, her tears had enclosed her eyes that fast.

"Hey, Sunshine, you okay?"

She was sobbing, holding her hand, while Riley drew closer, the barrel of his revolver holstered next to his hip. *Cold metal.*

"No! No! Get away! Don't touch me!" Maggie screamed.

"Sunshine, it's me. Riley. What's the matter?"

She drew back, crouched, a near crawl pulling away from his grasp, her face more terror than breath, a pulsing sob strained her voice. "Not the gun! No! Don't make me!"

Riley covered the revolver with a towel and placed it on the ground. "Okay, okay, the gun's put away. No one but me here with you, Maggie. I wouldn't hurt you. See? No gun." He raised his hands widely toward her. "Don't listen to those voices, Sunshine. Just listen to me. Riley." His calm voice and face passed into focus as she made her way back to Arizona.

Her body sagged into weary sobs that tore his heart. Then, as her sobs softened into sharp breaths, Maggie sat upright on the barn floor, hugged her knees, and rocked.

"I remember." She nodded slowly, staring at the floor. The monster she remembered stared back, not blinking.

"I just want to sit next to you, Sunshine. Okay if I go slow?" She felt him ease each foot closer, side stepping. "Can you tell me what you remember?"

She took a deep breath. "It's not nice."

"Did they...hit you with the gun...or threaten to shoot?"

She shook her head "no" as if shaking away flies.

"I wish they had shot me." Her voice wavered. Then the air slipped out too quickly, and a sob arrested her breath.

"They called it a new game. They pushed me onto my stomach in the van." She began weakly, but lost air again. She swallowed hard, watching the movie of herself living this, she felt the barrel getting closer...closer... "They knew I couldn't fight if I were on my stomach...they pinned me down. I couldn't see...they pulled my legs apart..."

Riley held his breath. He repulsed the image of Maggie

being pinned down by three males, as if it took three men to overpower her. The image of her, on her stomach...

"...and they pushed the barrel...inside..." Her words blocked her throat.

Riley sat stunned, his own breath choked back, that old feeling from Grace's suffering pounding against his brain, the anger with God, the arrogance of a higher being letting injustice like this exist, being raped with a gun. He felt his jaw set, box-like in anger and revenge.

Yet, what he did instead was tender, unnoticed by the grasshopper snapping by the barn entrance or by the wisp of cloud swiping the forehead of the sky. He pulled her close and kept rocking, so his fist wouldn't hit a wall, so he wouldn't grab the whiskey in the kitchen cabinet. He rocked away the horror so Maggie could think more about Christmas trees and Minnie Mouse. He pulled her tight to make it go away. Maybe for an hour. Maybe more.

CHAPTER
THIRTY-NINE

Maggie stood first, brushing the barn floor from her jeans. "I suppose we should finish those planks. Hannah and Griff will be here—"

"They'll be here soon enough. Let's get that splinter taken care of." He pulled tweezers from the horses' med supplies, washed the reddish wound, and when she was willing to place her hand forward, he held it again.

"Thing is, Sunshine, I don't pretend to know what has happened to you. But I do know you survived beating, humiliation, threats, physical and emotional damage that boils my blood." He tugged gently on the exposed splinter tip. "I've felt loss, including myself, after Grace passed. But I've also seen a colt survive its mother and turn into a fine horse. I've watched seasons change. And as hard as it is," he tugged slowly as the splinter pulled free from the skin, "there's always something new around the corner that eases pain." He pulled it free, nearly a half-inch of Grace's plank taken from below her thumb. "When you're ready, you'll see it too." He smiled.

"I want all the bad memories to go away, you know?"

He washed the spot with an antibiotic swab. "Yes, Sunshine, I want that, too. But unfortunately, that will happen only when you're finished remembering most everything. When you're ready."

She nodded, a flat smile creasing her face. The wound's bleeding had checked while he applied a bandage.

"You'll need to protect that today, you know. So, where're your gloves?"

Late afternoon, the horses pastured under watchful eye, the planks absorbed the orange oil, and Maggie readied the kitchen for the Grace meal. The memory of the gun followed her darkly until she pulled down Grace's recipe box.

Curious. Someone who collected recipes but didn't have time to sort them. How did she know her favorites and where to find them? Seemed to Maggie that would be something someone would automatically do. Something clicked. Sorting, alphabetizing, boxes with cards like this. It was almost instinct for her to reach into each section and sort the recipes in a way that anyone could use. But the thing that clicked was that some cards weren't handwritten, but typed clean and orderly, predictable as sure as *A* follows *B*. Something, she swore she knew at one time, before the gun, before the van, sometime earlier.

"Hey, girlfriend!" Hannah and Griff wedged themselves through the kitchen door with a box of dishes and food. Maggie jumped, so focused on the rooster recipe box, she hadn't heard her friends walk onto the porch. Hannah lifted foil-covered dishes from the box. "It's really a combination here, the fig appetizer—that was Grace's favorite—and the dessert, too. But I'm keeping that as a surprise. Room in the fridge?"

Griff handed over a large bowl. "My contribution. Grace's linguini salad. But I admit, Hannah helped."

"Looks like a restaurant, I swear." Riley followed through the door, gloves in hand. "Hannah, can you spare Griff? I need to build the table."

"We'll start that enchilada sauce! Which means, Riley, you have to share!" she joked.

The men approached the planks and sawhorses like a large outdoor puzzle. "I have to confess, I've been looking forward to this all day." Griff rubbed his hands together. "And you?"

"A little sad, a little happy. I see Maggie getting excited with the planning, her head together with Hannah's; she's like a new person." He lifted up a plank and balanced it onto the sawhorses, while Griff squared it. "Then, I notice there's someone missing who really should be in the thick of things."

He paused. "I mean, Maggie did a lot of that. She wants this to be a meal to remember," Riley continued, managing the second plank.

Griff nodded. "Gives her something positive to think about."

"She had a flashback this morning," Riley paused. "Almost didn't know who I was. She remembered a detail of the rape. She was raped with...one of the guns." He shook his head. "The other day, in Ten Winds, she recalled a gas station in a photograph—"

"Hannah told me. I know that place, about forty miles east. That gas station's been abandoned for years, so somebody stopping there wouldn't be noticed for days. And we've got a height for the shooter: 6'5". We know he's left-handed and around 240 pounds."

"I could think of at least six people right off the top of my head who fit that description." Riley centered the third plank.

"But this is someone with money either to own or to charter a helicopter to that mesa. Don't think he was from around here."

"Only helicopter I know is the one your office uses."

"Exactly."

"So, a tall, rich guy who pilots a 'copter and shoots left-handed." Riley completed the last plank while Griff squared it into place then approached his friend.

"This is what I think happened. The three guys in the van came to the mesa at a pre-arranged time for a meeting of some sort. They were set up, patsies, every one of them. The shooter and the helicopter weren't visible from the road. The outcroppings are too high, the angle from the road too steep. They never saw the shooter. As they got out of the van, he got off clean shots before they could react. State confirms from the van and remains that the bullets entered from a sharp high angle. I'm thinking the shooter, or whomever hired the shooter, used these guys as a crew for some job and something went wrong. The meeting was only to kill them and dispose of them with, hopefully, no one ever finding the evidence."

"To cover up something," Riley asserted. "Maggie remembers 'others' when she met up at that driveway. Maybe he was the boss, the 'others' were the ones killed."

"Because they were greedy...or missed a deadline..." Griff brought one of the benches to the table. "But there's something bigger than a van crashing down a ravine," he insisted. "Some kind of crime syndicate? Jewelry? Inheritance? Ransom? I may need some reinforcements to help me out with this."

"Like the state police?"

"No, like the feds." That single word swirled into the air between them and headed toward Maggie in the kitchen. The feds could open a door anywhere.

The table was covered with printed thrift store tablecloths, held in place with mismatched cups and plates, as if Grace had placed them there herself. Poke settled under the table, for a nap, and certainly, later, for anything that fell from laps onto the ground.

Nice job, Riley heard. *Hope I can make it through this*, he thought.

Hannah walked toward Riley. "We've got Grace's sweet potato casserole for Griff; Maggie and I just finished the enchilada sauce—your favorite. I made the fig and cheese appetizer, and Maggie has something secret she made...and Griff's favorite linguini salad, and I'm making a tossed salad with Grace's favorite dressing. Dessert is already done. What do you think? Will the table hold it all?"

"If not, we'll eat in shifts." He grinned.

She put her hand on his shoulder. "You know this feels right, all this celebration. I hope you feel it, too."

"Tell you one thing, the one who would really enjoy it won't be here."

Hannah's breath was slow and even. "Yes, she is, Riley. Just look around. We're all a part of her. It took Maggie to figure that out."

He looked away from Hannah's gaze toward the barn. It was all he could do to blink away the stinging in his eyes.

Maggie checked Grace's recipe one more time, checked the timer, then opened the oven door just as Hannah walked inside. "They look done." She hesitated. "Are they ready for the rest of the sauce?"

"Ahhh, they smell so good!" The aroma from the sauce steamed up from the pan, an earthy and spicy thickness to the tangy enchilada mix. "Let's cool them a few minutes while we carry everything out to the table. I think it's time to gobble down this feast! Thanks, Maggie, for doing all this. You know Riley would never have agreed to it if we suggested it. You got Riley to agree to something pretty amazing." Her beaming smile wrapped Maggie softly.

"Don't forget the tossed salad in the fridge! And my surprise!"

If the table were a prairie, the hot and cold dishes were landmarks of Grace's life. Riley looked at the choices, smelled the aromas he'd forgotten he loved. But one item remained uncovered.

"What is this one?"

Maggie beamed and removed the cover. "Ta Da! Jell-O salad! Carrots and celery and oranges in lemon Jell-O." She giggled. "It was in Grace's recipe box!" She defended her choice.

"I should have known." Riley laughed, not a little laugh, but one that she saw only once before, that lunch behind the gallery. That laugh that crinkled his eyes and wore away his sadness. As they sat, the memories sat with them.

"Now when did Grace make this appetizer, was it at the Horse Rally Banquet or the sheriff's picnic?"

"The picnic—remember? She ran into the Grange Hall yelling out, "Give me twenty minutes and I'll have this ready!'" Griff laughed.

"Yeah, she said she never 'cooked', she just 'assembled'."

"Now these enchiladas, here," Riley finally spoke, "these were from one of our dinners here. She told me 'It will only take ten minutes' so I had to hold the tortillas while she filled them. Meanwhile, I have hungry horses I got to bring in. No, she wouldn't hear of it...and forty-five minutes later—" He broke into a broad laugh.

"Yes! We drove up and Riley runs out the door, still wearing an apron, making a beeline with Poke toward the pasture." Griff joined in.

"By gosh, she got her enchiladas done. So, my hat is off to

you, Sunshine, for making these. I know the amount of time it takes. That sauce is perfect!" He took another bite.

"Now, didn't she make them with pinto beans, one time?"

"And hated it! Always served them with black beans after that." Riley reached for the casserole.

"We saw that on the recipe card in tiny writing," Maggie added. "Use black beans!"

In his mind, Riley saw her quick movements in the kitchen, shaking her head, mixing the sauce, tasting it with her pinkie just dipped into the pot. "Just right," she'd whisper, winking. And the casserole, when she cut the potatoes, she sharpened the knife too quickly and cut herself, vowing to call the manufacturer, then just as focused, finding the brown sugar.

Griff and Hannah's laughter brought him back.

"...Or the time she made the custard—"

"Oh, no! I'd forgotten! Oh, the look on her face—" No one finished a sentence, the laughter was so intense it took sentence breaths away.

"Okay, Maggie, she wanted to make egg custard, and, well, I guess she was in a hurry—"

"She never forgot that, either, always joked about it—"

"So, the custard is finished, and she puts nutmeg on top; I mean it really looked pretty!"

"She bit into it, and the look on her face!"

"She'd gotten paprika, instead—" Hannah choked with laughter. "God love her, she started laughing, her face was so red, she couldn't stop—"

"Or the time she made the linguini salad—I was like to die." Riley squeezed out a high-pitched laugh. "What was she thinking?"

"Oh, gosh, Maggie. She made the linguini salad, and instead of garlic—" Hannah broke into a wheezy laugh. "No, no, I've got this. Instead of garlic, she'd added horseradish!" The table erupted, all remembering the hot red faces, the attempts to swallow milk, water, and iced tea all in one sip. Hannah caught her breath. "I know we make her out to be careless in the kitchen, but she really was such a great cook." Hannah wiped her eyes with a napkin, while they all shared the remembered burn of horseradish splitting their tongues.

He could see it clearly again, Grace sitting right where Maggie was, the first to taste the linguini salad, halting her chewing, eyes round, face redder by the second. "This is horrible," she gasped, then grabbed a pitcher of milk, yes a pitcher, and drank two cups straight down. Her laughter didn't stop, then, insisting the salad played a trick on her.

Maggie caught the infectious laughter, slurping the cool lemon Jell-O past the crunch of vegetables. She felt it, too, as if Grace were sitting next to her, letting the laughter float up past the Emory's oak, down the road toward the sunset.

"Oh, I'd forgotten." Riley wiped his eyes. He then saw Maggie's lost gaze. "What are you thinking about, Sunshine? You must think we're a little crazy, huh?"

"I was hoping this would happen. I kept hearing about Grace from all of you. But you talked to me about her, you never seemed to talk to each other about her. I wanted to get to know her, too. I wanted to see you share her. It made me sad you didn't. But she's here with you tonight, don't you think?"

Riley stopped breathing for a second or two. Maggie drew back slightly, as if wounded by an arrow struck straight through him. But there was something different in his eyes, just then. He seemed to find Grace, so that arrow didn't pierce anything vital. Just went through like a silk thread, and out the other side, a narrow slit that could heal in another second. His glance scattered toward his friends.

"I think we've all missed nights like this." He spoke softly, cleared his tight throat. "It used to hurt to think about her, to try to bring her back, to call up memories, and maybe I forced that on all of you, too. She was such a special lady, you know. But tonight?" All he could do was shake his head.

"Look what you did, kiddo," Hannah whispered. "You not only brought her back. You brought him back, too." She gave Maggie a hug.

Hannah looked up toward the others. "Sooo, before I get too sentimental, here, I did want to share something very exciting, something I'm sure Grace would have celebrated, too. Ten Winds Gallery," she paused, "was nominated last spring in a field of twenty other nominations for the State Entrepreneurship Award, and we found out that we won! Got the call the other day!"

"Well, congratulations, Hannah, that's amazing!"

"So, sometime in the next month or two, we are going to have a bang-up open house—TV coverage, newspapers, Arizona Highways—and the governor to present it! In little old Copper Station, Arizona!"

"The governor? Here!" Riley raised his glass. "Well-deserved, Hannah! You've worked hard to make an impact on our town, and you finally got the credit for it!"

"Don't know why he's trying so hard—he's got the reelection locked!" Griff joked.

Hannah playfully slapped his shoulder. "Enough, you! This is *my* time, don't minimize it. Go get your own award."

"I already did," Griff answered and pulled Hannah into his lap. "I got you."

"Right answer." She kissed him. "Now who wants double-chocolate cheesecake?"

Riley swore she was there again, standing, maybe giving a toast, celebrating along with these dear friends and his new friend, sitting next to him. Grace had done it, Hannah had, too, making Copper Station a better place. Maggie? Of course she had, too, but she just didn't know it, yet.

CHAPTER
FORTY

Maggie

I'm sitting on the porch steps, Poke curled next to my thigh, the last plank stored in the barn, the horses safe. We make a party of washing dishes, dividing food among us, Grace is still here, a part of every thought, every movement. Hannah and Griff hug us goodbye, drive off, sitting close and golden in the front seat.

The cricket's rich rhythm is crisp. The stars pinpoint the sky, smudge the Milky Way. I lean against the baluster while the breeze occasionally fans the oak leaves. Riley walks back from the barn, not that slow, end-of-day walk I've seen him use. His steps are purposeful. Unlike me, he knows where he belongs.

The screams and beatings are distant, just now. Maybe I have control over those voices. I can sit back, let the evening paint the sky. I can take one breath, then the next, and the next, just to be content in this place, right now.

I look at the stars. Which one is Grace?

Riley sits next to me. He breathes in the evening. Poke's tail thumps two, maybe three times, then is quiet. Riley scans the sky—for Grace?—then smiles. His hand finds my shoulder. Part of me says I should pull away with every muscle and bone. But my body doesn't tense. Not at all. He points to Jupiter. It's always so bright this time of year, he says. He looks toward the barn.

I see his profile in the shadows, relaxed from the evening's laughter, like he saved up for years to spend all that laughter in one night. Somehow, I know what it's like for him. He's washed the hurt clean. He sits quiet at first, maybe finding Grace close to Jupiter, being so bright and all. The lines on his face are his story, silently telling of land and sky, his horses, his losses, his strengths.

He speaks, then, with the soft voice I suddenly remember from the hospital. His voice chokes again, when he mentions Grace, then, as quickly, mentions me, using profound words which I don't see how I deserve: unselfish, grateful, kindness. I see his shoulders quiver for a second and without a thought, as natural as brushing a hair from my eyes, I prop my arm against his shoulder. It's a moment that redefines me, one I remember again and again in the months that come. He leans his head toward my hand, his cheek brushes my fingertips. It should, but the closeness doesn't terrify, hurt, or damage. I allow this, maybe again. Close enough to hear him whisper.

"Thank you."

Somehow, I've helped Riley; I learned that today. As if what I do makes a difference. I like being stronger. I like being Maggie Fletcher. I don't want to leave her any time soon.

Poke and I sit just a little longer. We like being with Grace because Jupiter is so bright this time of year.

CHAPTER
FORTY-ONE

Coffee spilled its aroma through the kitchen as Riley formed the last pancake in the pan. The sun's pale morning rays opened the day like an envelope over the mountains. He peeked at Maggie as she opened the pantry door and, after a brief hesitation, scanned the contents as if sorting cans and labels. She spotted Poke's food bin, a scoop on the top, the reminder of her purpose. She drew out one, two scoops of food, dropped the kibble into the bowl just as he had shown her. He turned the pancake, but in his mind, he urged her to the next step. She brought Poke's water dish to the sink, smiled at Riley as if caring for Poke were as easy as maple syrup dribbling down the sides of the stack. Poke hit both bowls once they were on the floor. Atta girl.

Leaving Maggie for most of the day to attend the horse auction gave him no sense of guarantee that she'd be safe. Both Griff and he would be two hours from Copper Station and the way Griff told it, there were still people looking for Maggie. Who knew what the Arizona wind could blow in while he wasn't a yell away?

All the more reason to have Hannah check the house mid-afternoon when she got away from the gallery. He placed the plate before Maggie, then himself, straddling his chair, absently anticipating riding new horses. Surely, he was doing the right thing, this return to search and rescue. He'd gotten nothing but smiles from those who found out. And it needed to be everyone's project. Maggie helping, sure, but Hannah checking on Maggie, and Griff following through on any suspicious activity that was still lost in the crypt of Maggie's memory.

"Okay, so, I'll pack lunch once I finish here," he said out loud, as if everything else fell into place that easily. A two-hour drive, no telling how soon they'd find the horses they wanted, or when those horses would come up for bid, and how soon the paperwork would be completed, how quickly they could load the horses, let alone the two-hour drive back. "I'll be gone most of the day, Sunshine, so we'll make some lunch for you, too. How about that?"

"There're still a few leftovers from the Grace meal." No panic, no problem, it seemed.

"Hannah will be here sometime after 2:30, I imagine, so you two can spend the afternoon together."

"Okay."

"We should be back before dark."

"Okay, before dark. Got your gloves?"

He was torn like old sheets. He couldn't shake the feeling of abandoning her, like others had done. At some point, she needed to be at the ranch by herself—he'd need to run an errand, he'd need to meet with Griff—she needed to manage on her own, right? It just came a little sooner than he'd expected.

"I'll need you to clean the barn for our two new residents tonight."

"Okay."

"You may want to give Bliss and Cartwheel a snack. Don't want them out of sorts. I've got apples in the barn fridge."

"They'll like that. Snacks and cleaning. Okay."

"Want me to write it all down?"

"No, I got it. It's like any other day: clean the barn, snacks for the horses, out to the pasture for a few hours."

"And water. Make sure the trough is filled. It'll be a hot day."

"Okay. Got your gloves?"

He ran through it again when he rinsed his plate, filled his thermos with coffee, pulled together his lunch, loaded the truck with harnesses, blankets, a saddle and a bag of apples to make new friends. She had chores she could do to keep her busy. He'd never forgive himself if something had happened. He stepped up onto the porch. Was he thinking about those days with Grace or now with Maggie?

"You've done this all before. Bliss and Cartwheel are comfortable with you."

"Okay. I'll use apples, like you said. They'll follow me anywhere."

"Hannah will be by later and we'll have chili tonight for dinner. Should be done by seven, I bet."

"Sure, it will be fine." She squinted at him. "I'll be okay, honest."

"Good, good." He sighed, a deep rush of air. *That's settled then. She'll be okay.* Sure. "I guess, then...I guess I better get going. Griff's waiting with the horse trailer."

Maggie stood small on the porch, fingertips shoved into her front jeans pockets. The bruises were gone, the cast was off. She was actually smiling, shielding her eyes from the new sun. He waved awkwardly, got into the truck, started it up. In the few seconds he backed out of the driveway, he felt more settled behind the wheel. He'd driven all of fifteen feet when he heard Maggie running behind the truck. *I won't go,* he thought. *I don't dare.*

"Riley! Riley! Wait!"

He slammed on the brakes.

"Here." She extended her arm through the driver's window and opened her palm. His gloves. "I'm pretty sure you'll need these." She grinned.

He noticed flecks of color in her brown eyes, now. "I swear those gloves should be glued to my hips! Thanks, Sunshine, I'll see you later."

She stepped back. The truck rose up the drive and onto the highway.

Yeah, she'd be all right.

⁓

All she heard was a soft wind after Riley's truck disappeared from her ears. She felt the sun wash over her as it rose higher, the Emory's oak brushing the backbone of the sky above. She turned to see Poke staring from the kitchen doorway.

"Hey, Poke! Time to feed you, boy!"

She freshened his water bowl. Opening the pantry door, she lifted the lid from the food bin and counted out one, two scoops. Just like Riley. She brought the bowl close to Poke, his feet in his dancing-for-food excitement.

"There you are, boy," she cooed, scratching behind his ears. Just like Riley did. The pup buried his nose into the kibble, rarely coming up for air.

His rhythmic chewing was a welcome sound from the quiet house. She piled dishes into the sink. The warm water churned bubbles that slipped tickles between her fingers. She scrubbed and rinsed, watching a squirrel climb up the oak on the other side of the drive. The click-tick of its paws against the bark reminded her of a turn signal in a car...a van...

There she was, lying belly down in the back seat, her right eye already sealed from its swelling. Voices argued in the dark about turning left or right, click-tick, click-tick. Nausea lined her throat. *Hey, Kick, you got the girl? My turn next.* The seat was too warm against her face and her leg was cramped. The wind changed and blew a breath through the curtains across her face. She was back again, washing a glass while the sun traced the edge of the drive. *Kick.* She knew that name. She blew out a breath as she lifted the stopper in the sink. Air. Water. Flowing out and away.

As she dried her hands, she looked around. Poke was staring at her. "Oh, my gosh, Poke! I forgot to feed you, didn't I?" She reached for the food bin in the pantry and measured one, two scoops, just like Riley. Poke scrambled to his dish and chewed from the center of the kibble.

She wiped the counter when she spied Grace's recipe box. Something about that box...she held it, but this time, opened the lid, knowing that Grace must have done this a thousand times each year, knowing its secrets. But Grace's system of filing? The tabs extended like fat fingers above a strange mix of cards and clippings, as tight as a cabbage roll: *Appetizers, Bread, Pies, Cookies, Breakfast, Cakes, Beef*...she read.

Something did not fit.

Grace's order of things made no sense, whatever the order was she used. Maybe the order of how you eat, like *Breakfast,* then *Lunch,* then *Dinner.* Certainly logical, but where would the chicken recipes go? Or the salads? She closed the lid with one deep, simple thought emerging. Another thing she had known was coming back to her. Something she recognized as soon as it would open the door in her mind. Something from a long time ago, something useful.

Alphabetical order.

As sure as she knew her own skin, she knew letters followed letters, things fell into those letters and made categories.

"Alphabetical order. I *know* this. Alphabetical order. It's easy!"

She pulled one tab and the recipes following behind like school children, then another group and another, stacking each set on the counter, top to bottom, left to right.

"Appetizers, first, NOT chicken or bread or miscellaneous. I *know* this!" The something familiar pushed her urgently, confidently. She could fix this, a way to sort and maybe even...

"Cross reference." An idea intersected with alphabetical order, making a grid of order. She could complete this even better...

"Reference" another word. She ran words like a waterfall, words and concepts that opened a bigger view, not just cards with names. Her brain connected a thought to something that made sense, something important from before. There was so much "before" tumbling over the edge of those rocks, she couldn't grasp it all.

Sorting the *Beef* tabs, she cross-referenced with *Chicken,* then *Breads* with *Cakes* , with *Snacks*. Her hands flowed over the cards like a mountain stream. She knew recipes she'd never seen before and recognized which slot they needed to be placed. And she knew she was right, no second guessing, no checking with anyone. She was right. Skill. Confidence. Something so simple had once been vital to her. Somewhere. She knew it.

The flotilla of recipe cards and tabs were methodically sorted, stacked, and returned to the recipe box. She closed the rooster lid, feeling centered by alphabets and reference, not screams and dark slashes of recall. The roosters still faced in the same direction, the corner worn from use, but now the box seemed more complete, more functional with whatever she had done.

She rested her eyes, looking out the window, only then aware of the change in sunlight. What time was it anyway? Almost eleven? What had just happened with her morning? The horses! They were whinnying at the end of her ears, in the barn. The horses! Poke!

"Gosh, Poke! I forgot to feed you!"

For some reason, the water bowl looked nearly full. So, she pulled open the pantry door, lifted the scoop and the foot bin lid. She counted one, two scoops just like Riley. Within seconds of setting the bowl on the floor, Poke attacked the kibble.

"There you are, boy! I'm so sorry! Riley's been gone for hours, and I forgot my jobs already!" She scratched behind his ears, just like Riley. "I bet Bliss and Cartwheel aren't too happy with me. I promised Riley I'd clean the barn, too. Let's go!"

She rushed toward the barn, Poke immediately behind, finding impatient, snorting horses. They anxiously pawed at the barn floor, awaiting their water. The yellow coin of the sun reflected in the trough water until the horses chased it away while they drank. She added fresh water, bringing the coin back, rippling into smooth. They ate their feed and ran ahead to the pasture, ignoring Maggie.

Maybe she deserved that.

As suddenly, she heard only the whisper of a breeze that pulled a strand of hair across her face. This Arizona. How could she be centered in two places at once? Somewhere with sorting and cross-referencing mixed into reaching for a pitch-fork inside the barn.

She teased the soft hiss of new hay into the stalls; it pillowed onto the barn floor. Flakes of hay danced between shafts of sunlight, a dry yellow rain landing in her hair, on her shoulders, in the bend of her elbow. Hearty work, not like sorting cards. Being so connected to the horses, she pulled the rake faster as if to erase a faraway shadow tucked inside: three men, one named 'Kick' who pushed her into cramped, non-negotiable demands.

She remembered that she'd fought, she kicked, she bit, she elbowed, but the small space didn't help her. They used their anger against her face, her mouth. At some point her wrist snapped, too. She fought until exhaustion and their bodies overpowered her. Click-tick, click-tick, the seat belt. Click-tick, the turn signal. The horses whinnied off in the distance, brought her back to the barn, while a tear threatened her cheek.

Riley said it was over. But they always found her brain at the quietest of times. They knew she'd slip back into the fear in a second.

This morning slipped out of her hand like a ribbon in the wind, and she still had to finish the barn. She promised. She cut the twine on the new bale, pulling chunks toward her with fierce intent, digging in to create new beds for new horses. Poke broke her thoughts when he peeked around the corner.

"New horses, Poke. We'll be busy the next few months. You ready for new friends?"

She heard gravel crunching in the driveway and immediately thought Riley was back already. No, only the mail truck. Lester. Riley warned her about him: keep your distance. She retreated back into the shadows. Poke was alert, ears forward aimed like darts, a radar beam focused from eyes to tail toward Lester.

He placed one foot, then the other onto the driveway, emerging from the truck awkwardly, as if on a secret mission. Her heartbeat took over with each step he took. Lester circled as if lost, then turned toward the porch. She remembered those men looking over their shoulders, much like Lester, now, remembered swiping snack cakes and wallets from convenience store counters, then, backing out of the store before knifing into a run toward the van. Her heart skimmed faster.

Lester carried a small box and envelopes. Just as he set his foot on the lowest porch step, Poke's guttural growl warned Maggie that he meant business. Lester cupped his hands around his eyes, peering into the house. Maggie gasped. If it came to that, could she use the horses' toe pick to land a hit?

If it came to that? Lester was only one man, compared to the three that tried to break her. If it came to that? She felt her hand tighten a fist around the pick.

Poke growled intently. "Easy, Poke, easy." The adrenaline ticked through her veins, her heartbeat thick in her ears. Lester pulled gently on the screen door and it gave. He walked in. She felt a fight rise in her, the familiar fear and anger deepen. She took a step, then sank bank into the shadows. That was Poke's cue. He stalked the house slowly, first two steps, then three. Then four.

The screen door pried from the door jamb as Lester emerged. He stretched both arms leisurely overhead and tried to touch the eaves with his fingertips. Left, right, slid his eyes along the edge of the house, as if missing a detail or footstep. He strode toward the truck, tossing a cup of Jell-O into the air.

That's all it took.

Poke bulleted directly for Lester's legs. In under three seconds, the dog's mouth had anchored onto his pants cuff and tugged Lester off-balance.

"Get him, get him, Poke!" she muttered, having no doubt who would win.

Lester swatted, tried to pull away quickly, but Poke gripped harder, tugging with teeth bared, the growl deeper than his bones. In the final tug, the fabric tore, a small flag of victory as Poke tumbled backward. Lester also fell, then half-crawled, half-ran into the truck.

"Damn dog! That's my uniform! I gotta pay—"

Poke charged the truck. Lester geared into reverse and skidded sharply up the drive.

"Get outa here! Get outa here!" Maggie yelled as he sped down the road. Her fist wrapped around the toe pick, pumping the air. The sudden silence followed while the remnants of screaming reached the barn rafters and unsettled the pigeons. She had been the one screaming. She relaxed her hand and the toe pick dropped.

In trotted Poke, the dark ragged cuff trailing from his mouth.

"Look at you, the big man!" She leaned over to pet the soft fur. "I owe you, buddy, you know that? That'll teach Lester, huh?" She was half-giddy, half-tearful. Maybe Poke just saved her life. Well, it seemed that way.

He looked at her so intently, still biting the fabric, when she suddenly gasped. "Oh, gosh, Poke! I forgot to feed you this morning! Let's get to the house!"

When they entered the kitchen, Maggie noticed the mail and a box on the counter, "Refrigerate immediately" written across the package. She grabbed the fabric from Poke, put it on top of the package and shoved it into the fridge.

"Okay, Poke. Sorry, you're long overdue! Here you go, one, two scoops. You deserve that." She set the bowl on the floor. He sat, his tail a whisper across the floor. Then, he yawned and lay down.

"Hey, buddy, I owe you breakfast! You must be famished...Or are you mad at me?" She picked up a few pieces and brought them near his nose. He sniffed, then closed his eyes. "Go on, now...Poke? Poke?"

"Oh, no." Her blood iced. "Did Lester hurt you? Are you hurt, boy?" She felt his ribs and back the way she saw Riley do, but with no idea what to feel for. Poke wagged his tail. "Come on, boy! Try your food. Wake up, wake up, Poke!"

The dog moved briefly, as if already dreaming about chasing horses. She'd been so confident in the kitchen earlier, but that made her late, and that made her vulnerable when Lester arrived. Had it not been for Poke...if it came to that...

Hey, white bitch, hey, princess. Her memory jumped in with thoughts that Riley wasn't here, and Poke might die. *You didn't run fast enough this time, you slowed us down, bitch. We almost got caught because of you, 'cause you didn't listen.*

We gotta teach you a lesson. That raspy voice echoed from the dark place she hated.

She lay on the floor next to the dog. "Please eat something," she choked. "Please don't die," she whispered. "Please, I'll do right next time. I will." Her panic circled the kitchen, the voices following. She got up, touched all the counters, looked in the cupboards for medicine, a cold cloth, a chew bone...something for Poke to make it better. *Quick.*

Her circle enlarged to the living room—a pillow or blanket, maybe—opening end table drawers for something to help Poke and keep the voices away. A snack cake, a donut, a wallet to get her by. Her breath became short as she looked toward Riley's study, a place she never went, had no reason to. *Maybe, maybe he had a book, something with pictures to help Poke.*

The familiar leather-paper aroma swam inside her, an aroma she'd not been aware of for some time that saved her in some way, many times before, with answers. She focused on the titles, running her fingers along the spines, something stronger than the voices: *Your Dog and You, Training Search and Rescue, American Horse Breeds, The Dog Guide, Healthy Horses, The Manual of Equine Medicine...*

Hey, girlie girl. I like how you feel. It was Street, this time. Another name and voice that jumped in.

"Stop it! I'm helping! Leave me alone!"

She removed volumes from the shelves, knowing she'd done something like this somewhere. She found another book *Canine Anatomy,* but only flicked through the pages. No perfect answer anywhere. She grabbed three books: *Caring for Your Dog, Common Canine Illnesses, Home Remedies for Dogs.* Yet when the pages opened, all she saw was print running like ants down the page, mentioning nothing about one, two scoops or attacking a mailman. She set aside *Knowing your Dog,* stacked like layer cake on other cracked-open volumes. The weight of the pages between her fingers was like a friend pushed aside too soon.

SHE was the problem; she fed him too late. She carried a book back to the kitchen. Poke was still but breathing. She felt his nose—Riley did that, too. But was Poke's nose supposed to feel a certain way? "Don't die, Poke." She dropped the book and returned to the study.

She'd left a tornado behind: open drawers, lights turned on, cabinet doors left ajar, open books on the floor, five more on Riley's desk and papers spilled on Riley's chair. What had happened? It wasn't like this before, was it? Why couldn't she remember?

Panic was electric in her brain. Thoughts snapped, incomplete and sharp, shards of accusations and confusion filling up inside. Breath quickened. Hands and knees fought to keep going, keep going one more day, please, please...

Can't do anything right, bitch. Run away and you get hit, right? Damaged goods, my ass! Clean you up good and you're still worth a hundred grand. You fucked up everything. Everything.

"No!" she wailed. "I'm trying to help. I don't want Poke to be hurt!"

"Hello?" called a familiar voice from the kitchen. "Hello, Maggie?"

Poke barked, a pure powerful bark startled her breath back to the study, to the mess she made. "Poke?" She ran to the kitchen to see him sitting upright. Hannah stood in the doorway.

"Hey, girlfriend. I'm a little early, but I—hey!" Hannah looked around. "Kiddo, what's the matter?"

She was sobbing, exhausted, holding a book upside down against her chest. "I...don't know...don't know what's with Poke. He won't eat. I made a mess of things. I can't do anything right—"

"Hold on, hold on there." Hannah reached for Maggie's

shoulders and for a second she flinched. Poke's tail thumped. "Look! He's okay. He looks fine to me."

"He wouldn't eat. I thought maybe he got hurt, or I did something."

"Well, let's take a look." She ran her hands along Poke's neck, nose, forehead, ribs, belly. "His belly's full. This dog's had plenty to eat. In fact, I'd say he's a little bloated. When did you feed him?"

Maggie rubbed her forehead, across wet lashes and through her hair. "I don't know. I can't remember."

"Is it possible you fed him more than once today?"

"I didn't feed him at all...I was late because I was late with the horses and then Lester came and tried to get into the house—" Her thoughts raced past the barn.

"What?"

"I was in the barn and Lester walked into the house, but I had the toe pick in case he got too close—"

"Oh, God, Maggie!"

"But Poke attacked him and scared him off, but then I thought Poke got injured...I fed him late...or..." She stopped to catch her breath. "He didn't wake up after that, and I thought I killed him."

Hannah smiled, hands still resting on Maggie's shoulders, ready to earthquake into another sob. "Look, kiddo. See? Poke's sitting up, he's fine. Calm down. Here, take a breath. Did Riley feed him before he left this morning? Think back."

"No, it was up to me...I got up...came downstairs...Riley was making pancakes..." Her thinking scrolled through the early sunlight, the pancake on her plate, Riley's gloves in his jacket pocket. She remembered turning...toward the pantry. She blinked a pause.

"Oh, gosh," her voice faded. "I *did* feed him, before breakfast." Her face fell, betrayed by the hole in her memory. "How could I have forgotten? I could have hurt him..."

"But you didn't, see?"

"I could have killed him. Then Riley would have been mad."

"Oh, no, no. Those days are gone, sweetie. Riley keeps you safe. He'd never kill you. Riley loves—" She stopped short. "He loves *Poke* and how you care for him."

"But I kept hearing—" Maggie's brain stopped walking, stalled, let her take a breath and see her friend before her. Hannah. Hannah who was keeping her on the ground right now, instead of running two places at once in circles. There was no place for the voices then, moving back where they belonged.

"The horses!" Maggie called out.

"They're fine, too. Happy in the pasture, chasing grasshoppers and chipmunks, I bet. You did fine, your first day alone, considering. Look, you fed Poke, you took care of the horses..." She picked up the blanket and pillow on the kitchen floor to return to the couch. Maggie followed and recognized the tornado she had created.

Hannah scanned the mess in Riley's library. "Okay, let's take care of this first. Then tell me about Lester."

CHAPTER
FORTY-TWO

Maggie's face relaxed with Hannah's kindness. The voices, the fear were gone, but the remnant of her panic was scattered in Riley's living room and study. Her confusion had not been benevolent: books in disarray, pages open, books on the floor, chairs, tables, a cup on the floor, pencils scattered across Riley's desk, a lampshade tilted like a hangover, a cushion askew.

Hannah methodically entered the room, surveying the enemy, hands on hips.

"I messed up."

"No, no, Maggie, you had some confusion. We can take care of that."

"I thought I could."

"Give yourself a break. And it will get better, don't you think?"

Maggie released her grip on *Your Dog's Health*, set it on Riley's desk with the other books. "Wait a minute," she said. "I bet I know how to do this. Riley has a system, see? Dog books here, Horse books over here. And I remember alphabetical order, now, too. I sorted Grace's recipe box earlier this morning. I think that's when I got late and messed up. But I remembered alphabetical order..." Falling into a library quiet, she tilted each book to read the spine, then opened to the title page. This was familiar too, she realized. Checking the spine, the title page, scanning the shelves, running fingers over the bindings, with no hesitations sliding the orphan books back where they belonged. Inside, deep, she couldn't ignore the feeling that she had done this before Maggie, before that part was taken away.

Hannah stood back, amazed. The books looked random and chaotic, but Maggie sorted and checked effortlessly. Maggie couldn't remember if she'd fed Poke, but she remembered how to place the books and where they belonged. Hannah figured she would need to take pictures to figure out the patterns of Riley's books.

Hannah merely handed Maggie books, while she closed a drawer, straightened a pillow, fixed a lampshade. Yet, she remained captivated by the woman before her putting books back into a magical order. One by one, a red volume, a thick black leather book, a yellow or brown one, one with a black title, the one imprinted with gold, one by one, these books placed securely.

"Maggie, do you realize what you just did?"

She scanned the built-in oak shelves, a place she'd never been before today, as overwhelming as a promise, then shrugged. "Put the books away."

"No, no—it's the way you did it, all by yourself. I just brought books to you. It was...like a part of you woke up and took charge...like second nature."

"There *is* something, something from before. A stack of shelves and the aroma of these books, the pages and covers." Maggie absently looked back at the shelves, pulled one book out and traded with a black one on the shelf below. "Hmmm, maybe he won't notice." She turned to see Hannah again, focusing more on her friend. "Thank you, Hannah, for helping me."

"Oh, gosh, kiddo, you think I don't deal with shelves and disorganization at the gallery?" Hannah pulled Maggie's wayward lock back over her shoulder. "Look, we need to get the chili started before we check the horses. Think you're back on track?"

The walk to the pasture cleansed Maggie. She let go of the chaos and voices and Poke's lethargy, the stacks of books and the recipe cards. But not Lester.

"So what did Lester do?" Hannah asked. "Did he come near you?"

"No, I watched from the barn. He went into the house for a few seconds—"

"Actually inside? Without knocking?"

"He looked in the window. Then he went inside and dropped off the mail and took one of my Jell-o's."

Hannah bit her lips together and stopped for a moment. "You stayed in the barn the whole time?"

"I did. Poke didn't. He took after Lester when he came back outside. They had a tussle. Poke grabbed his ankle and tugged until his cuff tore off. I still have it. In the fridge with the medicine."

Hannah tried not to laugh. "I'd love to have seen that."

"Lester was mad, but Poke was madder and scared Lester into the truck. He drove off."

"And he never touched you?"

"No, Riley said to keep my distance. I stayed in the barn. Did I do something wrong?"

"Oh, gosh, no, Maggie. Lester was wrong. Riley will be

proud, and I'm sure he will have quite the discussion with Lester sometime soon."

The Arizona sun washed Maggie's skin as Hannah called the horses. They deserved treats. Lazy from the sun, Bliss and Cartwheel had little clue of the apples in Hannah's pockets. With a kick or two, they trotted toward Maggie for a rubdown, a signal of forgiveness.

She brushed Bliss and Cartwheel, the animals' warmth radiating, the twitches in muscles and the horses' satisfied deep breaths giving in to the relaxing welcome. Maggie liked Hannah's soft voice in the background, the humming of words between them. *Maybe alone wasn't such a good thing, yet. She needed to talk to Riley about that. Water under the bridge, he might say.* She kept the image. The river bubbling and moving under an imaginary span, moving like a lullaby she felt with her hand against Bliss.

The horses took another drink, settled into the corral, just as she heard an engine, a creaking trailer bending down the incline of the driveway. Griff gave a wide-palmed wave from the passenger window. Riley crept the truck and trailer toward the barn.

Maggie froze her gaze on the black vehicle approaching, then found the familiar again. Now, she shook away the voices, the gun, the hits, and grunts. Riley stopped the truck, opened the door and his silhouette against the late sun showed him stretching toward the sky. She liked doing that, too. She could do that here, in Arizona, at Riley's ranch. Reaching upward toward forever and stretching every inch without hurting.

He must have said something, because there was something comfortable between them. Maybe he called her Sunshine, or maybe Maggie. She was safe as the breeze, walking toward him. He moved toward her, opening his arms wide, his strong arms that could find a place for her to belong. The

Arizona sun spilled its apple-cider across the drive.

"Wanna meet Ranger and Justice?"

"New horses," she whispered from his embrace, her excitement leaking from her smile.

Riley unlocked the trailer, his calm voice heard inside as he led Ranger, a black horse, showy with fire. Justice, a dun, followed with ears alert and attentive to Bliss and Cartwheel nosing toward the corral fence.

"They're beautiful," Maggie whispered again. "Do they want a drink? It's fresh." She reached for Ranger, a cautious but firm touch leading him to the trough. His spirit was electric, taking sips, eyeing the pasture, then neighing his greetings.

"Griff, they're fantastic!" Hannah ran her fingers over Justice, the warm flesh soothing to her touch. "Good choices, guys. They'll serve you well."

"I think we need to give them a bit of exercise before they bed down," Riley said. "Got time before dinner?"

"We'll see you inside. Chili with all the fixings, cornbread, salad, and dessert."

"I'm famished." Griff chuckled and kissed Hannah again.

———

Their talk at dinner focused on the auction. Did you see Ranger's strength? Justice's temperament? The vet said they were healthier than any of the other horses. Good teeth, good bones, attentive, smart.

"So, how was your day, Sunshine?"

She didn't really want to say. She wanted to hear more about the horses. "Mmmm—" She looked at Hannah, who nodded. "Okay, I guess...I...got a little confused," she added softly.

"She may have overfed Poke, but he's okay," Hannah added quickly.

"I...kind of messed up your library—"

"But you should have seen her, Riley. It was unbelievable. She knew where all the books belonged and returned them by herself. I didn't help at all."

"Well, good." He nodded. "You're still in one piece, right?"

She looked at Hannah. "I guess so. More than I can say for Lester's uniform."

Riley looked up at Hannah, then at Maggie. "What's this about Lester?"

"Um, well, Lester brought some medicine today. And... well, he came into the house for a few minutes to set it on the counter."

"He did *what*? Where were you?" Riley and Griff both sat upright.

"I was in the barn. I don't think he saw me. You told me to keep my distance."

"By God, Sunshine, you did. What did Lester do?"

"He walked into the house and put everything on the counter..." She got up toward the fridge and pulled out the medicine and the fabric from Lester's uniform. "But when he came out, he had one of my Jell-O cups. Poke didn't like that and chased him down—"

"Poke in action! That'd be something to see," he said under his breath.

"I watched Poke and Lester. Poke had him by the ankle, then..." She gave Riley the fabric. "Lester was pretty angry. I had the toe pick in my hand if...it came to that..."

Riley stared at her for a few seconds, not a harsh, mean way, but getting all the understanding, pulling away her fear, imagining her armed with a toe pick if Lester came anywhere near her....

"Poke saved my life."

"That he did, Maggie. He might have saved Lester's life, too, come to think of it."

"You want me to file a complaint with the postal authorities?" Griff's voice was stone cold, like a headstone in winter.

"No, let me have the pleasure of taking care of this first. Then it will be your turn," Riley replied just as coldly. He rolled the fabric once and twice in his hand. "Maggie, you did everything right. You completed all your chores—"

"I ran a little late—"

"No harm done, right?"

"Well, I guess not. The voices came back and scared me, that's when I got confused—I thought I'd killed Poke!" she spilled, ready to let go of a sob.

"Obviously, you didn't. Look at him. He's had an eventful day, just like you. You're all right now? Poke saved your life. Pretty darn good day all around, I'd say."

She felt a relief she'd been holding, waiting for Riley to strike her or push her onto the floor because she messed up. But he was water under the bridge.

Poke moved closer to her chair. "Yeah, yeah, I'm better now." Poke put a paw into her lap.

"Forget it, Poke," she teased. "I fell for that look enough today." Maggie smiled, back from that dark place where she didn't belong.

CHAPTER
FORTY-THREE

MAGGIE'S JOURNAL

So, I guess I'm still a little nervous about the mess I made. Even though I tore up Riley's study and darn near killed Poke, he's not mad at me. He's angry with Lester. All Lester did was steal my Jell-O...well, and go into the house. Riley's not even mad at Poke for tearing up Lester's uniform. Says Poke's a hero.

I guess it was Riley's whistle that got the horses moving in the corral when they drove in. I didn't hear it in the barn with Hannah. I just saw the black and shiny coming toward me. I thought for a moment it was the van, but no, it's Riley's truck: the truck I squished pretend bugs in, I sat in and counted to sixty and Riley was proud. The truck moves slow motion against the sunset-fire. His smile inches back, the closer he gets to us. Hannah calls to Griff. He gets out first and kisses her.

I watch Riley, back to the familiar again, like a key locking into place. He stands, nods to Hannah, and stretches to grab the sky. I hang back, storing the horses' brushes. And the toe pick. I forgot to pick it up.

Still, he walks toward me, says something familiar. I can see his smile, his gloves are on, road-weary in his stance, letting the adventure settle a little. He walks closer, arms wide as if measuring a fish that got away. I can smell the good smells of horses and leather. He comes near enough with those wide arms and folds me in like a warm towel.

No voices. They don't dare come now.

But later, I'm dreaming a dark voice, a slap, a lunge, a push against me, squeezing me flat, and no breath. The voices are back, and I remember names. I hear a tap, tap; maybe someone's at the van door. Finally, someone sees what's going on and wants to break down the door.

...A soft voice asks if I'm all right...

I'm on the floor, tangled in a comforter. The voices would never ask me that.

Someone's checking on me, asking if that's okay. Don't be afraid. I'm checking to see if you're all right.

It's not a nurse or a doctor. The room is dark, which makes no sense because I'm in the van. I'm still foggy when someone approaches. I push him away. I think that was too easy.

Someone says Sunshine, wake up.

My arms fly against his chest. I don't know who this is to be so kind, I'm not ready for it. It's a joke, it's a trick. No one means this kindness, really.

I won't hurt you, the voice says. Wake up, wake up, Maggie. He doesn't call me princess or white bitch. The name Maggie clears the fog a little more. I'm not sitting in a van seat; I can tell now. I'm on the floor, a bed, a nice one beside me. I'm on the floor with no beer cans or snack cake wrappers but sitting on a soft rug that doesn't smell like pee. My eyes are wet as I look up. I recognize Riley in the dark.

"I don't want to go back there."

"You won't," he says. "You're safe here. The men are gone, never coming back." He's told me this before, I just remembered.

But they did today when he was gone, tonight when I dared to sleep. How can they be gone and still come back? He stares at me softly as if he wants to erase them from my dreams with his eyes, take those dark dreams that are always darker at 2:00 a.m. The kind of dreams that never seem to have options that time of night.

I blurt out the truth. "Hannah was being nice. She didn't tell you I couldn't remember my jobs, I was late with the horses, I almost killed Poke, tore up his library to find a book—ANY book—to help Poke get better, but I couldn't do anything. The voices told me I couldn't. They found me. She covered for me, and she shouldn't have—"

"You're still here, and you're safe; that's important." His calm voice soaks me. He says he never wants me to think of those men again. He says he'll take care of Lester, who was just two steps short of finding a toe pick in his neck. He rubs the back of my neck, and we rock and rock. He says it's okay, that I did everything right.

But I know the truth, just then. I'm not Maggie as much as I want to be. Someone else is trying to swim to the surface, gasp a breath of air, and hand me the safety line. To do that, I need to let the voices back long enough to remember it all. Riley says when I'm ready.

A muscle here and there backs down, twitches away the tension, brings other muscles with them. My breath is more even now, and I give in to sleep. I have no knowledge of being lifted back to bed, covered again, next to Poke. Somehow, the voices stay as silent as the moon.

CHAPTER
FORTY-FOUR

Pictures. It came to Riley so suddenly, he put down his razor, half-shaved, and stared at the half-Santa in the mirror before him. *He and Grace did something like this with Mindy Taylor, a young lady with paraplegia: a series of pictures to help her physical therapist when Mindy rode her horse Colonel. He and Grace took pictures, step-by-step of her managing the horse, mounting, and dismounting, riding. The therapist fine-tuned her exercises to gain Mindy's strength, to keep her posture and balance from those pictures. Why couldn't something like that work for Maggie? Help her focus? Keep the voices away? Help her remember?*

Great idea, Grace's voice said.

Not just the horses, though. Things like feeding Poke or making meals, doing the laundry, sorting and dispensing the meds. He rubbed his chin, finished the right side of his face and rinsed. He wondered where the old 35mm was. Maybe in the closet in Maggie's room, where so much of Grace was still stored. Those new-fangled digital things—now that would be quicker.

By the time he was frying eggs, the picture idea had cooked as well. He'd add Hannah to the recipe. She was good with a camera. The drug store in town processed film. Maybe Hannah could help him put the book and captions together—

"Good morning, Riley."

Maggie's face was streaked with shadows and regret from the night before. She walked to the pantry, scanned the shelves, spied the food bin, counted one, two scoops and placed the bowl near Poke's dancing feet, then balanced the water bowl across the room to splash it down by his head. She scratched Poke behind the ears, the way he liked. Then, she let him outside, retrieved her breakfast Jell-O. Through all that, as simple as it was, demons shadowed her.

Riley placed breakfast at her place setting. "I've got an idea, Sunshine. Tell me what you think."

～

"I'd love to help!" Hannah said over the phone. "My camera has been begging to be used. And I can get some great pictures of the new horses. Oh, this is perfect! Maybe the pictures of Ranger and Justice could be used for posters elsewhere to increase fundraising, too. Oh, yes! When can I come out there to do this?"

Leave it to Hannah to show up that afternoon. "Okay, I thought I'd start with you, Riley, holding up two fingers with the scoop of dog food near Poke's bowl. That tells a story with all the elements."

"Can Poke be in the picture, too?" Maggie giggled.

"If he can stay still for two minutes!"

She snapped Poke and Riley, then, Maggie making a sandwich and sandwich fixin's, sitting atop Cartwheel, and leading Bliss to the pasture, Maggie holding the pitchfork, the toe pick, carrying the water, raking the stalls, filling the trough with water, measuring the medicine in the vials, washing dishes, brushing Bliss...As routines took over, their wooden poses naturalized. Hannah clicked away, just another body in the background for telling the story. Their story.

"You're very photogenic, Maggie." She took a long drink of water by the corral. "I'd love to take pictures of you."

"But you are."

"No, not for the memory book, for fun. Just pictures."

In fact, Hannah was already composing one in her mind: Maggie sitting on Riley's front porch steps in late afternoon, when the shadows were soft, and the light was golden. The shadows didn't show on Maggie's face, after a day with the horses. Looking directly at the camera lens, head slightly tilted to the left, her hair hanging against her collarbone, holding one of the rope harnesses in her hand against her hat, with Poke sitting or lying on the top step next to her.

It would become one of Riley's favorites.

Theirs was to be a simple errand. Stop off at the library to return a book, do a quick check of new books coming in, then pick up the book Riley had requested about search and rescue in the high country. Maybe a quick stop at Marta's to grab raspberry-rhubarb scones for breakfast tomorrow. But no side trips. After all, Riley didn't need gloves now that Maggie watched out for them.

The library was a simple two-story brick building with large glass windows and a reading plaza bordered by cactus and boulders. Near the entrance with the large glass doors and the book return box, people soaked up sun and words together. Just then, something glided into a place, something Maggie Fletcher shouldn't know at all.

Once inside, Riley returned the book, a thick thud behind

a wooden case, then asked for a clipboard, the reference list he used like a roadmap. She looked around. Like Riley's study, but with bigger comfort, palpable curiosity, and inspiration. Her connection was tangible within the space and sunlight and pages.

The muffled conversation while people pulled books from shelves, shuffled pages, the tapped fingers along the spine as she had done with Riley's books, as people turned to the index or table of contents. She saw Riley do all this, too, but now she knew it was something she had done thousands of times before. Not just in Riley's study. Not here, but somewhere else that was bigger and filled with those leather-bound references she loved to look through. The demanding snap of a newspaper, the softened heel-strikes when walking down a corridor of shelves on commercial carpet, the pause of sunlight along a shoulder escaping across the sill. She knew this. Before Maggie Fletcher. She couldn't stop the sensation, now coming in waves.

The sound of checking out books against a barcode reader, the heavy thump of volumes tumbling into the return box, the stifled laughter behind a conference room door, maybe an office even, the sound of keys clattering against metal files, the shelves nearly to the ceiling in ordered rows, the tables and chairs inviting another chapter, the copy machine, a microfiche, the soft murmur of penciled notes on papers, the occasional erasure, the dropped pen, the crisp sound of pages curled under a moistened finger, poised to turn the page catching the last possible word, turning, turning, the smell of paste and paper and leather and cloth. But now the smell of a wet coat drying on a chair crowded into the Arizona space, the smell of electric-warm computers and latent pipe tobacco in someone's pocket. Now, the smell of ink and cards stacked inside card catalogues, a three-hour-old Starbucks cup nursed for those last drops of java while finishing the article.

She knew all this, all of it, absorbing the mass of it as Riley walked toward the card catalogue. Grace's recipe box, a smaller version, had captured her attention the other day, but the card catalogue, what she couldn't think of at the time, was there before her like a ship at harbor. Somehow, she knew there were digital catalogues to streamline his search, even though she hadn't seen any. The wooden card catalogue, the treasure chest of authors and subjects and titles, and maybe even who *she* was before Maggie Fletcher.

She stood and looked at all of this in seconds, pulling a random catalogue drawer open to smell the cards and ink, to look at the numbers, to see the organization. It all came back to her. In those seconds, tears flushed her eyes, an odd welcome home, joyous and painful, because she had lost it, too. The connection was, at the same time, clawing at her and pushing her away with disbelief. A portion of her life returned just as the tear formed on her cheek, just as Riley selected the book and walked toward her. Just that second.

She worked in a library.

Riley's face furrowed. "Maggie? You need to sit down? You okay?"

"Riley, I know this. I know this place. I know all this," she whispered.

"You haven't been here before, though."

"No, no, a library, any library. I've not only been in one, I *worked* in one." Her voice quivered like a quarter tilting and rolling on tile until it gyro-wobbles off the table and out of sight.

Riley pulled closer.

"As soon as I walked in here, I remembered working like this. I know what a microfiche is, I remember how to repair, catalogue, and check out books, I can research with card catalogues and cross reference with the internet or register a book collection online." Her voice caught up to her breath. "I did this! I know this!" she whispered intently as if convincing the very air between them.

He swallowed. "Do you remember where?"

When she shook her head "no," she needed a better answer. Wasn't it enough just now to know as certainly as the overhead sun that she worked in a place like this?

"So, you were a librarian? That explains why you organize—"

"I've always known this." She looked at him with such piercing certainty, he stepped back slightly. "Just by walking in here, I've never been surer."

"Whew!" Riley tipped his hat back. "Goosebumps, Maggie—look!" He extended his arm. "We've got to tell Griff—"

She raised her hand. "Not yet. I need to let it soak in. It's mine right now. And I'm not sure I want to share this with anyone other than you."

"Mind if I look through the card catalogue for one more reference before we go home, then?"

She took a calming breath, in a place that could nearly be as much home as Riley's home. "Know what? Let me see if I can help you." A smile broke through. "I bet I can do it."

"Thought you'd never ask."

CHAPTER
FORTY-FIVE

"Slow down, Ranger. You don't always need to be first." Maggie led him past the water trough, but the horse broke into a spirited run toward the pasture. She shook her head, like a mother after an errant child.

"Good thing I had my gloves on. He got away from me. What do I need to do?" She squinted at Riley already seated tall on Cartwheel.

"I think Ranger is my project for a while. He's younger, he's a little more impulsive, even a little goofy. I'll work with him to channel that energy. He's from good stock, just needs someone to guide him." They watched him in the pasture chasing grasshoppers.

"A little goofy," she agreed.

"But you'll help me. Ride Bliss with me out there and we'll practice cutting him off in those quick movements. We won't frustrate him; we'll make it a game. He'll have to outsmart us by slowing down, use his intelligence and speed. Sound good?"

"Don't forget your gloves," Maggie teased.

Bliss and Cartwheel knew they were working, once the

saddles were in place. Ranger hadn't learned that yet. As fast as Ranger was, Bliss was methodical, Cartwheel was more the teacher. Riley had both horses stand parallel to Ranger, too busy munching grass to focus on them. The older horses surveyed how Ranger tolerated them. If Ranger moved, Riley and Maggie rode directly to close in again.

She rode Bliss slowly, getting the hang of moving so close to the others. They ambled into the grasses reaching the horses' forelocks at times. The thick hoof steps against the soil made Ranger look up, grass dangling from his mouth like a hayseed's portrait. Maggie grinned. Goofy, all right. *Where was Hannah's camera when you wanted it?*

Riley used hand signals to cue Maggie. Back up, turn, come forward, left, right, slow, steady. The horses needed to communicate with each other with each move and change, rather than having Riley telling the horses how to react.

"He's teasing us," Riley whispered. "See his ears? He's focused on us, but he's pretending he's not. Watch his legs. See? He's ready to run. You come behind me and stop. Just watch Ranger. I'll move to his side."

Ranger didn't know who to watch: right side, left side, back and forth. He lowered his head, pretending to eat. Riley brought Cartwheel around in a less confrontational manner. The horse looked up at Riley, started to approach him then stared at Maggie.

"Can't figure us out, see?" He wants to run, but he doesn't know which way to go. Riley paused, shifted in his saddle. "Let's teach him his name. Call him, Maggie."

"Ranger. Hey Ranger!"

The horse shifted weight and looked up.

"Hi, Ranger. Good boy!"

Riley brought Cartwheel closer and reached towards him. Ranger shook his head.

"Oh, you think so, do you? Well, Maggie and I won't hurt you, boy."

Riley motioned Maggie to close the gap, developing a wedge for Ranger to run through.

"Hi, Ranger. That's your name—Ranger."

The horse saw his chance and bolted between them.

"Now!"

Maggie and Riley churned Arizona soil. Cartwheel blocked the black horse. Ranger stopped dead then turned toward Maggie.

"Run by him, Sunshine!"

Bliss didn't flinch. She loved this game, too, like playing chicken with a '54 Ford. Ranger swerved toward Riley. Riley's turn. Ranger figured out the game, started toward Riley, then swerved toward Maggie. They wove back and forth, running, starting, and stopping a good thirty more minutes until Ranger slowed and approached the two horses.

"Hey, Ranger, come here!" she called out. Ranger slowly walked toward her. "You like the name Ranger? It's yours." He lifted his head so she could rub behind his ears. "Do you like that name? A name is very important, you know."

He watched her lean from Bliss toward the big black. It was a marvel how she had fit into the horses' training with every bit of inspiration toward Bliss and Cartwheel's sensitivity. Using the calm of a river to focus Ranger's high energy. Someone watching from the highway might see instinct, she seemed that comfortable.

Riley thought back to when Maggie was a shell of herself, how the shadows held her back, how she'd grown in the past months to take on the sunshine. As sure as the dead ends would eventually untangle, something would take Maggie from this place, back to her library life. He told himself he was prepared. But just that moment, when he pretended he could do this all himself, he just couldn't imagine her away. She belonged here.

"Looks like he's catching on." Riley rode alongside her.

"We'll try something like that with Justice later on. He's a little more mature. These horses will learn fast. In fact—"

Riley saw the motion in the driveway. Lester had just driven up with the mail.

"Hey, Sunshine, do me a favor. Why don't you take Ranger back for a drink? I have a little business with Lester. You stay by the barn until Lester leaves. Understand?"

Riley rode Cartwheel closer to the house. "Lester." Riley tipped his hat, approaching the driver's side of the mail truck.

"You need to know our dog attacked me the other day," Lester said. "Tore my pants cuff clean off my uniform."

Riley looked down from his mount, drew a breath. "Is that so? Now why do you suppose Poke would do a thing like that?" He leaned forward on the pommel.

"Well, I just don't know. Maybe he's crazy! Came out of nowhere and attacked my leg. You know, I can file a complaint about your dog—"

"Oh, I don't think you want to do that, Les, do you? Because I might have to file one, too."

"Now, what does *that* mean?"

"I think you know. How many years you've been delivering mail?"

"Going on eighteen years next March," Lester said proudly.

"And in those eighteen years you've been delivering mail, you usually put it in the mailbox or by the door, right?"

"Well, sure, I can't place the mail anywhere else that isn't authorized. You know that."

"So it's never been the policy of the United States Postal Service to walk directly into someone's home to deliver the mail?"

Cartwheel's ears twitched. Riley squinted his eyes toward Lester, pulling within a few inches of the truck window.

"Have I ever authorized you to enter my home and place

mail inside, let alone, check my refrigerator and take Jell-O?"

Lester sucked in a breath. His eyes grew wide and looked at the house, as if it would excuse him.

"Seems you didn't leave the mail in the mailbox or even on the porch. You walked directly into my house and placed the mail on my counter. Poke was just protecting the house from an intruder, right?"

Riley's steely blue eyes bore a hole right through Les' temple.

"See that insulated box over there? By the door? The one you've used for—what?—eighteen years? To drop the horses' medicine inside if I'm not available? We set that up, Lester— what?—eighteen years ago, so you wouldn't leave it in the heat. Isn't that right?"

"Riley, I—"

"The very box you chose to ignore a few days ago, so you could walk uninvited into my home and steal Jell-O from my fridge for your time and efforts." Riley's voice rose and filled the mail truck. "Hell, Lester, my dog is smarter than you! He knew you were breaking into my house!"

"Well, the door was open!" Lester sputtered.

Riley's hand leaned onto the window of the truck. "Seems I could file a pretty strong complaint against you, when it comes right down to it."

"Well, he didn't need to attack me like that!"

"Why'd you go into the house, Lester? Looking for something? Looking for someone? Wanting to make an impression with your uniform?" Riley grabbed Lester's collar. "If I ever catch you wanting to make an impression like that again, our conversation won't be so polite. I don't care if the door had welcome lights flashing, you were in my house uninvited. And you stole from me. That's against postal policy, in my book."

Lester sniffed.

"Right?" He yanked Lester forward.

"Yes, yes, Riley."

Riley released his grip. "Now get on with your business. I'm sure you'll think twice about pulling a stunt like that again."

Lester handed Riley his mail, reversed the truck and nearly hit Hannah's car entering the driveway. He gunned his vehicle onto the road. Hannah parked near Riley's truck.

"What was that all about?" Hannah laughed, closing her car door.

"Oh, Lester and I—we just came to an understanding."

"Ohhh." Hannah nodded. "No more adventures, I take it. Hey, take a look! I've got Maggie's memory book! I couldn't wait to bring it here. Got time to take a break?"

Maggie brought Ranger and Bliss up toward the house, seeing Hannah full of smiles.

"I had to take a break," she said. "That gallery is stacked and boxed and inventoried for this open house, and I'm no closer to finding a path through the collections than I was yesterday. This is my excuse, and I'm sticking to it!"

"Let's take a look."

She handed a brown volume to Maggie, with the title *Your Arizona Friends*. "I didn't want to call it a memory book on the cover. This seemed a little more personal, like something you'd hold on to for a while."

"Oh, it's beautiful," Maggie whispered. The cover creaked slightly as she opened it, the sound Maggie loved and connected to the best books ever. The names *Winnie the Pooh* and *Wind in the Willows* peeked from her memory long enough to trick her thoughts, then tucked inside again. Lost.

The first page consisted of pictures of Griff, Hannah, Riley, and of course, Poke. Then, pictures of Riley's house, the truck, the barn, the corral, the pasture. Then Bliss, Cartwheel, Ranger, and Justice. Maggie giggled. They were all hams, those horses, all posing important and proud, waiting for their close-ups. Then, starting on the fifth page, a close-up of Riley holding two fingers next to Poke's kibble, Poke drinking from the water dish, Riley raking the hay, Maggie adding fresh hay and water, washing dishes, pulling recipes from Grace's recipe box, checking the medicine in the barn fridge, riding Bliss, leading Justice, rubbing down the horses...it was all there, including that picture of Maggie, after a long day, sitting on Riley's porch steps.

"It's beautiful, really. I know it can help me."

Hannah nodded. "It's all about you, Maggie, everything you love, everything you do, your strength, everything about Maggie Fletcher."

Maggie turned the pages again, remembering all the jobs she'd come to do with Riley, how the pictures made Maggie Fletcher clear again. Everything she loved that helped her belong.

CHAPTER
FORTY-SIX

Griff watched his normally confident wife, the woman who sought out artists, created a gallery, a business, the woman who went to schools and the county fearlessly to seek support of art classes, who set up open houses monthly to highlight talent—this woman was now second guessing the representative artwork for the governor's open house. Ten Winds Gallery, to be featured in state publications, on television, was taking more than baby steps. It was difficult enough to title the event, but "Summer's Harvest" celebrated the gathering of plenty that was Ten Winds Gallery.

The governor's staff had arrived for logistics—a brisk, immaculate, suited, and sophisticated machine. They stood out like a clambake in Copper Station, yet found the gallery space desirable, quaint, while easily measuring space and planning with cell phones and iPads. Within two and a half hours, the team created a schedule timed to the second, set expectations, planned media coverage, and finally, completed two short conference calls. In the whirlwind wake, Hannah's confidence switched on again. All Griff recognized was that Hannah had finally stopped biting her nails.

She completed the daunting task of making final selections that told stories of Ten Winds' artists. She crowded other backup selections in the storage room. Just in case. But her favorite was the enlarged portrait of Maggie, relaxing with Poke on Riley's porch.

The day of the open house distracted her once again with after-shocks of insecurity. Perfection and the overlooked details were her enemies. And a Phoenix TV-station was going to film it?

"It's probably because of the award," Griff soothed dryly.

"Oh, gosh I totally forgot about the award! What should I say?" She tapped her forehead.

"Relax, sweetie. Never mind me," Griff teased. "You go on and worry about things you have prepared for, things you have no control over, and everything in between. You've done everything to perfection, and you can't even enjoy it!"

She glanced sideways at him. "I'm doing it again, aren't I? I get into disaster mode every time."

"You said it, I didn't." She shook her head. "Just stay by me so I don't say anything stupid."

"Moral support, you bet."

***

"This is Jenna Marsh, reporting from Ten Winds Gallery here in Copper Station, Arizona, about two hours south of Phoenix. Tonight, we have the honor of highlighting the Arizona Entrepreneurship Award. Ten Winds Gallery features a collection of local artists' works, the brainchild of Hannah Hensley, an artist herself. From this pottery, the paintings, the weavings, to this simple photograph behind me of a cowgirl taking a much-needed break with her dog, Ten Winds shows why the governor will be awarding Hannah this award. And Hannah—the founder of Ten Winds Gallery—this must be a big night for you!"

Hannah was swept in front of bright camera lights. Behind her, the photo of Maggie stared directly into the camera. Hannah looked for Griff, but her confidence bubbled when focused on only Jenna and the artists.

Townspeople, eager to share their town, milled about within the small gallery space. First thirty, then forty, then more squeezing inside, then spilling into the street, staring at the camera from behind Hannah, smiling at Griff, waving at friends or family members, as warm as the hot cider served nearby.

"Hey, Sunshine, look at this!" Riley drew Maggie through the crowd during Hannah's interview toward her photo. "Now, *that's* a great picture!"

"Isn't it, though?" Griff leaned toward them. "Hannah hasn't exhibited her own photos in quite a while, but this one, she just couldn't pass up."

"It's a perfect picture, and I know the perfect place to put it, too. Stay here, I'll be right back." Riley's voice disappeared into the crowd. But a surge of people broke Maggie and Griff's space. She couldn't stand her ground. Then, applause. Voices. The governor had arrived.

How Maggie lost sight of Griff and Riley, just then, when a series of crowd movements separated her from them. It happened so smoothly, like a gear into place, a turned cog, the tiles in a Chinese puzzle. Suddenly, Maggie was pulled into a corner of the crowded room, looking into an unyielding screen of the back of people's heads.

The applause died down to pin-drop quiet. "Ladies and gentlemen of Copper Station, I'm Molly Swanson of the Arizona State Arts Board. I am pleased to be a part of your 'Summer's Harvest' to recognize one of your community members who has made an impact in business and the arts. The arts board's mission is to ensure the arts as an integral part of everyone's life. So, when I discovered Ten Winds Gallery last spring, I wanted the rest of the state to know what a treasure Arizona has here."

During the applause, Maggie squeezed against shoulders from the corner to keep her from thinking of the van. Too tight, too warm, bodies pushing. She worked a few steps forward, then sideways to her right. Was that Riley ahead?

"...this special occasion for Hannah Hensley and the artists who make up Ten Winds Gallery, as well as Copper Station that supports arts every day..."

More applause freed small spaces for Maggie to escape. A step, another, and now she could see part of Hannah's head and the TV lights.

"...and this year's winner of the Arizona Entrepreneurship Award is Ten Winds Gallery and Hannah Hensley!"

Hearty applause allowed Maggie a few more steps. She'd been holding her breath, holding her palms forward to prevent getting too close. If she could just get out of the van...

"...to present the award this evening, the governor of Arizona, the Honorable Boyd Mullengrath."

The applause rose again as he stepped forward next to Hannah. "It's quite an honor to be with such a talented group of artists that represent the best of our state, who not only make art a business, but make business an art. The impact of Ten Winds Gallery and the support of Copper Station are the powerful combination that provide art experiences for the whole community."

With the next applause, Maggie moved forward, finally seeing Riley's hat. She knew...if she could...just work her way...

"Hey, Sunshine," he whispered. "I thought I'd lost you." Maggie watched Hannah hold the plaque and award, beaming and posing for pictures; she was just as happy for her friend and—

Her bones froze.

She felt the buried pain inch back from her memory. The "who" of the three men who brutalized her world, intersecting with the "what" of a man, clean, untouched, black hair, mole on the cheek. The sunlight sprayed into her memory, too. The harsh, white shirt he wore assaulting her good eye. She found the choice difficult: keep the eye open and risk sun-blindness or close the eye and always wonder about that moment. Her eye blinked wide against the filmy moisture, as wide as a gun barrel, to remember his voice and his looking at her...remember...*Boyd Mullengrath*. He had a name.

Her panic glided toward her throat, mixing memory and the "where" of right now. The talking man, the man with the mole and the slicked-back hair was there in the driveway and here, now, standing before her. She was two places at once: the smell of her kidnappers' skin as they held her in place; the sour beer and urine emanating from the van, baking in the drive; the just-washed scent of soap combined with air-conditioned cool spilling from the front door; an iron and turquoise crucifix nailed just inside the front door.

Then, inching, too, the "how" of mixing the concoction she remembered with the flashes and cameras and crowd, a cell phone tinkling in the background, and Riley standing next to her, smiling with Hannah and Griff. She gripped Riley's arm, but this time she didn't have a swollen eyelid, a broken wrist, or a cast on her arm.

"Maggie, what's going on? What is it?"

She stared, bones shaking like a roller coaster gone awry, an earthquake in her stomach. "I know him. I know him. His hair, see? The white teeth, the mole—"

The governor turned his head to wave. Riley saw, now too, what she'd seen. The charming presence that he once had voted for, now, something sinister. He saw terror shredding her, right before his eyes.

"Riley, please, it's the talking man. Remember? I told you? I remember it, more...what happened...I remember...please, Riley, help me!" Had there been no crowd noise, she very well could have been screaming. Instead, she was shaking, as if she'd stepped into a freezer. The governor posed again with Hannah.

"The Governor?" he whispered. "Okay, tell you what. Stay back here in the hallway. I'll get Griff. Do NOT go anywhere."

He disappeared again into the crowd that divided into selfie shots with the governor and pockets of conversation. The governor worked the crowd, occasionally glancing at pieces on display, then interrupted to shakes hands, in his standard pose, one leg slightly forward, so a three-quarter shot would show his better side.

No more than three seconds of conversation between Griff and Riley turned Griff's face into disbelief. He found Maggie's face in the hallway, filled with terror, as if she couldn't hold a scream much longer.

"Well, here is something," the governor commented. He moved toward the photo of Maggie. "This is such a simple photo but look at that face!" He paused, with great intent. "Ms. Hensley, is this someone who lives in the area?"

Griff's eyes slid from Maggie to the governor to Hannah. He wanted her to stop, to rewind the governor into a different position, across the room by the mobile or by the baskets, so he would never, never, never see Maggie's picture.

"Actually, she's a friend of mine."

"Her face, for some reason looks familiar to me. Can you believe that? I don't know where I would have—"

Griff stepped forward. "Governor, it's a pleasure to meet you! I'm Sheriff Griff Hensley, Hannah's husband. We're so glad you could be here, tonight." He pulled the governor away slightly from Maggie's picture, while Hannah's perplexed face stared accusingly at her husband.

"Great to meet you, Sheriff. You must be very proud."

"Indeed, I am. Hannah has worked hard, and you can see the community cares about her. But I've got to ask you a question—I'm dying to know, how do you do it? What's the secret to winning the public over so quickly? I'm just a little fish in a little pond, and I know how difficult it is."

The governor smiled, teeth flashing. "Well, I do love our state and all the aspects—the history, the geography, fabulous cities, the sports, and activities. I come to places like Copper Station and meet people like you, I know I've got the best job in the world. Who knew there was such exceptional talent in this little town? Now this—" He returned to Maggie's photo. "This caught my eye immediately. There is so much of Arizona in her face, in her eyes. I was considering it as a purchase for the state collection."

Riley stepped in. "I'm afraid, it's already purchased, Governor. It's no longer for sale." Riley looked at Hannah's face, convinced that she thought he was as rude as her husband.

Maggie barely breathed. She felt the crowd press again. Were people staring at her? Was it the broken wrist, her swollen eye, or the bruises along her arms? She dropped her head and saw two boots...the governor's boots. She remembered those, too, polished hard like marble. It was coming back. Days in the van, tumbling like rocks inside her; being used by all of them for every whim. Their names crept past the memory curtain, flashing something like Parker...*Poco no, Paco! Paco* talked to him, while the others held her upright. Paco, Kick and....She remembered Paco went by 'Street'.

"Hey, you're the gal in the picture!" someone said. "Hey, you! Over here, Governor!"

Riley spotted Maggie and pushed toward her.

Maggie closed her eyes, swayed with the crowd. Maybe she could disappear. Maybe it wouldn't hurt anymore. Her stomach found a new place to live, near her heart, and she was certain she would never breathe again. She opened her eyes, and Riley's blue eyes met hers as he pulled closer.

"Stay with me, Sunshine. We'll get you out of here *now*." He reached for her hand.

"So it is, so it is." The governor offered his winning trademark smile. "Young lady, what is your name?" He extended his hand while tilting his head to obscure the mole.

She wanted to say, *"Damaged Goods, that's what you named me"* But she choked on her own breath. The TV camera bumped against Maggie.

"Governor, Jenna Marsh. Can we get a quick interview for tonight's newscast? It will only take a few minutes."

"Absolutely, Miss Marsh. Wonderful night, isn't it?" He dissolved into the glare of the lights.

Maggie pushed past Riley, Griff, and Hannah, out the front door, out to the curb, and emptied her stomach into the gutter. She was somewhere between sobbing and choking, catching her breath and giving it away. The fist balled up in her stomach, the one she'd reserved for Les, the one she wished she hadn't broken in the van. That fist was ready for the governor. She wiped her mouth when Griff leaned over.

"What is it, Maggie?"

"I was...I was the merchandise. Kick, Street, and Paco, that was their names. I was damaged goods, no use to him at all. We drove up a long driveway, to a home, with a turquoise and iron cross inside the door," she gasped for breath, "and he met us outside and said they'd spoiled the merchandise, just like that. He told them to get rid of me." Her sobs were harder, now. She looked at Riley. "Please believe me, please...I remember, I remember..." She slowly sank to the curb. She hadn't known Hannah and Riley had followed and were listening to her words. She didn't realize some in the street were staring.

"The governor? Human trafficking?" Griff said under his breath. "This could be big. Big, all right."

"What's up with Maggie? And you two...what's with withholding a sale to the governor? I could have jacked up the price—"

"Hannah, I need you to listen to me as you never have before. We just got a break in Maggie's case and it's standing as guest of honor inside your gallery. So, very calmly, go inside and act as though nothing happened."

"You mean...? Oh, my gosh. Maggie, are you all right?" She looked at Maggie curled against her stomach rocking on the curb. Later, she thought it was such a stupid question while Maggie was in pieces at her feet.

"I know that face, that voice, his boots, his hair, his mole, his white teeth that didn't belong with the rest of them, that face on the TV at Doc's office..." she whispered.

"*That* was the talking man." Riley shook his head, as if it had been obvious all along.

Griff stood. "Okay, Hannah, take Maggie's photo down immediately and hide it in the back. We'll get it later. Don't let the governor near it. Riley, get Maggie home. I'll call you later. I need to check something at the airport."

CHAPTER
FORTY-SEVEN

You could call it an airport. Three hangers, a small office/terminal/vending machine haven in one room with round tables and serviceable plastic chairs. Run by volunteer deputy Mitch Blankenship, part-time helicopter pilot for search and rescue, the airport serviced crop dusters and a few local pilots. Griff's car was familiar with the narrow, rumbly country road that snaked an incline to the top of Sulfur Mesa. The sky in Griff's rearview mirror completed its last daylight thought while Griff planned how Mitch could be a resource to add another link to Maggie's past.

"Hey, Mitch. Griff," he said into his cell phone, blinking with about ten messages he needed to ignore.

"What's up?"

"You still have some of the governor's entourage with you there?"

"Sure. Carload of young people with cell phones and clipboards came in and met him here when he landed. They look like they belong in high school. Oh, and the helicopter pilot for the governor, he's here, too. Now that's one big dude."

"Pilot been snacking while he's waiting?"

"Matter of fact, had a sandwich and, he's finishing off a soda right now. Something I need to know?"

"I need that can fingerprinted. I can explain later when he's not around. But I need you to grab it for me. Was there anything the governor touched when he came in?"

"Oh, I'm sure I can help you with that, sir." Mitch switched gears.

"Can you keep the pilot there?"

"Yes, sir, you bet."

"Okay, give me ten minutes. I'm on my way. I'll want flight plans for the governor's helicopter, for today and any others for that copter in the past few months."

"Can do."

By the time Griff reached the top of Sulfur Mesa, the night sky had opened a few stars and the breeze danced across the small runway. Around him mixed the smell of jet fuel with the high desert evening. The windsock tugged against the cables, a whip swallowing a breeze. Two overhead parking lot lights hummed, their eerie white wash spotlighting the concrete block terminal.

He stuffed a few items into his vest from the back of the car: baggies, a tweezer, even a DNA swab kit if he got lucky to get a sample. He strode toward the brightly lit entrance, seeing the young group sharing iPad and cell phone conversations. Two state vehicles were parked under that same light. On the other side of Hanger 1, he was certain he saw the rotors of a partially hidden helicopter.

The gray metal door squealed open from years of desert dust clinging to the hinges, and the assaulting bright interior flashed into Griff's eyes. Mitch nodded from the counter. The group's piecemeal conversation of unfinished sentences paused when he entered, surprised by another body interrupting their space. Griff assumed his casual-sheriff mode, despite the urgency he felt.

"Mitch, how goes it?"

"Oh, fair to middlin'. How about you?"

"Just making the rounds, governor in town and all." He turned to the group, whose heads snapped back down to their screens. "Evenin' folks." He tilted his hat. "Hope Copper Station is treating you all right."

Mitch nodded toward the group as Griff leaned closer. "Those four over there drove. I heard them say, they expect the governor back in about an hour. And then there's—"

The men's restroom door opened and a strapping man, approximately the same size as the Grand Canyon but with legs, walked toward the group.

"That monster is your pilot. Flew the governor in this afternoon. Not sure how they both fit in that helicopter. Kinda had to unfold himself to get out. You probably saw it on Helipad 1." He pulled a manilla envelope from under the counter. "Got what you asked for."

"Hang onto that for a sec. I'll be right back."

Griff entered the men's room, looking at the hard surfaces reflecting the greenish florescent light. He spied a soda can protruding from the trash bit. "Well, I'll be." He couldn't guarantee it had been the pilot's. At this point, he couldn't guarantee anything about Maggie after her discovery, nor could he pass up something handed to him after all this time. He pulled a baggie from his vest, used the tweezers to carefully lift the can into the bag.

The hair on his arms stood at attention, that electric alarm under his skin when he saw potential evidence. His senses were heightened now, hearing every little drop from the sink or gurgle from the drain. The sink, the ledge above, the towel dispenser, there had to be something more. He pulled tape from his vest, this time carefully placing it on the hot-water faucet handle...another from the towel dispenser handle. Two fingerprints, from a large hand, maybe even from Grand Canyon, himself. He hoped it would match the partial on the bullet casing from Mitchell Canyon. He could have been satisfied, but as he turned to exit, the payoff: a large, full palm print on the door. Plenty of tape to get that, too. He flushed the toilet to cover his purpose.

He nodded toward Mitch as he went back outside to a brisker upwind. He dropped off the pieces of evidence he'd already collected, then walked quickly toward the copter. Not sure of the make, he would bet a last dollar it was a Sikorsky, compact for two passengers. He pulled a tape measure along the skids. Nearly eighteen feet, a match to the length from the ghost copter in Mitchell Canyon. He bagged a dust sample along the body, another connection, perhaps. Handprints on both side handles were collected those on tape as well. As he scanned the soil outside the helipad, on the pilot's side, Griff made out several boot prints. No problem getting those if he moved quickly. But as he stood, staring at the sky, he became certain of eyes focused on the nape of his neck.

"Something I can help you with, Sheriff?"

The pilot seemed bigger outside the terminal for some reason. Griff let out a small breath. "Sheriff Griff Hensley." He extended his hand. "You're missing the party in town!"

"So are you." The pilot's grip was as if Griff had just put his hand into concrete. "Wally Cameron, Sheriff. You like this little toy?" A hint of a smile followed.

"You the pilot?"

"Yes, sir. Been with the governor for six years now."

"Now that's the perfect job! Flying anywhere in the state. I have to confess, I really wanted to take a look at this baby. Boy, our search and rescue could sure use something like this."

"Thought you had a helicopter."

"Well, not like this! I saw those comfortable seats. Is that a sound system?" Griff cupped his hand against the bubble of the cockpit.

"Governor likes a little music to relax. He can set up channels to pull in radio, music from his phone, and my chatter, too."

"So, this beauty isn't yours?"

"Oh, gosh, no! It's the governor's personal helicopter. He uses it for some state business, but sometimes, he just likes to get out of the city to get a bird's-eye view, know what I mean?"

"Like I said, the perfect job! Speaking of perfect, you've got the night for it too, clear sky, not too much wind. You heading back tonight?"

"As soon as the governor gets back."

"I suppose you follow the canyon and make a turn north of Cavern River Bridge, to get back to Phoenix."

"Aw, no, we always follow the river and highway all the way back."

"At least you don't have to drive back tonight. What, you can make it back in an hour?"

"Forty-five minutes, tops."

"Nice, nice. Well, I guess you're right. The canyon's a bit of a challenge, especially at night with those wind gusts."

Cameron tapped the edge of the helicopter. "This baby is a sweet ride. I'm used to night flying—I flew in the marines. This baby's got electronic everything—" Wally relaxed, stepped backward onto the soil, leaving behind a clear, right, boot print.

"No kidding! The marines?"

"Nothing like this, though; this is a piece of cake! It's so stable, you can land on a dime, even if the wind is kicking up. Well, just a few months ago, I landed this bird on a little mesa in Mitchell Canyon—" Cameron stopped. "Uh, no problem, no problem at all."

Griff had hooked Cameron and he took the bait: *"just a few months ago."* He wanted to pull out the cuffs right then and there, grab Wally Cameron and the governor and march them back into town before the moon rose. But, instead, Griff lowered his head, hid his face, as if the sand had caught his eye. "Well, I hope our little town did you all proud. It's been a real pleasure, Wally, just to get to talk with you." Griff extended his hand again, just then, on purpose, dropped his car keys on the ground.

"Hey, you can't lose those!" Wally bent over and picked them up with his *left* hand.

"No, I don't dare. Thanks again, Wally. Have a safe flight, now. Beautiful night for it."

Griff returned to the terminal just as two of the young people peeled out of the parking lot and drove toward town. He walked toward Mitch who motioned him into the bathtub-sized airport office.

"They're picking up the governor now," Mitch nodded toward the disappearing car. "I imagine he'll be back in about twenty minutes. So, what gives, Griff?"

"Remember that ambushed van we found in Mitchell Canyon? Remember we found evidence of another helicopter when we set down? What struck you about those marks?"

"A small helicopter, a two-seater, likely, but something you could manage in a canyon."

"The skids match the length of the one out back. I have a suspicion that helicopter brought two people either to meet with or dispose of the bodies we found."

"Mullengrath? What the hell for?"

"Can't say, yet, but for now, I need some evidence. Our pilot left a nice boot print out by the helicopter on the south side. There may be some of Mullengrath's prints, too. I need you to get those for me. And I'd love to get a fingerprint of Mullengrath's too."

"Got something better. When he arrived, one of the entourage had Mullengrath signing papers to fax back to the Capitol.

In his hurry, he got a nasty little paper cut on his index finger. You know those things can bleed like a stuck pig. So, you've got your DNA and fingerprint, too." He held up a small bag with a used bandage inside. "Hey, you asked for evidence. He changed to another bandage once the bleeding stopped."

"Mitch, you're beautiful."

"Now, as to the flight plan, I don't have anything filed for that bird in the last few months."

Griff felt his shoulders fall a bit, although wasn't surprised the copter would have kept that flight secret. Illegal, but hey, when you're the governor in your own private helicopter...This was too predictable and clean. He shuffled through the flight plan identification and registration.

"Hey, wait a minute! This says the helicopter came here tonight along the canyon ridge."

"So?"

Griff leaned closer. "Cameron just told me they followed the highway and the river." He stared at the report. "Okay, follow along with me here. What if, the helicopter flew along the canyon ridge, then took a quick detour into the canyon? What if they were, oh, say checking to see if the van was still there after all this time? If Mullengrath recognized the van was missing, he'd know we'd found it. He could get the state lab reports or destroy the evidence when he gets back." He stared at Mitch's blank face.

"He's playing us," Griff whispered. A brief flash of pride washed over him from Hannah's award earlier in the evening, but he couldn't help but wonder, what if the Entrepreneurship Award was a setup to fly past into the canyon on a legitimate flight to check on the van?

"I think they just drove up," Mitch said.

"Say, you've got that camera for the helicopter handy, don't you?" Griff slammed the flight plan report onto the desk. "I want one more piece of evidence. I think it's time to play the game for our advantage..."

The sudden flux of chatter as the governor and Cameron strode in heightened the energy in the sleepy terminal. Wally Cameron got another soda for the night flight back.

"People, you all did well. This went so smoothly considering the amount of logistics we had to get in place. I think the people of Copper Station—well! Sheriff! We meet again!" Governor Mullengrath extended his hand forward. "I wondered where you went to!"

Mitch leaned forward from the counter. "Now Governor, I hope you don't mind, but we don't have much excitement around this airport just every day. Would you mind if we could steal just a few more extra minutes for a picture?"

"Well, of course not!"

"Maybe we could get you and your aides. Mr. Cameron, would you join us, too? Oh! And Sheriff—you could be in the picture, too. I know you're in a hurry to get back, but a picture like this would add a nice official touch to the terminal."

Governor Mullengrath's practiced smile gleamed. Mitch focused the shot, gathering around a mounted propeller on the wall, the governor, his aides, Molly Swanson, Griff.

"How about this? Maybe, Governor, you could put one hand on the propeller. Sheriff, you do the same. Makes a nice frame. There...that's good. Okay, say 'parachute'!"

The flash captured quick smiles, the exceptionally white teeth, the mole on his cheek and even the bandage on his index finger. The propeller captured the governor's handprint.

MAGGIE

I'm shaking, all the way inside jangling out through my arms,
my legs, even my ears. Riley curled me into the truck, opened
the window on my side, knowing I needed to suck in the desert
air that shot across my face. I'm shaking and my foot taps like
the old days, so much so, that my stomach is shaking up in my
throat. The only thing I don't do is count. Almost, but I don't.
Riley screeches to a halt in the driveway, hadn't even cut the
engine, and I was already out. Up the steps, caged by the porch
rail.

All I can taste is the bile from the swath of vomit I left in
town.

All I can hear is the ringing—or is it screaming?—in my
ears.

All I can smell is Riley's cinnamon kitchen, a reminder that
I could be home if I could just settle.

All I can say is, "No, no, no."

It's like Maggie Fletcher just got stolen and I can't be sure
of me.

It's coming back, like getting drowned in pages and pages
of old newspapers, of the three grabbing me, into the van, not
letting me go, keeping me inside, unless I had to pee or they
needed to eat, or they wanted a beer at another convenience
store. It never stopped, their hunger and urgency. They never
leave my side unless I pee. They're outside the bathroom door
when I finally see the damage they'd done and how I got lost
after that. I wash my face in the sink, but don't recognize the
monster face in the mirror. I bend over to push my face into
the water, but I can't drown myself. There is no stopper.
Maybe someone tried before. I can't remember much before,
but I remember then, all of it: the van, the smell of the beer,

the semen and sweat, the donuts and the beer cans rolling on the floor when they slammed me down again. Again. Again.

Riley holds my shoulders to make sure I don't disappear. He tells me everyone has my back. Hannah, Griff, Riley. He reminds me this was a shattering clue regarding that son of a bitch, even though it's left me raw and fearful all over again. *It was going so good*, I thought, *just as I was discovering Maggie Fletcher*. Now, I know how dirty I felt, how I wanted to die, how I lost who I was because I couldn't ever face myself again. Riley holds me. Each new answer is the thing that drowns me with those memories.

I should run away.

Problem with that, he says, is that running from something never leads you toward something else. It just puts you in circles until you figure out what you're running from. Riley's right. I can breathe a little because I actually heard my Maggie Fletcher voice squeeze through my breath. A breath, now, two away from that woman I remembered: head slumped forward, torn and bloodied clothing, eye swollen, that incredible pain in my right wrist, the constant throbbing in my gut. That woman who was physically shredded into Maggie Fletcher coleslaw, with not a drop of soul left in her being.

Spoiled, damaged, merchandise. And now I remember who said that—not even to my face because that was one face he could ignore. Thing was, he was right. I was so damaged I could never be myself again.

Riley pulls me back outside to sit on the porch with Poke in an attempt to feel normal. He looks for Cassiopeia and suddenly I remember looking for Orion; it was something I did before Maggie Fletcher, before the van, long ago in some other place. I breathe a little more while Poke puts his paw in my lap like he knows something. Riley brings me cherry Jell-O. That's how Maggie Fletcher began.

I hold the Jell-O. It isn't shaking. Nor am I.

CHAPTER
FORTY-EIGHT

Griff's desk had taken on a life of its own, a landscape of files across the surface. Maggie's case had spilled into detective work like a flood. That intricate net of Governor Mullengrath's involvement pulled Griff in more. Yet, he didn't want this case to unravel when influence was stronger than the truth. Mullengrath's portrait stared towards Griff's desk, while silver shivered along his spine.

With the distraction of Hannah's gallery exhibition the other night, Griff was keenly aware that someone could have found a way to his office, his files, but his security cameras showed nothing and evening shift reported no one in his office. He couldn't help but check under the lamp, behind file drawers, under his desk and chair and, yes, even behind the governor's portrait, but found no listening devices or cameras. Just then, the fax machine hummed to life, punching papers into the tray. His phone rang.

"Sheriff Hensley, this is Dan at the state crime lab. I'm sending you a rather lengthy fax right now about the individuals in the Mitchell Canyon van."

"Coming through right now. Talk to me."

"Sorting the remains was difficult, but so far, we can confirm three individuals with positive DNA matches. There may have been a fourth person, and we're working on DNA from the seatbelt for that."

"Go on."

"We used what dental work we could, and the maggots for the rest. Crazy fluke. We'd been checking Arizona records with no luck. Once we consulted the federal list, we got a match. These guys aren't from Arizona. They're from New York."

"New York?"

"We picked up multiple traces of pollen from other states collected in the van undercarriage. But, yes, New York is one of the states that has pollen matches with what we found. As far as we know, that's the farthest east this van was."

Maggie could be from New York. She remembered a long trip in the van. New York was, what? Three days in good weather and someone driving 24/7. So, four, maybe five days in that van across country, over two thousand miles. That could fit with her story.

"You got names?"

"Here goes: Joseph Martin Hicks, white male, age forty-four, with previous records including gangs and prostitution. Gang name we think was 'Kick'. Then we have Charles Andrew Pitts, a white male, age forty, street name 'Pro'. Had priors in car theft, prostitution, and trafficking. And the third guy is Paco Felipe Valesquez, Hispanic male, age forty-three, gang name 'Street', with violations in drugs, theft, and trafficking."

"That's some list. So we've got three things in common: prostitution, trafficking, and New York City. Was the van stolen?"

"We can't get much with the VIN ground away, but when we checked New York records, we found no missing black van."

"And the female?"

"We're hitting a roadblock getting information about the female, but right now, we have to assume she was from somewhere along the route they took."

"So, did these guys meet in a bar somewhere, get to talking, and decide to kidnap someone?"

"Page eighteen of your fax shows three mug shots, from Auburn Correctional in New York. They served there. In fact, Hicks served with Valesquez on the same cell block, and Pitts showed up about eight months later. Their dates overlap."

"Well, I'll be. They were pen friends. I'll show these pictures to the female today, see if she can recognize any of them. By the way, you get my soda cans, saliva and blood samples? The fingerprints?"

"Think we got them by courier today. I'll get that on the schedule. Those should be easy."

"I've got a really stupid question. What happens to the vehicle, the bodies, the other evidence? I only ask because, of course, I want the findings kept confidential."

"Oh, always, Sheriff. The items are sealed and place in evidence. All of this is admissible in court, but we keep the results and preliminary findings for your eyes only or for legal teams later. We couldn't be very effective as a crime lab if we leaked findings."

"But you know as well as I do, some bigwig or senator who might want to know more could—"

"Whatever you're worrying about, Sheriff, this is too complex a case to let anyone but you or legal representatives in a trial see what we have on file. We'd need a court order to overturn that. That includes the governor himself wanting to see any reports."

Funny he should say that, thought Griff. He wanted to pursue that comment further, and might have at a local bar. He kept the questions tucked in a corner of his brain. "I do thank you, Dan. You've given me a bunch to keep me busy for a while." He replaced the receiver, awaiting an explosion.

⎯⎯⎯

Maggie and Riley were walking from the barn in animated conversation about Ranger and Bliss when Griff arrived. They'd been knee-high in pasture grass, teaching Ranger about keeping pace with other horses, holding back the reins a bit to keep him comfortable with a canter. Maggie's smile was tempered with caution when she saw Griff on the porch, his drawn face, his hands clenching a folder. Whatever it was, Maggie wasn't ready.

"I've got some pictures for you, Maggie. Just a few I want you to look at. This won't take long."

They walked into the kitchen, and he placed a small camera on top of the folder.

"What's with that?" she asked.

"I need to start recording your responses, now that you know more. This is very important. I need your permission to do this, and it could be used in court. Are you willing to look at the pictures and tell your story?"

"Do I have to say anything into the camera?"

"No, not if you don't want. We'll pretend it's not there. Just talk to Riley and me, like you normally do."

"Sure, okay."

Griff set up the camera, had Riley sit out of view, but close enough that he saw the red light blink.

"This is a preliminary interview with a woman we know as 'Maggie Fletcher', an alias because we don't know her real name. So, now you tell me your name."

She giggled. "Maggie Fletcher."

"Now, Maggie, I'm going to show you three men's faces. You need to tell me if you recognize them." He opened the folder and placed the pictures one by one in front of her. Slam! She felt their bodies pushing, shoving, twisting her sanity away. Her back stiffened, her shoulders braced, she sucked in a breath tightly, almost ready to snap that breath in two. She covered her eyes, all within three seconds.

"You said I'd never see them again!" Her voice was as thin and brittle as a torn newspaper insulation in the wall of a cabin.

"These are just pictures, Maggie, the men are gone. Do you recognize them?"

She sniffed then nodded briskly. "That's Pro, that's Kick, and this, this is Street. I finally remembered. And Street went by Paco when he was at the mansion with the governor." She had just dealt Griff four of a kind, all kings, and the jackpot was ready to cash in.

Griff checked the camera, making sure it was capturing the deal. "You're certain these are the men that took you into the van? The ones that assaulted you while transporting you to Arizona over the course of several days?"

She rocked against the back of the chair, hugging herself. "I wanted to forget them forever," she whispered. Riley's hand reached over to her to keep her from sinking farther. "Yes, yes, those are the men."

"Okay, Maggie. We're almost done. I'm hoping you can remember more details now, a smell, a color, a place. You once told me 'Hamilton', but I wasn't sure if that were a town or a person. Anything about that?"

Riley looked accusingly at Griff, as if saying "enough is enough."

"I only ask because you are remembering more. For the first time, you might reel in a few details that you hadn't thought of. If we could record them...you wouldn't have to think about them again."

Moments before, she was Maggie Fletcher, riding Bliss in

the sunshine, now she was losing Maggie to those monster demons. That other woman was on shaky ground; someone Maggie wasn't even sure she liked. The voices had wiped her raw enough, and yet, if Griff were right, this might be the end of it. This would be the time to tell whatever she could remember, despite who she was. Griff would finish his job. She looked at Riley.

He nodded toward her. "Reliving this is pretty horrible, Sunshine, and Griff can't make you do this. But he's right. If you want this all to go away and be behind you, you need to tell Griff whatever you can remember."

"But I don't like her! I don't want to remember her!"

"You know what I think? I think you don't know who that other woman is because these guys took her away from you. I think you don't want her to go away, it's Pro and Kick and Street that you want to go away." Riley dug a bit to have her think of her other life, a contrary direction to lead her away.

"See, when Bliss was little her mama died. Bliss remembered her mama night after night and cried for her. Grace was in the barn all night, sometimes, trying to get her to eat, to drink, to rest. Bliss had memories that were sad, and she couldn't move on from them, until she looked around and decided to walk into another day. And you're like Bliss, right now. You've got some bad memories to walk through, some real unknowns. But on the other side, we'll still be here; I told you that. You see how happy Bliss is now? Cause she let go of her sadness and moved on. You've got to do this, Sunshine. When you're ready."

"Like Bliss..." She wiped her face with her arm and hands then took a breath. "Okay...I remember...a parking lot. The sun was shining. It wasn't hot. I heard birds, too. I was carrying something bulky. It was heavy. My arms were loaded down..."

CHAPTER
FORTY-NINE

RILEY

Riley, worn after listening to Maggie about those days of spare sunshine, took a short walk toward the barn. If Grace talked with him now, she'd likely recognize his anger was arrowing into revenge against those three excuses for humans. But there was something else she would sense from him: his awe for Maggie, her survival. How a fishing trip turned his life around.

"You know you're a part of me, Grace, always will be. I don't always feel your presence, can't always pinpoint you the way I did. It kills me a little every day that I can't. I tried my best for Maggie, bringing her here, something you understood. And even though Maggie lost herself, I lost what I was with you. I watch her pulling those dark memories as if remembering her grave. But she still finds a smile for me. I couldn't have been that brave.

"When she came here, I didn't expect all this and Griff warned me it might happen. I'm fooling myself to say that Maggie isn't as important as I thought. She's not a project to finish, she's someone I look forward to seeing every day. In everything we do. I can't find wrong in that.

"If Maggie has another life, she needs to return to, well, that's something you could face better than I ever could. If her happiness takes her away, I guess that was the point all along.

"Did you have landmarks, too, that I didn't notice or pushed aside? You were strong, too, facing your cancer. And maybe I didn't listen enough to clear the air about saying goodbye. Maybe that's why you've been so good about listening lately.

"When Maggie stopped talking today, the exhaustion wiped her muscles soft, letting go of the fight that she'd kept in her all this time. I couldn't help but feel my heart switch gears. Not pity anymore when she finished, no, I admired her for facing her darkness and walking through it. That's pretty damn brave. Something someone could love."

CHAPTER
FIFTY

By the time Griff set his coffee mug on his desk—the very mug he'd purchased from Hannah—his double-shot Americano had grown cold. He was distracted by the stack of papers collecting on the fax tray, spewing sheets onto the floor before he arrived this morning. Which meant the state crime lab had completed DNA testing on the soda can, blood samples and fingerprints. And maybe a match to a lone shell casing at the canyon.

He pulled the CD of Maggie's statement from a briefcase loaded with about three dozen folders ago and let it drop on the desk. Her exhausted face ghosted his mind, after her marathon of memories, that dark dungeon that provided clues and answers at the same time. Like pennies, those details saved up a clue at a time. In that shiny disc, he recognized her testimony would convict Boyd Mullengrath before he earned another vote. After the storm she'd been through that washed her clean? He couldn't help but love her a little himself.

The stack from the fax tray reported DNA samples completed for "John Does one and two," ambiguous monikers that represented Mullengrath and Wally Cameron. The pilot's DNA was in the system as part of a background check performed by the governor's office. A red flag jolted him. Someone in the crime lab might have recognized the name and notified the governor, despite what Dan said. Sure enough, the fingerprints matched for Cameron. He'd handled the bullet. That son of a bitch Mullengrath had to have been close enough to duck at the rifle's report. Now, he'd have to prove it.

———

By mid-morning and three bitter sips of coffee later, Griff had investigated the Auburn Correctional files online, finding Hicks and Valesquez had been admitted within a month of each other. Pitts showed up months later. Pitts' mug shot, a sullen SOB, contrasted with Valesquez's picture that showed a bit of comfort, and Hicks' picture that hinted fear. But this was what caught Griff's eye: Hicks and Valesquez were not only in the same cell block, they occupied the same cell for more than five years.

That discovery cracked like Cameron's rifle. Bang.

But meeting for a game of hoops and talking during a card game and sharing signals or codes on the inside is one thing; getting money to front an operation is something else. So, who had a tie to Mullengrath? What was the New York-Arizona connection that owned not only the three but a governor as well?

His day was consumed by the computer, with background checks on persons with common enough names: Hicks, Pitts or Valesquez. He swung back and forth between Arizona and New York, eventually focusing on Valesquez, with fewer hits between the two states. He looked up. Governor Mullengrath's image seemed to whisper "Sucker!" taunting him with those white teeth and perfect smile.

He found a Dr. Chris Valesquez who got his medical degree

and residency completed in Columbia, but he didn't fit the darkness suggested by Maggie's past. Here was a Bo Valesquez who worked briefly in New York, then Chicago, St. Louis, Houston. Then employment history stopped. Job history was sporadic—mostly fast-food restaurants or diners—brief, intermittent, in the mid-1980s. Social security number led him to 1965 when Bo was born, and no military records to be found. This Bo was a drifter, all right. Just the kind of person Griff might look for.

Paco was younger than Bo Valesquez, if there were a connection, and easier to find because Paco was a frequent flyer. He seemed to love prison. A lot. There was no picture of Bo, even a driver's license. Curious with all the drifting he did. Griff scanned newspapers in New York, then Chicago and St. Louis finding no connection between the two...until Houston.

Local Man arrested for Drug Trafficking in New York

Griff raised his eyebrows. Well, I'll be. It was Paco again, arrested in New York in 1987 for transporting marijuana and cocaine from Houston in the wheel wells of his pickup. His nice new truck? Someone else could afford that, not a released prisoner. So once again, Paco worked for someone with bucks. Paco apparently sold the marijuana for upwards of six figures, but the cocaine had disappeared. That left Paco hanging again and back to prison. Felt like a setup. That was about the time that Bo disappeared, too. But still no Mullengrath in the picture.

It took another seven years before Paco was released, Griff found in the Auburn records, but in a matter of months was rearrested for trading drugs for prostitutes. When he returned to Auburn, that's when he met up with Hicks and Pitts. What seemed obvious to Griff was that Paco was taking the fall for someone, either he was too stupid, or he was working the system to find more players and connections. But where was this Bo Valesquez?

Before the internet made everyone's life so nauseatingly accessible, Griff knew it was fairly easy to get lost. Work in McDonald's for four or five years in four or five states, no one follows you. Short-term employment, moving from job to job, staying long enough to make enough cash to move on. It was cash, too, no credit cards or checking accounts. Just like Bo Valesquez. Thinking like Bo, Griff would go to a place large enough to blend into a crowd, say, a circus, in construction, or on a ranch where you didn't have to explain much to the next fellow because no one was asking. In the '80s, one didn't have to think globally to make some cash.

So, Griff turned to Houston for announcements: county fairs, amusement rides, boxing matches, where someone could make an extra dollar and get lost as quickly. He became print blind after a few hours, reading ads and notices, and nearly missed the small ad, late July, 1987. A coincidence this was about the time Bo Valesquez disappeared and Paco returned to Auburn? The ad was black with white print, a traveling rodeo on a circuit through Oklahoma and Texas. They were hitting smaller towns outside Houston for no-name talent, inviting riders who were willing to pay a hundred bucks to enter and maybe get a bit of cash if they lasted eight seconds. Stories like this were always good fillers for the larger papers when a local athlete made good.

"Bo Mullen from Houston...local bronc rider Bo Mullen from the Xbar6 ranch...new on the rodeo scene Bo Mullen..." The name was too close to Mullengrath's for Griff to overlook, so he switched gears again. Who was Bo Mullen?

"Bo Mullen won the $150 purse on the final ride of the night. He drew 'Backbreaker', the horse out of J-Circle Ranch. But the horse was no match for Mullen's control. He lasted nine seconds, one second over because he claimed he never heard the *signal. A crowd favorite, Bo Mullen's talent is..."*

Bo Mullen, bronc rider. Bo Mullen who suddenly appeared from a ranch out of nowhere, maybe a step away from Boyd Mullengrath if the wind were right and the shadows didn't lie. Or just another quirky coincidence. A picture, about the size of a postage stamp showed Bo Mullen, hatless, riding the arch of a hard-riding bronc, but it didn't help. But the Xbar6 ranch could.

Griff was riding this track and it seemed the trip might be worth it. Bo Mullen had no social security number, let alone any documentation that he'd worked for Xbar6. So, Griff searched for Bo Mullen's driver's license. And there, in Enid, Oklahoma, he found gold. September, 1988, Bo Mullen applied for one. The scanned picture tracked through his fax. Bo Mullen, 6'2," 197 pounds, black hair, brown eyes, thin, muscular, a mustache...and on the contour of his left cheek, a mole. It was unmistakable.

Bo Valesquez became Bo Mullen, who then became Boyd Mullengrath.

Griff imagined a new scenario. Maybe Bo Valesquez kept the cocaine, sold it for millions, but lived simply and under the radar while Paco, *his brother?* paid his debt, and got a payoff when released from prison. What's four or five years in prison when someone has a million dollars for you on the outside?

After all this, Griff rubbed his face with his hands. His next step: getting DNA from Mullengrath's blood sample to match with Paco's. The phone jolted Griff from the chill that just dripped down his back.

"Sheriff? Dan again, from the state crime lab. You know those boot prints you sent me? The soda can? We got a match through military records, although we ended up matching in our system as well. Those boot prints verify this guy is tall, about 6'5". His DNA from the soda can matches to a very tall marine from Vietnam, a Walter Cameron."

"Don't tell me: Cameron was a helicopter pilot and trained as a sniper."

"How did you know?"

"Let's say a lucky guess."

"And that Walter Cameron? We've got a match with some-one living here right in Phoenix."

"No joke," Griff deadpanned.

"No joke, honest. You want me to send that to you?"

"Oh sure. My desk can always use a new piece of paper. Oh, and Dan, I have another favor. That DNA you got from our 'John Doe One'? See if that DNA has any match to Paco Valesquez. Just a theory I have."

"I can do that right now. Let me pull both tests up on the computer."

As much as Griff had grown to hate computers with their tiny little brains and frustratingly complex maintenance, he'd give a new pair of eyes to find out the two DNA samples matched. Clicks and hums over the phone gave Griff more confidence he was on the right track. He looked at Mul-lengrath's photo on his wall. If this weren't a match—

"Okay...just a moment...Sheriff? You're not going to be-lieve this!"

"Try me."

"DNA samples that you took of John Doe One and those we have of Paco Valesquez are a 99.9% match! How did you know?"

"It's my lucky day. Can you send me that comparison, too? We just hit a jackpot!"

Bo Valesquez was Paco's older brother. Paco took the fall for Bo, as Bo racked up an untraceable income. But even more chilling is that Bo Valesquez as Boyd Mullengrath was willing to kill his own flesh—and abandon the body—to cover his as-sociation with Paco.

"So, who is this 'John Doe One,' now that we've established

he's Paco Valesquez's brother?" The voice over the phone reminded Griff he was still on the line.

"Can't tell you right now, it's early in the investigation. But I'm counting on you, Dan, to keep this extremely confidential. We'll keep the name 'John Doe One' for now on that sample, but no one, and I mean no one else is to know. Is that clear?"

"As clear as my testimony in court will be about these two. I'm sending the faxes now. Oh, and the dental records for the female? Everything is shut down by the FBI in that regard. They must be doing an investigation in New York and no locals or state agencies can access anything, yet."

"FBI? Really?"

"No one, except another FBI office can make a request. You know, the FBI talks to the FBI. States? Counties? Not so much."

"I'm getting the faxes, now, Dan. I thank you for all your efforts these last few months. You've been more than helpful."

Griff replaced the phone receiver into the cradle, finally blowing out a boulder of air that had lodged in his lungs. What a complicated mess he'd stepped into: brother against brother, across-state human trafficking, hidden drug sales and false identities, all in the name of money, what he thought all along motivated the killings. Boyd Mullengrath saw Maggie's picture during the gallery open house, but more important, he didn't dare recognize that Maggie had survived. Griff's case had to be airtight, no slip-ups, no missed details, no overlooked evidence. The prosecutor would be in Mullengrath's pocket and could tear Maggie to shreds all over again if Griff missed one tiny spark of truth. And yet, as tired as he was, he sat back smiling. This was the most challenging investigation Griff had ever been involved in, from a stop along a country road to check on what someone had thrown from a van. All because he couldn't forget that young woman's battered face and torn body when he unrolled the carpet that warm night.

Griff shook his head. The fax machine hummed alive again with two sheets of paper with similar DNA: Paco Valesquez and "John Doe One."

"What the hell did I get myself into?"

CHAPTER
FIFTY-ONE

MAGGIE

Sometimes I look at my hands. I open them, at first touching, palms up as if I were opening a book. I see lines and branches but sometimes I see calluses and creases from my leather gloves. I see a scratch or even a small bruise from holding the reins or cleaning their hooves or currying the horses. My hands feed them, water them, touch their foreheads or their backs, and I love how they respond to my touch.

Part of me remembers a time when I held my hand up to block a slap headed toward my cheek. Or another time when my hand rubbed a bruise near my eye. I remember better these days. Riley says it helps to, and I don't have the panic I used to. Griff asked me questions, and I remembered more than bits and pieces: Rolling Rock beer cans, Snickers candy wrappers, McDonald's double cheeseburger wrappers, cheap restrooms with dirt mopped into the corners and a broken latch on the bathroom stall door...those things came back and he said they were important. Street's face, Pro's stubby fingers, the arch of Kick's eyebrows, the smell of old carpet.

But today, I watch my hands be comfortable, reaching for saddles, tugging on my gloves, lifting hay with a pitchfork, fingers wrapped tight around the handle. And when I take a deep breath of early autumn Arizona, I look up because I can.

Hannah leans against the corral fence while we watch Griff and Riley. Ranger and Justice are in the pasture, the men riding, the thick, soft rhythm of hoof against cold earth. The fog, a lost white breath from the mountains, disappears as the sun rises. Griff changes directions in the pasture with Justice, Ranger going forward, then sideways, then stopping to Riley's signals. Stop, start, reverse in knee-high grass. Somehow those horses are quick to trust Riley and Griff in every move. I know that trust, a solid core inside me that no slap to my cheek or no slamming to the floor can touch. Sideways turn, turn back, run forward, stop, back up.

Sometimes from my bedroom window I watch Riley walk the driveway toward the barn. He stretches his arms to the sky like I do sometimes, grabbing a piece of turquoise.

Riley continues to the barn, the sun throws a shadow, a flag of breath puffs from the horses, an eagle flies overhead and the moment passes. Griff rides past me and Ranger nods. Riley's boot creaks into the stirrup, and Hannah watches with me in the beginning light, her hair the black silk down her back. Shadows fall away while the two horses communicate in the high grass. The horses and men gradually become as small as my thumbnail when they near the rocky outcropping at the end of the pasture. The moments pass like treasure.

My hands grip the fence, that solid piece that holds its ground. The fence fits here. Solid. I wonder if I can be that way, someday.

It's another day to be Maggie Fletcher, the way it should be.

I'm lying awake at 3:00 a.m., writing this down. I saw a face in my dream, just now, just waking up. A man's face, I think. Quick as a hummingbird wing, a blur. When I focus, the blur seems to be from before the van, in the white somewhere; someone with close-cropped brown hair. It was a face that Maggie Fletcher wouldn't know. I feel a tug away from what I know with Riley and the horses and Poke. I have a question, a doubt, all from that hummingbird wing.

I remember brown curly hair, tee shirt, and sitting next to me. A summer afternoon. I don't remember eyes or mouth or voice, if he is tall or if he wears glasses. Someone who didn't strike me. It was as if that face were telling me I knew it and yet, when I look again, no face was there.

There was a drop of happy in that face when it found me, as if I should be happy to see it, but I don't know why. Then I sat up in bed awake, with no screaming or fear, my breath sucked out of me until I remembered to breathe again. I had to write this in my journal. Maybe it's a brother or a cousin or a co-worker or a newspaper carrier or a pharmacist...someone I know. Somewhere in the white...

CHAPTER
FIFTY-TWO

VINCE

Vince had wanted to say these things to Tess, but instead, he opened his sock drawer where he hid Brenniss' picture. Was it an apology? Or just trying to sort things out?

...I don't remember your face much, unless I look at my favorite picture of you here, as if it keeps you preserved. Actually, I'm lying. When Tess started staying the night, that picture seemed to stare at us. Awkward. So your face hides next to my socks, where you smile at me in the morning. I make sure I open the drawer when Tess is in the shower or making toast, nowhere near that comforting smile. I still long for a smile from you no matter how frozen, while still stuck in that familiar groove of you. And yet, when I'm with Tess, I feel like a fresher version, like I've found the perfect waterfall to tumble across my weary skin.

Tess can be lying there, her hair tousled around her face, her soft breath like a kitten's and I feel lucky she's next to me filling that empty spot I had all those months. Have I truly given up hope since finding a place for Tess in my life? Or will I always feel a little torn, a little divided until you walk through that door? Then Tess turns in her sleep, absently rubs her sleepy face, and I'm focused again on today, not yesterday or what could be. I'm done hurting right at that moment.

There she is, my girl, walking toward the kitchen to make breakfast. There she is, bangs spilling over her eyes as she pulls the omelet from the pan onto my plate, smiling as we sip espresso and talk about our Saturday. I used to say those exact things about you but now, it's Tess. It's a rhythm again, a chord in me that I like hearing, feeling the change of seasons or a bus ride or tasting my favorite deli sandwich. I like the today, the routine, where I won't be ripped apart every step I take. Not many will understand that. I'm not sure you would either.

CHAPTER
FIFTY-THREE

Griff was as nervous as a long-tailed cat in a room full of rockers. His breath seized as he rode the elevator to the Attorney General's office. Phoenix wore a layer of late autumn to add to Griff's sense of uncertainty. His heart pushed against his chest as he strode into the AG's office, arms weakening from the weight of files and briefcases. The right thing to do was to dump this into the State Attorney's lap, but he knew he was tied into this investigation like barbed wire.

He sat in a quiet corner to homestead his confidence. The drive from Copper Station was the most certain thing he'd ever done in his career, knowing full well that the road led to this moment. He checked the large briefcase a third time as it stood at attention near his left leg, the set of files in another folder in his lap. He picked them up, shuffled through the contents, set them back against his chest. He straightened them again, as if they needed that cowlick combed before a school picture.

Griff had made an appointment with State Attorney Preston McNee under an assumed name to keep suspicion low.

Would Preston remember him from a law enforcement conference two years ago? From fishing a year ago, when McNee tried out the river making a nice dent in the fish population? They emailed periodically, but that was no guarantee that he could walk into the State Attorney's office as Phil Wilson, in hopes that McNee would welcome him with open arms.

And why should anyone be suspicious? In Griff's favor, he was a small-town sheriff with evidence poised on one of the most despicable crimes he'd ever encountered, in his opinion, worthy of a grand jury. Why should he be seen any differently than a cattle rancher at that particular moment? His boots had a catch of authentic dirt along the heel. Maybe that scuff was convincing enough that he was someone to ignore.

"Mr. Wilson? Attorney General McNee will see you now." The exceptionally thin receptionist smiled. He followed her toward a large walnut door, she with file in hand, tip-tipping in her impossibly high heels. She opened the modern chrome door handle with a solid click.

"Attorney General McNee? This is Phillip Wilson." The two men nodded. Griff wanted to tip the brim of his Stetson, but his arms were occupied.

"Mr. Wilson, would you care for some bottled water or coffee?" Her smile split bright red lipstick around glossy teeth, about the only thing that looked healthy on that young woman.

"Sure, I'll take some water. I'm a little dry."

She walked toward a panel on the wall, tapped it open to reveal a refrigerator with water bottles stacked like sentries. She not only opened the bottle; she poured it as well.

"Thanks, Sandy." McNee waved her out, and she quietly exited the room. McNee stared through desert-colored eyebrows and waited a sunset-length of seconds before he extended his thick hand.

"Griff, how the hell are you? What's it been—a year? I still haven't gotten back to Copper Station for another round of fishing. Hope you haven't taken the last of the trout this summer. How's Hannah?"

"Pres, glad you could see me. Hannah's doing great. Gallery's doing well. I suppose you heard about the Entrepreneurship Award?"

"I thought that was Hannah—saw it in the paper! I'll be darned. She really built up that gallery. You're looking like you need a vacation. What's with this 'Phil Wilson' business?"

"Been busy with the new search and rescue horses—we got two more...and this." He lifted the files onto McNee's desk. "Really could use your help."

Preston's eyebrows converged into a fluffy landscape across his forehead. "Okay, I wondered what all the mystery was about." He eyed the stack.

"It's a long story, and it gets more complicated and bizarre the more I investigate. Had to fly in under the radar today."

McNee's eyebrows rose. "I'm all yours. What do you have?"

"Suppose I had information implicating a government official in a crime so inhumane it would make your skin crawl? Suppose I had a witness, one that could place the official in the crime and DNA evidence in another crime in an attempt to cover up the crime? Suppose I told you in these files, there's murder, false identity, and human trafficking? Who would I need to involve to get this guy locked up?"

"FBI involved?"

"Not yet, but that may be my next step."

"Not necessarily, but that might add credibility. Sounds like you've been earning your pay, Griff. You came to the right spot. Let's take a look." McNee smiled at his old fishing buddy while he pressed the intercom. "Sandy, hold my calls."

An hour and a half, three bottles of water, and a round of scotch later, McNee ordered in lunch and cancelled afternoon appointments. Griff had the bait and McNee had bitten: the canyon pictures, the DNA evidence, Maggie's statements and identifications, the mug shots and prison records, and yes, even stomach contents of maggots.

"So, Bo Valesquez is Bo Mullen, is also our illustrious and popular Governor Bo Mullengrath, and is the one financing human trafficking?"

"Until he killed his own brother Paco. I don't know how many women prior to Maggie may have been kidnapped or used up. We may never know."

"You'll need financial records. That's where the FBI comes in. This Maggie Fletcher willing to testify?"

"Yes, but we need to protect her six ways to Sunday. Mullengrath may still believe she's dead. I don't want him to think otherwise." Griff sat back for the first time discovering a comfortable leather back massaging the tension in his shoulders. "I honestly don't know if she can manage testifying more than once. I want this to be rock solid."

"She's safe right now?"

"Absolutely."

"Defense may have a field day with her memory. If she can't remember who she is, if she's going by a false name—"

"But by recognizing Mullengrath, she's started to recall more. And the DNA picks up the rest."

McNee took one, two breaths. He looked at the ceiling, closed one eye while chewing on his lip, as if focusing on an imaginary bullseye.

"FBI will have to be in on this, Griff. Kidnapping, across state lines, human trafficking." McNee's mouth drew into a pucker, switching left to right as he seemed to think of options, possibilities, implications. "I've got a few friends at the FBI office here."

"Does Mullengrath?"

McNee shook his head. "Don't think so. He'd have too much to lose with his multiple identities. That explains why he's so distant. Rarely attends our functions, only the ones *he* initiates."

"Would the FBI let us keep Maggie safe where she is? I have to say, her wellbeing, her peace of mind in all this is crucial."

"This is big—I mean BIG, Griff. Let me make a few calls. Can you stay? The other attorneys could weigh in at our meeting tomorrow, hearing it directly from you. I'm sure we have enough for a grand jury. We can get some warrants, I have no doubt."

"I'm counting on you." Griff shook McNee's hand again. "I've been married to this investigation for nearly six months and I'm ready to get something accomplished."

McNee lit a cigar and downed the last of his scotch. "I tell you, Griff, this is really big!"

CHAPTER
FIFTY-FOUR

"Vince, this is absolutely thoughtful for you to help me. My heart hasn't been much into holiday decoration, I confess. Oh, I'm sure it's the same for you." Betty's smile tightened when she pulled tissue wrapping from a small silver bell. "Oh Lord, I forgot about this. This is one of Brenniss' ornaments."

Her frail voice, like the tissue itself, whispered and dissolved as she reached for the chair, her bell a strong memory for Vince as well. "This was her first Christmas ornament. It was always the first one on the tree and the last to come down." She wiped her eyes. "This whole box of these ornaments were to be yours this Christmas to continue your own tradition. But now..." Betty looked around the room. "Oh, this Christmas business isn't going well at all, is it?"

The skeleton of an artificial Christmas tree reached out to Vince in a plea to look more Tannenbaum. Milt seemed to be the only one who could make sense of how to assemble it. These traditions were lost on Vince once his parents died. They felt a little like wallpaper paste, that thick goo that meets up with a layer of new paper over the old. The tree was a scraggly, witchy thing to him, compounded by a kink in his back.

Yet, Vince sat next to Betty, restored the bell into the box and carefully closed the lid. "Why don't we do this? I'll put the box in the corner, and we'll leave the decorations for another time...when Brenniss is back."

"She's out there somewhere. She'll be back." Betty's eyes closed as if making a wish. "The first Christmas is the worst." She looked around the flickering fireplace. "So what should we do with this mess? I planned something festive for my Tai Chi class next week. But what's a tree without ornaments?"

"Okay, how about this? I'll assemble the tree and add the lights. Then your Tai Chi class can decorate it any way they want."

Betty's eyes slit upward in a twinkly smile. "That's perfect! We'll do an ornament exchange! You're a genius!" Vince's face drew a blank of how brilliant he'd been. "See, each person brings an ornament, hangs it on the tree with a number attached. Then after refreshments, people draw numbers and take home the ornament they received. Nothing but good memories, see?" Almost childlike, Betty stood and walked toward the tree and placed two branches into the false trunk, something that had confounded Vince for the last twenty minutes. A twitch in his memory told him he was forgetting something, but he continued with the last branches and wove lights throughout.

Betty patted his arm on the way out the door, telling him he saved the day. By the time he drove into his parking space, he was humming a Christmas carol. The condo lobby had also sprouted a tree while he was gone. *Okay, so the season is served, just let me sip it when I choose.* He checked his mailbox, still with something slipping silver through his brain that he'd forgotten something, left something unfinished. He watched the elevator door swallow the lobby tree in front of him.

When he slipped his key into the lock, the solid tumblers gave way too easily. Did he forget to lock the door, or—Brenniss? He tossed his coat on the chair and faced...Tess. Tess standing hands on hips in a brighter-than-red Christmas dress that fit her more like a stocking than a dress.

"Wow! Don't you look fine?" He gave a puzzled twist of a smile. "Are you supposed to be my Christmas present?"

"And WHERE have you been?"

"Been? At Betty's helping her with her tree." It sounded more like an excuse, an apology, when he meant it more as fact.

"You honestly don't remember, do you? You're over two hours late!"

He shook his head.

"Kent? Dave? Jerri? Pat? Drinks at Trendz? Christmas?"

He blinked once, then twice. "Oh, shit!"

"Seriously?"

"Oh, God, Tess, I truly forgot! Well, actually there was something nagging at me that I'd forgotten something, but...well, let me change. There's still some time—"

"I've been waiting nearly THREE hours! YOU told ME to meet you here, for God's sake." She slammed her clutch onto the sofa. "Here...waiting for you...so you could finish your Christmas tree somewhere else!" She yanked her red shawl from her shoulders, rolled it into a ball and threw it at Vince.

"Tess, I said I was sorry! My bad! But we still can make it."

"What gives, Vince?"

Vince ran toward the bedroom. "I know exactly what to change into. Ten minutes, tops!"

"That's it? That's all? You've got balls, I can say that. I spend money I don't have on this dress, get my hair done, my nails, wait three hours, no way of knowing where the HELL you are, and here you are decorating a Christmas tree—!"

"Actually, I just assembled it—"

"I DON'T CARE if you stuck mouse ears and called it Mickey! A Christmas tree, for God's sake! And not just any tree. Your *fiancée's* Mom's Christmas tree! I thought you said you moved on, at least you convinced ME that you moved on!"

"Hey, okay, okay. I forgot, and I apologized. I'll make it up to you—maybe we can host a party here." He shrugged on a pinstripe shirt, buttons flicking through his fingers.

"You want me here when it's convenient; when it works for you. So where does that put me?"

"HOLD IT!" he screamed. Her eyes snapped wide at such a sound coming from calm, mild-mannered, smooth, reliable, lovable, confused Vince. "ENOUGH already! I don't want to have a shouting match with you! You're acting like yours is the only injustice here! I'm not perfect, okay? These last six months have been hellish, but I've tried to make a place for Betty who, like ME, doesn't have family anymore."

Tess rolled her eyes at the mention of Betty's name.

"Christmas has NEVER been a favorite holiday for me, but right now, Betty is the only family I have. So, forgive me, if it allows me a smidgeon of Christmas spirit...to forget the pain, to move on... No matter what I decide, it's wrong." He flipped the tie around his collar and Windsored it in place.

He saw her face snap, the tight spring exploding in her. Not like a spring, dizzy and spilling out of its case, breaking against glass. But an icy, Everest, severe break. He'd gone too far; this was a total disconnect.

"Tess—"

"Never mind." She closed her eyes and inhaled sharply. "I sure don't want to be the 'wrong thing' in your life."

"Tess—that came out wrong. I'm sorry."

"You've been saying that a lot lately. Maybe you need to figure out who you want to say that to." She picked up her shawl and flung it around her shoulders. "I'm out of here."

The slamming door pushed his anger right through him,

left a hole hanging right there in the middle of his chest. Tess...his friend? A distraction? Someone that filled that empty space? If Brenniss walked through the door right this minute, what the hell would he do?

He walked back into the bedroom. Tess held the mirror up to him once in a while to remind him he was still among the living. He needed that in-your-face truth right now. Okay, that's what he'd do. Put on his coat, get into the car and chase after Tess, all the way to Trendz if he had to, to salvage some of the Christmas that he promised to celebrate with her. She might be walking. He might be able to flag her down, give her a ride so they both could arrive together. He would take the blame for their late arrival. She'd probably be cold, in that thin, skinny, eye-popping, Marilyn Monroe red dress and shawl that snaked across her shoulders like a lazy thought. His apology better be good.

Maybe he could save the day a second time.

CHAPTER
FIFTY-FIVE

"Griff, this is Special Agent Cody Bishop from our regional FBI office here." Preston McNee stood by a man dressed convincingly in a crisp dark suit and shiny black shoes with black hair combed to the side. His brown eyes took no nonsense. Griff hoped his handshake might convey the same seriousness.

"Agent Bishop, I'm grateful Pres could arrange a meeting so quickly."

"Hate to break into your Christmas holiday this way, but it's an honor to meet you after all this time."

"Pardon?"

"You're the same Griff Hensley that worked for the Indianapolis Metro Police Department a while back, correct? I have to say, I cut my teeth on the Tom Philpott investigation. When Preston called about this evidence out of Copper Station, I recognized your name right away."

"I'll take that as a compliment."

Cody sat with the rest of the men in Preston's office. "So, really? A human trafficking ring?" His eyes set full-bore onto Griff.

"Mullengrath is identified as part of it. We have a witness who escaped from him. He doesn't appear to realize that, yet."

"Is that what prompted this investigation?"

Preston poured coffee as Griff talked about the van and Maggie but watched quietly when Griff pulled out the ER pictures. Cody looked carefully at her face, as if he might recall her story. They drank tepid sips as Griff showed the DNA evidence and listened to Maggie's heartfelt recall along the highway of her ordeal.

Cody sat back, snapping files open, lifting pages, comparing one file to the next, as if making an inventory of Griff's evidence. "And she identified Mullengrath, too."

"I can tell you," Pres interrupted, "Griff left no stone unturned. Our next step is to seize Mullengrath's books, his financials, his records. And I think we all agree, we need Mullengrath behind bars. Period."

"So, this Maggie Fletcher. We don't have her name in our missing persons database."

"And you won't. We still don't know her name. Maggie Fletcher is the name she gave herself. 'Jane Doe' was taken." Griff smiled. "We didn't send out posters or descriptions in case someone wanted her dead. We kept her safe."

"A safe house?" Cody's eyes slit into a question.

"Not officially. But she's safe. She may be from as far away as New York. That van traveled over two thousand miles; she could have been picked up anywhere. It just made sense with my investigation—"

Cody waved his hand. "You don't have to justify anything to me, Griff. I understand. So, how I see it, we need to find out who she is, but keep her identity quiet until after the trial." Cody was ready to follow this highway to Mullengrath's door.

"Griff did all the dirty work, with few resources, I might add." Preston nodded. "Seems like he's handing something to you on a silver platter."

Cody raised his hands. "Give me a few minutes."

He pulled a laptop from his briefcase, punched in passcodes and a voice-recognition clearance code and in a matter of minutes started the questions. "Okay, this Maggie Fletcher. You found her sometime in early June, right? So, I'll estimate the possible abduction around late May, even mid-May..." He typed in information, hit ENTER two, three times. And waited. The screen went blank through a six-month data search.

Within thirty seconds, a report appeared on the screen in an official blue background: descriptions of a mall, a van, a kidnapped woman.

"Well, I got a hit from New York. There's no way you could have retrieved this, Griff; it's accessible only through the FBI. Let's see...Young woman, thirty-five years of age abducted by three men outside a local mall, a suburban area outside of NYC, placed into a black van....description fits...timeline fits...and we'll get a picture here soon on page two..."

The men gathered around the screen.

"Oh, my God," Griff whispered. "It's Maggie, all right." Her smile was more certain, she looked softer, not as edgy with sudden movement. She was a confident young woman, looking forward in her life.

"Well, your Maggie is really Brennis Tripham, a librarian working at the New York Public Library, as an archivist...working on authenticating a newly found letter attributed to Alexander Hamilton—"

"Say again!"

"Hamilton, Alexander Hamilton. What?"

"Cody, she remembered only two things when she first woke up: 'Hamilton' and 'white'. I thought Hamilton was a town or a landmark, not THE Alexander Hamilton. She just remembered working in a library in the past month. That all fits!"

Cody read on. "...Abducted from Whisper Tree Mall...carrying items she purchased which included...you ready for this, Griff? She was carrying a wedding dress. She was about to get married."

"White! That's the 'white' she remembered. I'll be."

"Exactly. You need to tell this young lady that we've found her identity and we can get her home."

"After she testifies."

"We can take her into protective custody within two hours."

"Cody, we're asking a favor on this one," Preston interrupted. "Griff says she's willing to testify, but she's still pretty vulnerable. Griff will introduce her to her former identity slowly, but in court she needs to present herself as a reliable and confident Brenniss recalling these events. The governor's defense would have a field day if she seems to be unsure."

"Plus, our trump card is that Mullengrath thinks she's dead," Griff offered. "She's safe where she is, out of Mullengrath's face."

Cody's eyes narrowed, then he shifted from one hip to the other in his chair. "I see your point, guys, we need to protect our witness. My thoughts jump to her mom Betty, not knowing her daughter is alive."

Griff nodded solemnly. "We're just asking to extend her anonymity during the trial."

"I'm thinking the same way, Cody," Preston added. "Brenniss needs to testify, no distractions, and I might add, in a closed courtroom to keep the media out of it. Once the trial is over, she can return home. The transition will be easier."

The pause was deafening. Cody looked back and forth between Griff and Preston, both men committed to what was right, both honest men, both men of integrity. "Thick as thieves, you two." He half-smiled. "But starting tomorrow, know there will be two undercover agents in Copper Station making sure Maggie—or Brenniss—is not harmed. One thing goes wrong, we step in."

Griff shrugged. "There's a quiet little hotel near the hospital. They'll be comfortable there."

"Understood. Deal."

"I'll put in a call to the New York office when I leave here and start the process."

As Griff drove home in the pale December light, he knew the first thing he needed to do was swear in Riley as his deputy. Riley wouldn't rest if he weren't in that courtroom during the trial. The second thing he had to do was explain to Riley that Maggie wasn't just Maggie anymore. Some Christmas present.

CHAPTER
FIFTY-SIX

Friendship is more than sitting back on a summer's afternoon and laughing at stories and secrets, being comforted in the change of seasons or the oncoming storm. Friendship is a rope that weaves in and out of lives, sometimes barely touching, sometimes stronger than steel. The rope works through calluses and blood, through a cold night to calm the wind.

Maggie felt that security when she brushed Bliss. If Bliss were a human—sometimes Maggie thought that way—she very well could be Maggie's best friend. Riley gave her more freedom which curved confidence into her life. He asked her questions about the horses, included her in decisions. It made no sense then when Riley returned to the barn, a cloud cutting across his face the way late autumn does sometimes.

"Griff and Hannah are coming by later." He opened the barn fridge and reached for the Tetanus vaccine. "I'll give this booster to Bliss before I go in. We'll meet up at the house."

It was as though she'd been kicked in the stomach, hearing his business voice, seeing his neglect of eye contact.

"What's up?"

"Bliss' booster was due the first of the month. Now that it's colder weather—"

"No, why are Griff and Hannah coming?"

He stopped the plunger in the needle and looked directly at Maggie, a stone for a face. "They need to." He returned to the hypodermic and finished the draw.

She put the brush and comb on the shelf. She saw Bliss' eyes soften as she nuzzled Maggie's neck. A deep breath still did not convince her that nothing could be that bad.

Once Riley entered the kitchen, he immediately began preparing the coffee. "You like it here, Sunshine?"

"Of course."

He nodded, dried his hands then went upstairs to change clothes.

She kept answering his question in her mind. *Of course, I like it here. It doesn't hurt to wake up, I can feel the sunshine even on these cooler days, I can breathe, I belong—what's not to like? Wait a minute!* Her head snapped toward the stairwell, retracing echoes of Riley's heavy steps. Riley tripped over his feelings if there were another question to ask.

Griff's truck pulled into the driveway, the dust kicking up like a newborn colt against the air. Hannah looked worried. Griff's face was dark, his eyes squinted against his thoughts.

They're here, she tried to call out, but her throat went dry. *It can't be that bad*, she told herself again.

"Hey, girlfriend, I brought pumpkin cheesecake." Late autumn frost, that's what Maggie thought was in Hannah's face.

"Griff, Hannah." Riley came from nowhere, shook Griff's hand in a way that was formal, like greeting someone at a funeral. "Why don't we all sit down?"

"What's going on?" Maggie whispered.

"It's simple, Maggie." Griff said. "You helped get an FBI investigation against the governor started. They're working on getting warrants for his arrest as we speak."

"That's good, isn't it?" She didn't see a celebration in any-one's face.

"We all think he committed some horrible crimes and needs to be arrested. That's the good thing. But the scary thing is that we don't know if he had others help him."

"He did. Paco and Kick and Street."

"Well, I mean people in high places, other government of-ficials or businessmen or even people from other countries. We don't know if anyone, anyone but us, knows you're here." Griff shifted his weight in the kitchen chair. "There likely will be a trial once he's arrested. And you'll need to testify."

Maggie knotted her hands together.

"Sunshine, if someone wouldn't want you to testify against the governor, someone could come after you—"

"But you won't let that happen, right?"

Griff spoke with the weight of Arizona granite on his back. "Never. We would never let anyone take you against your will. But Maggie, the FBI has finally figured out your identity. I'm thinking you'd like to know who you were."

She looked toward Riley. "What if I don't like her? What if I don't fit?" *Sunshine, do you like it here?*

"Know what I think? I think you'll take a shine to her, be-cause an awful lot of you is already acquainted with her. You just don't realize it yet." Riley half-smiled, more than he shared in the barn.

"We know you're safer here and Mullengrath needs to stay behind bars. We also know at the trial you can tell your story to the jury. Riley has said all along that once we got things figured out about who you are and where you're from, it's up to you to decide what to do." Griff added.

Riley turned his head away. "That hasn't changed," he mumbled.

Maybe I should have said something with more meaning about how getting up every day had so much to do with Riley, she thought.

Griff eased back in. "This is where it gets complicated, Maggie. You have other family in other places. You may want to return to them. If that's where you'd be safe and happy, you need to consider that."

"And leave the horses and Poke and all of you?"

"You've been remembering your other life, in bits and pieces," Riley continued, "like a jigsaw puzzle. You remember the fancy coffee, you remember the library...well, come to find out there's reasons why you remembered that."

She looked at Hannah, at Griff, and back to Riley. They were pulling the floor this way and that, keeping her off-balance as she sat there.

"We were able to trace the three men—Paco, Kick and Street—back to New York State and eventually, we found out that's where you're from," Griff said. "There's been a missing person report on you for about seven months. The FBI found it. Your name is Brenniss Tripham, you worked in the New York Public Library, and you were about to be married to a young man named Vince Caldwell. That's part of your life, too, Maggie."

She took a breath to say it was all a lie. That wasn't true. There's no such name as Brenniss whatever. She was Maggie, she was Maggie, all right, and she could prove it.... And then the name "Brenniss" swung around again toward her, like a big rubber band about ready to smack her brain on recoil. *Brenniss*, her brain whispered again. A memory of her dad and mom, sitting somewhere, near a garden and lush trees, green everywhere.

"Brenniss," she said slowly, letting her tongue move up and down through her name, a slow roller coaster of sounds... walking down the stairs of a large home...riding to school with her dad..."Brenniss"...She tried again, more quickly...her mom calling her name from a doorway... "Brenniss Tripham." Each time she tried the name, there was something else pulled into the puzzle: a blue flowered bedspread, vacuuming the hall-way, writing her name on a check.

"Say it again to me," she asked Griff. "So I can hear it in another voice. It sounds familiar."

"Brenniss Tripham."

A lightning bolt tore through her forehead and landed squarely into a storm of recognition. "Oh, oh, my gosh! My mom and dad called me 'Bren'." Faster, the memories tumbled like an avalanche, overtaking her down a rocky mountainside with no control. "There's a brick home, with shrubs and rho-dodendrons and roses on a patio and oak trees and maples and lilacs and big green lawn no one uses out front—" She sucked in a breath.

Riley reached for her hand, but his face looked sad. "Sounds like a lot of lovely memories"

"When you're in court, you'll have to testify as Brenniss. All the things that happened to you in the van were as Bren-niss, not as Maggie. Understand?" Griff nodded to her.

"Okay, but...can I be Maggie here?"

Riley patted her arm. "As far as I'm concerned you can be Maggie any time you want, but the law wants you to be Bren-niss in that testimony. Very important, Sunshine. They can create all kinds of problems if you say you're Maggie."

"I've got something you might want to see," Griff added. "The FBI found your driver's license and your library em-ployee ID card." He turned the paper so she could see.

"Oh, my, that's...well it kinda looks like...I mean my hair is longer now and I guess I lost some...I look..." What were the words: happy? Accomplished? Driven? Satisfied? Confident?

"I look so...innocent."

She looked up, straight at Hannah, remembering her walk into her hospital room with a bag of clothing. It seemed like yesterday. It seemed like years. Hannah's shoulders sagged.

"Do you remember Vince? Your fiancé?" Griff tilted his head.

"I was walking out of the mall...that's what I was carrying...my wedding dress...my final fitting that day, and it landed on the asphalt...white..." Her wispy voice faded.

"White," repeated Griff. "The one clue you knew that never made a connection until now. So about Vince. He'll be someone you'll likely want to contact...after the trial..."

Riley's hand loosened, pulling away warmth, as if he didn't have the right, just then, to be supportive, the intimacy unfair. A lost scarf, a lost hat, a lost coat would be just as cold as that moment.

But Maggie held on, pulled his hand back. "Can we stop for now?" she whispered. "I've had enough to think about, and I can't track it all, all the things jamming into my brain all at once." She wanted to say she still felt like Maggie Fletcher, that nothing had changed. She wanted to tell Riley that he didn't need to pull away, just yet. She liked it here, but more than "of course," more than "great." She wasn't sure of this Brenniss stuff, the name that came with postage stamp memories, one on top of another, jumbled up inside her. She just tried to breathe as Hannah sliced dessert and poured coffee, there at that table, with the only people she knew who cared about her.

Did she like living here? It seemed so certain an hour ago.

Riley squeezed her hand again.

He lowered his eyes to the folder that Griff had closed then looked at Maggie's sad face. He realized, as that rope of friendship frayed a little at the edges that she might never be Maggie again.

CHAPTER
FIFTY-SEVEN

RILEY IN EARLY MORNING

I've expected Maggie to call out thin cries during the night, fighting off her demons. I've expected her to be jumpy, to fall into those early patterns that, even though they ground her into pieces. I've expected her to be taunted into a corner of her memories when she had no fight left.

Instead, I've been the one unsettled, less patient with the horses. I'm the one that forgot the coffee pot was still on until what was left looked like liquid tar. Maggie giggled at that because, for once, it was my fault. And normally, I just look away at her mistakes, but I don't tolerate mine too well. I'm the one who couldn't find a comfortable place in the saddle, or in my bed. I'd doze, I'd wake up—that kind of unsettled. Unfinished.

She worked so hard to belong here. And now she did. And I liked that about her.

I can't bring myself to call her Brenniss. It doesn't fit with dust and splinters and toe picks. She may be Brenniss, and I couldn't fault her—it's a nice name and all. But, she's still struggling with Brenniss, too; I can tell. It's almost like she didn't know who'd speak up when I asked a question: Brenniss or Maggie? "Maggie" fits her stride, the way she lifts the saddle onto Bliss, the hard dig of the shovel or the rake when she cleans the stalls. She'll always be Maggie to me.

So, I was sitting on the edge of my bed, looking down at my feet at 3:30 in the morning, trying to figure out if today would be the day I'd call her Brenniss for the first time. I asked her a couple days ago if it would help things to call her Brenniss from here on out? And she looked at me with that confused smile that seems to visit her face more often lately and told me she wasn't sure. Said she was remembering pieces of her Brenniss life, but it wasn't enough yet to feel like Brenniss. Lost between two names.

So, there I sat on the bed thinking about her sad, confused face and what the hell I'm supposed to do. And I swear, just then, I felt the bed shift a little as if someone just sat down next to me. I looked up to my left, toward the foot of the bed.

There was Grace.

As plain as day, sitting there smiling at me like she knew what I was thinking, like she never left me behind at all, like she'd just come upstairs after a long day. She looked healthy and strong, as if she were ready to start her day with four horses and still make breakfast and better-tasting coffee than what I've pulled off recently.

Grace. What are you doing here?

Thought you might need some help. I know where you live, too.

She didn't glow like a ghost in the movies. She didn't float near the window or walk through walls the way some are known to do. She wasn't wearing a white gown. No, she wore jeans and a flannel shirt. Just like she would have yesterday or the day before if she'd been here.

I can tell you want to fix things, she said. You tried to fix things with me when I was dying. You wanted to find the one thing that the doctors failed to find and make life perfect again. Remember? You couldn't do it and you blamed yourself for losing me.

I didn't know just then if I was angry or regretful. I missed her, that's for sure, but she was making sense about making things better. What human being wouldn't do that for the one he loves?

But you didn't fail. Did you know that?

Of course, I failed. You died. I couldn't stop that. I remember thinking that, and maybe I said it, too, but I just don't remember talking. It was as if Grace and I were thinking the same thoughts on the same frequency, like pulling in a radio station from Chicago or some place in another time zone.

But you didn't fail. You prepared yourself for better times. You saw the sadness and the finality, but you moved on. You proved you're loving and gave yourself permission. That's what living is.

Is that what you came here to tell me?

You're in a fine pickle—

A mell of a hess. She used to use that phrase. And I just used it, nearly three years later.

Because you don't know about Maggie.

See? Even Grace called her Maggie.

You want to fix things with her, too. Find the one solution that lets her be Maggie and Brenniss all at the same time. You want to do this because you feel you couldn't do that for me. The difference is, I was at the end of my life, a little string tied to you that unraveled and frayed. Maggie is tied to you, too, but she's getting stronger, like a braid, all woven and beautiful. She's getting stronger because of you, not in spite of you.

I'm thinking braids and strings and getting a little

confused, because it's 3:30 in the morning. Then Grace asks, Do you like having Maggie here?

Well, of course. She helps me out and she's getting healthy again...

You know there's more to it than that, Riley. Be honest.

What the hell does that mean?

You're only fooling yourself, Riley, if you look at her only like a partner and a helper of day jobs. It didn't work for me, and it won't work for Maggie, either.

Now I was mad. Grace had this down-to-earth smile, the one I remember as being the most honest she could be. That kind of smile with no judgment, the one that said whatever I might say back would be all right. I'd forgotten that I loved that about her.

"Are you saying that I'm in love with Maggie?" Now that time, I must have spoken out loud, because my voice bounced off the walls and ceiling. I looked to my left again.

No Grace.

I wasn't sitting on the edge of the bed either. I was lying flat, eyes wide open, staring at the ceiling, as if I'd been lying that way all night, mouth as dry as a corncob in November. There was Poke, sitting upright and staring at me, his nose on my pillow.

In my head I kept hearing that question over and over again, like a recorded message. I realized it was similar to the question I'd asked her a few days ago, when I was ready to shut down, ready to give up. I just needed to hear it from her that she wanted to be here. And know what? I answered the same way.

"Of course."

CHAPTER
FIFTY-EIGHT

Christmas needed to be like a silk parachute, something smooth, effortless, didn't create problems, and kept someone from landing too hard when he least expected it. Vince thought about parachutes as he gathered his client reports for the morning meeting.

He wanted to fly under the radar this season, a little like Santa, not get pulled off course by a downdraft, not miss the mark for a distant safe landing. No surprises, no deep meaning for the season, just another snowy red and green day with a late breakfast. Tess was getting pretty good at eggs over easy.

He pushed the glass conference door open with his back, then turned to face Kent, Dave, and the new intern Jackson as they bubbled a light-hearted conversation about a picture Kent held.

"...So, she decided to use it for her Christmas card! Honest! Take a look!" One by one, the group peered at a photo Christmas card, then chuckled.

"No way, that's so lame."

"Well, it *is* her fifteen minutes of fame, right?"

"She's not serious, right? Really?"

Kent shook his head. It's so cheesy, it's funny. "Vince, you gotta see this."

"What's up?"

"You know those Christmas card photos people send out? Okay, so my cousin who lives in this little two-dot village by some Indian reservation in Arizona sends me her picture this year." He flashed the photo showing an interior shot in orange and rust tints. A young woman in jeans and a peasant blouse showed a wide smile, and her left hand extended in a "peace" sign, while her right arm was around the arm of a tall man with dark hair.

"Get this! This is the governor! The governor of Arizona! She met him at some local function, got this picture taken. She used it for her Christmas photo!" Kent cackled again. "I mean you can barely see her face, the light is so poor."

Vince tried to focus on her smile, but he didn't have the energy.

"It's priceless!" Kent laughed.

Vince smiled. "Maybe she's got something going on she didn't tell you about."

"Did she kiss him? What's that on his cheek?" Dave pulled the picture from Vince. "I think it's a mole! That dude has a mole on his cheek. See?"

Vince's attention was again drawn to the Christmas photo. He could have done something pathetic like this, he thought. Sitting at my desk, files piled high with a caption like "having a wonderful time at Christmas. Wish you were here." The cousin's grin in the picture was framed in brown shoulder-length hair. The governor's appropriate and rehearsed smile was a little too forced, much like Vince's smiles these last six months. Yet, there was something familiar about that scene, too. Before he took a third look, Kent returned the picture to his suit jacket.

Morning meeting droned through new accounts and projects, end-of-year projections, but always finished with friendly one-upmanship, teasing about teams or sports or hobbies. Always a great way to go back to the computers, clients, and cold calls.

During that patter, Vince's mind's eye jumped back to Kent's picture. One thing in that picture, suddenly focused so clearly. Kent's cousin was standing in front of a large portrait, something like a cowboy sitting on a fence or something. But the cowboy was familiar: the eyes or the face. It struck him as familiar.

As the conference room emptied, Vince caught up to him. "Hey, bud, show me your cousin's picture again." Kent shrugged, pulled out the photo and walked with Vince into his office.

"Man, I didn't realize my cousin was so popular!"

"No, wait. Wait a minute!" No longer distracted by the cousin's smile, Vince looked past her left shoulder. There was the picture of a *cowgirl*, he was mistaken. And it was a photo, not a painting. He'd just looked at it wrong. She wasn't sitting on a fence, but a porch instead. The hat in her hands, her head tilted to one side. Someone he knew tilted her head like that when he'd ask a question. "Do we really need to go to the baseball game?" Her hair was longer in the photo, her face more tanned, her smile less certain as best he could tell, staring at a pose no larger than his thumbnail, embedded within a crowd on a wall. He knew those cheekbones, those eyes, the lips he'd kissed hundreds of times.

It was Brenniss.

"Kent, Kent! Who is that? In the picture!"

"I told you; it's my cousin—"

"No, no! Behind her, in that photo, see? On the wall? Who—who does it look like?"

"It's so small, I'm not sure..."

"It's Brenniss? See?" Vince's hand shook.

"What? No way!" Kent pulled the picture closer, raised his glasses above his eyebrows then closed one eye. He blinked. He looked again. "By God, Vince..." he whispered.

"It's Brenniss!" Vince's voice notched nearly an octave. "It's her! It's her! I know it is! She's still alive!" Tears rivered creases as he looked again. Her face a little uncertain, but he'd seen that half-smile before.

"The town—what town was this picture taken in?"

"Hell if I know. Some little one-horse town—"

"Call your cousin!"

"Holy smoke, Vince! Slow down! You don't know—"

"Call her now, Kent! My dime." He handed Kent his cell phone, eyes wide open, now causing others' heads to turn.

"Okay, okay! Hold on, though. I've got to call my mom. She'll have Hayley's number. I don't have it."

Kent needed a squint-eyed moment to recall his mom's number. Busy. Kent tried two more times, while Vince's face heated, mouth gasping short, small breaths, as if that made the connection work faster. He tried a third time.

"Hello, Mom? Yeah, good, I'm good. What? Oh, I don't know yet. I might be there either the twenty-third or Christmas Eve. It all depends—"

Vince's face inched toward purple.

"Uh, yeah, hey, Mom, I need to—well, Dad and I can do that, too, you know—once I get there."

Vince glared.

"Okay, Mom? Mom? Listen, I'm calling for a favor. Um, I need Hayley's address and phone number. I don't have it....Yes, I'm at work, but I need it right now." Kent rolled his eyes, his best attempt at apology. He covered the phone and whispered, "You know how moms can be." But the truth was, Vince didn't. If breath were left in Vince's body, it sucked into his throat, holding like a tight rubber band stretched across his neck.

"Yeah, cousin Hayley...yeah, I got it Saturday night...well I guess it's the governor, that's what she said..."

Vince listened to the squeaky tin voice from Kent's mom but the blood was too thick in his ears to figure out what she was saying.

"Sure, there's time to still send a card...Yeah, yeah, I'm ready..." Kent wrote quickly, the voice directing numbers like a traffic stop.

"So, Mom, do you know where this photo was taken?"

"Come on, come on," Vince whined.

"It looks like some kind of art show. A gallery? Really?"

Vince tried to grab the notepad, but Kent was still writing.

"Two Stone? Two Rivers? Okay, I'll try to reach Hayley...No, I'll call you again later on...I promise! Okay, okay, I will...Sure...Sure...Gotta go, Mom! I'll call you later. Bye!"

Vince blew out the air that had knotted his lungs.

"Okay, Hayley lives not far from a little town called Copper Station, in Arizona. Now, Mom says there's a gallery in Copper Station but she doesn't remember the name of it. Two Stone gallery? Something like that."

"What the hell is Brenniss doing in Arizona?" Nothing fit together at all. "Okay, then, call your cousin. Now."

Kent stared at the man he often considered his best friend, a man with an impossible hope buried for months.

"NOW! Call her, damn it!" Vince screamed. Outside the glass wall, people craned their necks for a clue. Tess, at her desk, shifted her eyes from her computer screen to Vince, back to the screen, back to Vince.

"Sorry, Kent." Vince's voice broke, the first sign of anything broken in Vince for months "It's urgent, you know that. I wouldn't ask if it weren't."

Kent waited for the pick up, an agonizing few seconds for Vince who hoped Hayley wouldn't let voicemail take over. It had to be Brenniss in that picture. He stared again at it. He could see it now, a bit of friendly Brenniss with such a tentative smile.

"Oh, hello, Hayley?" Kent nodded toward Vince. "It's your cousin, Kent. Calling from New York." He winced sour. "No, sorry I didn't realize it was 6:30 in the morning. Sorry. But I have a crazy question about your Christmas card...Yeah, I got it...Yeah, it's pretty wild...I...well...I...yes, the governor."

Vince nearly ripped the phone from Kent's hand, stopping only because he had no air in his lungs to initiate a question.

"...Yeah, I've been showing it around here in the office; you're pretty famous, you know...Facebook? Well, of course. I'll have to check it out..."

Vince tapped his fingers on the computer monitor.

"Well, it's about the photo, Hayley. I was wondering where you had it taken?" He nodded then wrote *"Ten Winds Gallery in Copper Station"* on the notepad. "It looks like a nice function, yeah. So, do you remember when it was taken?"

The pause was too lengthy, like that parachute was never going to open.

Kent wrote *"October."*

"So, here's the deal. I have a buddy, actually, my best friend, here at the office and he thought he recognized the person in that photo hanging behind you in the picture...yeah, the black-and-white one...Do you happen to know who that was who posed for the picture?" Kent's smile faded. He shook his head "no".

"Really? Really? Well, I'll take her name and number, sure. That would be great..." Kent gave a "thumbs up" sign and wrote a name *"Hannah Hensley, owner"* on the bottom of the pad. "That'll be a big help, honest! And I'm really sorry I called you so early, but you really did help, Hayley. We'll talk again Christmas, all right? Great. Okay, bye." Kent handed him the paper.

"Okay, the function was at this Ten Winds Gallery in

Copper Station in October. She didn't know who posed but did know that Hannah owns the gallery. She'd likely know if it's Brenniss." He handed Vince the note. "Now...can I please get to work? I've got an interview in about ten minutes—"

"Sure, sure, Go! Thanks, bud, thanks for making all those calls, but can you leave your cousin's photo?"

"What the hell for?"

"Evidence! I may need to convince the FBI to investigate this little spot in Arizona. Maybe this is the break we needed." Vince had already swung his jacket from the chair, pocketed his keys and wallet. He extended his hand for the photo.

"Where are you going, man?"

"FBI headquarters. I have a date with Arizona," Vince yelled, his voice floating like a parachute over the heads of the employees staring at him. He ran toward the elevator, punched the button again, again, again until the doors opened and invited him in.

Tess stood at her desk. Kent's eyes caught her ashen face. She held tears back when she ran to the elevator, too, pushing the button for the next car. There was no parachute at the moment that Tess could hang on to, coming in for a harsh landing.

"Well, everyone. You're not going to believe this—" Kent's voice broke. He looked at every face in the dead silence. Except Tess' face. The elevator door had already closed.

CHAPTER
FIFTY-NINE

Vince had options and he didn't know what to do first: call Ten Winds Gallery, call Betty, call Agent Stanley, or get onto the next flight west toward Arizona. Because Brenniss was alive. He had proof.

While driving to the FBI office, he searched his phone for Agent Stanley's number to reintroduce himself. "Agent Stanley, please. This is Vince Caldwell. It's urgent. It's about Brenniss Tripham." All because of a fluke photo.

"Hello, Vince. Stanley here. What's this urgent thing you mentioned?"

"I admit it's a little crazy, but my friend just got a Christmas photo in the mail from a relative and it appears Brenniss is in the background. I'm on my way..."

Vince heard Stanley sigh. Things like this happened all too often, especially around the holidays.

"...a photo on display in the background. I'm about six blocks from your building and traffic couldn't be more uncooperative, but please, look at that photo. Do you have ten minutes? That's all it will take."

Stanley took a deep breath, hoping Vince would too. The important leads had dwindled including the flake of hope he still clung to. It couldn't hurt, he supposed. "Okay, Vince. Ten minutes as soon as you can get here." No more than ten seconds passed when the desk phone buzzed again.

"Stanley? Agent Cody Bishop from the Phoenix division on line three."

"Stanley here. What's Phoenix doing today, Cody?"

"Carl, I understand you've been working on the Brenniss Tripham kidnapping case since May. I'll be brief. We have discovered her here, alive, in this vicinity."

"What? You're kidding? I just got a call from—"

"She had been taken cross-country, was so badly traumatized during her kidnapping that she lost her memory of her previous life. She's living safely on a horse ranch about two hours from here. She's healthy and recalling details daily about her kidnapping, which we believe is part of a human trafficking ring. At this time, we are asking you to tell no one, not even her mom, just yet, as we need her full attention during an upcoming trial."

"What the hell? You just drop this in my lap? Where have you been these last six months? I've got her fiancé showing up in ten minutes believing he has a picture of her in the background in someone's Christmas photo!"

"Stall him. I know this is unusual, l but we really need her uncompromised testimony. And we need you involved at this end of the investigation. She's integral to identifying the leader of this ring, possibly the governor of Arizona.

All Stanley could say was "Go on."

"Any emotional connection right now to her Brenniss past may affect her testimony. So we need to keep her identity a secret until the trial is over. That means her fiancé and her mom. Once the trial is over, you're more than welcome to transport her back to New York. We'll even credit your division with preliminary investigation."

"Generous. So, you haven't contacted Betty Tripham at all?"

"You'll get to do that, just not yet."

"So, I tell Vince...?"

"Well, first off, I want that picture. Your investigation is the earliest piece of the puzzle, and, to our benefit, the governor thinks she died a few months ago. A picture like that could leak a theory or rumor will run like mercury. The media will have a field day, soon enough."

"Okay, but not telling family? That's... well, I understand it. I'll make sure I get the picture. I'll tell Vince we're working on his lead. That might calm him for a bit. And you'll give weekly reports?"

"Now that I know who's been in on the New York investigation, we'll include you in conference calls, I'll send daily faxes if you want. We aren't even revealing her identity throughout the trial, for *her* protection, not for any benefit of the FBI."

"My team gets included in the conference calls, too, and I want everything Phoenix has so far."

"You got it; you'll get it by courier by tomorrow evening. Looking forward to meeting your team during Thursday's conference call, Stanley."

"All right, Bishop, we'll play your game for Brenniss' sake. But right now, I've got to deal with Vince who is wound tighter than a clock. I'd rather be fishing; I can tell you that."

"Later."

He hung up the phone gingerly, as if any sound would announce to New York City that Brenniss Tripham was alive and well. God, he'd give anything to look into Betty's eyes in time for Christmas and reassure her. But his team would certainly be able to pull it off.

"Sir, Vince Caldwell to see you. You want him here in the

conference room or in your office?"

"This will be fine." It was not lost on Agent Stanley that the last time they'd met, Vince had iced him out the front door of the Tripham home, and from then on, he'd taken a keen dislike to the young man. Vince approached the conference room, his handshake was spidery thin in his excitement.

"Thanks for seeing me on such short notice. I can't believe this fell into my lap. Just this morning—"

"Let me see this picture, son. What do you have?"

"A co-worker received it in the mail, a Christmas photo of his cousin posing with, I guess, the governor of Arizona. See? That's Hayley, his cousin, and that's the governor." Vince's shaky hand could barely contain the position on the photo.

"And here—behind Hayley, see? There's a photo on the wall? That's Brenniss. See? She's posing like a cowgirl? See? Right there?"

Agent Stanley peered closer, not only at the Brenniss picture, but at the governor, himself. Cocky son of a bitch, he thought immediately. No wonder Bishop wanted anonymity for her. "I don't know, Vince, it's a little blurry. Let me get a magnifying glass."

He took the picture from Vince so easily. Magnifying glass in hand, Stanley looked at details in the portion that Vince stated was Brenniss. "But this is a cowgirl!"

"My friend Kent said his cousin worked near a little town called...Copper Station, in Arizona. The photo was from sometime in October."

Vince had Stanley's attention now. "Arizona, huh?" He put the picture down near his pocket. "You know Vince, Arizona is a long way away from New York. You have no way to connect her there from here, do you?"

"I DON'T KNOW! You're the one doing the investigation!"

"Mind if I keep this? The lab can enhance it, get better resolution for a clearer picture. You said Copper Station, Arizona, right?" He needed to stall Vince, Cody said.

"In fact, verifying this picture will take time, even with all our technology. How about you leave it here and I'll do my best to get a clearer image from our lab."

"I'm not losing that picture!"

"No, of course not. We'll take good care of it. But do me a favor. You can't tell anyone right now about this photo, even an inkling about Brenniss being alive. No press. No interviews. Not even to Betty. Not until we can positively verify this picture. I need your word."

Vince's eyes fell to the picture. "But Betty has a right—"

"You say one word to her and I'll arrest you for obstructing justice, Vince. This has always been an extremely sensitive investigation. Your word?"

"Well, okay. If it brings Brenniss back sooner. Sure, okay." He left the building with satisfaction that *he* gave the FBI a lead and was part of the wall of silence that would keep her alive until she returned home.

Within three minutes of the door closing behind a reluctant Vince, Stanley had the picture in the lab. The computers copied, scanned, then enlarged and enhanced the cowgirl. The background was washed into neutral sepia, the shadows and people's faces fell away. She was sitting on a porch step, a dog sitting nearby, as if she belonged there. The western hat she held was dusted with hard work, her eyes steady into the camera. Her head tilted as if asking a question. With computer measurements of facial landmarks, there was no doubt: it was Brenniss, all right. Perfect match.

Within the hour, Agent Stanley pulled together the crew for a briefing. The quiet conference room became an infusion of activity. Maps coated the table surface, pictures were scattered across the table. He set up a conference call to the Phoenix office, sending copies of the enhanced photo. All agreed to keep Vince at arm's length whenever possible. No investigation needed a firecracker like him around. Within two hours Bishop and Stanley developed a plan to protect and retrieve Brenniss when the time was right, after the trial's verdict. And without the help of Vince Caldwell.

CHAPTER
SIXTY

Riley slowed in mid-December when the cold hit the canyon. The wind blew a chilly breath that left a frost across the pasture. He'd ordered more feed and hay, with Maggie taking charge of the pitchfork while he checked the horses for any respiratory problems. Maggie made each day count with Ranger and Justice. The surprise of snow didn't hinder their training. He'd bought her a few sweatshirts and a vest to wear during the horses' training when her tee shirts didn't cut it anymore. She always had her gloves.

"Sunshine, what do you think about having Christmas this year?" he asked after dinner one night. The dark sky visited early these days while the wind danced through dry oak leaves in the driveway. The closed kitchen door checked the oven's heat.

"I don't know. I hadn't really thought about it. We've been busy."

"Well, I could buy you some things you might need."

"Need as Maggie or as Brenniss?" After she said it, she realized her words pierced like an arrow right through Riley's generosity. It was just as taunting of a question when she asked herself. Did she want to stay Maggie and turn into Brenniss when it was convenient, like on the stand in the court-room? Or did she want to be half-and-half? And what the hell was Brenniss, anyway? Just the other night, she remembered Brenniss talking with her mom during a holiday dinner, and some poor slob sitting next to her with a cold. Awkward, all that sniffling and sneezing. *Was that Brenniss being snobby? Or was that Maggie hating the sniffles, wishing they would go away, so she could hear her mom's voice?*

"Sorry, Riley. That was a bit snippy, all because ...I don't know who to be these days."

"Why don't you be yourself?"

It was a joke, right? He was kidding, right? She tilted her head, the same position she had in the picture while she was sitting on the porch. Only this time, her face sank into a pool of doubt.

"What I mean is, you love working with the horses, you have a rhythm here, and a place where you fit in. That hasn't changed, honest. Don't let your discovery of Brenniss make you walk on eggs. You are still your own person; it's still up to you. She'll come in on her own time. Don't force her into you."

"I hate thinking I might turn into someone else. It scares me."

"Well, I think of you of Maggie. Always will. I don't expect you to be Brenniss, here."

She smiled at the thought of something that might last for always. Riley seemed to know what to say, even on a December evening, that made it feel like August. The horses, too, were a constant in the changing wind and season. Bliss didn't mind if breezes were cold, Cartwheel didn't mind if she were Brenniss or Maggie. She was still...herself. Riley was right, being afraid of yourself is two breaths short of crazy.

"So, I was thinking, if you wanted a Christmas tree, we

could take the afternoon today and go out and chop one down. Bring it back, dress it up for a few weeks." He looked at her sideways, waiting for that childlike joy that had glowed through Grace this time of year.

"You know? I always feel sorry for the trees having to die just for a few weeks of Christmas." Her face crowded confusion.

"No tree, then."

Her face brightened. "I have an idea. Why don't we decorate the horse's stalls? Put some greenery in there, just the boughs we trimmed around here. It'll make the barn nice. We can give the horses presents. Just gifts for them." It wasn't fair, it seemed, to be getting more things from Riley, just now. He'd done more than his share these past six months. But the horses? They'd enjoy a few extra apples, maybe, or a load of carrots, just in time for the chill that was coming.

Riley's smile broke for the first time in weeks, as if his smile relaxed all the way to the canyon and back. "Sunshine, I have to admit, that's a wonderful thought. We can be Santa for them. That's a great idea!" He found a chuckle in all the fear and confusion he'd had and let it bubble past like a spring runoff. "By damn! That's what we'll do! I like that!"

She felt golden with the idea floating about her. What's a new blanket to a horse? Or a bough of pine draped across the stall door? Or an extra apple or carrot, or an extra-long rub-down? The horses know it's kindness, love, compassion. Takes the chill away. Keeps the heart warm. Opens the door for all kinds of possibilities.

CHAPTER
SIXTY-ONE

"Agent Stanley, Vince Caldwell on line two. And Cody Bishop is on line one."

Sonofabitch. Legitimately not taking a call from Vince was its own reward, a little like winning a year's worth of bourbon in a drinking contest. He snapped his finger onto the keypad to the blinking line two. "Hey, Vince, I'm really sorry, but I'm in a conference call with Washington, DC, and I can't talk right now. How about if you leave a message and I'll call you back when I can."

"But Agent Stanley, I just want—"

"Sorry, Vince, the President's waiting." He switched the line to his secretary who was more than willing to give Vince the attention he deserved.

"Hey, Cody. I just lied through my teeth to avoid talking with Vince Caldwell. He thinks *he's* part of the investigative team, now. Hope this is good."

"Looks like the State Attorney will sign the warrants against Mullengrath, and we'll serve them in the next day or so. We'll seize files at the governor's office and at his residence and arresting him and his pilot Wally Cameron. It may make national news, I don't know, but it certainly will have all of Arizona abuzz tomorrow. You know gossip is more powerful than a Starbucks."

"The public loves to see someone fall from grace. How is Brenniss doing in all this?"

"Making it through the winter just fine. We've had a few snows, and she's out every day with Riley training those search and rescue horses. That guy knows what he's doing. I'm tempted to hire him for here in Phoenix. Our guys in Copper Station are big fans of his."

"I'm looking forward to meeting him, soon. He'll be a hell of a lot better than Vince to carry on a conversation. Talk to you during the conference call Thursday."

"Sure thing. Take care."

Agent Stanley held the receiver, reluctantly returning Vince's call.

"Hey, Vince, sorry to be busy at the time you called. What can I help with?"

"You got anything new...about the picture, I mean."

"Oh...well, our lab is *very* meticulous with our technical analyses. That picture may be used in court, so it has to be perfect. That means it takes extra time."

He heard Vince's voice retreat. "Oh, sure, I understand."

"We've contacted the original photo company that processed the photo, to develop a timeline to confirm that was an original photo. Those details, see, add credibility to *your* lead. Glad you're keeping our confidence."

"I guess I didn't realize how involved this investigation could get. Thanks, Agent Stanley." Vince replaced the phone and ran his hand through his hair. So much for a Happy New Year. All New York offered in January were monotonous skies, intense storms that closed down highways, stranded subways, and low-light days. The bright Christmas colors of red and green gave way to gray, white, black. Happy new year, indeed.

Change of season in Arizona is cast in the sky and the sun. The clouds bring snow to the high country, keep the sun prisoner for a few days at a time. The dry powdery magical snow fluffs with footsteps and fails with snowmen, the kind that flies with the next wind into the next county. The sun wins out at some point, the snow gradually melts in quilt patches of stones and hard sand. Maggie had looked up all winter long until she noticed the changes. The stars changed their positions, the rivers took on snowmelt, and if she were lucky, she saw an eagle return early to start the season all over again. Christmas lights at some point looked dated, when the sun lasted a little longer in the sky. She gathered the drying pine boughs left for the horses' Christmas. He noticed she was looking toward the canyon every so often, a little lost in her gaze as if she were searching for another memory or connection to her past. Then she'd blink, catch his eye and smile. Her smile alone would warm the sun a few degrees that time of year.

Ranger and Justice adjusted to the snow and sometimes slippery dead grasses underneath. They were building instinct, building how to pace themselves in the weather, whether a snowstorm blew in for a day or the sun stayed for a warmer afternoon. They learned the quick scan of the environment, the quick decision of walking forward, or holding back a step before trying a turn. Then a day happened, when spring hinted at lifting that winter cold from a shoulder, sweeping the breeze with a hint of fresh that someone can't help but inhale. It's a wonder of the change of the season, how a person grew in a matter of months, how a person put the season away until next year, even though it was only a day ago that winter visited the sky. Just look up. It's coming around the corner.

CHAPTER
SIXTY-TWO

"Good Morning, Phoenix. Russ Witter coming to you live from KOEP-TV. We've interrupted regularly scheduled programs with this special report. We have breaking news, live, coming from the State Capitol complex. Our reporter Jenna Marsh is there. We have very sketchy information with reports coming in about arrests by the FBI. Jenna? What can you tell us?"

The television screen immediately went blank. Viewers heard shuffling and the sound of voices fading like a windy day's breath. Then came a woman's voice. "Are we on yet? Are we on?"

"Apparently the team is still setting up." Russ scanned the news desk rather than looking directly into the camera, a technique he used once successfully as a student. "Jenna, if you can hear me—"

"Russ?"

"Jenna, what do you have at the State Capitol complex?"

As quickly, Jenna Marsh's face, a deer-in-the-headlights look, unlike her composed and coifed persona that viewers watched for, filled the television screen. In her left hand, she held a mismatch of papers. Behind her, a gathering of black vehicles with tinted windows was parked awkwardly to block West Washington Street. FBI agents, in blue anoraks and with furrowed brows, passed boxes, cartons, folders, and manila envelopes marked "EVIDENCE" toward an awaiting van.

"Russ, it looks pretty chaotic, here. We're hearing reports of a very sudden development regarding the governor. As you can see behind me, there is a strong FBI presence here, descending on the Capitol this morning with warrants to arrest some government officials. At this point we don't know who or for what. FBI agents are wearing their side arms, so we have been cautious about approaching the perimeter."

"Jenna, those boxes appear to have the word 'EVIDENCE' on them. Do you know what the evidence is about?"

"Despite this presence, Russ, the FBI has not shared anything yet, although we expect an FBI announcement sometime around noon. Some anonymous observers told us that the boxes do contain files of some sort, but no official word. The FBI has shut down this portion of the Capitol complex, asking workers to leave the building." She turned her back to the camera and speechlessly watched the steady train of agents loading files into a van.

"If I can interrupt, Jenna—"

A third voice, faceless and unidentified caught Russ Witter's attention. "I've been told we have another reporter—who is it?" He looked around the studio awaiting the ghost in his ear to confirm. "Is it Mark? Mark?"

"Russ, this is Mark Gresham on my cell at the governor's mansion. We are still setting up here, but we are observing a similar situation with FBI agents gathering items, mostly paper files, documents of some sort, some computer disks, taking pictures of the location and removing items from the mansion. It's a steady parade of boxes, a laptop, folders."

"Okay, Mark, any ideas if these two incidents are related?"

"Agents showed up at the mansion approximately the same time as at the Capitol, so, yes, I have to assume—Wait! I can see, it's one of the governor's assistants being led down a sidewalk to an awaiting car. He is in handcuffs—"

"Russ, Jenna again. We just got this." The studio shifted back to Jenna's perplexed face. "There is a pause in the flow of the items being transported and it appears...it seems there is someone other than an FBI agent emerging from the Capitol. Are you getting that shot? You have it? Wait...There! It's Governor Boyd Mullengrath, agents either side of him, walking toward the sidewalk. Of course, Governor Mullengrath announced his bid for reelection just months ago. We have a live shot now at the bottom of the steps and, yes! He is handcuffed, also! Governor Boyd Mullengrath leaving the State Capitol at this moment in handcuffs. I'm going to try to get closer..."

As Jenna drew closer, an onslaught of other reports, photographers, and camera operators jostled for position along the yellow-tape barrier.

"Governor, can you say what this is about?"

"Governor, did you call in the FBI today?"

"Are you being arrested?"

"Does this have to do with election finances?"

"Governor! Governor!"

Governor Boyd Mullengrath flashed an easy smile, but his voice faded as quickly as blue smoke. "I'm sure we have some miscommunication. I'll cooperate any way I can—"

Jenna turned back to the camera, but the camera man followed Mullengrath to the open door of a black SUV.

An agent cradled the governor's head forward, a gentle gesture at first. But with his head forward, Mullengrath's face changed. The smile dissolved into a whispered "no." His eyebrows darted forward then back, snapping against the reality that cameras were following. His face sank, his shoulders became defenseless, an authentic panic that had never surfaced to the public eye even in his darkest of times. The car swallowed him into the back seat before the shiny door slammed shut.

—

Griff watched it all with his deputies from a tiny TV set in his office. He recognized Mullengrath's effort to stay calm, to exude confidence, while breathing air as a man arrested for federal crimes.

It's happening, Griff thought. Time to tie down on this bronco and get ready for the ride.

Once his office emptied, he reached for the phone.

"Riley? You anywhere near a television right now?"

"No, what's up?"

"Mullengrath was just arrested by the FBI."

Silence. He could drive a train through Riley's silence and still not awaken a sleeping baby. "Riley?"

"Yeah, yeah, I'm here."

"You may want to make sure Maggie is safe. FBI is releasing a statement at noon. If there's any retribution, it could be in the next few days."

Riley let out a heavy sigh. "I know this is the right thing, but right now...jeez."

"May want to stay close to the house today. I'll be by later."

As warm as the early spring sun was on his back, Riley's blood was a frozen stream through his veins. He urged Maggie to finish up for an early lunch. As they walked toward the porch, the mail truck pulled into Riley's drive.

"Mr. Bedarte? You've got a package." The face wasn't Lester's. That frozen stream in his veins sludged to a halt, hair standing on end.

"Maggie, you go on in." He nodded, then turned to the driver. "Where's Lester?"

"Oh, he's on vacation. I'm taking over for a while till he comes back." The postal worker handed him the package of medication for the horses. Then in a lower voice, the man said, "Don't worry, we've got you covered." He smiled, handed Riley the package and his mail.

Riley stared at him as if he'd just spoken Portuguese to him.

"I think you know may know my boss, Cody? From Phoenix?"

Riley's blue eyes went from ice to thaw. "Ohhh, Phoenix. A Phoenix replacement, I see." He nodded in unison with the postal carrier. "I'm sorry I didn't get your name."

"Just call me Dale. My partner in town is Roy. That's all you need to know."

"Well, it's a pleasure, sir. I have to admit, it's nice to see someone other than Lester in that truck. I hope he's enjoying his vacation."

"Long deserved, I'm sure. Now I understand, if you're busy, I'm to put the medications in the insulated box over there?"

"That's correct, Dale. Looks like we'll get along just fine."

"See you tomorrow."

"Ladies and gentlemen, I'm Special Agent Cody Bishop with the Phoenix branch of the FBI. I'm involved with the ongoing FBI investigation involving a gentleman identified as Boyd Mullengrath, Governor of Arizona. At 8:30 this morning, FBI agents entered the Arizona State Capitol complex to arrest the governor, age forty-seven, on multiple charges that include kidnapping, racketeering, prostitution, and murder. We are also investigating charges of human trafficking and attempted murder. Governor Mullengrath surrendered without incident at 9:02 this morning and is currently in custody. We also have arrested one Wally Cameron at 8:59 AM, at the governor's mansion, as a possible accomplice to murder, age sixty-three, an aide to the governor. Governor Mullengrath has promised full cooperation. We have secured the area and are in the process of removing potential evidence at both locations. Since our investigation is ongoing, I cannot entertain any further questions at this time. We will provide information as we are able to share it. Thank you for your cooperation."

Griff watched Cody Bishop turn away from the makeshift podium, the flashes from cameras stabbing his shadow against a blue backdrop. His profile appeared stone-like, but Griff saw Cody rein in a hint of satisfaction when he folded the statement in half. Griff looked up from the television set to see the picture of Boyd Mullengrath hanging on his wall. Before Griff could check it, he felt the same hint of satisfaction in his own face.

A text photo from Cody buzzed his cell phone. *"Is this the turquoise cross your witness remembers from the governor's mansion?"* Framed in the doorway entrance washed with shadows, hung a large iron scroll cross with turquoise accents. Maggie described such a cross as she peered from her swollen eye, when she'd been presented to Mullengrath. One more ragged piece of memory turned into evidence with that picture. He'd show it to her later.

"...And that's what we have at this time, ladies and gentlemen. In summary, these are very shocking allegations our state has heard today, presented by FBI Special Agent Cody Bishop against Governor Boyd Mullengrath. The governor of Arizona was arrested just a few hours ago on the steps of the Capitol building." He gathered scattered notes before him on the news desk. "This unbelievable story began this morning at 8:30, when—"

No, Griff thought, this story began in May last year.

CHAPTER
SIXTY-THREE

BRENNISS

In the last few weeks, I've not always slept well. Not nightmares, rather anticipation the way it curdles and boils up. Griff has coached me about the questions I might be asked, shared pictures of things that I didn't dream, but really did exist during that awful time last year. I often fail when he says things like *"Brenniss, what do you remember about the van?"*

This Brenniss thing. I think he's talking to someone else. I miss the question.

The trial seems so abstract about something going to happen but never does. But, my testimony, Griff says, will be the turning point that could convince the jury about the governor's guilt. I guess I know that, but so much hinges on Brenniss. And I'm not sure I'm her, yet.

I turn back the page in my journal and look at the name. I try writing it again:

Brenniss Tripham. Brenniss Tripham. Brenniss Tripham. Brenniss Tripham.

My fingers create a tripod to hold the pen. It bobs up and down for the curl in the *e*, the bumps of the double *n*, the sassy snap of the double *s*. Familiar to my hand when I write it, yes. But it still looks funny to face me on the page. I recall writing my name across the top of my favorite white paper for a book report, for work contracts, and credit card receipts. I've even remembered signing a document when I took possession of a rare book or manuscript for the library. Funny how a signature can bring back memories just from the muscle patterns. *Brenniss Tripham.*

I think about what a courtroom might look like, even the severe seats. A closed courtroom, no distractions, Griff promises. Each time I practice a question, I've come to associate Griff's smile with "You're doing fine; keep going." Riley will be there, too. Riley's smile means "I'm proud of you." But I'm not sure if it's Brenniss or Maggie he's proud of.

Griff says I can take notes with me, to look prepared, to be sure of myself, unshakable. But I can't use them during the testimony. I want to be believed: every ugly, gritty, miserable detail, not because I WANT to remember, but because I NEED to. I need to stand strong. I still have scars. Some aren't so visible. They need to be washed clean.

But out there, beyond the trial, I may have to decide between Brenniss and Maggie because no one else can. Riley and I have talked about it a little; he's always told me it's up to me. I'm living a life I don't want to lose. I'm afraid if I become Brenniss, I'll forget Maggie, just like I forgot Brenniss when I was Maggie. I remember portions of my Brenniss life that must have been pleasant. At some point, it will be a little like Solomon's baby. I may be forced to make a choice.

I think I fear that more than the testimony itself.

CHAPTER
SIXTY-FOUR

February, such a feeble month, with at worst, twenty-nine *gray* days, that drizzle into March. The snow recedes along sidewalks, the morning suddenly breaks over the skyline canyon and filters into a window not visited since early fall. Some offices with lunch-break gardens and trees, may reveal a robin, a nest that wasn't there two days earlier, bringing a soundtrack of spring. The universal exhale of stale winter evaporates against the palest of suns. Despite threats of a March or even April snow, most realize that the planet has tilted toward the sun again, and there is no turning back. With that, New York finds more people venturing out, not because they have to, but because they want to.

"Vince, line one." Tess' voice broke Vince's concentration, a voice that startled him back from figures and lines and projections and charts. March's gray flannel sky tattered the morning past his window, while he ignored the arrival of spring. It couldn't come soon enough, he had thought earlier in the day, and yet he was poised nose nearly to screen as his computer hummed numbers for his new client.

"Hello, this is Vince Caldwell."

"Hey, Vince, this is Special Agent Stanley. Just wanted to thank you again for getting the photo to us so quickly. Wanted to give you an update. The lab has the image in their system for analysis and hope to have verification soon. But I did want to let you know that my team will be out of town in a few weeks, and we won't be able to talk."

"Is it Brenniss?" Vince's hope lit a candle spark under a basket in a dark corner of an unused barn.

"You know, son, we've got other cases besides Brenniss to work on, and there's one that has our attention elsewhere. So I can't—"

"Can I get updates?"

"Since when did you work for the FBI? This is confidential!"

"Oh, sure, but I thought...well, never mind. But, I do need to ask about something. Before Christmas when I was there with the photo—did I leave a maroon plaid scarf somewhere there?"

"Maroon and gray plaid? I've been wondering whose scarf that was. It's hanging on the coat rack in the conference room."

"That's it, I'm sure. I've been looking all over for it. Never thought about your office until yesterday. Mind if I come by and pick it up?"

"By all means. We'll have it downstairs at the reception desk for you. Come by any time. And thanks again, Vince. I'll get back to you after a few weeks when we get back to New York."

Carl Stanley gathered his evidence, and the agents assigned to Brenniss' case and meet with Cody Bishop in Arizona to see this trial through. Boxes of files, the tiniest of receipts, cell phone records, maps, diagrams, and, yes, even Brenniss' wedding dress were scheduled to be part of this. The last thing he would think about was Vince Caldwell. He closed down his computer, gathered his laptop and headed out the door for a plane with his name on it.

———

Vince hunched his shoulders against the wind gusts stepping into his vehicle. Late March had its own version of winter—blustery, monotonous, soggy—despite the calendar stating spring had arrived. The wind felt old, as another round of storms crept around the corners behind him, certain to bull-seye New York before evening. March was approaching, an army setting up reconnaissance on each corner fighting back the winter's influence. The sun glinted off the FBI office windows, as he found himself thinking about last summer, when the sun never found him. He was ready for warmer weather, even mentally promised himself he wouldn't squander the season this year. He drove past the automatic door into the FBI garage where a valet waited for him, as if he were the only one showing up today but knowing full well he was on a camera in someone's office.

He overheard a familiar voice in a nearby bay on the phone: *"We do have sign-off...we'll pick it up after 2:30...yes, Phoenix Sky Harbor International, all right?"* Vince glanced quickly toward the voice and saw Agent Stanley pocket his cell phone and slide into a tinted glass van. *Phoenix?*

Despite that overheard exchange, Vince proceeded toward the receptionist's desk, a male directing Vince to wait while he was on the phone. "I'll be with you momentarily, sir."

"Stanley's team just departed, sir, for the flight. Thanks for checking." The headset remained craned around his head, while he turned to Vince. "Now sir, thank you for waiting. What can I help you with?"

Vince approached the console—an uncanny coincidence

just handed to him no thicker than silk, no heavier than a feather—and leaned forward slightly. He barely found his voice. "You have an item for Vince Caldwell, a maroon and gray plaid scarf?"

"Sure, let me look." The receptionist leaned partially under the desk, sorting through a bin of outgoing information.

Funny that Agent Stanley would have to go to Arizona... for another case? Knowing Brenniss was there, too? Vince's brain twisted slowly like stepping slow motion into the space created by a moving jump rope. Brenniss. Copper Station, Arizona. Phoenix. Wait a minute...The rope slipped into place for Vince to dance over its edge at the right time in perfect sync. No way there was ANOTHER case in Arizona. Stanley *lied* to him to keep him in New York.

The receptionist sat upright with a packet holding Vince's scarf folded neatly into quarters. "Caldwell? I'll need you to sign for this."

Vince barely could hold the pen as he scribbled his initials. "Perfect. Thanks so much. You don't know how helpful you've been."

"I'll call for your vehicle."

Vince half saluted and calmly walked toward the car, despite his heart racing double time. Again, he found the door open, engine running, with no one else in view. The interior was wiped clean, warmed sufficiently against the late gray in New York.

Silly, he thought. I won't need a scarf if I'm headed to Phoenix.

CHAPTER
SIXTY-FIVE

The dry heat baked Vince's wool jacket to his shirt as he stood in the aisle of the plane, now on Phoenix soil. Only now, he felt a moist regret of this impulse driving him, texting to Mr. Whitten that he'd been called to Arizona. Perhaps Whitten and Mast believed that. He'd tried to text Tess three times during his layover, but she ignored each one. Once inside the airport, he recognized she wasn't here covering for him, with arrival or departure times, not keeping his files straightened and complete. Instead, he focused on Brenniss.

He squeezed between urgent groups of men and women, a seeming crush of people in Phoenix this time of year. A convention? Ohhhh, maybe a golf tournament? And just at that moment...Was it Agent Stanley around the corner? He ducked into a newsstand, grabbing a newspaper behind a shelf. The headline shouted *Secret Star Witness to Testify*. Well, there *was* the trial he heard some people talking about.

"You buying that, sir?" the young woman behind the cash register called to Vince. Her smile was sincere, but knowledge-able; she'd most likely seen people read papers before, then leave them behind, unsold. "You can buy that here."

"Sure! Sure! I...uh...I'm heading downtown, and I want to find some great place for dinner. Should be something in the paper, right?" He fumbled for his wallet, pulling out his last fifty. When he handed it to her, he saw her face fall. Fifty—really? For a ten-dollar edition? He could read her face as if she'd texted her response across her forehead. Instead, she used her best customer service face and slowly counted his change. As Vince moved toward the concourse again, the man he thought was Agent Stanley was still ahead of him. He called for his hotel shuttle, hiding his face behind his paper as Stanley proceeded out the door. Cautiously he picked up his only luggage, a carry-on with a few short-sleeved shirts, underwear and spare toiletries and dodged a backward glance from Stanley through the glass.

Once outside, he leaned against one of the pillars to soak in the Arizona sun splashing across the newspaper headlines, a splash that he wasn't prepared for, after months of New York's winters.

God! What a story! This governor dude was in deep and there was some mystery witness key to his conviction. He saw the governor's picture, not much different from the smile in Kent's picture of his cousin arm-in-arm with...a murderer? Kidnapper? Human trafficker? What a piece of work this guy was! Kent needed to warn his cousin to hang out with a better crowd.

"...the female who will testify has evidence regarding kidnapping, but the FBI investigation will not reveal her identity. Their statement describes this woman's kidnapping by multiple assailants which she can possibly connect to Governor Mullengrath. To protect this woman's identity further, the courtroom will be closed during her testimony."

Vince read it again: young woman who will testify was kidnapped... He looked up.

Vince choked.

"Mr. Caldwell? Vince Caldwell? I'm your shuttle ride from the hotel. May I take your bag?"

He looked around for Stanley and his crew. Nothing. Between the words he just read and the Brenniss he knew, Vince was not able to utter a sound due to the lock on his throat. He nodded toward the driver and stepped into the shuttle.

"Welcome to Phoenix, sir! I hope you didn't have to wait long. Getting to the airport isn't too bad this time of day, but the traffic into downtown is ridiculous now that the trial has started. We may need to take a round-about way to get back to the hotel. Please be patient, sir." His eyes met Vince's shell-shocked look in the rearview mirror. "Where are you from?"

He found a thread of his voice, a little wavy thing like Silly String curling out of his mouth. "New York City, actually." He waved the curled newspaper. "Wow, I was just reading about that trial. What a mess!"

"Lord have mercy on that girl! Mm-mmm, these are crazy times. The governor is running for office again, a shoo-in until this broke. He won't be able to buy a vote. Whatever happened to that girl sounds bad, but...they say the governor killed his own brother in this!" The shuttle leaned toward an entrance of multiple lanes channeling toward a warm western skyline.

"Well, what I read so far, the FBI is not sharing much. So, do they think the woman had anything to do with the murder?"

"Oh, no, no, no. FBI says they have DNA evidence to tie the governor to the murders and then to this lady. See that picture on page four? That's the van she was in!"

"Damn! That's flat as a pancake! How'd she survive?" Vince stared at the van that he wondered was the same one in the grainy security video he'd seen a thousand times. *This van? His Brenniss? No way.*

"She wasn't in the van, then. See, there's already been

testimony from the FBI that Mullengrath killed the gang that included his brother. She was long-gone before that happened. I guess they were trying to sell her, you know, like human trafficking?"

The facts were swimming thorough Vince's head like an Olympic trial meet, too much, too fast, too many lanes to watch. And Brenniss? First she's in the van? Then she isn't? What the hell did Agent Stanley keep from him all this time? Vince's blood flashed to ice so quickly. No wonder Stanley didn't want him to know the details.

The driver ducked his head to slide through a yellow light, then continued. "Sounds like she's been in hiding, like the governor may have had a hit out on her. Nobody knows her name right now or what she looks like."

Vince looked around the walls of the shuttle and imagined being stuck in the same spot with HIS driver for multiple days. Then, how the van just flattened into an accordion fold, only to be catalogued and filed like Brenniss' library documents. "So, she'll be testifying?" Vince asked quietly

"Yeah, sometime tomorrow." Vince heard an exhale from the driver as he turned toward the Capitol. "Oh, boy. Well, New York, welcome to the circus!" Vince saw people gathered on corners with signs, "Pray for Mullengrath," with others selling shirts in makeshift booths, "Women speak the Truth." Carnival or social movement or exploitation, the mayhem became more crowded along the streets. What the hell did he get into?

In a twist of a second, he knew he could connect with Brenniss....tomorrow at the courthouse. That would work. He'd get into the courthouse plaza, stand outside the main door to wait for her, then she would be walking toward the entrance when she saw him. Her mouth would fall open, maybe even mouth his name "Vince," and she'd cry, after all the months of not knowing. Maybe by tomorrow night, they could fly red-eye back to New York.

CHAPTER
SIXTY-SIX

"Son of a bitch, who are these clowns?" Griff uttered behind the wheel. Riley sat beside Maggie in the back, his hand on her shoulder, reminding her to breathe. Theirs was an anonymous vehicle with darkened and tinted windows like a filmy mourning veil on the way to the courthouse. *Same as the van, Maggie thought. My life keeps meeting crossroads in a black vehicle.*

"Can I open the window at all?"

"'Fraid not, Maggie, uh, Brenniss" Griff continued. "I'll just crank up the AC a little more. It's stuffy in here, I know."

"Damn claustrophobic, with all these freaks here," Riley added.

A piece of me ready to scream all the way to hell and back without an open window.

"Breathe, Maggie. Just breathe." Riley caught her gaze and took the wild fear away. *I like that about Riley, I'm still Maggie.*

"Almost there, Brenniss," Griff whispers. He wove through vendors and protestors, unnoticed, turning into a ramp that led to an underground parking garage, as dark as a spider's underside.

Just for a second...*Hey, girlie girl...*

Riley took a breath, then the click of the seatbelt latches. No rap music. No arguments about stopping for beer or which way to turn.

"Waiting for the all clear, Brenniss, then we can go in." This is the official and aloof side of Griff she rarely saw, a second nature for him.

"I'm doing fine."

Two agents nodded determinedly at Griff, then Riley. They opened Brenniss' door into a florescent shield of sickly light along a concrete corridor. Another agent, Bishop, warmly shook Griff's hand, then Riley's. While his soft smile turned toward her, Brenniss saw how young he was. *And my life is in his hands.*

"Brenniss, are you ready?"

"I've been through worse. I hope they believe me."

"You've got a jury who wants to hear your story, Brenniss." He guided her as if she were silk, away from the vehicle. "Your story will solidify the evidence we've already shown. They need to hear *you*. They need your honesty."

"It's brutal," she said, feeling her voice cracking like an egg ready to spill its contents.

Once inside, they walked toward a small elevator labeled "Prisoner Entrance."

"Could I go to the bathroom?" she asked. It wasn't much bigger than the toilet and sink. So much like looking at a distorted face in a scratchy tin mirror in a bathroom. She washed her shaking hands, trying to clean the soreness from her swollen jaw, not making sense of the terror she'd lived and imagining how she could crawl through the pipes under the sink to escape. But now her eyes were clear. Her hands shook as she dried them, from nervousness, not fear. Her mouth felt as dry as Mitchell Canyon in high summer.

She opened the door, took a deep breath.

Riley put his arm around her shoulder. "Let's go, Sunshine."

Shine."

She walked into the oak-paneled courtroom with Bishop to sit behind the prosecutor's table in front. Sounds echoed: the polished wood reflected noise and light. No one else was in attendance, like a funeral: quiet, respectful, everything focused on the front of the room. Brenniss could almost hear the dust collecting as it filtered through the sun past the window blinds. The jury entered like a choir.

The prosecutor assured Brenniss with a liturgy of instructions: *one question at a time, yes or no, elaborate only when I ask you. Look directly at me, no staring or sarcasm, no signs of anger. You know more than anyone how to answer the questions I'll ask.*

"Ready?"

As if on cue, another door opened, and the dead quiet returned except for a slow shuffle and chains rubbing each step. All she saw was a tall man wearing orange flip-flops, with dirt along the edges. Brenniss knew who it was.

The judge entered, sat, and for the longest second, made eye contact with Brenniss and the barest of nods. *What am I supposed to do with that?* She tucked that nod into a mental pocket for Griff later.

Called to the stand, Brenniss felt the Bible warm to the touch and suddenly thought of Perry Mason. There was always the crazy lady in the last thirty seconds who admitted to the crime. But when she sat, only Riley and Griff were before her, and no lady with a smidgeon of a hat on her head. Just Brenniss with a heavy collection of truth she just swore she would share.

She was asked to spell her name, and for a second she

thought it was to trick her memory. Beside her was a pitcher of water, a full glass, and a box of tissues. She took a breath and realized taxpayer money provided that for her. *Touching that someone knows the basics to clean up rape.*

"Exhibit twenty-nine, your honor," the prosecutor continued. "This video was taken from a security entrance where Ms. Tripham exited the mall, and the time and date stamp correspond to the purchase of the gown."

For thirty seconds, Brenniss watched the surveillance video, thinking how small and silly she looked, arms flailing and off-balance as if rollerskating. She heard someone gasp. But the question she'd secretly asked herself again and again told her she couldn't reverse the tape: *How could I have stopped them?*

"Exhibit twenty-eight, your honor." The prosecutor carried what looked like a small tent toward her, unzipped the zipper and pulled something long and white from the inside. It flooded back, just as she dropped the water glass, shattering behind the stand. "My wedding dress," she cried out. Then sobs convulsed her. She reached out to touch the fabric. The Brenniss she almost was.

"A break, your honor?" The prosecutor handed her a fresh glass, she held with shaking hands. The prosecutor walked to the jury and handed someone a tissue.

Another breath and a sip of water, she whispered, "I'm okay, I'm ready."

More questions then about those first few hours.

"Did you fight back?"

"Did they hit or beat you?"

"Did they humiliate you?"

"Did they rape you?"

What Brenniss wanted to say that they took pieces of me away.

"Did they rape you multiple times?"

She finally pushed a spit of air forward. "I lost count after forty." She lay down the truth and for some it was hard to hear. In quick succession, she wanted to see Riley's eyes to remind her of something kind and sweet. She started shaking as she verified details, followed by more video and sworn documents. The prosecutor continued about the seat belt and how they eventually beat the Brenniss out of her.

"Over a period of four days," she answered.

There were fingerprints, a piece of the van, a hair or clothing fiber, even a photo of the van that all substantiated what she said. Then, DNA evidence between Mullengrath and Paco Vallesquez, from maggot stomachs. *Somehow, it seemed fitting that Mullengrath deserved no more than maggot guts.*

"You arrived at a mansion after that fourth day. Was there anyone there?"

"There was a man at the door, and behind him a turquoise and iron cross behind him on the wall. He called me 'used merchandise'.

"Is that man in the courtroom?"

She nodded yes and for the first time, looked at him with two good eyes, a set jaw and healing scars that were itching for revenge. She looked at his dark hair and the mole on his cheek. She pointed with a strong thrust, her hand not shaking.

Boyd Mullengrath clenched his teeth and looked away. But she still stared.

"Did you go somewhere else after this encounter?"

She spoke softly of the putrid air in the van, being rolled into a carpet and her exhaustion. How she was ready to give in, ready to die.

A little after 4:00 p.m., Brenniss Tripham stood down, met by the prosecutor who shielded her from Mullengrath's face as he returned to his cell. She stepped toward Riley and saw his eyes were rimmed in red. But Griff, not looking at her, nodded again and again as he stood.

"You were amazing," the prosecutor whispers.

She was still not sure who Brenniss was.

CHAPTER
SIXTY-SEVEN

BRENNISS

Today, I'm warned by the prosecutor that the defense will attack my memory. He will take issue regarding anything I say I remember to discredit me. I'm not on trial, he says. The defense will object to every effort to paint Mullengrath guilty. You've got this. He says this gently, not like some prophet calling for Jesus with a jutted jaw and a vein visible underneath his forehead. He says it with confidence and a smile. I believe him.

I sit in the same spot as yesterday. Most of the broken glass is cleaned up, although I see a few slivers caught in the corner. I did that. That may always be here, kind of like a memorial. There's Riley and Griff and the prosecutor. All in a bullet line of sight. Outside I hear crowds, horns honking, the rise of a chant. "She speaks for those who can't." The judge's gavel snaps near my ear, like a flag catching the wind.

He reminds me that I've already sworn the truth.

"How convenient," the defense attorney begins, his arms crossed at his chest, "that you would suddenly be available for testimony, how your memory fell into place at this particular time."

Convenient? This mess? Truthfully, I'd rather be riding Bliss or Justice, the early sun warming my back while the slow river sparkles.

"Objection," the prosecutor says. There was no question offered yet. I've not even said anything yet. "Badgering the witness." The judge tells the defense attorney to turn his statement into a question.

"Brenniss...Now, do I call you Brenniss or Maggie?"

"I'm Brenniss Tripham. I testified yesterday as Brenniss." I take another breath, but an objection slices thorough my thoughts. *I was ready to accept Brenniss, right then and there as if it were nothing but the truth.*

"All right, then, Brenniss, is it not true that you had little recollection of these events until recently?"

Another objection, but this time, the judge allows the question to hear my side of how the puzzle pieces fit together.

"It's true, but the events of the kidnapping, the rapes—"

"Just answer the question—"

"Objection."

I get an image: two wolves circling a carcass. I'm right back to being a piece of meat being prodded and sampled and objected to, even though I've said only eight words. They pounce on each other, leaving the carcass staring dead to the sky. I look at Riley. His face is the kindness I've forgotten.

"Let me ask you this, then. What were your first memories when you were fully awake?"

"White," I say immediately. *I know this one.*

"White?"

"Yes, more recently I figured out I was remembering the

color of my wedding dress, the white as it fluttered to the ground when I was pushed into the van."

"Yes, yes. Your wedding dress. Did you remember the abduction?"

"Objection. Your honor, she answered that question with details in her testimony yesterday. I remind the court of the multiple exhibits we've presented to substantiate the witness' recall."

See? I think. The courtroom works like that. Ev-i-dence.

"Yesterday, you testified that you endured four days or so of ongoing rape from three assailants, is that true?"

"Yes."

"We saw pictures of that van in various gas stations and then after it had been destroyed. Yet, you remembered the floor, the seat, the seat belt, even your injuries."

My head skids to a stop, because I was told to answer questions only. So I wait for a question. The judge gets it and intercedes. "Is there a question, sir? If there is, you need to form it before the sun goes down."

"Yes, your honor. You remember those things about the van and your injuries, correct?"

"Yes."

"Was Governor Mullengrath ever in that van?"

"Not to my knowledge."

"Objection!"

"Did Governor Mullengrath rape you?"

"Objection! Your honor, we established the assailants in that van in previous testimony. We provided evidence including DNA determining the assailants were indeed in that van and were connected with the defendant. The prosecutor has never claimed the governor physically raped this woman."

Sustained. *I can tell the judge is getting a little tired of what's going on. He uses the word "antics" and "theatrics" in the same sentence. In the corner of my eye, I see a jury member* write something on paper.

"Do you know if Governor Mullengrath is in this room?"

"Yes." *This is too easy. I know I'm being setup.*

"Would you point him out?" I point my finger toward him again.

"You are saying this man did not physically abuse you? Did not pin you down, tie you down, break your wrist, punch you? Slap you? Kick you?"

I pause only because it's damning to me. "*He* did not."

"Yet, you testified you were raped over forty times. Do you remember the fourteenth time you were raped? The twentieth?"

"Your honor! Objection!"

"The thirty-eighth? Can you remember them all?"

Objection, objection, objection. *The defense attorney has a point. After a while, it all blurred together. All I saw were teeth, hands, lips, eyes. I remember it, but not like a catalogue description with pictures. But I let them sort it out, teeth bared, spit crossing between them.*

The judge draws the two attorneys to the bench. I hear him say that the defense is spinning its wheels, he's warning him. *I look at the clock. I've been sitting here for two hours. I look at Riley. He's nodding carefully, just for me to see. I look at Mullengrath, who studies his flip-flops. I look at the jury; they look angry. I bet somebody is missing out on a school meeting, a great sale at Walmart or a golf game.*

A lightning bolt of thought hits me. *I know there must be something I could say, once and for all, something profound that would seal the deal, stop this sorry defense attorney dead in his tracks, show that my memory isn't punched into holes like Swiss cheese. Just one thing that I could say about this whole miserable experience that would stop him, mouth gaping open, with nothing more to ask, looking like the fool that he is. Riley kept telling me it was my choice; it was all up to me. For once I want that to be true more than anything else in the world, right now.*

The defense attorney returns to his legal pad, traces his finger down the page, as if something will remind him of another stupid question to ask. He forms a cage with fingers touching together, held across his chest.

"Brenniss," he turns toward me, "I just have a hard time imagining that you could remember anything at all after the brutal treatment you received from these thugs. You testified yesterday that often you didn't know one day to the next. Is that true?"

"Yes, after a while, it was all the same."

"Just answer yes or no please. Yet, you remember meeting the governor, correct?"

"Yes, at his home."

"Did you say a greeting to him or introduce yourself?"

"No, I couldn't talk. My jaw was broken."

"Brenniss, yes or no. Did you know he was the governor?"

"No, not at the time."

"How did you know that it was his home?"

"Paco said we were heading to his brother's home. That's where we stopped. Paco was the governor's brother—"

"Your honor! I'm asking the witness to respond in yes or no answers. She is taking liberty with the facts."

"You asked this, sir. But I will remind the witness that yes and no questions are preferred. Do you understand that, Brenniss?" The judge turned toward me, not reproachfully, but more like a grandfather reading a story, making sure I understood who the Big Bad Wolf is. *I nod yes, but I get the feeling the judge won't hold me to yes or no much longer.*

"You referred to Paco, correct?"

"Yes."

"Also identified by DNA as Paco Vallesquez, correct?"

"Yes."

"What happened to Paco Vallesquez when you arrived at the governor's mansion?"

Now I'm confused because there's no way I can answer yes or no to that one. I shake my head.

"Is that your answer? Your head shake?"

"No."

"Then, let me ask again. Once you arrived at the governor's mansion, what happened to Paco?"

"Do you want me to answer yes or no?" I hear the jury stifle a few giggles, and the judge leans over to me. "Go ahead, Brenniss. You need to elaborate here. The court will allow an answer more than yes or no."

Well, good, I think, it's about time. "Paco knocked on the door, and the governor answered, then came outside where we were standing by his steps. He looked at me, then talked with Paco for a while."

"How far away from them were you?"

"About two feet."

"Could you hear what they said?"

"For the most part."

"How in the world could you hear this, Brenniss? You had been repeatedly traumatized over four days! You testified that you were in pain, and you hadn't eaten and were thirsty. How did you manage to hear what they said?"

Oh, I know this one, too. And it's one that I had only told to Griff and Riley. So now I get to tell the attorney and Mullengrath and the jury, too. "The pain in my wrist, in my gut, and in my chest kept me alert. I was out of the van for the first time in days, other than walking into restrooms or convenience stores. So I remembered clearly trying to stand up, but having to be held in place. I heard his words clearly. I remember looking at him because I had no choice. Kick pulled my hair to raise my head back. I saw a man with dark hair and a mole on his cheek—that man," I point to Mullengrath, "answer the door and embrace Paco and call him 'brother'. Then he looked at me and asked 'what's this?'"

"Your honor, this witness is babbling. I must object—"

"The defense attorney opened this line of questioning," the judge says firmly, "regarding the witness' recall. She is telling what she recalled. I'll allow it." The judge looks at me, his hands folded over each other. *He has nice, clean fingernails. Obviously, he doesn't work with horses or drive vans.*

"Please, young lady. Go on."

"The governor smacked Paco against the side of his head and asked 'What did you do with my merchandise? I didn't pay you for a joy ride. You were supposed to teach her a lesson, not destroy her.' Then he said, 'Get rid of it.' I remember his calling me 'it'. He said to dispose of the merchandise because I was damaged goods."

Silence.

"That's amazing you can remember all that so clearly," the attorney says with a smirk. "And the only other ones to counter your testimony are dead." He shakes his head.

Now, I know that's not true, because Mullengrath is sitting right there. We could just out and out ask him. But I also know that's the last thing the defense attorney wants is for Mullengrath to open his mouth.

The defense attorney tries again. "You testified that Governor Mullengrath didn't rape you, didn't slap you, didn't kick you or cause any of your injuries, is that correct?"

"He didn't inflict those injuries on me directly, no."

"Then tell me this! What else from your memory do you remember that Governor Boyd Mullengrath didn't do?"

Now there it is. My brain just simmered into position. The attorney just opened the door with a welcome mat right in front and even handed me some lemonade. I look at Riley, prop my shoulders back a bit. He knows something is coming, but not sure what. I take a breath and look at the defense attorney.

"He didn't offer me water or a change of clothes. He didn't call the police—"

"Your honor, I object!" The defense attorney's eyes are on fire.

"Your line of questioning, sir!" the judge spits. "I'll allow anything the witness describes as the defendant not doing."

"He didn't seek medical attention for me, he didn't offer me a chance to wash up, a phone call, an offer to take me home, didn't offer me a chance to cool off inside, offer to remove me from the van. That's how I recall it."

The room is still. "He didn't even recognize me as a human being." My voice wavers into water. My stomach churns as I look at Mullengrath. His eyes are nearly slit shut, but he is staring at me all the same.

He knows.

CHAPTER
SIXTY-EIGHT

Riley

When I look at a new horse for search and rescue, I use slow eyes. Those movements and twitches, the horse's stance, the head position. They all tell stories. I look at the coat in the sun, in the shade. I watch the back as it accepts the saddle, the head as it sniffs the air, the foot as it paws the hay, the flick of the tail, the clarity of the eyes.

My slow eyes are working today as Mullengrath enters the courtroom on this second day, so there is tension drawing the room tight like a shoelace. Mullengrath's stiff leg movements and darting eyes remind me of a nervous horse up for auction. My slow eyes see his stiff jaw, hands permanently clenched with the weight of the arm cuffs. He stands as his leg chains are looped though a table leg. I can tell his fear is brittle like frozen burlap stretched its limit. If he were a horse, I'd want control of him with a bridle and short reins.

When the judge enters, Mullengrath takes a skittish breath as he holds his head more erect. He is the horse that's been beaten, but still ready to rage. His muscles tense, his eyes focused ahead. He's looking to run, a hard, relentless path toward escape.

Maggie's eyes meet mine as she sits. I nod. She knows a storm is approaching. This memory will last forever, the blizzard she's grateful she's lived through, but never wants to experience again. I'm proud of her, braver than most.

Mullengrath slips into focus again. He's a horse sensing a tornado, pulling at the reins with a stout neck, not accepting the rise in the wind, a part of nature he can't fight.

Maggie will do this, I now realize. I'd had my doubts. But now I see her strength. Later, she'll go back to the hotel room, relax, the storm over, the wind relaxing like a bad dream. It will be finished today. She's ready to show the survivor she is.

I watch Mullengrath with slow eyes as he tries to pretend he is still in control. But, now Maggie stands her ground in a furious storm that even the judge won't accept. Maggie looks up again. I nod again and she seems to focus, ready again.

I look at Mullengrath's head now; my slow eyes see it. A defeated horse will lower its head, show submission, become listless. There it is. Not his head, but his shoulders sagging. There's a crease down the back of his shirt, as if a dull knife were making a slow entry. I see it with my slow eyes. He's given up.

Maggie finishes another six hours of testimony with her first memories in the hospital.

"Someone talked to me in a low voice. I wasn't being pummeled or touched or probed or slapped anymore. It was quiet. I smelled clean. I was lying still, and I heard a comforting voice. The voice talked about an angel, a woman better than anyone deserved. I knew that when I finally opened my eyes, I would still hurt, but somehow, I was safe. I knew the nightmare was over. I finally opened my eyes and saw a window in a small room. The sun and blue sky warmed me. I could look up and see the sky because no one was holding my head down. The voice returned and offered me Jell-O. It was the best thing I'd ever eaten."

Maggie looks at me, a start of a smile, then a head tilt as if to ask...

Griff whispers, "That's it. She's done it."

...as if to ask if that voice were mine.

I thought she'd never ask.

CHAPTER
SIXTY-NINE

Vince studied the map while waiting in line for the guided State Capitol Museum tour. When the line advanced him toward the front, he found a reason to stall until he saw Brenniss. He was a tourist, staring at the rotunda, staring down two different hallways where reporters paced by the oak doors of the courtroom. He pulled his phone toward his ear, an imaginary and important call, while he listened to the gossip and projections about Brenniss' trial. Like the reporters, he focused on Brenniss to emerge from the door. Just one or two seconds was all he needed to show that he never gave up hope. He was *this close* to hearing her voice again, seeing those eyes that were smaller than dust specks in Kent's Christmas picture.

A policeman rose on his toes, like a blue jay, and looked in Vince's direction. Vince casually punched in numbers. If he'd planned better, he would have brought a file or a newspaper to look convincingly nonchalant. Slowly, he edged toward a narrow hallway leading to the restrooms. The cop turned, moved on.

Who was this guy in the restroom mirror? Circles coursed under his blank eyes, his face sagged with fatigue and effort. About to splash water on his face, he heard a commotion outside the door, random voices, an agitation, a dust devil of questions getting louder. By the time he emerged from the hallway, the buzz saw of the crowd caught him up into the sea of faces.

He bobbed his head upward looking for Brenniss. He nearly missed her.

In the corner of his eye, farther down the bathroom hallway, a nearly invisible door creaked open, unnoticed in the mayhem. But there was Brenniss, book-ended by two men, walking further down the bathroom hallway toward a door marked "PRIVATE."

"Brenniss! Brenniss!"

The trio walked in unison toward that door as if they planned to explode through it, leaving splinters behind.

"Brenniss! Over here!" His heart stumbled into a marathon pace. He waved his hand, but it was lost in the forest of cameras and confusion.

One of the men tapped on the door; it opened from the other side. She was swallowed into the darkness while he was sucked into the opposite direction. Vince turned, planted his feet to break free from the group. First one foot then twist the second to support his balance and direction toward the "PRIVATE" door. His last chance, as the crowd ebbed.

The door handle caught but didn't open. Locked. He tried again. He pounded on the door.

"Brenniss! Brenniss!"

The door snapped open. Agent Stanley, his coarse short hair, his scowl, his earpiece, and his gun, emerged from the green hoodie he wore. Suddenly, Vince realized this man was the size of a bear, close enough he could feel each thick finger grab his arm.

"What the hell are YOU doing here?" he bellowed. "You

were to stay in New York, you idiot! Are you trying to blow this thing wide open?" Vince lost balance as the bear yanked him through the doorway onto a parking garage ramp. Concrete so hard that Vince skidded painfully to his knees, worse than sliding into first on a pop-up fly. Just then, a black car drove away. Brenniss was inside, shielded by someone in the back seat. His Brenniss.

The shock of being thrown sideways stopped his breath and his brain. "You didn't answer my question!" Spittle landed like freckles on Vince's face.

"You let her get away!"

"That was the idea! Hold your damn voice down!" Stanley pulled Vince's arm behind his back, then brought his mouth to Vince's ear. "Do you realize how hard we've worked to keep her identity from the press? Your stupid move might cost her life. I nearly shot you!" Stanley adeptly pressed him in place against the concrete wall. "I ought to arrest you here and now for obstructing justice and put you out of your misery," his voice hissed.

Stanley waited for Vince to take three breaths, then leaned back an inch, his face as threatening as a bulldog. Two more men, casual in janitor uniforms approached the ramp then looked around. They spoke into their shirt cuffs. The PRIVATE door jammed open against the concrete wall, this time with Mullengrath like ham in a sandwich between two guards. He walked halting jerks down the ramp toward another waiting car.

"I don't care what that bitch said!" Mullengrath yelled toward the closing door. "They can't prove it! I didn't pull the trigger, I told you that!" Gloved hands pushed his head near his chest. He slid clumsily into the car, which jetted up the garage ramp into the sunlight. All clear.

Vince felt his fingernails dig into his palms, two fists of frustration pressed to his side, the only thing he could move at that moment.

"You—Vince," Stanley growled. "Get in." He held another car door open. "Now! Or the cuffs go on you, too!"

Vince slid into the car, blood returning to his lower arms. Stanley ducked in and the car accelerated before his door was closed.

Stanley leaned toward Vince to look through imposing eyebrows. "We. Had. A. Deal. You were to stay in New York, damn it."

"I needed to see her."

"You idiot! She turned evidence against the governor of Arizona! Can *you* guarantee her safety at this moment? He may have another sniper trained on her—on YOU!—right now. We can't afford to have you plan a romantic rendezvous, WHAT were you thinking?" Stanley's face turned a deep red, and the sound of his voice would carry to Texas, if the windows were open.

"But nobody knows her—"

"As long as you don't blurt out her name in public the way you just did! That's because we have a team of eight agents working very hard to keep her alive!"

"Well, I didn't know, you never told me!"

"Why do you suppose THAT is, you moron? It's not *your* business to know! Your job is to stay in New York. Period. I ought to toss you out into the desert and leave you there." Stanley's eyes narrowed. "No, I've got a better idea. You are with us 24/7 until she gets reunited with her mom."

"But my hotel room—"

"Already located it, collected your belongings and stripped it clean." The car pulled into another office building parking lot. "You'll stay with me."

"But—"

Vince felt a hand wrap around his throat. "You. Me. The same room. It's either that, or I arrest you for interfering with a federal investigation. That's a long time in prison, Vince, and an awful lot of romantic rendezvous, if you get my drift." Stanley's left temple showed three veins pulsing with each breath. Vince leaned back against the seat.

"That's the first smart thing you've done all day, boy."

CHAPTER
SEVENTY

"We'll rest here before we leave for home under the cover of darkness." Griff unlocked the adjoining hotel room doors. "FBI is paying for meals, so we'll order room service.

Maggie walked through the connecting door then felt her body drain that last spark of adrenaline. She sat on her bed, the weight of months of memories lifting like wings from her shoulders. She blankly stared out the window, much like those first days in the hospital—empty, free, uncertain, at peace. Her fingers rose to the bridge of her nose, pinching that spot, the familiar habit she once had.

She took two breaths, then saw Riley at the adjoining doorway. "Maggie?"

"Yeah?" She looked a little lost, as if the focus in her were an unwinding kite string.

"Thought you might need to talk."

Her smile returned. "I've been talking for two days. I'm not sure it made any difference—"

"Of course it did." He leaned forward. "Then let me do some talking. You just listen." Her brain, still spinning from all the questions, was not picking up what he wanted to say.

"When you first..." He held his breath.

"Riley, what is it?" She understood his struggle, those first words that get confused.

"Okay, here goes. I first met you trying to put the pieces of your life together. What you didn't know was that I was wandering as much as you. We both, I guess, got through those dark times together, didn't we?"

Maggie's eyes pinched in confusion. Just then, Griff poked his head through the door. "Maggie? You want salad, chicken, or pork chops?"

"Salad, maybe a cup of tomato soup, too? And Jell-O if they have it?" Her weary smile relaxed with the thought of Jell-O.

"Riley?" Griff turned his head.

"Oh, I'll take the chicken, I guess."

"You got it."

Maggie focused her eyes, as if pulling the last bit of her energy toward Riley. Why did his shoulders buckle just now?

"I've maybe said how I'm proud of you, not just for surviving, but for being brave. You found something inside you that you could rope onto, hold on to all those rough memories. You pulled your way past it. Most people would have given up and let that dark piece of life take over. Not you. Not Maggie."

Her smile was weak, and he wasn't sure she had the energy to listen just now. But he was ready to say this. He might lose his nerve if he didn't. "Listen to me, Sunshine. I've been thinking about your leaving and all, and I need to say this. You've found a place to fit and ...well, I just...I know now...I can't help but say I lo—"

"What do you two want to drink?" Griff interrupted again.

"Iced tea, I guess. Thanks, Griff." Maggie kept her eyes locked on Riley's face, but her brain was thinking about riding Bliss.

"It sure will be good to get back home." She leaned against

the pillow, closed her eyes, her eyelashes resting comfortably. "I miss Poke, Bliss and even Ranger...no, I miss the quiet. Don't you think, Riley?"

He almost got it past his lips, headed toward her heart. But instead, "So you want to stay there at the ranch for a while?"

"I've never thought of any place else." She smiled again.

As they rode home in the dark, Maggie relaxed by herself in the back seat. She curled her legs up while she listened to the conversation and the music on the radio. The men were courtroom quarterbacks in their conversation.

"We've got him, I'm sure." Griff nodded so hard his shoulders rocked. "The state testimony with the DNA identification, the testimony Cameron placing Mullengrath at the canyon—"

"Governor's got, what? Twelve counts against him?"

"No, seventeen! Don't know if all those will stick, but I'm pretty damn sure he won't be running for reelection any time soon. Feds did a powerful job."

"On your evidence, Griff. All your work, you know."

Maggie leaned her head against the open window, cobwebs forming in the backseat of her brain. Her eyes stretched toward the sky, the deep blue punched with stars. She thought of sitting on the porch, Poke sitting close, the Emory's oak whispering a breeze. No traffic, no horns, no demonstrators, and no voices from the past jumping in on her. She felt a breath sink into her lungs. She was going home.

"That defense lawyer set himself up. I watched him put that noose around his own neck and pull tight. I couldn't believe it!"

"But Maggie turned it back toward him. I watched that jury. Their faces told Maggie's story, too. Did you see that, Maggie?" Riley turned toward the back seat. She was asleep.

"You know what's next, don't you?" Griff said softly.

"We wait for the jury's decision."

"Well, yes, but after that. What are you doing, friend? Letting Maggie think she's going to stay on with you? The feds are already in Copper Station—"

"Yeah, Roy and Dale. One of them is delivering the mail while Lester's on some kind of vacation."

"I mean it, Riley. You have to start thinking about her going back to New York."

"Her decision, Griff, I told you. I won't stop her." But he shut his tired eyes for a second. "Doesn't make it easy, I know." It was too late about the hurt. He felt it open his heart, ripping seams, one stitch at a time.

CHAPTER
SEVENTY-ONE

Brushing Cartwheel's mane was like heaven to Maggie after swallowing that tornado in the courtroom. Cartwheel's tail softly swished in rhythm to the brushing, the late spring morning easing above the river and toward the pasture. Those soft sounds and the horses' nickering was this side of perfect.

"I won't be long in town." Riley pulled on his gloves. "If you can get these horses exercised this morning, we can work Ranger and Justice this afternoon. Got a lot of catching up to do. You'll be okay?"

"I can handle it." She stopped to look at the silhouette in the barn doorway. "Thanks, Riley. You know I couldn't have done all of this without you, don't you?"

He tugged his glove tighter. "Maggie, we did this together, that much I know." He stepped forward out of the sunlight. His eyes stung. "This working together has really brought us...closer..."

She looked at Riley's eyes, the same eyes she'd seen dozens of times, but this time a strong wind of feelings whipped through her. His lined face told stories of kindness and caring;

shoulders that carried burdens gracefully. His arms had wrapped safety around her this past year. Then, briefly, a younger face emerged, a smooth smile, a face from some time ago, a face with brown eyes...But she blinked, ready to say more about how she felt she was a part of something here at the ranch. All that came out was "Thank you."

"Well...well." Riley looked past her. "When I get back, let's go for a quick ride. Maybe we have some things twisting around inside that we need to say."

"Sure, sure, that's good. We...we need to talk, huh?" Her smile blended into the barn's stolen sunlight.

"Okay, I'll be back with supplies—yes! I won't forget the Jell-O!" He chuckled. He reached for her arm, leaned closer, and kissed the top of her head. "It's time we figured out what's coming up ahead."

He walked toward the truck from the barn. Just like that, she wanted to drop the brush, run after him—not out of fear of being by herself, but to keep that moment frozen between them—climb into the truck, ride off to town with him. But she stopped two steps, for some reason, waving a soft goodbye as he turned onto the highway.

***

Griff's phone rang around 10:30 while he was typing up a missing teen report.

"Griff? Cody Bishop. Don't know if you were watching the TV or had the radio on."

"I hadn't even thought of it; what's up?"

"Jury came back with a verdict."

"Already? You're kidding! We've only been home two days."

"Found Mullengrath guilty on sixteen counts, just came in. Your diligence laid the groundwork for all that compelling evidence. That and Brenniss' testimony."

"Damn! Damn! I'll be. That's great news!" Maybe his soul was weary, but it was baptized by Maggie's case. "Just proud to have been part of the team," he said quietly.

"You're a bit of a legend around here."

"Well, thanks, Cody. I don't mind telling you I aged about five years during that investigation. Once the state lab got enough evidence that triggered Maggie's memory—"

"No, I'm giving credit where credit's due...so, I was thinking, have you ever thought of being a part of the FBI? We sure could use someone with your skills."

Griff chuckled. For a man who had all the answers, Cody Bishop sure didn't know him well at all. "Cody, I take that as a compliment, and I thank you. But it's like this: I like getting up in the morning, having breakfast with my wife, and driving to the sheriff's office. Copper Station gives me time to breathe, time to look for the runaway I'm searching for today, time to take a ride on my favorite horse. Go fishing on a river that's a bit of heaven. You let me know when you'd like to try on my life for a day. Riley and I will be glad to take you out on the river."

"I knew as much, but I thought I'd offer. But there *is* another reason I called, though. Special Agent Carl Stanley will be headed to Copper Station today sometime. He'll want to meet with Brenniss, give her a chance to talk to her mom, finally, then pack up. We have a private jet waiting for her to return to New York. Can we ask you to get that all arranged?"

Griff's stomach took a quick elevator ride toward his gut. "Arrange" what? Pull Maggie—okay, Brenniss—from a situation that she loves, that Riley loves..."arrange" what? Clean up the mess?

"You do understand Cody that Maggie has made a few friends here. Could she have a day or so to get ready?"

"This is one of those times, Griff, where I need you to say

you'll help arrange anything we need. We told Betty just this morning that her daughter was alive. She is beyond happy and is by the phone, waiting to hear from her. I need you to do this as quickly and painlessly as possible."

Griff sucked the air into his lungs. "Okay, I'm on it. Let me type up this report," he said sharply. "Thanks, Cody." He immediately dialed Riley's home number. Let it ring, oh, maybe a dozen times...no answer.

What was happening here? Maggie leaned against a hay bale. She worked both horses steady in the new grass and along the sloping hillsides. The horses felt sure beneath her, the sun was a warm, faithful hand gliding them into the spring. She didn't need to think about the shadows anymore and the horses seemed to know it, too. But it was more than the horses and the sunshine. She finally saw a future, unfettered with names and faces she hated. But there was more. The future felt more like Riley than anything else she knew.

She curried the horses, checked their feet, their teeth and rotated their meds, just the way the picture book reminded her. Her jobs were getting to be second nature, that's how much she fit. She liked the certainty of it, nothing hanging on unfinished.

By midday, she returned to the house with Poke, just as Riley drove the heavily laden truck toward the house. "Hey, Sunshine! It's like Christmas!"

"What's all this?" She giggled.

"Hey, I got to thinking about steaks on the barbecue. Forget the meatloaf for tonight!" He looked up toward the canyon. "Glad I got back early. Storm clouds drawing in. I bet we'll get a thunderstorm tonight after dinner. How were the horses?" He handed her a small grocery bag.

"Bliss and Cartwheel both needed a good run, so I rode them through the pasture. Then I brushed them and—oh! A few of the vaccines were close to expiration. Lester delivered more today. I haven't had a chance to pick them—"

Riley stopped at the kitchen counter. "Les? He's back? He give you any trouble?"

"Not at all. I stayed in the barn...although I think Poke was willing to take him on again."

"Hmmm, Les is back..." Riley walked toward the truck again for another load. That meant Roy and Dale were no longer in the picture...which meant..."Hey!" he looked up. "I even got some ice cream for sundaes."

"Hey, you had me at 'steaks'!" She pulled two more bags into her arms while Poke followed her.

"I ordered more feed," Riley added. He pulled the horses' meds from the refrigerated box on the porch. "I picked up a few more supplies for Ranger and Justice. I'll get these vials down to the barn later."

Unloading the truck was nearly finished, the last bag in Maggie's arms when she looked up toward the road to see a sliver of dust, then a thick cloud rise. Three dark cars were hell-bent at the bend in the road, coming toward the house.

"Looks like a tornado driving up the road, huh, Poke?" She looked away, then looked back. In that split of a breath, she heard Kick's voice back in her ear: *come on, bitch! Get the hell out of here! It's the cops! Get into that van!*

The cars slowed toward the mailbox by the drive, but she saw Paco pulling up his pants around his hips while her stiff legs wouldn't let her stand. *Bitch, I'll slice you open if you don't move your sorry white ass! I said get going!*

Riley was inside, didn't see her spill the bag back onto the truck's front seat, didn't see her run as she'd never felt her feet go, down through the alleys and buildings with oil and diesel and garbage in the air. Her heart clenched around her lungs nearly to the barn now and moving toward the pasture. Riley didn't hear her run or her fear because he thought it was all behind her.

Poke sped after her.

But Riley did hear the commotion of motors in his driveway and pushed open the kitchen door, to face three dark cars blocking the truck, dust flying uproad like a scream. He pulled his revolver from the drawer. Mullengrath's men, maybe?

"What the hell?" he breathed. His eyes swept the truck. Maggie was gone. Or had they taken her already? In the corner of his eye, he caught Poke rounding the corral toward the pasture.

"Maggie! Maggie!"

"Mr. Riley Bedarte?" The older man stepped forward, a familiar face from the background in the courthouse. Riley brought his gun to his side. Four agents raised their automatics.

"Who's asking? I'll warn you, I'm armed."

"We see that. You need to put down your weapon."

"I will once I know who I'm talking to."

"We see that. I'm Special Agent Carl Stanley of the FBI, New York. I need you to put down your weapon."

Riley slowly complied.

"Is this where Brenniss Tripham has been staying for safekeeping?"

"You ought to know. You've been watching the house for a month, now."

"Is she here?"

"That's just the thing. Your cars just scared her off. She ran somewhere toward the pasture. If you let me—" An explanation took too long.

"Brenniss Tripham, also known as Maggie Fletcher. We are here to collect her and return her to her rightful home."

It sounded like a damn crime. "Now wait a minute! I'm not the one who kidnapped her—"

Stanley raised his gun. "Mr. Bidarte, you could be arrested for obstructing justice, if you do not surrender her. We are here to carry out our job of retrieving Brenniss Tripham. Now, step back and we can figure out where Brenniss is."

"But, that's just it: Maggie isn't—"

A fourth car pulled into the dusty drive, rocks chipping upward. Griff jumped out of the sheriff's car.

"Stanley! Stop right now!" Griff flattened his palms outward as two agents turned their guns on him. "What the hell is going on? This guy's on *your* side. No need to come in here like outlaws and threaten the man."

"He said he was armed."

"Well, so am I, damn it!" Griff walked toward Agent Stanley and touched the barrel of the agent's gun, pushing it calmly downward. "And so is just about everyone in Arizona! He did the law-abiding, responsible thing by letting you know he was armed, right? He had no way of knowing who you people are, trespassing on his property with guns drawn and making demands. Now tell your black suits to stand down. Around here, we get a lot more accomplished by being polite."

Stanley nodded, and drawn barrels were lowered. Griff looked at Riley as he approached him on the porch, a stored breath escaping like powder from his mouth.

"Now, my guess, gentlemen, is that this can be taken care of more amicably if Riley, here, felt safe enough to invite you in."

Riley glared at Griff.

"Riley?" The wind blew up a sudden gust from the river.

"If you don't mind, gentlemen, I was putting my groceries away. Can I at least walk to my truck to get the last bag?"

Agent Stanley stepped aside, placing his gun back into his holster, then he and two others followed Riley and Griff inside. "Valley, you stay with the cars. Rinaldi and Lindsay, guard the back entrance of the house. Shearer and Schmidt, check the barn." Low clouds blotted the sun. Stanley entered the kitchen piled with boxes and bags; the refrigerator door was still open.

"What the hell, Griff?" Riley hissed. "Maggie panicked when she saw the cars—"

"I've been calling you for the past two hours to let you know these agents were on their way. I didn't know they'd be here before me! So where's Maggie?"

"That's what I'm trying to tell you! She ran off! I think she went up toward the mountain, but these clowns wouldn't let me get a word in edgewise!"

"Do we have a situation here?" Stanley interrupted as Riley put down the last grocery bag.

"You want Maggie? She must have had a flashback and took off when your cars were barreling down the road."

"We'll get a group together and start looking for her."

"Good luck with that," Riley mumbled. "No, *I'll* start looking for her." A whip of wind intensified down the road.

"Mr. Bedarte, are you hiding Brenniss?"

Riley slammed the refrigerator door so hard, the canisters on top rattled. "No, thanks to you! I never did kidnap her, as you well know, and I never forced her to stay here. You scared her off, and she's getting farther away each minute we waste here."

"We can get a search party together—"

"How many of your agents can ride horses? Or track a mountain trail? Or read animal tracks while they wave automatic weapons at a woman who's living a flashback? Not a good idea."

Griff interrupted. "How about two familiar faces with Ranger and Justice doing the job they were trained to do?"

"They haven't been trained to climb those steep surfaces yet with packs. Not sure that would work out." Riley shook his head. "Let me go, Griff. She trusts me. I'll take Bliss. She'll recognize Bliss. That horse has been up the mountain hundreds of times."

Outside, a car door opened. "It's hot in there! I want some

air! Where is she anyway?"

"What's the fuss out there?" Griff asked.

"Gentlemen, I have another headache that I was hoping would leave on its own." Stanley pushed open the screen door. "What's going on out here?" he barked. A young man with brown curly hair was held in place by Valley. "I told you to stay put, boy!" he barked again.

"You going to make him sit in that hot car?" Griff asked.

"This, gentlemen, is an uninvited guest, none other than Brenniss Tripham's fiancé, Vince Caldwell. Any objections, Sheriff?"

Stanley could have just as easily shot Riley in the gut right then and there. His stomach went hollow, he felt the blood fall away, his eyes snapped shut just as a blast of wind shut the screen door behind him.

Griff squinted toward the canyon. "Good God, what is he doing here?" He shook his head. "Look I don't have time to sort things out now, especially with those clouds gathering as quickly as they are. We're due for one of our spring thunderstorms, oh...I'd say in the next two hours. Riley had better get going."

Stanley saw those same clouds like fists bullying their way along the sky.

"All right, Valley, you and Caldwell come inside. Maybe he can help put groceries away."

Riley's voice was low and cold as he shifted his feet. "Come on in, son," Riley said wearily. "You must be thirsty." He drew a glass of water.

"Where's Brenniss?"

"If we're lucky, she's near a trail on that mountain behind us and I'm going to get her."

"I'll go, too!"

"Son, can you ride a horse?"

"Well, no."

"Then you're not coming. Put my groceries away."

"I didn't come here to put away your groceries—"

"Oh, for Christ's sake!" Riley's automatic instinct brought his fist squarely against Vince's jaw and knocked him to the floor. Just for a second, he swore he saw a smirk cross Stanley's face.

Riley pulled a few supplies, the first aid kit, a lantern, some dry clothes, a rain slicker, and blankets along with his gun and started out the door.

"Do you need your revolver, Bidarte?" Agent Stanley stepped forward. Valley, by the door, brought his hand to his holster.

"Actually, yes, and a shotgun, too. There's a cougar in these parts that is roughly the size of one of your sedans over there. I may need to defend myself or Maggie." His eyes bulleted toward Stanley's. "Right, Agent Stanley?"

"Of course, of course."

"Now, I'm walking to that barn, saddling a horse, and going up that mountain. I'll likely be back after dark if that rain comes in." Riley slammed his hat on his head, gathered his supplies and marched toward the barn.

Stanley turned to Vince on the floor. "Get up and put these groceries away. And keep your mouth shut," Stanley barked. "We'll wait until he comes back."

Riley felt a spit of rain along the back of his neck as he readied Bliss with the blanket and horse packs. He needed to find Maggie's tracks before the rain soaked the trail *and* before Many Devils noticed she was in his territory. Riley galloped Bliss toward the outcroppings, finding Maggie's footprints within twenty-five yards on the trail. Instinctively, the horse focused on Maggie, sure footed in her pursuit. Finding Maggie and Poke's footprints together into the thick growth was a relief. That dog was her best defense until he could catch up to them.

Bliss cleared the rocks with ease. "We've got to find Maggie," he whispered into her ears. "She's up here somewhere with Poke. Steady, girl." The rain intensified and the ranch and valley slowly disappeared below with its cars and guns and personalities and everything Riley had hoped wouldn't be decided in a lightning flash.

CHAPTER
SEVENTY-TWO

MAGGIE

All I know is I'm here. With Poke. I don't remember how I got here.

It's raining and I'm in stands of pine trees so dense that I barely see the trail, what there is of one. All I know I've been running, and I don't know why. Maybe for hours. Maybe with Paco and Street and Kick. But then again, that can't be true. They're as dead as some of the branches overhead.

I'm breathing hard. The steep trail leadens my feet and wearies my breath. Maybe I can stop here. Poke's face is soggy with the downpour. I remember Poke, but I don't know how, yet. He stays with me, but I'm sure I'm lost. I sit on the trail, the runoff pools around my hips and legs. A sorry sight, I'm sure, sitting on a sandy trail, water seeping into my skin, clothes plastered against my back, my hair snaking water down my shoulders. It's getting darker.

How do I know Poke?

Wait a minute...there's Riley in there somewhere. The name Riley stirs a comfortable place I want to be.

A rip of lightning crosses the sky, with an immediate jump of thunder like a cannon shooting down the trail. The storm announces itself above me. I look up and watch elongated raindrops spear toward my body. I barely see the slick trail below me, but there's a war going on overhead. I may be here for a while.

Does Riley know that? Am I supposed to be here?

A shiver runs electric through me from the cool rain. Poke crawls to an overhang of branches just off the trail. He stares at me. He's a smart dog, letting me know with that stare that I need to follow. The thick needles are surprisingly soft, surprisingly dry, and I can curl up here while my mind clears. If I sit here long enough, maybe I'll sleep, maybe I'll figure out Riley and where I'm supposed to be—

The police! They were after us! We heard sirens and I needed to run, even though I wanted to be found. I still want to be found. But sirens didn't make me run this time, and it wasn't night when I started running. It was hot daylight, with something safe nearby. But I ran anyway. Something scary was coming toward me.

Now it's raining hard, and I can't run anymore. I can't remember. I'm tired and cold-wet. The jumble has come back like it once was. I remember laughter, dry sheets, and sunshine, but now it's all jumbled. I look across the trail. Two eyes stare at me through the branches and growth. The face is large in the shadows, not human. Poke is on alert. It's not Street or Paco. The head profiles into a cat's, while Poke softly growls from his belly, some primal communication. The cat turns and pads further into the pines, up the mountain, no more than a ghost.

Now something is coming up the trail, slow measured

steps, something that sounds familiar, something I know. I just can't bring it up to the front of my brain...the sound, like big certain raindrops...now, now I remember, horse's hooves...Bliss, that's her name. Gentle, sweet Bliss. I rode her fast, just today, I think. The world flew by me in the green pasture, the shoots of grass meeting her feet...something else with Bliss, though, because she's walking heavy. Something good and kind and—

Riley.

I remember, now, he never gave up on me, he believed I could be someone whole again. Poke whimpers then puts his paw on my arm, letting me know I'm safe. Now I'm shivering, I've been sitting too long. Poke looks up, ears turned toward the trail. He crawls from the branches, sits tall right there in the rain, looking toward the noise. Something is coming. He ducks his head as he leans forward, a quick movement to show he wants to run toward the something, but he needs to protect me. His tail sweeps the pine needles along the trail, a quiet wet swoosh.

I see a pale light bobbing up and down, glinting in Poke's eyes. A candle? A lantern? That would be something Riley has at his house, I remember, he keeps lanterns in the barn. For emergencies. This must be an emergency, then. For search and rescue, I remember. I can continue to shiver here. I can move my legs that have turned into Jell-O. Jell-O. I like Jell-O. Riley has Jell-O. Had it from day one.

Day one was when I rode home in the truck after the room at the hospital. Day one was when I met the horses...Bliss... Bliss' thick steps clicking against the rocks, along the sand trail, more steps like a heavy heartbeat. I remember more. The light is a soft spotlight on Poke. He ducks his head two, three times as if he'd love to run toward the light. His whole body wiggles. He does that when he's happy. I remember.

Coming up the trail, four hooves stop in front of Poke. The

light hits full on Poke now. He lets out a cheerful bark. Two boots step down. "Well, hey, Poke; there you are, boy."

The voice is soft, one I heard once when I was sleeping in crisp, dry, warm sheets. When I wasn't running from anything. When I wasn't running toward something. That voice, like honey, spreads hope over me, something I didn't know I'd lost. Poke dives toward me. A gloved hand pulls back the needle branch.

Now, I remember. Riley. His weary, soaked face flashes a smile.

"And there's Maggie." That's who I am. I remember, now. Maggie in jeans and boots and tee shirts and sweatshirts.

He pulls me into a warm blanket as I stand, how important warm is, coming back to me. The running was over a long time ago. It's all there now: the horses, Riley, Griff, Hannah. I stare at him as puzzle pieces click into place: the gallery, the governor, the trial...the fast cars pulling into the drive...

All from my name Maggie and Riley's weary smile. It all comes back like a warm wind in the middle of the storm. Something I could love.

CHAPTER
SEVENTY-THREE

"You scared me, Maggie, running off the way you did." Riley's poncho was a drum for the constant rain. She stared intently at his face while pulling his face from her memory.

"Some sort of flashback, I'm guessing. Believe me, *I* could have nightmares about the jokers back at the ranch." He rubbed her arms, adjusted the blanket around her neck. She looked at him with darting eyes between raindrops.

"The ranch—home?—you know, where you've been staying with me? Remember? You came from somewhere else before you came here."

"The van took me?" she whispered.

"That's right. Well, the FBI figured out your name, remember? Brenniss? Remember New York City? See, they were the ones that rode in like Jesse James a few hours ago. To talk with you about New York...about going back, understand? Back to your family. But first I've got to get you off this mountain." The rain splattered around them. He reached for a towel and started to dry her hair.

She stopped, looked at Bliss' saddle as if it were a mental

TV set, seeing Christmas trees and brick fireplaces and sweeping lawns bordered by curved streets. A Brenniss home.

He dried her hair to a damp mop, then snapped a rain poncho open, like pulling magic from the Bliss' saddlebags.

"Maggie, there's a young man waiting for you," he whispered against the rain. He kept his eyes on the seams along her shoulders, as if they were more important than her gaze. "Says he's your fiancé." Maybe she would deny it, right there, standing next to him in the downpour.

"Fiancé?"

"Guy named Vince? Remember your wedding dress?"

"Did I know a Vince?" Her face twisted the question. "Vince...Vince...I don't think—do I?"

Riley's heart tugged on a slice of hope as he rubbed down Poke. He tried a smile, thinking that would help, but he just stopped, stared at the trail. "He seems to think you do." What he really wanted to blurt out was "he seems too young for you" or "you can do better." But instead, he took a breath and steadied onto Maggie's face, her eyes stabbing directly into his.

"It's always been your choice, Sunshine," he said evenly. He was waiting for her to say something about how there was no reason for her to leave, right there in the midst of an Arizona thunderstorm. He was certain she'd come to that conclusion by now, all that time running up to this place. Her memory was sluggish in the rain, slow to recall their connection they felt earlier in the day. He reached for the hood on the poncho and lifted it over her head. He leaned forward slightly, toward her face a quarter inch closer, then hesitated. They held that gaze until he found the words.

"What you say we head back, Sunshine? Can you walk part way?"

"I suppose."

"Once the trail levels out more, you can ride Bliss." He lifted Poke onto the saddle. "Let's head home then."

The sun had lost the war with the thunderstorm, disappeared into the canyon to reconnoiter for another day. The sky was battle-torn by how the rain had divided the day. Maggie, Poke, and Riley were not totally aware of what they should celebrate as the rain's constant hiss thoroughly soaked the ranch, creating rivulets in the flat drive. Poke and Maggie were shivering again, but she felt a brief warmth from the bright light ahead of them inside the kitchen. One FBI vehicle remained. It was all true. Someone was here to change her life on a dime again. The sinking feeling entered her stomach. Riley helped her from Bliss, then up the porch steps, the wonderful wooden creaks that welcomed each step into the first dry reprieve she'd had in hours.

Chairs stirred inside as Maggie removed her poncho and blanket, while Poke accepted another quick rubdown. Griff and Hannah met them by the door. "Maggie, there's someone here to see you," he whispered, as if at the entrance of a funeral, but all the while staring at Riley's face, already registering loss.

"Brenniss Tripham? I'm Agent Carl Stanley from the New York City division of the FBI." He flashed his badge, and she immediately flinched toward Riley. "We've been waiting for you. I'm glad you're safe." Stanley nodded in Riley's direction. "You are Brenniss Tripham, aren't you?"

Maggie stood trembling from the cold, the harsh light, her clammy skin, the unfriendly tone from a stranger. "Also known as Maggie Fletcher?"

She looked toward Riley, still in the doorway, a weariness in them both. He nodded.

"I'm Maggie Fletcher." A kitten would have been louder.

"We have been looking for you since you were kidnapped on May twenty-eighth of last year. We are ready to take you back home to New York. Your mom is waiting for you...in New York."

"What?" As if it weren't enough to be shivering, soaked, confused and cold, some stranger was babbling about New York.

Hannah leaned toward her and gently put her hands on Maggie's shoulders, the only decent thing Maggie's skin felt since she walked into the kitchen. "Perhaps, Agent Stanley, we should get her out of these wet clothes and offer her some of the dinner you had earlier."

Only Hannah could make her voice sound like a butterfly and a wasp at the same time.

It had only been a few hours since Maggie had seen the pinpoints of three black cars racing up the road and now, the kitchen had turned into a circus of dirty dishes, cell phones, computers, and tossed suit jackets. Riley seemed a stranger here, drawing coffee to warm himself, almost as an afterthought before bedding down Bliss. She didn't remember inviting any of these people into his home, let alone being responsible for feeding them. They all seemed to be in such a hurry...

A flurry of a fireball, an explosion of energy emerged from the couch in the living room—*Riley's* living room—while Maggie surveyed the bizarre gathering. A burst of flesh with curly brown hair and brown eyes, a rumpled shirt with sleeves drawn to the elbows shot from the other room.

"Brenniss! Brenniss!" Vince yelled, running into Maggie with arms slapping a soggy embrace. Tears trickled from his eyes. "Brenniss! I'm here, I'm here. I knew I'd find you!" He reached to kiss her. Maggie's face twisted as if tasting a sour pickle, as if spitting a bug from her mouth. Bewildered, at best, repulsed at worst, she pulled away.

"Bren, it's me!"

She stared. A face that didn't know her but claimed it did.

"It's me. Vince—from New York! Come on, babe, ME!" She felt a lasso wrapping around her, ready to pull her tight into someone else's happiness. But there was no smile, tilt of her head, or softness in her eyes. Instead, prisms of incomplete memories, in a dismal and damp room. She sensed an expectation, too, that she was supposed to say or do something.

"Do I know you?" She meant it as a true question to help her memory. But all she saw was his face change into disbelief. "Sure! Vince! Vince." He pointed to himself.

Brenniss saw his smile, but a flatter version. He looked at Agent Stanley, waiting for an explanation. Stanley looked away slightly. The only other sound in the otherwise dead silence was Riley taking another sip. Vince focused on Stanley, too, awaiting the ice-breaking comment that would fix everything, the trick question that revealed it all. But Stanley rubbed his head, staring at the kitchen light, jaw slightly off-center.

"I'm sorry...I'm...I'm not sure..." She stepped back into her own puddle on the floor, staring at the young man's face. In his eyes, she saw a snippet of sitting in a restaurant.

"I'm...I'm..." her teeth started chattering.

"Come on, Maggie." Hannah guided her toward the stairs. "Let's get you changed. You'll feel better." She started up the stairs, legs dead-tired now, grateful for Hannah's strength.

She saw Riley turn out the door toward Bliss, and despite the rain and all the cold she felt, she wanted to go with him.

"Her name isn't Maggie!" Vince yelled. "It's Brenniss!"

Maggie took one look at Vince, daggers piercing from behind her tired eyelashes while the residual warmth in her core switched to anger. "Listen! I don't know who you are or why you're here. All I know is you're very rude to my friends." Drained, she felt Hannah's hands, the only warmth left in her body, guide her up one more step, then another.

"Well, for the love..." Vince muttered.

Outside, hearing it all, Riley pulled his collar up, tucked his hat low, and smiled as he climbed into the saddle. Good girl, Maggie. Thank you, thank you, Sunshine.

By the time Maggie returned to the kitchen, she was wrapped in a sweater and jeans as well as Hannah's encouraging words. The tension was as thick as the clouds overhead, a fence separating everyone. Griff by the coffee pot, Agent Stanley on the porch on his cell, Hannah toward the sink, Riley eating his dinner, Vince in the corner folding a paper napkin. She stopped at the bottom of the stairs and pushed her fingers onto the bridge of her nose.

"Got a migraine, Bren?" Vince interrupted the silence, his napkin crumpled in his hand.

"What?"

"Whenever you have a migraine, you pinched your nose." He smiled weakly.

She turned to Riley. "How's Bliss?"

"I rubbed her down really well, gave her an extra apple, checked her hooves."

She nodded. Bliss was more important after a long, wet ride than trying to remember a name or a migraine or a voice. She sat at the table, feeling unwelcome from all the stares and strangers. Riley slid a dinner plate toward her. She realized she hadn't eaten since breakfast, her stomach suddenly raw.

"I'm really tired right now." She sat at the table. She stared at the meatloaf. "You all are expecting me to say something about how happy I am. But frankly, this is all still very new, and I can't make a lot of sense of it. My memory doesn't work like a light switch that switches onto every detail in the room. It gets triggered sometimes, more like a flashlight, a beam on one thing that may not come to me right away. It takes time. I'm sorry I ran away today, and it caused so many problems—"

"Maggie, it's not your fault," Riley whispered.

When she bit into the meatloaf, she remembered just then, Riley had promised steaks and ice cream, and a ride later on in the day along the river. She still felt twisted inside, the way Riley meant, and they were about to unravel it all. Nothing got done today the way it was supposed to. She looked at him with such sadness and regret that she couldn't swallow.

"I told our 'guests'," Riley looked around with a sharp eye, "that anything can trigger a flashback. You thought those cars were a threat, so you did what you remembered to do...that simple." Instead of giving her a hug to make the storm disappear, he asked, "Want some Jell-O with dinner?"

She smiled, followed by a clap of thunder echoing through the canyon.

⸻

Agent Stanley stepped back into the kitchen from the porch and surveyed the silence. Brenniss, nearly too tired to eat, finishing her meal; Griff making small talk while helping Hannah with the final dishes; Vince looking bored. He tried to ignore his disdain for Vince, but it seemed to be taking over the room by most everyone else.

He extended his cell phone toward Maggie. "It's for you. It's your mom. I told her we'd call when we got here. Sorry it's so late."

Maggie stood and Riley turned. "My mom?"

"New York, Brenniss. Understand she hasn't talked with you for nearly a year. She sure would like to hear your voice. Go ahead—on my dime." Stanley nudged the phone toward her again.

She held it gingerly, a hand grenade of emotions. "Hello?"

"Hello, hello, Brenniss? Bren, is it really you?"

The sudden flash of that voice in eight words, the voice

that tucked her in at night, that rose above the others' applause at a piano recital, that sang in church while sharing the hymnal, that encouraged her to stand tall for her prom picture, and just as tall for her graduation picture—that voice whose last words were that Brenniss took her breath away, that voice nestled through the roughness of the past year and softened a place in Brenniss' heart like a down comforter.

She sucked in a breath. "Mom? Mom?" Her knees buckled as she slid down the kitchen wall to the floor, next to Poke. Dry sobs hacked deep inside her lungs, choking her words. That voice, she remembered, was a thread that pulled into her heart, cozied her yesterdays, the way a mother's words do.

Maggie didn't know which of her mom's questions to answer first. "No, no, I'm okay. Are you okay?" The words didn't just form on Stanley's dime, but hearing those sobs spoke volumes. One thing she *did* know, a mom never gave up on her child, even more, there wasn't anything more powerful than her mom's voice.

Riley helped Maggie to her feet, guided her into the living room for privacy. She looked at his face through her tears and reached for his hand, not wanting him to leave. He sat carefully, then pulled her hair back over her shoulder.

"So, how's Dad?" she asked after a breathy pause. But her face fell, she looked at Riley as if a car had just driven through the front door. "What? No, NO!" The sobs percussed her chest again. Riley rubbed her back, what seemed a useless gesture just then.

Her dad filtered into her memory—so much easier with her mother's voice next to her ear—the tall correct posture, a man of few words, sitting by the Christmas tree, handing out foil packages with elaborate ribbons, or behind the camera, directing a pose, now fading...fading past the light.

Maggie found her voice again and tried to explain Arizona. Slowly Maggie slipped into a different place, a detachment that was more Brenniss than the woman Riley had come to know. Maybe Griff had been right all along. Brenniss' life had a quality that didn't fit her life here, a Brenniss life of Christmas and chickenpox, through algebra and college that Arizona could never be a part of. Maggie felt that fluent and easy connection with Brenniss that Griff had warned the others about.

"...but you'd love them, all these wonderful, special people..." Maggie tapped her hand on Riley's and smiled in his direction, to keep him close. "Well, Riley and Griff found me, got me the medical attention. And Griff's wife Hannah has been like a sister..."She was smiling that sunshine smile now.

"Riley helped me recover here at his ranch. He has horses—no, Riley says I'm a natural. We've been training some new horses for search and rescue for Griff's sheriff's department—no, honest, I ride them, too!"

Riley heard her mom say something about coming home and seeing Vince.

"Well, that's something I'm still trying to figure out, Mom—just, who is Vince? Well, I remembered the dress, sure, but, I don't remember much about him. I mean, I look at him and he looks a little familiar, kind of like seeing an actor you hadn't seen for a while...well yes, yes, he's right here! And I still don't remember him...Yeah, here, with the FBI, right now. He's, well...rather rude."

She heard Riley snort a chuckle. Her hand was still inside his, the one that fisted into Vince's jaw earlier. He squeezed her hand to let her know he was still here. Maybe there was still time to talk with him tomorrow, instead of running off crazy.

"Sure, if you want to...hang on a second...he's in the kitchen..." Maggie rose and called out, "Vince? My mom wants to talk with you." She handed him the phone.

Vince's eyes widened again, the same look after Riley had hit him, blindsided by knuckles and flesh. He brought the phone close. "Hi, Betty, I—Honest! Look, it was an opportunity I needed to take. I thought I could let you know once Bren and I—"

Maggie watched Vince dig himself deeper into the ugly hole he had made for himself. This someone she was supposed to recognize was getting dressed down by *her* mom. Better than handcuffs, when you get down to it.

Vince thrust the phone toward Maggie, a corner of shame along his mouth. "She wants to talk to you."

"Mom?" How complete she felt saying that word again and remembering her guide, her past, her foundation.

"Yeah, I know...I just can't quite...see what I mean?" She led Riley back into the living room, while Vince just stared at the two of them. "Okay, yeah, I know it's late. I don't want to hang up, but I'm so glad to hear your voice again and—well, soon, I guess. We'll talk more. Here's Riley's number..." Saying goodbye was awkward as she returned to the familiar skin of Maggie again. "My mom wants to thank you. Maybe when we talk tomorrow," she whispered to Riley.

"Brenniss, are you going to ignore me?" A sneer formed along Vince's upper lip.

Maggie stared at him. She tried to find the thread to wrap around some recognition for this sorry man. His tousled hair, his eyes the color of a well-blended mocha took her to a windy day some time ago.

"Look, babe. We met at the New York Public Library where you worked. I work west of there, at Whitten and Mast. You and I dated nearly a year. I proposed to you that weekend on the beach. Any of that sound familiar?"

"A beach?" Maggie stopped. She tugged that piece of memory into a picture of sunset and wind. "The sun was setting..."

"Right! You remember!"

"But we were looking for something..."

"Your scrunchy...your hair thingy...we combed the beach for nearly two hours looking for it." His voice, instead of registering fact, slid upward, a plea, a question. "Remember now?"

She shifted her eyes into brief splashes, like the ocean she was recalling. A warm day, a beach, windy, soft dimpled sand underfoot, her hair getting into her face...yes, maybe a scrunchy, ...maybe a proposal...but she only saw herself there, herself only, no one else, including Vince.

"Maybe bits and pieces, Vince. They're all disconnected, like a jigsaw puzzle thrown onto a table. Sometimes it takes weeks before those pieces tell a story."

"I've got weeks, if it means being with you. Remember the condo? We lived in a condo."

"A condo in New York? With big windows?"

"That's it! See? You're remembering—or how about Trendz? I bet you'd remember if you got back to New York. You'll come back, right? Tomorrow?"

She looked into his eyes, but all she saw was weary. "I'm so tired. I have to get up early tomorrow. I don't know anything else right now other than horses and hay, and Riley saddling Justice. And Hannah's cheesecake. I have to sort through the condo and the restaurant...I need to think about it all. Maybe it will make sense, if I give it time." She nodded.

Riley turn back into the dining room just then. Something about the sag in his shoulders told Maggie that he had lost something.

CHAPTER
SEVENTY-FOUR

A morning after a thunderstorm makes a person want to take deep breaths and reach up to the turquoise sky, reach for a handful of that perfect blue for a little bit of the morning to tuck into a pocket. Even though Riley was tired from the events of last evening, he found himself stepping off the porch at 4:00 a.m. doing that very thing: reaching for a handful of precious sky.

Maggie deserved to sleep in, considering all the confusion she'd been led through. Riley wanted the early morning quiet to sort through what he needed to do or say in the next day, to find some answers. The only way he knew how, a ride along the river, the way he and Grace used to.

"Hey, there, Ranger. What do you say we go for a ride?" The black horse barely visible in the barn shadows jerked his head up and down. Riley lowered and cinched the saddle, his favorite worn saddle full of journeys that Grace had given him years back. Back when things were simpler, when a man didn't have to struggle with his feelings the way they were twisting up inside right this minute.

Riley leaned into the saddle and raised himself onto Ranger, then headed toward the river while the house was still quiet with no conversation or accusations.

What do you think, Grace?

He was sure his wife's voice would jump right in, just itching to tell him about fairness, because at that moment, there didn't seem much fair in this corner of Arizona.

He trotted Ranger across the highway and sloped down the banks toward the river. An eagle flew past him, low, to snatch a fish along a pool where the fish were lazy. Another and another found their way to catch breakfast for their young.

Maggie intruded past a trout or a whisper of a feather gliding from a nest.

Have you been totally being honest? Grace's question slid in next to Maggie.

I was ready to be honest yesterday. Dinner and talk got interrupted by those suits and that high-strung, judgmental, selfish idiot named Vince.

Well, *that's* honest.

I was going to tell her how natural we were together.

Honest? That's all you got?

That, that, I'd—

Honest?

Riley sighed. "That I loved her."

Your timing sucks, you know. It wasn't Grace's voice. It was his.

He let his thoughts ride along the river's edge, feeling Ranger work his magic.

A pair of eagles was about to fledge. Wouldn't be too long, now, another few weeks at the most and they'd leave for some mountain in Wyoming or Montana. He may not see them much till next year.

Because they always come back.

He stopped in the saddle, stopped cold. They...always... come...back. A little calm came over him, no bigger than a spring breeze, as if that was enough for him to know right now. He turned Ranger toward the highway, for home. Within a few minutes, he saw Maggie open the kitchen screen, let Poke free, then start toward the barn herself. He rode quietly toward her. "Hey, Sunshine."

"I wondered where you went. The phone rang and woke me up about 6:30. My mom. I looked for you, but you were gone. My mom wanted to talk with you."

She stopped by the barn. "Can you believe I'm saying that with any kind of conviction? For real? It's so natural to say, 'Oh that was my mom.'" She sighed at the change in her. "I'm a little late on checking the horses, but I fed Poke."

"Already fed the horses early." He dismounted Ranger and led him inside, leather creaking comfortably. "Couldn't sleep."

Maggie leaned on Ranger's flank. Her face was flat honest. "What should I do, Riley?"

He removed Ranger's harness and bit. "We are in a pickle, Sunshine, that's what Grace called it."

"A pickle; I've heard that before."

"This is how I see it," he continued while removing the saddle and blanket. "We both like working with the horses, we both like living here, caring for the garden, we make a good team...there's Hannah and Griff...all of us...But you've been given an opportunity to return to the life you once had. I'm sure your mama said as much when she called."

He brushed Ranger, but Maggie only listened.

"And you've given me an opportunity to weigh in—"

"Be honest, Riley. You haven't told me anything I don't already know."

"Didn't your mama weigh in too?" He paused brushing Ranger. "I see your face give in to some old feelings after you've talked to her. I know your mama wants to see you and

I bet you want to see her, too."

"Honest, Riley."

"I've been trying to do just that these last few hours and it's tearing me up all the same. This is how I see it, Sunshine. Your life was interrupted by horrible events, events that changed your life. You're strong, Maggie. You may not think so, now, but I think about those eagles and how they start out. They are pretty damn vulnerable, and yet, they become strong and do amazing things. You may have some things in your former life that may have been just as strong, that you still need to sort through."

"But I like my life right now!"

"I'll be honest. It's a great life, and I've had a chance to get to know you better than anyone around here. I like having you here, there's no doubt. But your former life...maybe you were content with that, too—"

"A condo, Riley! I'm not sure I want to return to that."

"See, that's my pickle. Did I make it too safe for you here? Too comfortable? Have I somehow made it harder to make your choice? And is that fair to you?"

"Don't you want me to stay?"

He brought his steel-blue eyes from the floor of the barn to meet hers, dead straight, but only a whisper came out. "Sunshine, of course I do. I don't want you to leave because this is the wrong place to stay. I want you to stay because it's the right place to be." He paused in the quiet of the barn. "And you may not be able to make that choice until you return home and find out for yourself."

He hated himself for saying it, but like those eagles trying out the wind, he knew it was true. From Maggie's face, he could tell she knew it too. She looked sideways at the horses, as if they would offer advice as well. She traced Poke's shadow with her boot.

"How can you be so sure?" she whispered, a pinprick of

betrayal trailing through her voice.

"Aw, Sunshine. Contrary to what I'd like to believe, I'm sure about only a few things. I'm sure these horses love to run on a sweet spring day like today. I'm sure the sun will rise up over the river tomorrow morning and set west of Mitchell Canyon in the evening. I'm sure that there are dark days in our lives, but somehow we find something or someone that makes our lives start up again. I'm sure the eagles love the river because Mother Nature provides enough fish to feed their young, that summers are hot, that fishing is a pastime for kings and fools, that I like cream in my coffee and a good pair of gloves." He smiled at her. "And I'm sure I love your smile, as much as I love your being here. But I'm dumb as rocks when it comes to being sure about what's right for you. And unfortunately, that's up to you."

She looked directly into Riley's eyes again. "So you'd like me to stay."

"All along, I've said I wanted you to be safe and happy. With Mullengrath behind bars, we're pretty confident you're safe now. And I haven't seen you happier than when you're with the horses. You fit here. Yes. Yes, I'd like you to stay."

"I'm not sure I'd feel safe and happy with Vince. I'm sure I don't want to marry him."

"Then don't!"

"But you said to go back to my life—"

"Safe and happy means *your* choices, Maggie." He tossed the harness and bit by Ranger's stall. "I know your mama wants to see you. Focus on her instead."

"I can do that?"

"Sure. You could stay here and always wonder about your mama each and every day, but your heart won't fully be here with the horses, here on the ranch, until you see her, be with her again."

"Sooo, I could go home to see Mom and reconnect with

her." She spoke slowly.

"Then, you still have choices to make about your job, Vince, whatever comes up, because you at least have a place to be safe and happy—at your mom's house."

"So, maybe I could go a week or two."

"Take as long as you need, Maggie, because you can't live a half-life full of regrets." He stopped the practical Riley for a second, the other feelings starting to surface, the ones he feared would influence her beyond reason. "Truth is, Maggie, I've never known anyone like you. And that includes Grace, too. There's a part of me that doesn't want to lose...this."

"And you know that...that I..." Her shoulders dropped, unable to say that her life had become so much more with him.

He pulled her close enough to feel her hair tickle along his throat, feel the warm of the Arizona morning radiate from her skin toward his face. "Yep, Sunshine, I know." His eyes stung as he looked up. Overhead, an eagle was making a wider circle from the barn back toward the river. He wanted this moment to last a little more than a lifetime, thinking about how a lifetime could fit between here and New York.

"Now, I have a feeling Agent Stanley will be driving in pretty soon. He'll want to talk with you about all of this." He looked to see if the eagle would make it home. "Let's have some breakfast." He smiled.

"With Jell-O," they both said simultaneously.

———

Washing the breakfast dishes, Maggie's recollections burst like the bubbles in the sink.

"Riley, how far is it from Arizona to New York?" She pulled the drain stop to let the water flow away.

"Oh, I'd guess about 2400 miles."

"So, if I left here, I just couldn't turn around and come back."

"Sure you could." He smiled. More than anything, his selfish side wanted that very thing. "You could come right back, I wouldn't mind at all. But even an eagle takes a season or two to decide what direction to go. Depends on your home, what you remember, what you want to keep in your heart. You need to find some happiness there, too."

A pair of shiny black cars inched like beetles into the drive, dust licking the sky as if last night's gully-washer was already forgotten. "Looks like they're back." Riley sighed. "Maybe they won't draw guns on me today."

Agent Stanley got out of the car, a bit reluctant with Vince tagging along. The agent's face was stern, threatening the young man with few words. He held up his hand to push Vince away, to stay close to the car.

"Riley?" Agent Stanley knocked at the door.

"We were expecting you, sir." The door ached open, wanting to keep the cool air inside the house.

"Brenniss, good morning." He hinted a smile. "I understand you talked with your mom this morning."

"Yes, sir."

Agent Stanley stepped back, hands clasped forward, as casual as an FBI agent can stand. "I need to apologize to both of you for coming in like thugs yesterday. Sometimes our job gets more important than the lives left in the wake, and we get a lot of criticism for that. Truth was, we scared you off; the last thing I wanted to do. We never meant to threaten you, just wanted you to get home safely. So, my personal apology, from my agents and myself, I apologize."

"Thank you." Riley nodded.

"See, Brenniss, I've been with your investigation from the first day. I was at the crime scene and got to know your mom and dad fairly well. What you don't realize that your testimony has started the governor talking about other women that were taken from their lives, just like you. We may be able to bring other women home. We want to thank you for that."

She glanced out the window toward Vince. He was looking at his shoes like a six-year-old standing before the principal. "So, what about Vince?" she asked.

"I can't fix that for you, unfortunately. He chose to make his life miserable coming out here; we never told him where you were. He made things far more complicated than they needed to be right now."

A pickle, Grace might say, she thought.

"Vince isn't winning many votes around here, either," Riley added. Agent Stanley chuckled.

"Well, Riley and I did some talking, and...after talking with my mom..." She looked at Riley.

"Are you thinking about New York?" Stanley's voice was a soft as a child's, the easiest person to talk with at that moment.

"I do want to see Mom, see her face again, be with her again and—" Her throat caught dry. "Would I be able to see her?"

"Absolutely! You both waited a year to be reunited. And we can make sure Vince doesn't interfere. He may still have some questions to answer at the FBI office. My assignment is to get you home—and I mean *your* home—safely to your mom. We could leave today—"

"No!" She looked at Riley, speaking a little too loudly. "I mean, no, not today. How about tomorrow?"

CHAPTER
SEVENTY-FIVE

Riley swallowed hard. Goodbye had floated through the air for months like cottonwood seeds, like moths diving after lights. His stomach tripped over the word "tomorrow," as real as if Maggie had thrown a rock in his path..

"Tomorrow works out fine," Stanley continued. "Are you sure that...will...give you enough time?" He looked mostly at Riley.

"It's always been Maggie's choice." But his eyes were directed toward Poke.

Maggie's eyes had tears, ready to take it back.

"Well this is what I'll do. One of my agents will take Vince back to Phoenix tonight and he can fly out the red-eye—"

"He won't be flying with me?"

"Oh, no, Brenniss. He came and will go back on a commercial flight. He's not our priority; you are. Bringing YOU home."

"So, what time? What time should I be ready?"

"Well, we have the plane already to go, but it's in Phoenix, so we'll need to drive there first. Does...9:00 a.m. sound too early? No later than 9:30."

"Can Riley come too?"

Now there was a simple solution, have Riley come along, and for a second, Riley was ready to say yes, in a minute, he'd do it. But he had the horses and Poke to keep him here. And postponing goodbye by a few hours was more agony than a person needed. "No, Sunshine, I better not. You need to keep focus on going home, and I'd be at best, a distraction. I've got too much to do here, besides. But thanks for the thought."

That's when goodbye really hit her; so final that tears choked her voice into a tight knot, dry as Arizona sand in July.

Agent Stanley clasped his hands tightly. "Well, then, I'll call our office in New York, the airport in Phoenix, and get clearance for tomorrow morning."

Poke's head popped up and stared at Riley as Stanley drove off, a silent Vince in silhouette in the back of the car. It was as if Poke wanted Riley to stop her from walking out the door. "I wish I could, Poke, I wish I could."

"Riley, I need a favor this afternoon." She focused past the screen door, down the drive, maybe even across the mountain.

"Name it."

"I want to ride Bliss and Cartwheel once more. Let's take the horses to the pasture and give them a good workout."

He smiled at her tentative face, the one he remembered when she first was unsure how to be, how to make a decision without someone pushing her around. Her face clouded with uncertainty.

"Only if we take, Poke."

"Deal!" There, it came back. Her sunshine smile.

⌒

Ranger was faster than Justice, Justice less impulsive. They worked the horses to find that spark in both of them, the sure-footed judgment they'd both need on any Arizona landscape.

First, Maggie rode Cartwheel to cut off Ranger, to teach him to attend to Riley's touch and commands. Ranger wanted to take to the sky if he could. But when Maggie brought Cartwheel close, Ranger leaned to slow or corner, too, sharp as a dime and kicking his head up with a wide eye. Justice needed a push from Bliss to pick up his speed. Once competing with the mare, he beat Bliss' stride in the pasture grass. The horses tried a thirty-foot rocky outcropping at the far side of the meadow. Ranger more willing to take the challenge, Justice being more methodical. Both horses, chests leaning forward, formed the balance with their riders and packs, showing their readiness for challenging terrain when duty required.

Even Bliss and Cartwheel seemed to sense a sadness between Riley and Maggie riding along the river, a strength, a resolve as well. Riley took the lead, then Maggie joining alongside once the river trail widened like an open window. It was the darndest place to be. This was where Riley had planned to stop the day before to share his feelings, hoped she would say the same. This is where—

"Riley?"

"Yes, Sunshine." The spring rays filled his face.

"What will you be doing this time tomorrow?"

Right then, he swallowed. "Tomorrow" grabbed his throat and wouldn't let go. He swallowed a second time, a third, trying to moisten his voice into something natural and fearless.

"Not sure, Sunshine." That was the best he could answer, as useless as anything else he could say.

"Do me another favor, then. Ride one of the horses. I couldn't bear it if you weren't doing this very thing every day at this time."

His eyes squeezed away moisture as he tilted his head upward. "You've got it, Maggie. Every day, this time, I'll ride one of the horses." He looked at her, wanting to find her cheek and kiss his promise right there. "Rain or shine, I promise."

And I'll be thinking of you, she shook away the thought of being 2400 miles away. She wanted it *just like this*.

———

By the time they returned, the river fell a little silent, the sun felt a little cold, the breeze too spare as it whispered into the kitchen. While Riley prepared dinner, Maggie slowly began packing.

I would have done it all over again, no doubt, Riley thought. Stop by the road's edge, sit by her side, bring her hope, help her through the darkest nights. We both needed to be in this place, to travel toward goodbye.

But, while preparing the potatoes, he stopped, wiped his hands, and turned toward the stairway. His legs felt like water with each step up, until he stood outside Maggie's door. He tapped lightly, the way he always did, not to startle her. The door yielded slightly. He watched Maggie standing over a suitcase on her bed, filled with folded items. She faced out the windows but was miles away.

"Maggie?" He stepped into her room. "Sunshine?"

She turned to face him, tears gliding slowly over the sunburn tinge in her cheeks. Her whisper was broken. "This is the hardest thing I've ever done." The folded tee shirt collapsed against her arm.

Riley moved closer, wrapped her with his sadness. "I know, Sunshine, I know."

"This is something I need to do, but—" Her mouth gaped open, a silent sob forming. She tipped her head against his chest, rare and comforting with him. For the first time, this close to him, she listened for his heart, less than an inch from her ear. She shut her eyes tightly, trying to memorize the sound to carry with her tomorrow.

"So, you do what you *need* to do," he whispered back. "I

understand. You need to pack. Get ready."

"I don't know what to take, what will be at home when I get there, what Brenniss will be like." She squeezed the bridge of her nose, that automatic move that used to bring comfort, but now seemed as useless as high heels in Riley's driveway.

"Then, stop packing for now? I'm making some baked potatoes for dinner. You want steak?"

"And Jell-O." She pulled away slightly. "It'll be our Grace meal together."

Riley turned toward the door. "No, Sunshine. It's our Maggie meal."

When the horses were settled for the night, Maggie returned to the suitcase, yawning wide on her bed. Everything she chose was tied up with a ride with Riley, with feeding Bliss or Cartwheel, or chasing Poke. Tufts of goodbye were folded in each tee shirt or jeans pocket. There was still plenty of room for her heart and a few tears in the suitcase. The horses whinnied from the barn. They knew too.

"Thought you'd like this," Riley said from the doorway. In his hands, a tray of Jell-O cups.

"What would I have done without you?"

"I remember the first Jell-O you had at the hospital. You weren't talking yet, and your first words were 'that's mine' when I reached for the Jell-O on your tray."

"I thought you were going to steal it from me. Paco would do that, if I didn't eat a Twinkie or a donut, he'd take it. I'd hated being hungry, but I couldn't stand all the sweet stuff. Ah, but Jell-O? Like heaven!"

"You were afraid of all of us. You'd hide your Jell-O under your covers and eat it when we were out of the room. What you didn't eat, you'd save in your nightstand drawer."

"I was a little hoarder?"

He laughed full from his heart. "You scared us because you wouldn't talk, you wouldn't tell us anything. I stayed with you those first few nights, because truthfully, I didn't think you'd make it."

She sat back a little rubbing the spoon against her lip. "I remember your voice, then, although I didn't know it was you. I realized I was still alive, but it was too difficult to open my eyes. Then when I did, nothing seemed the same, and I couldn't remember anything else, and I was afraid all over again. But you were always there."

"Doc noticed your vital signs were more stable when I talked to you, so I kept going."

"I remember a swollen jaw and my broken wrist. My insides burned like a hot knife ripping through me."

"You were hurt bad, Maggie. Those guys tore you inside out. Doc had a difficult time with the surgery. But somehow, you stayed strong....Do you...do you remember how you chose your name?"

"When Lester came by that time, you said I was Maggie Fletcher."

"No before then, in the hospital. Here..." he leaned toward her suitcase and pulled out her jean jacket. "See that?"

She held it up, waiting for the puzzle piece to stand out.

"Check the label."

She giggled, reading "Maggie's Closet" in a low voice. "I was named after a jean jacket?" She laughed harder. "No way!"

"Hey, your choice!" His hand brushed hers. "But you know? Maggie fit you, just like that jacket, a thousand times over."

"I liked being Maggie Fletcher." She looked at the lines on his face. "I still do."

"And I like Maggie Fletcher being here." He watched her

pure smile, the one she wore when she wasn't worried, when she rode the horses. Poke jumped onto the bed and curled by her feet.

"That dog," Riley pointed his spoon at Poke, "that dog adopted you the moment he saw you. Remember coming home from the hospital? You couldn't get into the truck, so Doc found some bedding, we put it in the back of the truck, and you rode home with Poke in the truck bed."

She turned her head slightly. "Poke was with me? I remember looking at the trees overhead, watching them and grateful for sky. When I was in the van, the windows were always blocked off. I couldn't always tell if the sky were blue or gray, let alone day or night. Poke, huh? My little guardian! Always my bud." She reached for another Jell-O cup.

He thought of that new Maggie, not the one sitting next to him, no, the new Maggie from last year who ducked at sudden movements, at faces too close, like a prize fighter when the shadows were a little too quick. And here he was, sitting next to her, relaxed, wishing he had done this a while ago.

"You must have thought I was a nutcase!"

"No, no, Maggie, I never did. Spent too many times caring for horses that had been abused. I saw how you needed to heal in your eyes, too. I have to admit, though, it wasn't until your testimony that I realized how badly you'd been treated. I could only imagine up to that point, and I never felt it was my place to ask. No person, no animal ever deserves to be treated in the way you were—"

"You accepted me. That's what it was. Even Vince can't do that."

His lips curled tight. "I know your name is Brenniss and your life with Vince before you came here was something that must have been special. Or you wouldn't have said 'yes' to marrying him...I can't and I won't judge any of that because I didn't know you then. But, I know Maggie, strong, in spite of her scars. Maggie will know what to do when the time comes. It's all—"

"—up to me, I know. I believed you then and I believe you now."

"God, the night of the barbecue when you got into the truck on your own? I was in awe of you."

She scooted closer to Riley, leaning against his shoulder, uninvited. It was the right thing to do.

"I could never have asked you to do that, and here you were, all on your own, leaning into the truck, sitting inside for over a minute. I stood there, so proud."

"Riley?"

"Hmm?"

"Let's just stay like this all night, just talk like we always wanted to do."

Like yesterday, like last week and maybe after that first nightmare, he thought. He smiled and handed her another cup of Jell-O.

The night carried sounds of a cougar making its way through the spring, Many Devils' scream echoing through the ribs and spine of Mitchell Canyon. The night pasted the moon above the river, smiling into the season of leaves and blooms. An owl drifted by Maggie's window sometime after midnight. Ever so slowly, the Big Dipper poured its stars into the high clear blue broth of the Milky Way. Now, they owned this night together, she and Riley. Catching up like old friends who hadn't seen each other in years. No one could take this night away.

Maggie first noticed the softened shadows against the mountains. Had Riley noticed, he didn't say, one more way to deny the coming day. A robin broke the silence.

"Oh, my." She sighed. "It's today, isn't it?" She paused.

"But I guess it's always today." She looked up from his shoulder, still hoping for one more day.

"We still have some time. Want to help with the horses?" His smile hid his heart telling him not to move, not to break the magic, not to make it dissolve away. "How about the horses and Poke, too? Then we can have breakfast and do whatever else you need to—"

"Visit my mom."

"See your mom, right," he whispered.

The sun peeled the eastern horizon away, first with a sliver of light, then splendid rays sifting through the clouds to spotlight the river. She focused not so much on her last time with the horses, but rather preparing them for Riley's ride later on in the afternoon. In a way, she could still be with him. The morning warmed the fresh hay, the barn roof clicked its expansion in the warmth, like a giant clock ticking seconds, a regular day. She fed Poke one, two scoops of food, only feeling the dog's stare after he finished. A dare to stay.

She pulled her last items into her suitcase a little before 9:00. Agent Stanley couldn't have been more prompt. She saw him with two other agents exit the car and heard Riley meet them at the door. She felt her first sob escape just then.

Riley's footsteps were heavy as he drew near her door. Brave, that's what she needed to be, do this easily, walk away in celebration because she would be back soon. But she couldn't pull it off as soon as he opened the door.

"Maggie? You ready?" His voice cracked once.

She nodded yes, then no, and ran into the bathroom to sob against a washcloth covering her mouth. She looked at Maggie Fletcher in the mirror, and saw a little Brenniss in her eyes. *Who are you?* She once asked, but now she had two answers.

She walked back with tissues. "I'll take a few of these, if you don't mind." Her tears had already started.

"Hey, leave me a few. I promise to use them." He smiled. Her suitcase was upright, closed, standing taller than Poke by Riley. The dog looked up and cocked his head, as if asking once more if she were sure.

"Okay, I guess—"

"I'll get your bag—"

"No, let me. You stay here." She reached for her suitcase, then reached for his hands instead, something she'd never tried doing before. His hands clasped hers, not in a rough way, but one that invited an extra minute or a lifetime. "Riley, I just wanted to—" Just this once, she was sure she could do this. She leaned forward, almost a sway, then pulled back as if she were too close. She started again, forward nearer his face.

She stopped, sucked her breath because wanting to be so close was something new to her, unexpected, a surprise. Slowly. Easy. No, maybe she couldn't do this. Yes, yes, she could. She blinked, swallowed, then closed her eyes and held her breath. She slowly brought her lips to the corner of Riley's mouth, where a tear had stopped along the crease. She swallowed again, then moved slightly forward still, her lips grazing the corner of his mouth, the tear, and his lip touching hers. A second, maybe two then she pulled back, grabbed the suitcase and turned out of the room.

Her footsteps gradually fell away. Poke ran out of the room after her.

He could not move. In all the months of not being able to approach her, of her fear of being too close, of pulling away from a group or a crowd, she surprised him again with the Maggie he'd come to love. He still felt a soft wing of pressure where her kiss had landed.

He heard the kitchen chair scrape on the floor, some soft words about her trip, the kitchen door opening. Stanley was on his cell phone, Maggie was petting Poke as the other agents stowed the suitcase in the car. "I hope you are looking forward to seeing your mom. She'll be waiting at home. Okay, let's go."

She turned quickly, sat in the back seat, and the car started up.

Only then, Riley found his legs, moved toward the bedroom screen. He looked at her as they pulled from the drive.

"Don't go, Maggie," he whispered.

But the car was moving too fast for a whisper to land on her ears. The car was too efficient in getting her to her destination. And too powerful for Poke. For nearly a mile, the dog ran like an arrow alongside, then behind the car, barking to warn Maggie about leaving. The car accelerated enough around the bend, enough that Poke lost speed, then he finally stopped in the middle of the road, watching the trail of dust diminish against the sky.

Maggie cracked open the window to watch the river one more time. An eagle flew along the bend, then circled back.

CHAPTER
SEVENTY-SIX

MAGGIE

Poke is charging the car like he's the last line of protection for me. He doesn't want me to leave, and he isn't afraid to let anyone know. Come to think of it, Poke would have been the best defense I would have against the black van. I'm imagining his flash of fur and barking, teeth bared even; no one could have ignored that loyalty, that fierce persistence. Slow tears sting my eyes hearing his barks get softer as we increase distance. I can imagine—I don't dare look back—his wiry little body sitting in the road, watching this car disappear into a black dot.

I can be in two places at once, right now, sitting in the car, but thinking about walking to the barn, sitting atop Bliss, looking out the bedroom window, eating meatloaf and Jell-O in the kitchen. I can be sitting near the top of the mountain, the other night, Poke by my side in the rainstorm while he saved my life. He stood like a soaked rag mop, like a sentinel pulling Riley toward me until Bliss stopped, and Riley reached for me in the rain. Like that, I can be there again. I don't want to forget.

It's not lost on me here, in the back seat, the parallel: a black van with three men, now a black car with three men with earpieces. No, I'm not being raped. I'm listening to a radio with scratchy conversation, not rap, but like in the black van, the sky gives me no clue where I am. They think I'm returning to people who know me better than myself, not like Riley who was willing to learn about me.

I'm leaving a place that I love where I could plan a life; that's a parallel, too. With Riley, I wasn't trying to establish a relationship until I walked down the steps to the kitchen and out the kitchen door. With Riley I recovered, but the hurt started up again when I stepped into the black car.

I keep my eyes closed, remembering Poke coming after the car...Riley's face when we rode horses yesterday, remembering the engine starting up as we drove from Riley's door, the cast of shadow across Riley's face when he promised to ride the horses again this afternoon, the smell of Bliss when she stands in the tall grass, the sun warming her back, the wild eye of Ranger when he runs. I think I did that before, remembering my mom's voice, the wedding dress as it fell to the ground, the sound of my cell phone rolling like a skipped stone across the asphalt.

You just get to thinking like this when everything familiar is pulled from you and you really don't want to talk much.

~

"Brenniss, our protocol at the airport is for you to stay in the car until we sweep the area. I'll open the door for you, and we'll accompany you onto the plane. We're here to protect you from this car to the jet in Phoenix, to de-boarding in New York, until you arrive home."

"Okay."

Again, Agent Stanley softens. "We have clearance to preempt any commercial flights, so once we are on the plane, it will be only a matter of minutes before we are in the air."

Safe and happy, right? Like with Riley. *All this for me. It's like a disconnected dream, one of those you get after eating pizza or shrimp too late in the evening.*

I look down at my boots and there's a bit of dried mud on the corner of the heel. I don't want to lose it, a bit of Riley's Arizona mud to take with me.

"I'll get you home, Brenniss. You'll be with your mom, tonight."

"Thank you." Sadness hovers over me like a drone.

"Anything you need right now?"

"Um, do you have a small baggie?"

"A baggie? Why, sure, I'm sure...where do you keep your baggies?" He shuffles around the consoles. With the FBI, they have things catalogued and stored. Stanley hands me a small baggie, then curiously watches as I scrape the dirt into the baggie and fold it up. I store it inside my boot. I think he's figured it out. Riley's there. I'm here.

I focus on seeing my mom, a small hope blinks an eye open. There seems like enough room for Riley and my mom at this moment, but I can't balance it yet. But I feel like a package, maybe a bomb ticking away like the incessant rhythm piercing my left eye. I don't say much the remainder of the trip.

———

While waiting on the tarmac by the unmarked hangar, fatigue suddenly sits in my lap. No wonder. I've not slept in over twenty-four hours, my clothes still smell of Bliss and Cartwheel, which I crave with each inhale, and the baggie inside my boot is beginning to stick to my leg. I'd give anything for some Jell-O right now.

Agent Stanley checks the four directions as he walks toward the hangar door, like a ceremonial pipe to the four winds to offer prayers. *I could use a prayer; please help me find my way.* It's as good a prayer as any, although I have a feeling the four winds don't show up too much in New York. I'm tired of being lost. My passenger door pulls open and the furnace of the tarmac slaps my face.

"Okay, Brenniss." I walk swiftly, something my legs don't remember. I remember seeing mule deer surrounding a fawn on the floor of Riley's pasture one time, protecting it from all directions. I try to be as invisible.

"Go ahead and have a seat here." He points to an enclosed, windowless room, with leather office recliners in formation. It's quiet, but I notice my headache is crawling to the other eye. I haven't had a headache since I'd been at Riley's. "No windows." He pointed out. "Walls are bullet-proof, too. In case of a sniper."

"Sniper?"

"No need to worry, Brenniss. You'll be safe. We just take every precaution. We'll be taking off in about ten minutes. You need anything?"

"An aspirin? Maybe a blanket. Suddenly, I'm very tired."

I settle as Agent Stanley said I would. He treats me like a princess, like his daughter who maybe just had a baby or won an Academy Award. This is a blind adventure I'm taking to be with my mom. How strange not to be sitting on the porch, already missing the horses' whinnies or Poke barking, or to feel my fingers reach toward Riley's tomatoes, or to see the river from my bedroom window.

There's a sensation of hummingbird wings as my weight shifts in the chair. Reclined, I smell Cartwheel and suddenly I'm razoring through the pasture. I feel the leather saddle cup me as real as yesterday. I hear the ease of Riley's gloves when he wraps the reins across his palm, and I feel the soft, curled comma of Poke at my feet. And on the tip of my lips, I still feel the tear I captured from Riley's kiss.

Somewhere in that dream, I leave Arizona behind. Sneaking through the sky at 30,000 feet, I lose Maggie somewhere between Highway 160 and the Four Corners.

CHAPTER
SEVENTY-SEVEN

While Griff watched a special report announcing the arrival of the "Kidnapped Bride," Riley cast a shadow along the river. Cartwheel loped along the banks; the river shifted the current near the horse's feet. At the same time, a black sedan silently and unnoticed drove along familiar streets, past a shape of a tree Brenniss remembered, a doorframe she remembered visiting for trick or treat. Her neighborhood memories flowed like quicksilver: here and gone, lost, and shifting under her fingertips until scattered beyond her grasp. She didn't have a formula to trigger it all into place. She still carried Riley's voice in her head. *Focus on your mom.*

The graceful lawns were no match to the river and the canyon, and she couldn't help be in two places at once again. She still could do that.

The car slowed, leaned to the left, and she opened her eyes to a large brick Georgian-style home that she immediately remembered with the green door—she helped her dad paint that door one weekend. Her mom had agonized over paint samples, so certain they used the wrong shade of green.

The engine stopped. "Wait here," the agent reassured her. "Wait until your mother steps back into the doorway. Then, we'll come for you."

Already, her suitcase was with the other agent; he rang the doorbell. A tiny-framed woman answered, tried to peer into the car, then put both hands to her mouth as she stepped further inside. Brenniss knew that gesture, hands to her mouth. Her mother used it when she was in any kind of emotion: fear, anger, joy, love. That was Mom.

"Brenniss, come with me," the agent said softly.

She walked the curved brick path toward the door, sensing Riley walked with her.

"Oh, Bren!" her mother cried.

Mullengrath, the agents, even Cartwheel and Riley disappeared. Those tiny arms enfolded her, the sun slipped away from the doorway, the door drawn shut.

Riley's house was too quiet as he readied for the night. He looked up at the picture above his dresser.

There was Maggie, frozen from last summer, sitting on the porch steps next to a distracted Poke, western hat in her hand, her head tilted to one side as if asking Hannah if she looked all right.

His heart was equal parts of love and emptiness that this was the only reminder he would have of her. Of course you looked all right, Maggie. Those eyes looking right through the lens straight to my heart. You never really knew how much that smile gave me every day. I called you "Sunshine" for a reason.

CHAPTER
SEVENTY-EIGHT

As if in a museum, Brenniss walked through the home's entry, absorbing the memories that flooded through her. The formal dining room, the kitchen and pumpkin pie, the garden full in bloom, the welcoming staircase to her room.

She recognized the patterns of the posters in her bedroom, although couldn't remember if she actually attended the concerts. Life on hold, a mild tribute to the missing, a portion of her soul still available in the room for comfort.

She placed her suitcase on the bed, although she still didn't quite fit in the familiar. It would be about now that Poke would wander into her room, that she'd watch the horses from her window. It was too quiet.

"Does it look familiar, Bren?"

Brenniss startled. Instinctively she turned in quick fear, then recognized her mother's casual face. "Some of it does, but I guess it had been a while since I lived here."

"You had an apartment in the city for a few years. You lived above a coffee shop called 'Merry Beans'—"

"Oh, my gosh! I remember Merry Beans! I've been trying

to remember that name. Merry Beans, that's it."

"We have lots of catching up to do." Her mom sighed. "I hope you don't mind having dinner in the kitchen. It seems less formal. Are you hungry?"

Other than a sandwich and a prepackaged salad Agent Stanley gave her on her flight, she hadn't eaten since Riley made her breakfast. Riley. "Why not? Do you have any Jell-O?"

She looked confused. "Well, I'm...not sure..."

Betty reached for the salad she'd prepared in the fridge, moved some packages aside, past the whipping cream and organic dressing. Brenniss stood back, remembering the cabinets and their contents, the large gatherings her father and mother hosted, the endless plates and bowls set onto the dining room table.

"As a matter of fact, I do have some Jell-O. I totally forgot! Is cherry all right?"

"Ahhh, perfect!"

"Although, I'm not sure if it's expired—"

"Oh, Jell-O never expires!" She opened the silverware drawer for a spoon.

"I just don't know where to start, Bren." Betty concocted a dressing. "I know I'm a little nervous, not sure what to say or not say." Brenniss nodded from the counter.

"You mean my life in Arizona? Or do you mean Vince? He expects us to be instantly connected, that everything will be as it was. Mom, I don't think he gets that I still need to reconnect to myself." She rubbed the bridge of her nose. Damn headache.

She tossed a salad of spinach and raspberries, nodding her head slowly. It felt like another precious Wednesday night, with Brenniss casually sitting at the counter. Maybe talking about the mundane was the best place to begin.

"Remember these?" She held up her palm stained with the beautiful fruit. "I saved a few in the freezer from last year."

"*Your* raspberries?" She took a pinch of two from her mother's hand. "These are like little rubies, you know. They're so good."

"You and your dad would go out early Saturday to pick fresh raspberries—"

"—for the pancakes! Yes! Yes, I remember." She nodded. Somehow these memories were much more pleasant than the ones she'd fought against last year. New York increasingly felt more welcome.

Her mom placed salmon in the broiler. "I can tell you that Vince was very supportive while you were...gone. I couldn't have gotten through the loss of you *and* of your dad had it not been for him. And the holidays!" She then faced Brenniss. "But this business of going to Phoenix without telling me, without letting me know? I guess...I felt slighted, pushed aside, with no good explanation." She could tell Brenniss didn't have an explanation, either.

"*He* felt slighted because I didn't return to the condo to-night with him. He didn't understand at all that I wanted to be with you just now. But then, he doesn't have anyone, I guess...I forgot about his parents..." She pressed her fingers more tightly, right there, to massage the headache away.

"Headache, Bren?"

"No thanks, I have one already." She giggled. "I just can't shake it."

"Your migraines. You always had terrible ones. I may still have some of your prescription upstairs..." She checked the salmon and removed it from the broiler.

"You know something odd? I just realized this...I never had a migraine the whole time I was at Riley's...the whole time..." Her voice drifted, as she swallowed the last of her Jell-O.

She looked at her mom's kitchen clock, mentally counting back the time zones. Maybe he finished his ride on Cartwheel or Ranger. She could see clearly his sad face from yesterday, only yesterday, when the sun was full and clean along Mitchell Canyon, the river a silver ribbon. Riley's eyes caught the sun just then, and he promised...

"So, tell me about this Riley. Tell me about the man who saved my daughter's life." She served the elegant simple dinner and drew next to Brenniss at the counter.

Brenniss was in two places at once, just then, sitting in Riley's kitchen serving up a meatloaf or sloppy joes, as well as sitting at her mom's counter, eating a meal that reminded her of summer barbecue, lemonade, chasing fireflies.

Her mom continued. "I'm grateful to him, you know, and I've never met him."

Brenniss' smile shifted again. The smell of leather and horses, the sure steps against hard soil when approaching the barn, the patience when she couldn't get into his truck, the nightmares, the Grace dinners, their wide, deep laughs wider than the river...details she never, never, never wanted to forget...but, where to start? ...Of course...

"He has blue eyes, almost a steel-gray blue..." Betty sat back and watched her daughter in the midst of an Arizona visit. "He has no pretense. He carries a beautiful honesty, could always say the right thing when I had such horrible nightmares and never held guilt over my head for those, either. When I did something well, he let me know. I wasn't able to sit in his truck for a while...See? It reminded me too much of the van, but he practiced with me every day. Every day. He worked hard, loved his horses and Poke—that's his dog who actually took a shine to me—cared deeply for his first wife Grace, who died of cancer a few years ago. He never quite got over her, he loved her so, sometimes just broken beyond grief for her. He always loses his gloves, he taught me to ride a wonderful horse named Bliss, to feed, care, and work the horses. He just got two new horses for search and rescue—Ranger and Justice—and I was helping with the training. He enjoys the river, lives simply, rarely watches TV, never uses the internet—we just didn't have time, working or caring for the horses all day. He has a huge library. He let me heal at my own pace, always wanted me safe and happy, knew it was always up to me." Her voice faded again, because, just for a second, she could hear him say it, too.

Her mom swallowed another bite of salmon. "Sounds like you miss him."

She blinked once, then twice. "I guess I'm just discovering that, too. He was everything that helped me get better and leaving him was so difficult to do. Seemed like I had so many more things to accomplish before..." A memory slipped in: Riley and she sitting on the bed just the night before, no! just this morning! A world away, now. After another bite of her meal, she returned to the kitchen counter, next to her mom. She reached for her mother's hand.

"Maybe Vince isn't as important in your life anymore. Maybe you've found someone that is."

Brenniss looked up, a secret unfolded right there between the salmon and the salad.

"Mom, I came here to reconnect with you, to fill in the spaces of the life I had here. It's just an empty place where Vince used to be."

"You know, we've all changed through this experience, Bren. I'm a little more independent, you have more confidence, it seems. I don't know how you came through all that trauma." Betty embraced her daughter. "Here you are, so close to me. I can hear you sigh and watch those little expressions sneak back across your face. Do you know how wonderful that is? I haven't seen them in nearly a year. I wasn't sure I ever would again. But keep your heart open, Bren. You don't owe Vince anything at this point."

Not much later, Brenniss returned to her room for a welcome night's sleep. She was troubled by giving Riley away as the day closed. She found the suitcase open on her bed, her meager belongings blushed an Arizona fragrance: dry high-desert sweetness mixed with leather and dog fur and pastures and a river's edge and...

In the bottom of the suitcase, the sight of it caused her to gasp. Riley must have slipped it in when she wasn't looking. Her memory picture book. The note read:

"Thought you'd like this to remember

how far you've come.

Love, Riley"

She sat on the edge of the bed, hugging the book like an old friend, like hugging Riley, himself, as if she could bring back all of her friends in the pictures instead of the longing in her heart. If it were that easy, that he would be as real as this New York suburb or her mom's tickle of laughter when she said good night.

This morning she had been in her bedroom, saying good-bye to Riley, something she still felt razor through her. Now, she lay on her bed, curled like a question mark, hanging on to that book, under the covers as tears made tiny rivers down her cheek.

CHAPTER
SEVENTY-NINE

Text message to: Tessa B.

Vince C.

I know I screwed up. Do I still have a job? Should I show up tomorrow?

SEND 8:40 p.m.

Text message to: Vince C.

Tessa B.

Talk to Mr. Whitten and Mr. Mast. Act contrite.

SEND 9:00 p.m.

CHAPTER
EIGHTY

Early the following week, Vince called the Tripham home to invite her out for a dinner. "We need to talk, Bren. I just want to figure out what we need to do, what *I* need to do. This is really awkward."

"I know, Vince. I never meant it to be. Dinner would be a nice time to understand about where we are."

"How about Casey's? Where we went on our first date. Do you remember?"

She paused, wanting to immediately say 'no', but then a flick of a room with white linen table cloths, wide windows that took in part of Manhattan. "Um, Casey's sounds fine. I bet I'll remember once I get there."

"So what have you been doing these last few days?" Vince pretended that small talk would make the agents in the car across from Casey's go away. He wanted the past year to melt away, to have "now" in front of them, the only thing that was worth knowing about each other. He saw her face tanned and lean and hoped the evening would trigger memories that would bring him back to her. Now.

"Oh, visiting with Mom, and over the weekend, we visited my dad's grave at the cemetery." She shook her head. "I have to say, *that* was pretty emotional. Nothing's been easy, Vince, like trying to capture butterflies." Soft jazz wove into the restaurant's background, like a friend tapping her on her shoulder.

"That whole thing was such a shame—his passing, I mean." Vince nodded. "I don't think any of us realized how fragile he was. She called me that morning, after Milt died, and I got over there as soon as I could.

"She said you helped her through the holidays, too. I'm grateful for that, you know."

Vince quickly flashed to Tess in that red dress throwing her wrap on the couch in a fit of anger. But he looked back at Brenniss, a quick easy smile forming on his lips. "You'll never know how difficult the holidays were for us. It was good we had each other."

He absently played with his fork. "So, where does that leave us, Bren? I mean I've been a part of your life these last few years. Don't you remember anything?" He held his hand up. "Sorry, maybe I'm coming on too strong."

Vince pulled the napkin sculpture apart to lay a flat comfortable shelf across his lap, awaiting the wine he'd ordered.

"*Wicked*—I think I remember. Witches, right? We went to Broadway. I remember something about green, right?"

"Right, right." His voice deflated like a balloon as the waiter arrived with a bottle of wine to sample.

Brenniss felt encouraged that they weren't arguing or drawing lines. But she waited for something more than trying to conjure up her past. She couldn't last a whole meal if this continued.

"You look lovely, by the way." He nodded to the waiter to fill both glasses, and like a ghost, the waiter dissolved into the background. "Although," his eyes drifted toward her feet, "I don't get the cowboy boots."

"Oh, you know I didn't own a dress in Arizona. All my clothes were work clothes, and these boots for the ranch work. This happens to be one of the dresses still hanging in my closet. It's a little big, but—"

"You used to hate cowboy boots," he added with a nervous chuckle.

She tilted her head. "No, I don't remember."

While they ordered, Brenniss looked out the restaurant window and recognized two agents in a car across the street. Agent Stanley had warned her about the shadowy protection. She welcomed them more than Vince did although, but felt out of place, looking at the others at their tables, an extra piece of jewelry, a crisply-turned cuff, or hair gelled so that it would never yield to an Arizona breeze. The piano and quiet voices were magical, but the sparkling lights reminded her of Riley's sky. Movement outside the window caught her eye.

"Oh, my God—a horse!" Her voice was a little too loud against the jazz, something a tourist might utter when staring down the streets.

"Sure, you remember the horse patrols, right?"

She stared out the window, watching the horse, a red dun, a female, a chestnut line somewhere and the long black sweeping tail moving slowly through the traffic. Brenniss absently took a bite of salad that had appeared before her.

"That horse has a limp, right back leg. Could she have thrown a shoe?" She assumed, like Riley, Vince would know the answer.

"Hellooo." He waved his fork. "It's you and me, Bren. Forget about the horse, okay?"

"But that horse shouldn't be—"

"Let's just talk about us, okay?" He reached for her hand. "I'm sure New York's finest know how to deal with their horses."

"Mmmm, maybe so. You're probably right." She glanced back up at the horse walking farther down the street.

"So I was interviewed a few times," Vince resumed. "Let's see—*Good Morning, America* and the *Today* show. I've been talking about how you're glad to be home, that we're getting reacquainted. Like now."

"Oh, right, right. It's hard to explain how sometimes I get a flash of something we did...it's hard to sort out. You're very patient." She took a sip of water. "But I'm not sure how much patience either one of us has, Vince." She looked around the room. "This is lovely. But for the life of me, I'm struggling right now, trying to pull memories out on demand. My memories get triggered by something I taste or see."

She ate another bite of salad. "I was in the hospital after I was found. I woke up and I didn't talk, I didn't even know who I was. It took me nearly a year to get to the point of recalling enough that I could testify." She set down her fork. "I'm just not sure you'd want to wait another year...or another before we could establish a life together."

She said it. She said what they both needed to accept as their life.

"Bren, I never gave up hope." He sat back in his chair and exhaled a stale sigh. "So, it's the guy in Arizona, right?"

Pow. Right back at her.

"Maybe. I just don't want to get back together based on something I can't even remember. It's not fair to you, Vince."

"So, you're thinking of me, not you." He crossed his arms.

"Look, Vince. We're different, now. I can't make that kidnapping go away. It's part of my life. We are not the same people, are we? You're different, aren't you?"

Vince's head dropped, his own memories less fresh of Brenniss saying 'yes' on the beach, instead recalling how Tess took so much flack for him at Whitten and Mast.

"Yeah, yeah, sure I am. I've learned I don't do well with

tragedy in my life. I need some stability these days. I want to blame you, but I know it's not fair. It was all out of our control. And, what hurts more is that you can't remember it, not that I've lost you. I sure as hell thought we could pick up as soon as you got home." He put down his fork. "I can't help but feel a little betrayed."

Brenniss nodded. "We both hurt, Vince. You're a nice guy, and I know we'll both heal. But I don't think that will be something we'll do together."

"Okay, then." He crumpled the napkin onto the table. "I admit I hate this is how we end, being it's all up to you, Brenniss. But at least you've been honest. You know the crazy thing? I've got an interview with *Newsweek* next week. Any suggestions what I'll say?" He looked at her several seconds. "No, I didn't think so." He caught the waiter's eye. "Check please."

CHAPTER
EIGHTY-ONE

Vince's better judgment told him he was a bit of a pauper rather than a prince, as he stood outside the familiar door. The short spring shadows dappled fingerprints of sunset across the door. He paused before knocking, something feeling like cement in his arm. Should he? He'd asked several times to see her, but tonight, there was more a hint in her voice that she might consider letting him past the doorway. Maybe it was pity. Maybe second thoughts. Maybe she finally would warm to hearing his side. He raised his arm and rapped his knuckles against the hollow-core door.

Forever, it seemed, to hear footsteps approach the door. How to apologize? For being such a jerk, for being impulsive, for hurting her. She once invited his spontaneity. But now, their conversations were open-ended. Even though he dreaded talking, he needed to, but...well, maybe she wasn't home anyway. He was about to turn away, when the doorknob twisted, clicked open, and the door widened a slice to see the surprise splash across her face.

"Well, hi, Vince. What...what are you doing here?"

"Hi, Tess. I need to apologize. I was...hoping I could talk with you."

Quite frankly, she was tired. She felt like a rubber band: stretched, pulled, wrapped double around Vince's life to hold him together, then boomeranged across the sky to land somewhere close to the gutter, until found at a later date to start all over again. Certainly, she benefitted by feeling strong, purposeful, and needed. But these sad, drawn eyes were not how she remembered his face. She extended her head past the doorjamb, looked up and down the apartment hallway.

"Where's Brenniss?"

"Not with me. Look! Before you slam the door in my face—"

"You've got reports for me to type? At this hour? You've got to be kidding!"

"No, no, now hear me out. I've been thinking and...well... can I just come in for a while to talk, instead of standing out here?"

"Talk," she repeated. One word sounded like a piece of iron tossed on the floor landing near his feet. She looked past Vince, trying to avoid those eyes. She'd heard it before, hadn't she? But it was another Tuesday night with no plans. A bit of loneliness was no match for 'a talk'.

"Okay, Vince. Come on in. We'll talk."

Vince sat at her breakfast bar, an elbow of a shelf, large enough for that second cup of breakfast coffee and the morning paper. Her apartment views weren't meant to be expansive or inviting, yet a degree of welcome lingered. "I know you think I shouldn't be here. I don't have any business to show up—"

"I didn't say that, Vince."

"Honestly, I'm not sure why I'm here." He looked up from his hands to see the mix of curiosity, welcome, and anger in Tess' face. "I mean, I haven't treated you as well as I'd liked."

"Got that right. What are you trying to say, Vince?"

He felt the stiletto of that comment jab him. Usually, this was where Tess told him she understood, how difficult it must have been for him, how he would have a better day tomorrow. He raised his eyebrows, opened his mouth even, but frustration grabbed his throat. "Brenniss and I, well, we've broken up."

She crossed her arms, eyed him through a cocked eye. "Okay, I know you didn't ask, but I'm telling you anyway. Maybe this roller coaster you've been on hasn't been your doing, but you set your dreams on fire to try to fix it. You planned on Brenniss falling into your arms when she came back."

"Ouch! What *is* this? Beat up on Vince week? She dumped me!" He looked at her, his anger impulsive and hot. "Remember, you're talking about the woman I love!"

"Make that the woman you *loved*, the woman you adored, you idolized. She's not that woman, not anymore. Maybe she never was." She poured coffee into pottery mugs, the swirling brown liquid tickling up the sides of the stoneware.

He sat, staring at the cup. "Tess, all along in this, you always 'got it', you know? You figured out how torn up I was. You picked up the pieces and handed them back to me. I couldn't always put myself back together, but somehow things made more sense when we talked. You knew I couldn't be perfect."

"Boy, I'll say. But you expected me to be."

"What?"

"I'm the one that finished the report or corrected the projections or handed the summary to you at the last minute as you joined your client. I jumped in to save you every time. Your ambition? Where the hell did that go? You expected everyone around you to understand that your ambition was on a life preserver somewhere, and we could rescue you in the meantime. Yeah, I'm pissed because you nearly cost me *my* job while you flitted off to Arizona. You had no right to use me like that."

"I made some stupid decisions, that's why I'm apologizing." He looked at her, cup in hand. "Tess, you don't understand. She doesn't remember me. I thought I could bring it all back."

She paused, watching him swallow the choke he held around those last words. Her heart skipped twice, but then her focus returned. What she wanted to say was that she didn't remember him, either. "Look, Vince. I can't imagine what she's been through. I know I wouldn't be the same person after being kidnapped and raped and living three-quarters of the way across the country in Colorado—"

"Arizona."

"Whatever! Some remote single-horse town that moves at the pace of a snail. I'd be bored out of my skull! Sounds like hell to me."

"But, that's the weird thing. She liked it there! She won't go anywhere now without cowboy boots—cowboy boots!—she hated cowboy boots."

"Do you?"

"What?"

"Hate cowboy boots!"

"What's that got to do with anything?" he screamed.

"My point, Vince. The guy I saw last year, so lost and confused, was looking for Brenniss and would have welcomed her back as if you could find her in the library stacks again or in the garbage dump. You waited for a year for Brenniss to return, in her beige slacks and black top. You didn't see cowboy boots in the picture. You put your life on hold, you sold your job down the river, you compared me to her, even convinced me we might have a future together, all because you were hanging on to Brenniss waltzing back into your life, exactly as she was. She's back, Vince! She's back and you're complaining about cowboy boots?"

He sipped slowly. But there it was: how she hit the truth

in ways he couldn't. She was right, he interrupted his life with a year-long dash after his name. At the other side of that dash, Brennis wasn't there.

"Okay, it's not *just* about the cowboy boots, but it is a betrayal, of sorts—if you think about it—by the punks who stole the woman I loved, and by the woman who came back in her place." His voice squeezed tight in his throat.

"So then, *why are you here?*" Tess whispered. "You held on to me like a lifeline, you dropped me faster than a box of horseshit, you opened doors for me only to shut them as quickly as soon as a hint of Brenniss was back in your life. And where was I?"

"This isn't about you, okay?"

"Let me get this straight: *This* is an apology? So now what?"

Vince stared at this woman he swore was his ally.

She shook her head. She gathered the still-warm mugs of coffee and poured the liquid down her sink. She rinsed out the cups, waiting for Vince to make a squeak, a chuckle, a protest.

"Wrong answer, Vince. I'm dying to know the answer, myself, so let me know when you've figured it out." She grabbed him by the shoulders and firmly pushed him to the door. "Good night, Vince."

He stood outside Tess' building a full eight minutes, with coffee still flavoring his mouth. His own memory collapsed into traffic lights and the neon parade of colors. He couldn't connect to the sidewalk, there was no anchor in his life. He approached his car, then unlocked it, an automatic separation of metal from metal. When the door closed, that final tight fit insulated him from traffic rhythms.

Now what? Tess had asked.

Now what, indeed.

CHAPTER
EIGHTY-TWO

BRENNISS

These are the things I know:

I like being with Mom; the connection was never broken, even though I forgot it for a while.

I've been back for six weeks, but I'm still confused. Being home hasn't entirely cleared things up.

I don't fit at the library, have no desire to go back. As much as I remember from there, it's a good place and I loved being there. But I just don't want to go back and be *that* woman that people might whisper about.

Vince is not part of my life, although there are fringes that come in a little more clearly because I'm not trying too hard. I remember the condo better and an occasional concert from a slice of music I hear. But it's still not enough.

My dad is dead. All this happened not just to me, but to my dad, too. There's only a tiny sliver of his face I remember unless I look at our photo albums. There's an occasional echo of a laugh or a stern face talking about homework or finishing college or helping out Mom. He didn't have it in him to tolerate my disappearance, he didn't have the strength. I'm the survivor.

I remember our house as if I'd never left. The house is like a bathrobe to put on after I've been cleansed.

But I miss Riley's house. Sometimes I can be two places at once, but I miss how the windows in the kitchen caught a breeze, no matter how hot the Arizona day was. The way my window looked toward the morning.

I miss the sun gliding on my skin as I rode Bliss or Cartwheel. How they seemed to put up with my clumsy learning until I could ride those horses no matter what day it was. I miss the sweet leather smell as saddles are set, the anticipation of that first step into a stirrup, and the acceptance of my body onto their strong backs.

I miss the Arizona storm that stampedes over the sun, through the sky and drenches you to your bones, but you still find your way home.

I miss the taste of the river after a long afternoon ride, the sun tipping Mitchell Canyon about ready to lose its balance into the peaks.

I miss working with Riley, getting Ranger and Justice strong in their movements so anyone would believe those horses could find lost souls. I miss the simplicity of the day, where there's nothing to figure out when you take a breath or offer a smile.

I miss Griff's matter-of-fact way of telling you the most awful details, so despite that, you know you'll make it through another day because the crime wasn't mine. I miss Hannah's cheesecakes and how she captured a landscape with the right f-stop and film speed, then turn it into a piece of her heart.

I miss Riley, his gentle way with the horses, the way Poke

looked up at him, his reassurance. I miss Riley guiding me through nightmares without a single judgment, without a question or asking a justification, and finding me somewhere between the grave and the dawn. No, I miss Riley because...I love him. Simple.

There, I wrote it down so I can't take it back. I wrote it and it's a surprise to see. I look at the words again. I love him. It softens my heart, lets my heart relax into the simple place instead of being two places at once. I look again and I know I'm not trapped anymore.

I'll be going back. I know that now.

In high school, I planted a plant in a glossy red Italian pot. For two weeks, the leaves withered and fell away. I'd killed it, I was certain. Then a few weeks after, when the sun was a promise, in one day sixteen shoots pushed through the soil in such a vibrant green I couldn't ignore the plant anymore. In those two weeks, the plant had sent down new roots, invisible but strong.

When you pull a plant away from the soil, you see those white healthy roots, soil still clinging. It sounds like something ripping apart, a seam that wasn't well sewn. It must hurt like hell.

You spend time growing roots first. Then you grow toward the sun.

CHAPTER
EIGHTY-THREE

Brenniss walked up the stairs from the kitchen. She knew these steps, worn with generations of footsteps. Then she heard a tip-tip coming up behind her. Poke. Making sure she got to the top of the steps. She knew there was something in her room she needed to see. The door was ajar, the gauze curtains catching wisps of breeze and settling again.

A woman sat in a chair near her bed, reading *Sense and Sensibility*. Her head was wrapped artfully in a colorful scarf, weaving down across her shoulder like a gloss of hair. Someone she didn't recognize, but ought to.

Hello. I've been waiting for you. She smiled. Come in. Welcome back.

The woman's smile was gracious, like a soft pillow for Brenniss' tired head. That smile revitalized Brenniss after such a long journey. Her welcome was genuine, wiping away any doubts that Brenniss fit there so easily.

I'm looking for something, but I don't know what, Brenniss said. I'm not sure I lost it, but I don't seem to have it right now. Even though she was Brenniss, she felt more like Maggie saying these things.

Oh, I know what you're looking for. You haven't lost it at all, you know. It's still here. It's been here all along.

Here?

Bliss and Cartwheel are out in the barn, hoping you'll go see them. I think Riley's there, too. He's told me lots about you. I never doubted about you, I can tell you that right now. I couldn't wait to meet you. We have a lot of catching up to do.

Brenniss felt she belonged next to the woman, but her feet wouldn't move. I don't want to interrupt you. You're enjoying your book. I'm sorry, do I know you?

No, but I know you, the woman said. And I'm so grateful you found your way back here. I knew you would. Forgive me, the woman said and extended her hand. I'm Grace.

Brenniss sucked in a breath as she sat upright, shaking from the ghost falling away from her dream. Grace seemed so real...so friendly...someone she didn't fear at all. It was just so sudden to hear her name in a dream that was so true.

She turned on the bedside lamp and for a second looked for Poke. Silly. She wasn't in Arizona, she wasn't having nightmares anymore, and Riley wasn't across the hall. She almost looked out the window for the barn, too, thinking she was ready.

Down the hall, down the staircase, she carried her photo memory book like a friend toward the kitchen. She foraged for a Jell-O pack, like at Riley's. Now, at the counter, she opened the book, like taking a breath for a sentence ready to form.

Riley, Hannah, Griff, Poke, Cartwheel, Bliss—they all looked at her from the pages as if asking why she wasn't there. Riley held up two fingers and the dog scoop. Poke sat on the front porch, tongue snapping against his snout. There she was—Maggie—sitting on Bliss, arms outstretched.

Maggie, not Brenniss. Maggie, not the confused girl in white sheets hoarding her Jell-O, but the woman helping Riley with Ranger and Justice. Maggie who sat tall atop Bliss, used the curry brush and the toe pick, knew when to give the horses water, when to check the vaccine in the fridge. Maggie, trickling wisps of hair from her western hat. Maggie the confident one. Brenniss wasn't anywhere in the picture.

"Can't sleep?" Her mom chuckled and approached the stove. "I'll make some chamomile tea. I used to do that right after your dad passed. I'd leave the kitchen light on, in case I needed to walk through the dark house at 2:00 in the morning. What are you looking at, there?"

"Oh, it's a photo album of sorts. When I was first recovering, I wasn't able to remember or organize very well, so Hannah," she pointed to Hannah's picture, "came up with the idea of a photo book to help remember the sequences of things I needed to do. Like here. Here's Riley showing me I needed to use two scoops of dog food for Poke. And here, the different steps to saddling the horses. See Bliss? That was my favorite horse. And she knew it, too."

"What a great idea. They all look lovely, Bren. These people here, I owe them so much. They cared for you when I couldn't..." Betty's voice wavered, her eyes stunned with tears. "I can't ever thank them enough, you know that. You had an army to care for you! So who's this again?"

"Okay, here, we'll start with Poke, Riley's dog. And here's Riley." A smile broke across her face. "And Griff, the sheriff; he's married to Hannah who took these very pictures—"

"And she owns the gallery?"

"Right, right! It's a tiny little thing, but it is filled with beautiful artwork: paintings, photos, pottery, and beadwork."

"So here, you couldn't remember how to feed a dog? My word, Bren!"

"Well, that's how it was at first. I couldn't remember those little things, even if I did them two or three times a day. But they all helped me." Brenniss ran her hand over the pages to pull them back into her life again.

"So this was Riley's ranch?"

"He and Grace owned all this. Here's the house and...the barn...the pasture and corral...and my good buds Bliss and Cartwheel. Now here, see that turret over the front porch? That was my room. I had the best view of the river..." Her voice faded.

Brenniss' face softened, a smile creasing her lip as she scanned the photos. She didn't see Betty sit back and watch for one, two breaths.

Her mom poured more tea. "Now, that looks delightful." She pointed to a picture showing a picnic table spread with an assortment of tablecloths.

"Once a month, we had Grace dinners. We kept Grace's memory alive by making her favorite recipes. See, when I first got there, Riley, well nobody, would talk about Grace except to me. I got tired of tiptoeing around her. So, Hannah and I planned this first Grace dinner—that's this picture—and it was so much fun. I heard stories that...well, you just expected to see Grace pop up, with all the memories and great food they shared. Riley got into it, too. It was good to see him smile about Grace instead of frown."

"A Grace dinner. What a great idea! Maybe I'll have a Milt dinner, sometime. Bring together some of the old gang. Talking about your dad wouldn't be so bad if the others could add their memories, too, you know."

Brenniss' full smile opened more when she stared at Riley's picture of him in the truck with Poke. That smile had been held hostage since being home. But now, it set free.

"So, all these people and animals helped the Maggie part of you become strong enough to return to me." Betty sipped from her cup. "And maybe the Brenniss part of you is strong enough now to return to Copper Station. What do you think?"

Brenniss stared at Riley's picture. "It would be good to go

back, Mom. I've found enough of myself to be your daughter again." She looked up. "I guess that's what mattered."

"Well, don't count me out. I'd like to meet this Riley, myself. And meet my other daughter...Maggie. I think I should do that before the wedding, don't you?"

Brenniss looked up. "Wedding? Mom, I told you, I can't go through with—" She stopped, looking squarely into her mother's face.

"You know you love Riley. You've wasted too much time in New York already, when all you want to do is go back." Her mom's hand gently tapped hers. "Bren, I think there's someone in Arizona who misses you as much as you miss him." Her eyes slipped sideways to Riley's picture.

Brenniss stuttered a breath or two, thinking about her journal and the "I love you" she admitted. And Grace, welcoming her back in her dream...

"What are you waiting for, dear one? Do I need to give you permission? Why don't you give yourself permission to be happy for a change? Lord knows, you deserve it. It comes down to this, sweetheart: it really is up to you."

Mom had just spoken magic words, as if they'd been floating in the house like fairy dust for six weeks without Brenniss catching them. Her mom was smiling, eyebrows raised, awaiting an answer. Suddenly the weight of Paco and Street and Kick were dropped from her heart like a stone, only dust left behind.

"Riley told me that, whenever I had to face a fear that it was up to me."

"Wise man. So what are you afraid of now?"

She shook her head. "For the first time in a year, not a darn thing." Her mom's hug sealed her path, the one west, the one toward a sunset.

CHAPTER
EIGHTY-FOUR

Riley contemplated the news he'd heard from Griff that Many Devils had been captured after fish and wildlife found him threatening some hikers. He knew right then that cat, living somewhere between legend and nuisance, would not last long anywhere near a hint of captivity. When Griff curled into Riley's drive that morning to drop off his fishing gear for a late afternoon turn along the river, he didn't expect there was more to the story.

"Got my gear and I'll meet up here after work. It'll be perfect later along the river."

"I could try my level of failure out there. Don't think I've improved much."

"That's a mediocre 'yes' if I've ever heard one. I'll bring dinner along. And, hey! Why don't we bring the horses?"

"Horses and fishing, now you're talking. Go ahead and leave your gear in the house. We'll load it later."

Griff turned toward his truck, then doubled back. "Oh, say, I forgot something. Something I have a feeling you'd be interested in." He reached into his shirt pocket and pulled out a bag, tossing it to Riley. "You realize that if you ever marry someone, you might need one of these."

Riley peered into the bag. "Does this mean we're engaged? I thought you were taken." He pulled out an engagement ring, an expensive one at that.

"You are looking at one of the last things they took from Many Devils. Wildlife had no choice but to tranquilize him, but he required at least four darts. The medication was too much for his system and he died. So wildlife did an autopsy."

A part of Riley fell, secretly hoping that Many Devils would have worked his magic again toward his freedom amid the canyon that he seemed to own. "Did they find any evidence from the van?"

"Sure, some snaps, buttons, and fabric …. and *this* engagement ring lodged in the lining of his gut." Griff pointed to the ring in Riley's hand. "You realize there's only one hand in that van that could fit that ring."

"But she wasn't in the van then."

"We think one of the gang took it from her maybe to sell it for cash. Maybe he died with it in his hand or pinkie that Many Devils couldn't resist. Could have easily swallowed it."

Riley held that ring tightly in his hand, willing Maggie to his. Many Devils had clawed his way into Riley's life multiple times, and now, this final time, included Maggie in the story. As inhuman as it was to have Maggie live the captivity she did, so was it to expect Many Devils to accept a cage, even for an hour.

"Just thought you'd like to know. I'll see you later today." Griff strode back to the truck.

Riley took the silence to remember the Navajo saying that the dust devils rising from the Arizona soil are spirits. Those dust devils that turn clockwise are good spirits: the loved ones you are forbidden to talk about, once they have moved to the other world. But counterclockwise dust devils are evil spirits that need to rise from your home. Many Devils was a bit of both, he figured. And now he had both, a bit of Maggie and a bit of Many Devils in the lifeline of his palm. He suddenly looked toward Poke who met his stare.

"All right, all right. I'm daydreaming again. So shoot me. Anyway, we're only working Cartwheel and Ranger today, before it gets too hot. Summer will be here before you know it." He advanced toward the barn.

Poke always ran in the center of the drive, automatic and bullet-like, usually stopping just inside the barn door. Once in a while, he'd stop short, like today. He slowed his pace, circled back ,and sniffed along the edge, near where the grass cradled the drive. Hopefully not a dead critter or a snake just waking up in the warmth.

Poke had not only stopped, but sat, paws extended.

"What is it, boy?" He looked more closely in the sandy soil...just some paw prints and—

He stopped breathing. All the countless visits to the barn, the times Poke stopped in that same spot, and he never paid attention, he'd walked right by. It took Poke to be the diligent guardian of a clear, but weathered outline of Maggie's boot, maybe from the last day she was here. Emotion flooded his heart.

Try as he could, he went through each day, thinking she was just a footstep behind. Each day, her voice was a little harder to remember, her smile a heartbeat or two away. These last few weeks, he never lost hope that she'd be rounding the river bend and find her way home. He blew out a sharp breath, took another and stood, staring again at that boot print.

"How about that, boy? She's never really been far away, has she?" He chucked the dog's chin. "Guess you do miss her, after all. Thanks, Poke. Thanks, boy."

Knowing she made peace with whatever New York kept for her, Brenniss packed her meager wardrobe willingly. With her mom in her heart, there wouldn't be anguished phone calls and updates and unfinished business after she left. She was going to the place she wanted to be, not because it was the only alternative for her safety. She was going to her home.

"Just let me know when it's my turn to visit." Betty winked. "I'm so happy for you, Bren. This feels so right." Brenniss called to give Agent Stanley an update that she would be returning to Arizona.

"Good that you called," Stanley replied. "That's perfect timing. It turns out Mullengrath has made several confessions these last few weeks. I'm flying to Arizona tomorrow. There's room for you on that flight. Would you consider joining me?"

"You mean, just like that? Go back with you?"

"I have to confess, Brenniss, I always thought you wanted to go back to Copper Station and...well...truth be known...and I can say this now, so as not to sway you in any way...I never cared for Vince, anyway."

Early morning in New York meant just after midnight in Copper Station. She had a whole day to get there, including the drive to Riley's home. For the first time in a long time, she looked forward to the sun breaking through the trees. She looked around her old bedroom, mentally boxing up the memories of her old life. How easy it was to pick up her suitcase.

But saying goodbye to her mother tore her again. "I feel like we just got reconnected. I don't want to go away from you too soon, you know."

"Oh, Bren, you'll always be with me. Go live the life you deserve. Just give me a call when you get in."

"I'll take good care of her, Betty. We'll make sure she's safe. We have our own jet, just like last time," he smiled. Then, slowly, Agent Stanley reached for Betty's hand. "You've been a trouper through all of this, and I thank you. Truly, you made my job so much easier. We don't always get to see happy endings in this line of work, and I'm glad we could do that for you this time."

"Well, Agent Stanley, I appreciate your bringing Brenniss back to me, even for a little while. Please, don't be a stranger. Keep in touch."

"Carl. My name's Carl."

Once Brenniss and Agent Stanley boarded the jet, he opened a map and gave her a rental car reservation. "Once you're clear of the airport turnoffs, just follow the highway north for about two hours. You'll see the side road for Mitchell Canyon and Copper Station."

"I'll know it when I find the river outside of town. You've been so kind, Agent Stanley. Do I still need people watching me once I get there?"

"We'll make sure there's someone close by until we get all of Mullengrath's confession. By then, we'll have an idea who might be a threat. Just know we'll be in the area."

"I kind of don't want you to be out of my life, just yet. I've gotten used to you, you know?"

"Well, you never know, Brenniss. You may see me again, sometime. Now, buckle up. We're going home."

While she napped, she dreamed of Riley talking with Grace. She's in good hands, Grace said. I'll be around, but you have someone else to focus on now. I always wanted you to be happy. It was always up to you...

She awoke to the smell of coffee, feeling she was between two places right now. Somewhere on the other side of Grace, somewhere closer to Riley. She napped again, until Agent Stanley nudged her to fasten her seatbelt, just a whisper over the Four Corners.

Suddenly, her heart skipped as if it were paper caught in a gust of wind. She left Brenniss behind somewhere in New York and now, seeing Riley again, would Brenniss want to sift back into her life? Here on this mosquito-sized white mark you see in the sky, would Maggie survive? But then, she thought of Poke and Bliss and Cartwheel. And Maggie slipped back beside her. I'm going home. Because it's up to me.

Once they landed, Agent Stanley walked her toward her waiting car. He clasped her hands almost like a prayer.

"You know, Brenniss, we've been through a lot together. I'm honored that we could bring you back to New York and now back home. You know what else? I'd be honored to visit you and Riley when I make it back to Arizona again. Yours is a story I've been proud to be a part of." His smile was genuine, and in the sun, there was a watery tint in the corner of his eye.

"You're welcome any time." And like that, she hugged him with no second thoughts, no fears. She'd left them behind in an empty space in New York.

She drove onto the black road ribbons, through thinning traffic until she was in the wide spaces, feeling her own smile again, looking up because she was ready to. The miles slipped under the vehicle, much like final memories of Vince as he evaporated.

Over a rise, she drank in the inverted bowl of turquoise sky, her first reminder that Arizona's rugged beauty had not forgotten her, the reddish rock fingers edged the highway before her, a book awaiting her new chapter, inviting the pen's first stroke...

...I have two names: Brenniss and Maggie...

She felt Maggie slipping back into her again, someone she hadn't invited into her skin for weeks. This Maggie felt wiser, more certain of who she was, more certain that Brenniss was part of her, too. In a few more hours, she wouldn't have to imagine the shimmer of the Emory's oak tree along the drive, how that eagle always found the sky when she looked toward the river...and Poke...sitting by the bed at night, when her body gave into the fatigue of the day.

And Riley...what will he say? She had connected with her past, just as he told her, only to connect with her future. Before you know it, that connection is a life. Just as Grace had told her: she hadn't lost it. It had been here all along.

Maybe all she had to say was that she loved Riley. That would cover it all.

She pulled Stanley's map like a paper bridge across the steering wheel. Looks like an hour to Copper Station. She'd been awake for more than fifteen hours, but only a half-inch of road lay ahead. Maybe she would get there in time for an afternoon ride with Bliss and Cartwheel. Talking's always easier when you're riding a horse. And that would be a good place to start.

Riley absently brushed Justice's mane, a habit he acquired after seeing Maggie's boot print this morning. The horses were exceptional in their workouts today and deserved every brush and rubdown before relaxing in the pasture.

She'll be coming back. It was a voice coming from deep within him. It wasn't Grace. It was his voice, so convincing and sure, he believed it.

He gathered his tack, his gloves, blankets, and saddles for his and Griff's ride tonight, but his skin started jumping. That feeling that nudges you when a thunderstorm shifts the breeze, charges the air with anticipation. Something was coming down the canyon at breakneck speed, like when life gets pulled different ways only to come back where you started. The horses sensed it too. But the sky was clear. The ride along the river that would settle him.

One more thing: He'd grab some fresh tomatoes from Maggie's tomato city for dinner along the river, maybe some carrots for the horses. Neither Griff nor Justice could refuse something fresh from the garden.

"Come on, Poke. Help me pick some tomatoes. I bet there are some carrots with your name on them too." He stepped off the porch, ready to turn the corner toward the back of the house, just as an eagle overhead caught his eye. Maggie's eagle, he swore it was. The first eagle to come back, although it seemed a little early. Kind of like that eagle always knew when Maggie needed a careful eye watching her.

"Let's go, Poke."

Maggie recognized Copper Station's road sign, briefly stopped for a breath as she anticipated the town around the corner. Riley's house was less than twenty minutes away. She turned slowly right, the only direction she needed to go, and curved into Main Street, past the hospital, the library, then toward Marta's and the Post Office, past Ten Winds Gallery. She drove slowly enough to see Hannah inside, handing a cooler to Griff. He opened the door and got into his beater truck just behind Brenniss' vehicle. She wanted to yell, flag down Hannah and him to ease her nerves. But she had a few more miles still in her, toward the river and to Riley's.

As she curved along the bend in the river, she felt her heart quicken, remembering how Poke had run this far to follow her when she left. In her rearview mirror, she saw the outline of Griff's head. He hadn't a clue she was leading him...or did he just look again? Just another mile or so—she saw the ranch up ahead. Just as she looked toward the barn, an eagle swooped past her driver's window and climbed up again over the river, as if to greet her. She couldn't hold back anymore, as if the river itself had found her cheeks, as if tears deserved to find their way there.

Griff had started toward Riley's, following a blue car that poked its way through town. But once along the curve, it sped up as if the car were racing hornets. License plates weren't local, probably Phoenix plates, but it was headed toward Mitchell Canyon. Certainly a sedan didn't quite fit the—wait a minute!

Griff looked again at the driver's silhouette: the hair, the shoulders and for a second, her profile as she looked toward an eagle flying nearby.

It couldn't be. It had to be.

When she slowed, then turned sharply into Riley's drive, he knew there was only one person who would show up at Riley's all on her own. Just like Riley believed she would. Griff pulled over to the side of the road and got out of the car. "Well, I'll be."

Maggie had already spied the horses in the pasture, but when she saw Riley in the garden—the garden with the tomatoes that were bigger than her fist, he promised—she choked a breath. Riley. Home. Yes, she was. After weeks of indecision and second guessing, she was *Home.*

She crunched the car to a halt in the drive. The Arizona quiet that she loved filled the open windows. Mid-July shadows carpeted the house, hinting that the heat was done with its daily visit. All she heard was the river behind her, a sound that would have gotten lost in downtown Manhattan. But here, she sat, taking in the sound, knowing tomorrow she would awaken to its music. Her breath calmed the giddiness darting under her skin. She opened the car door slowly, placed her boot squarely on Riley's soil, much like that first day at the ranch when A-ri-zo-na come into her senses like honey. She hadn't lost it. Grace had said so.

She heard a scuffle from behind the house. Poke jabbed past the corner, then stopped straight on all fours, alert and wary. He stood his ground. His sharp barks were meant to threaten, ears alert forward, tail strong. His bark pulled his front legs off the ground nearly a half-inch. Such a fierce little guy! Just as she remembered.

Maggie squatted next to the car, arms extended toward his nose.

"Hey, Poke, hey buddy. Come say 'hi' to me."

The dog stopped at her voice, turned his head slightly as if pulling up a memory and cataloguing the familiarity. He took a cautious step, as in disbelief then sniffed. Before the inhale was complete, he bee-lined toward those open arms. He couldn't stop with one dog kiss, he covered her face, squirreling and wiggling his joy. He probably would have hugged her if he could.

"How you doin', boy? How you doin'? I sure missed you. You've been taking good care of the horses, huh? And how about Riley?"

The dog yelped, arrowing right back into Maggie's heart.

"So, you helping Riley in the garden? You s'pose he needs some help from me?" Her hands were shaking, excitement, anticipation around the corner.

She stood, the dog's ongoing performance at her ankles because a dog's joy is never exhausted. She took one step toward the house, then saw a shadow in the back as it edged the perimeter.

"Poke? Poke! What's the matter? What's all the ruckus?" Riley's voice called from around the corner. "Poke? What's going on out here? What's all the commotion?"

With his hat pulled against the Arizona afternoon, Riley had focused only on tomatoes and carrots, losing sight of Poke. Until he heard barking. *What was happening out front? Poke never yelped.* Rounding the porch, he didn't recognize the shiny blue car, the driver's door still open. Poke was making crazy dances with all four legs against someone standing by the open car door.

Someone.

Maggie.

He stopped cold, holding the basket of tomatoes as if his life depended on it, despite his blood draining to his toes as if a plug had been pulled. He'd waited for this moment for the last six weeks. His throat cottoned his words into dry syllables. "Maggie?"

"Riley." She smiled back, the tentative air filling up between them like a balloon too full and ready to explode. He couldn't read her, she was still ghostlike to him. He gave nothing away in his face yet.

"I couldn't figure out what Poke—" He took a sideways step and finally set down the basket, a large tomato bobbling against balance and rolling onto the ground. He had marks in his hands from the basket handle because he wasn't wearing gloves. "Sure is good to see you." A blanket of warmth fluttered between them.

"Thanks, Riley. Place looks great. So do you. Those our tomatoes?"

"None other! Look at the size of these! Had to pick a few for tonight." His first smile. He relaxed into another step forward.

She pulled away from the car door, still along the fender. He waited for her to speak, but saw the words weren't showing up. They seemed to be moving in a slow dance, like ninth graders at their first party, not knowing those first steps. The silence didn't make him brave enough to take the lead. He wasn't clever enough to break the huge wall of ice that comes at a time like this. The silence stood like that awkward teenager.

He tried another tune. "So, how's old Vince doing?" Aw, that was a stupid question, you idiot.

"Oh, God! That was a disaster waiting to happen...We had a talk over dinner that didn't last past the appetizer." She put her hands in her pocket, kicking a shuffle step forward.

Riley sidestepped, looking at that eagle flying parallel to the river.

"Moved on, I guess you'd say."

"Okay, okay." Now was the time to say something, that first profound statement that would put Vince to shame. *Why didn't Grace give him some pointers about this moment?*

Maggie took a breath, then tilted her head. "I...I had a dream about Grace the other night. At least I think it was Grace. She was sitting up in the room where I stayed. I was looking for something. She said I hadn't lost it; it was here."

"That so? She talked to you? Grace was like that. Would come right to the very question you had. Sometimes people step aside and let you find those things on your own. The people who care step in later to make sure you're on the right track."

"But... but we don't need to talk about Grace or Vince, do we?"

"No, Sunshine, I don't think we do right now."

"So, as I was driving here—"

He was staring at her, not in a mean way, or a way that indicated anger. The afternoon sun lit up his blue eyes and he was leaning toward her next words.

A deep breath. "Okay, even though the Brenniss part of me showed up with my mom, but it didn't take long to realize that I needed Maggie in my life, too. So are Poke and the horses and Griff and Hannah, too. But mostly you, Riley. Like you said, I needed to get my Brenniss life settled... I'm not broken into a thousand pieces anymore. I've landed here because it's the place I belong." Her voice quivered in the clear dry air.

"Go on."

"I hated that lost and broken brought me here, but I loved what my life became. So when Grace looked at me and said I hadn't lost anything here, well, it just fell into place. For both

Brenniss and Maggie." She took another step forward.

He tilted his head back toward her, one step closer. "So what did you figure out, Maggie?"

Her smile warmed the sun. "Okay...here goes." She blew a breath. "I don't have to be Brenniss or Maggie, just me. And just me loves you, Riley." There, she said it out loud to the person it mattered to most. That was easier than she'd thought. "But I need to know that when I walk into that house, it can't be because you feel sorry for me, or because you're trying to protect me, or help me get better. It's got to be be—cause—"

"I love you."

"Right. We've got to—"

"No, Maggie. I'm telling you. I love you, right here and now. I loved you the first time you tried getting into my truck, the first time you fed Poke, the first time you gave an apple to Bliss. My God, I've loved you ever since. Grace let me know pretty darn early that she thought I was a fool for letting you drive away, so I think she decided to turn to you to get this all untangled. You didn't lose us. We're still here."

"Oh." She forgot Vince and Paco and Street and Kick, and even how tired she was standing there. In fact, standing there made no sense. Her legs loosened, she rushed toward him, folding into his arms. His face drew close, something she couldn't have tolerated even a year ago. He pressed his lips onto hers, gently at first, knowing she needed that reassurance, then more urgently to let her know he'd never let her go again.

From the highway, Griff tilted his hat back. "Well, I'll be," he whispered. "Guess I better let Hannah know we'll have something to celebrate."

Riley stepped back. "You don't know how many times I wanted to do just that. It just never seemed—"

"It's the right time now, Riley."

"Well, damn, anyway!" His mouth broke into a smile as wide as the river, as wide as the canyon, but his eyes stung tears. "Welcome home, Sunshine. This is your home, our home. Always will be. I love you so."

They walked in step toward the porch while the thread of their lives pulled together like a slipknot. "You must have been traveling all day. You drove?"

"Agent Stanley was headed back to Phoenix and let me ride on the jet. Mullengrath is spilling evidence, and he needed to be in Phoenix. Oh, hell, it doesn't matter if I grew wings and floated here! I'm here!" She leaned toward him and kissed him again. "Oh, I told Mom I'd call her when I got in. She wants to meet you, you know."

He picked up the tomato basket and stepped onto the porch. "Wise woman. If I'm going to ask you to marry me, she needs to approve, don't you think? Let's get that phone call going so I can talk to her, too. You must be hungry, though. Want some tomatoes?"

She paused, her hand on the screen door. Then, a giggle, the one he had nearly forgotten made its way past her smile. "Got any Jell-O?"

"Thought you'd never ask."

ACKNOWLEDGEMENTS

My experience has been any accomplishment relies on a team. I wish to acknowledge my 'readers' Jimmy B, Becca R and Dorothy R who gave me helpful and encouraging feedback, and Heidi M. Thomas who celebrated each step with me with her knowledge and support. My thanks to the Atmosphere Press team are not sufficient. You made sure I understood each step and gave me feedback upon which I could risk yet another step. You have all made this journey enlightening and valuable. Thank you all for your support and encouragement.

ABOUT ATMOSPHERE PRESS

Atmosphere Press is an independent, full-service publisher for excellent books in all genres and for all audiences. Learn more about what we do at atmospherepress.com.

We encourage you to check out some of Atmosphere's latest releases, which are available at Amazon.com and via order from your local bookstore:

Icarus Never Flew 'Round Here, by Matt Edwards

COMFREY, WYOMING: Maiden Voyage, by Daphne Birkmeyer

The Chimera Wolf, by P.A. Power

Umbilical, by Jane Kay

The Two-Blood Lion, by Nick Westfield

Shogun of the Heavens: The Fall of Immortals, by I.D.G. Curry

Hot Air Rising, by Matthew Taylor

30 Summers, by A.S. Randall

Delilah Recovered, by Amelia Estelle Dellos

A Prophecy in Ash, by Julie Zantopoulos

The Killer Half, by JB Blake

Ocean Lessons, by Karen Lethlean

Unrealized Fantasies, by Marilyn Whitehorse

The Mayari Chronicles: Initium, by Karen McClain

Squeeze Plays, by Jeffrey Marshall

JADA: Just Another Dead Animal, by James Morris

Hart Street and Main: Metamorphosis, by Tabitha Sprunger

Karma One, by Colleen Hollis

Ndalla's World, by Beth Franz

Adonai, by Arman Isayan

The Journey, by Khozem Poonawala

ABOUT THE AUTHOR

Linda Fifer grew up in Ohio with writers and musicians in her family. She graduated from Kent State University with BS and MA Degrees in Speech/Language Pathology, then moved west. She has written a musical, songs, poems, being published locally including *Spokane Writes*. Now retired, she completed her debut novel *The Road Between Two Skies,* an uplifting story of a woman who discovers her strength when faced with demanding challenges. Living in the west with her husband and two dogs, Linda is inspired in the nature surrounding her.